The C̶ Arn̶...

Tormod Cockburn

A "Mysterious Scotland" novel.

Set in Wigtownshire, Southwest Scotland

Mys.Scot

First published by Mys.Scot Media in 2024

Copyright © Tormod Cockburn, 2024

The moral right of the author has been asserted.

Print ISBN: 978-1-915612-15-1

E-Book ISBN: 978-1-915612-14-4

Cover photo: Prancing horse, by Pixabay, licenced by Canva

This is a work of fiction. Names, characters, places, and incidents are the products of the author's imagination or are used fictitiously. Any resemblance to actual events, locales, or persons, living or dead, is entirely coincidental.

For updates and free books, we invite you to join our Readers Syndicate. Either click the logo above in a digital copy or see details at the back of this book.

Mys.Scot

Dedication

For my mother, Liz. An artist, and the first person to nurture my aspiration to be an author.

Also by Tormod Cockburn

The Bone Trap
The Ness Deception
The Stone Cypher
This Jagged Way
The Ice Covenant
This Emerald Veil
Dark Sayings
The Crystal Armour
The Torn Isle

Chapter 1

Portpatrick, Wigtownshire – Present day

As the clock passed ten, Annie Wallace had been missing for three days. With his lower back grumbling and his head buzzing from too much caffeine, DS Archie Dewar knew the little girl was running out of time.

PC Hart finished her phone call and stood to update the situation board. 'That's mountain rescue finished at Quarry Bay,' she reported. 'No sign of Annie.'

Dewar nodded. 'Any word yet from the crew at Drumbreddan?'

Hart checked her sheet. 'Sorry, Sarg. They've stood down for the night.'

'They what?'

'Sixteen hours on the cliffs, boss. Their skipper has called a time-out until first light.'

Dewar wanted to feel annoyed. He hadn't slept in almost forty-eight hours. At this stage, with the little girl running out of time, taking a rest seemed like admitting defeat. 'Ah cannae blame them,' he muttered. 'They must be knackered. Any news from the guys down on the Mull?'

Hart swallowed. 'The crew searching the cliffs below Drummore finished and found nothing. The guys scanning the moor are still looking.'

Dewar shook his head. 'The wee girl's text said she was near the water. Walking the moors seems like a waste of time.'

'They're just interpreting what she said. Whether she meant she was right beside the sea, or perhaps could see it at a distance …' Hart paused when exhaustion crashed her logic.

'This whole peninsula is near the bloody sea,' complained Dewar. 'And the phone company says her mobile is still off?'

'Aye. The device was third or fourth-hand. Her dad reckons it'll be out of battery by now.'

Dewar nodded an acknowledgement while Hart slipped away to answer yet another ringing phone. He turned to look at the map and for the third time in as many hours, used his forefinger to trace the search area. Despite the difficult terrain, they were running out of places to look. 'Annie, Annie, where are you lass?' he whispered to himself.

'DS Dewar is busy at the moment,' said Hart, casting her gaze to the ceiling. 'Caller, if you could give me your name and a few details, I could track him down.'

Dewar watched her struggle to find patience. These late-night calls were the worst.

Hart held up the phone. 'Some old fella. Says he'll only speak to you.'

'Drunk?'

'Don't think so. Just garbled.'

Dewar stepped over and took it from her outstretched hand. 'DS Archie Dewar at Portpatrick. To whom am I speaking, please?'

'Archie. It's Shaun. Down at the dogs' home.'

'Evening, Shaun. Do you have something for me?'

'Are you still lookin' for that wee lassie?'

'We are.'

'It's just that two nights ago I was walking some of the hounds and spotted a light down at Clanyard Bay.' The old man stopped to cough. 'Didn't think much about it at the time, but then I got to wondering …'

Dewar considered this. If Shaun was remembering his timings, then he'd seen this light twenty-four hours after Annie's disappearance. This fact, combined with the location being further than the lass could possibly have walked, made it an uninspiring lead. But at this stage, any tenuous hint was better than pacing around the room fretting about what to do next.

'What kind of light, Shaun?' he asked, for the sake of extracting further details.

'I dunno. Something small. There's been a big new rockfall down there. All these damn storms have been hacking at the cliffs.'

'And was the light down on the rocks near the sea, or up on the cliff top?'

'About halfway. There's a narrow footpath skirting the stone. I'd say it's somewhere down there.'

'Shaun, I'm going to send a team to your position. Are you at the kennels right now?'

'Aye.'

'I know it's late, but can you meet us at Clanyard in twenty minutes? We'll need to fix the location of whatever you saw.'

'I can do that.'

Dewar hung up and passed the phone back to Hart. 'Am I right in saying we've no search parties available for immediate deployment?'

She shook her head. 'Everybody's dead beat.'

'Then grab your jacket, Constable. It's you and me.'

Dewar didn't rush the short journey down from his "Command Centre" in Portpatrick Village Hall. Simply, he was too tired, and the likelihood this would be another false trail left him disinclined to risk life and limb on the Mull's poor roads. They'd drive to Shaun's location and use the farm path to reach the shore. From there, the clamber to where Shaun saw the lights would be an ankle twister in the dark, but they'd go and do their duty. And afterwards, when they likely turned around with their tails between their legs, it would be time to consider winding down the search.

As they pulled over into the layby, they could see Shaun talking to a haggard-looking man in a red jacket.

'Ah shite,' spat Dewar.

Hart seemed startled. 'What, boss?'

'Annie's dad.'

'He'll have heard from Shaun,' said Hart.

'Aye, Shaun is a straightforward enough fellow, but Bram is a sleeve-tugger. Let's see if we can't shoo him away home so we can work in peace.'

Dewar parked up and got out of the car, pulling his cap on firmly and standing as tall as his fifty-eight years would allow him. 'Bram,' he barked. 'You should be back at the house with Karen, waiting for news.'

'News, Archie, there's never any news.' Bram's voice was shrill and resentful. 'And I need to be doing something, while there's still time.'

'No offence, Bram, but you look awful. You should be in your bed.'

Bram pulled a pained smile. 'You're no' so fresh yourself, pal.'

Dewar drew his hands to his hips. 'Technically, this is police business. I could have Hart here arrest you and haul you up to Stranraer for the night.'

Bram bit his lip and gently shook his head. Then he pulled out his phone and activated the home screen before thrusting it in Dewar's face. A picture of a pretty seven-year-old, with tousled blonde hair and dressed in a football top stared back at him. 'You've seen the time, Archie. If this is Annie's last night alive on Planet Earth, I'm damn well gonna spend it on my feet looking for her.'

'And by doing so, in your exhausted state, you'll be putting yourself in danger and hampering our search for your daughter.'

'They're saying the *Little People* took her.'

Dewar dropped his thumbs into his duty belt. 'What people, Bram?'

Bram's shoulders bobbed up and down. 'You know. The cave people.'

'Och, come on, man. Who's filling your head with nonsense?'

'Just folk,' Bram spluttered. 'Folk who remember how the *Little People* behaved back in the old days.'

Dewar darted a glance at his colleague, then back to Annie's father. 'I'm busting my gut here trying to find your kid, and you're keeping me back, blethering about evil fairies?' He jerked his thumb over his shoulder. 'Go home, Bram.'

But Bram didn't budge. 'That's where you're going now, isn't it? Shaun told me before you arrived. You think she might be in the caves.'

Dewar scowled at Shaun. 'Routine enquiry. Just chasing down each and every possibility.'

'And if there's even a chance she's down there, I'm coming with you.'

Dewar suppressed a growl, then turned to the man who'd phoned in the sighting. 'Shaun. The night's not gettin' any younger. Can you take us to where you saw the light?'

These days, Gill McArdle didn't run much in the mornings. Not that he wasn't fit. Nor was he putting on weight, but he was a morning person while Salina liked to burn the midnight oil. So, when it came to toddler management, Gill's shift started officially from 4 am.

It was almost 7 am now, and this morning's gig had started an hour before, which these days counted as a lie-in. Gill was wide awake, down on all fours in the family lounge and had engaged "hunting mode." With less than stealthy steps, and fearsome-sounding growls, he announced loudly, 'Here comes the tiger.'

Josh's smiling face popped out from behind the sofa and disappeared again with a giggle. Changing tack, Gill padded heavily to the other end of the sofa and made to creep up behind his son. 'The tigerrrrr is verrry hungry,' he announced. Reaching the furniture and peering behind, he saw no sign of the boy. But the channel between the sofa and the wall beckoned him forward so he decided to press on through.

Expecting to find Josh, crouching just out of sight, he was surprised to find his son had escaped.

'Raarrrr,' came a fierce sound from above him. Gill looked up and realised he'd been outmanoeuvred.

'Morning you two,' said Salina, appearing bedraggled but still beautiful. She bent at the knees to receive Josh as he barrelled off the sofa and toddled over to greet her.

'Thought you'd take a longer nap,' said Gill, extricating himself from behind the sofa.

Salina rubbed her forehead, then leaned in to kiss him. 'Yeah, well. All the jungle noises weren't exactly restful.'

'Ah. Sorry. Can I compensate by fixing you some breakfast?'

She nodded and together they went to find food for them all.

Sitting either side of the highchair a few minutes later, they took turns scanning their phones for messages and having a food-fight with their son.

'That kid,' said Gill, through a mouthful, 'seems to be able to flit around like Lorna. One minute he's just out of sight in front of me. Next moment, he's coming at me from behind.'

'Hmmm,' murmured Salina, unconvinced.

'Sometimes he can escape to a different room. I'd almost swear he can walk through walls.'

Salina didn't look up. 'Well then. With all these rough games you're playing, let's hope Raphael doesn't give him a sword anytime soon.'

Gill took his turn to steer another spoonful of cereal towards the child's mouth. He knew his son was utterly, astoundingly, totally amazing, no matter what Salina thought.

'Oh, thank goodness,' Salina suddenly exclaimed, looking up from her phone.

'What?'

'They've found that missing child, and she's alive. You know, down below Stranraer.'

Gill felt a burst of elation for a family he didn't know and would likely never meet. This was good news. Hearing any anguished parent's despair had taken on a whole new dimension in the eighteen months since he'd become a father.

Arriving at work, Gill dropped his case on a pile of post and turned to say a few words of greeting to the guys already at their desks.

There was no sign of Cassy, however a sticky note on his desk marked 'Urgent,' confirmed she was already in. There was no number, just a name, and Gill already had it on speed dial.

'DI Lillico,' came the businesslike response.

'Morning, Alex. Returning your call.'

'Thanks, Gill. How's the little one?'

Gill started to unpack his case while he spoke. 'We're gradually dissuading the little mite from his nocturnal habits. Exhausting, but lots of fun.'

'And Salina?'

'Champing at the bit to be back at work.'

'Will the university let her work part-time?'

'You must be kidding. They've got some deep dives around the Canary Islands starting this September, and Sal has told them she wants to lead the crew.'

'Excellent, listen.' Lillico cleared his throat. 'We've got an emerging situation down here. It's complicated and for a bunch of operational reasons, I can't tell you much about it. Suffice to say, there's an archaeological angle and given your expertise, I've persuaded the local Superintendent to let you look at it.'

Gill mouthed 'Hello' to Cassy as she returned to her desk with a coffee. 'Alex, I haven't worked a case with Police Scotland for two years. What's different about this one?'

'You wouldn't be working the case as such. But in the light of what we've found, there are questions that need asking, and I think you're the guy to tackle them.'

'Okay. When and where?'

'I'll need to see you down here ASAP if I'm going to stop it being shunted onto someone else's desk. And as for location, I'm working from a temporary police command centre in Portpatrick.'

'Near where they found that little girl?'

'Aye.'

'Can you tell me anything at all?'

'Absolutely nothing until you're standing in front of me, apart from advising you to bring waterproof trousers and a torch.'

Gill was silent for a moment, sensing Aura moving nimbly behind him.

'Gill, are you still there?'

'Yeah. Let me check in with Salina. All being well, I'll see you this afternoon.'

Chapter 2

Setting out after an early lunch, Gill followed a series of characterless motorways across the central belt until he joined the progressively narrower roads winding down into the far southwest corner of Scotland. Driving into Wigtownshire, he noticed how much wilder and greener it was down here, more like Ireland than Scotland. And remote! Working his way down a narrow finger of land known as the Mull of Galloway, with coastal cliffs pressing in on both sides, he observed its sparse population, feeling further from Edinburgh than many Highland regions.

As requested, he met Lillico in a waterside hamlet called Port Logan, and they travelled the remaining short distance in a police vehicle. Arriving at a field crowded with police vans, he noted their different liveries. When Gill gesticulated at one marked, "Bomb Disposal Unit" Lillico just shook his head.

'Does this place have a name?' asked Gill, for the sake of conversation.

'Not on any map I've seen,' said Lillico. 'But the locals know it as Clanyard Bay.'

Carrying jackets and hard hats mounted with torches, they followed a stoney path to reach the beach. Picking up a route marked by police tape, they bore right along the shore, picking their way across one hundred metres of boulders to reach a low cliff. Lillico stopped to point out a massive stone slab that, in recent times, had calved away from the cliff. It now stood, thrusting a pinnacle of unweathered rock towards the sky, reminding Gill of the Old Man of Storr. Forty metres above their heads, good grazing land stretched into the far distance.

'This stretch of coastline is eroding,' said Lillico as they arrived at a gap in the rock face. 'We're guessing Annie was walking the coastal path and slid into a narrow ravine that recently appeared.'

'What was she doing out here?'

'She lives in a village called Sandcrest on the other side of the Mull. She's mad keen on dogs and the working theory is she was creeping up on the commercial kennels that lie just beyond this headland. She might have used this route to come home in the dark and we're thinking the change in the terrain caught her out.'

'You don't seem very sure.'

'Well, the lassie hasn't spoken since her ordeal, so I'm left to figure it out for myself.'

'Was she hurt?'

'Cuts and bruises, but no serious injuries. She'll be okay.'

They'd reached the mouth of the cave and flicked on their torches as Lillico led the way. It was tough going, wet in places, and after a few scrapes, Gill was relieved he wasn't wearing his best trousers. About twelve metres in, they came to a branch in the cavern. Blue tarpaulin shrouded the entrance to the left-hand fork where two forensics officers stood comparing notes. They were tall men and seemed outsized for the cave's limited space. One nodded at Lillico but stopped speaking until he and Gill had passed further into the caves.

'That's *Alpha* cavern,' whispered Lillico, meeting Gill's gaze after a lingering glance back at the improvised screen. 'And as for what's behind the curtain, please don't ask.'

Continuing through the narrow cleft in the rock, they came to a small gallery, illuminated from above by a ragged gap in the roof. The cooing and fluttering of a few pigeons gave the place a little life, flapping at the light edges of the otherwise dark grotto.

Lillico pointed to a rocky outcrop, about four metres above their heads, and a further six metres shy of the open air. 'Do you see that ledge?'

'Aye.'

'That was Annie's home for the best part of three days. It's a miracle she didn't break her legs falling down there. There's a little bit of moisture dripping in, so I imagine she got something to drink.'

'Fortunate she didn't fall further.'

'Aye,' said Lillico, holding his phone aloft. 'Annie managed to get a text out to her dad before her battery died. If she'd fallen further, she wouldn't have had reception.' He swung a forefinger at the void around them. 'By the way, we're calling this *Bravo* cavern.'

Gill gave a sharp nod. Whatever Lillico had to show him wouldn't be far away.

'How are you with confined spaces?'

Gill winced and formed a harmless lie. 'Yeah, fine.'

Lillico was at the back of the cave now and dropped on all fours, facing a triangular-shaped gap in the rock face. 'And now I'm taking you into *Charlie* cavern.'

'Christened after our Dundonian friend? Ailsa will be so excited if you've named one after her.'

'No, Gill. We're using the NATO phonetic alphabet.'

Gill abandoned his nervous attempts at humour, and taking a deep breath, he followed Lillico on all fours.

They emerged into a poorly lit cave that Gill sensed was a more spacious place than the one before. Formed by an arched ceiling high above a steeply rising bank of sea-smoothed pebbles, it dipped on the seaward side into a pool of agitated water. In contrast, the top end narrowed into a dark cavity beyond the reach of their torches. Lillico nodded at the far wall. 'First things first. Have a look at that.'

Suddenly aware he was in an area of scientific importance, Gill took a deep breath and stepped carefully towards the facing wall. Carved images, scratched across the smooth canvas of sedimentary rock, overlapping, jumbled, and sometimes expansive. Human figures, in simple clothes, engaged in hunting, fishing and copulating. Depictions of individual faces, and representations of the moon at various stages of its monthly cycle.

'Fascinating,' he said, after a time. 'I can't think of cave art on this scale anywhere else in Scotland.'

'Do you think it's Pictish?'

Gill shook his head. 'More recent.'

'What makes you think that?'

'The absence of typical Pictish symbols, plus the presence of houses in some of the etchings.'

'Houses?'

'Yes. They're very faint,' said Gill, raising a forefinger to highlight what he'd seen. 'And always at the furthest margins of each scene.'

Lillico leaned in closer. 'I see.'

'Oh, and here's a horse and cart.' He found himself nodding. 'Alex, this cave is precious. We need to record it and preserve as much as we can.'

Lillico flashed a weary smile. 'Thought you might feel like that.'

They were interrupted by splashes in the water and turned to find two men in wetsuits and snorkels emerging from the chalky green pool.

'This is Murray McGovern and one of his crew,' said Lillico quietly while the two men waded out of the water. 'They're experienced cavers and have been making sure we don't accidentally kill ourselves down here.' He broke off the conversation to assist the younger of the two men struggling to clamber up the slimy stones. In turn, Gill stepped down to help the older man.

The man offered Gill a smile of thanks. 'I'm Murray. And you are?'

'Gill McArdle. Consulting archaeologist.'

Murray nodded. 'Well, there's lots to see.' He jerked a thumb over his shoulder. 'And once you're done in *Charlie* cavern, Donnie and I have been probing what could be a route linking this place to another gallery. The cave walls are smooth, suggesting it was once a watercourse or something, though it's currently blocked with rubble.'

'Thanks,' said Lillico. 'Will you guys still be around for an hour or two?'

Murray nodded. 'As long as you need us, Detective.'

'Great. I'm going to show Gill the main event.'

Murray shuddered. 'Knock yourselves out, boys.'

'Main event?' asked Gill.

Lillico's gaze drifted toward the higher reaches of the cave. 'You've seen the artwork. Now come and meet the artists.'

They left the divers to struggle out of their gear while and picked their way up the sloping rubble to the apex of the cave. Someone had installed a battery-powered lamp, and after a warning nod to Gill, Lillico switched it on.

'I've alerted the Procurator Fiscal,' said Lillico. 'But I thought someone should see these guys *in situ* before I write a report. Perhaps speculate on who they were and what they might have been doing down here. Apart from decorating the walls, obviously.'

As Gill's eyes adjusted to the harsh white light, he was briefly speechless. 'They're both tiny,' he said at last.

Lillico nodded. 'Just over three feet tall.'

'Kids?'

Lillico shook his head. 'Look closer.'

'Their arms and legs appear on the short side and the skulls are heavier than a child's,' murmured Gill, leaning close to the remains. 'I see bone ossification, and the skull plates are fused. Meaning these guys were … adults. But their small size; it's kinda weird.'

'Any theories about who they were?'

Gill scanned the remains. 'Deceased dwarfs, Alex? The last redoubt of a Victorian circus? Honestly, I've no idea.'

'Okay. I'm going to let you look around for a few minutes, then I'll need to take you back outside while the forensics guys finish in *Alpha* cavern. Will you be okay to stay in the area? I should be able to let you back in here tomorrow afternoon at the latest.'

Gill nodded. 'I can do that.'

'Great. I'd recommend talking with Murray. If you want to go exploring in here tomorrow, he's the guy who'll keep you safe.'

'Thanks, we'll have a chat.' Gill pointed back at the etchings. 'I'll be available as soon as you can let me back in.'

Lillico had intended to drop Gill to his car in Port Logan, but when he completed the long trudge back to the cars, he found there was another visitor already waiting for him. Apologising, he arranged with PC Hart to give Gill a lift back into town, then turned his attention to his next appointment.

'DI Shona Fallon,' said the woman, showing him her warrant card. 'PSNI Counter-Terrorism.'

'My Chief Super said someone was coming over,' said Lillico. 'Thanks for joining us so quickly. If you want to follow me, I'll show you what we've got.'

'Hang on a second,' she said, in her Ulster brogue. 'I get that we're in Scotland, and your governors can pick whoever they like for Senior Investigative Officer, but I'd have expected this job to go to your local counter-terrorism unit. I've looked you up, DI Lillico. *Special Investigations*? What the hell is that when it's at home?'

Lillico sighed. He'd had to answer this question a thousand times. 'We pick up all the weird cases. The stuff nobody else will touch with a long stick.'

Fallon didn't look convinced. 'I've read your preliminary crime scene report. What makes this cave so special?'

'Oh,' he said with thinly disguised irritation. 'That'll be because of all the dead fairies.'

Twenty silent minutes later, having completed the walk from the cars to the caves for the third time that day, Lillico signed the logbook and led Fallon inside *Alpha* cavern. Allowing his guest a few seconds to let her eyes adjust, he swept aside the blue tarpaulin, holding it so DI Fallon didn't get pigeon crap on probably the only jacket she'd brought with her. She didn't step very far, preferring to survey the scene from a distance.

'Oh, this feels like the good ol' days,' she said, quietly.

Lillico came and stood beside her so he'd a clear view of the arms cache. 'If you're referring to the Ulster Troubles, please enlighten me. What was good about those days?'

Fallon shrugged. 'Oh, ye know, they were predictable. The same stupid old bastards doing the same stupid things.'

Lillico said nothing.

'I haven't seen one of these for twenty years. Not since the dying days of the RUC.'

Lillico coughed in the damp air. 'Take this as a compliment if you want, but have you really been a copper that long?'

For the first time since she'd arrived, Fallon smiled. 'Joined up at eighteen. To save you the maths, I can retire with thirty years service in four years' time.'

Lillico thought about this. 'That's generous for a full pension.'

'It's danger money.' She shook her head. 'Or at least, it was, back in the day. New recruits don't get the same deal.' She took a few steps forward and addressed one of the forensics guys. 'You got a schedule for me?' She took the handwritten sheet and used the light of her phone to read the contents.

'One hundred and ninety-eight cases of M16 assault rifles, making just shy of twelve hundred guns, plus eighteen cases of ammunition.' She looked up at the CSI. 'No detonators? No Semtex or C4?'

Beneath his PPE, the man shook his head.

She pointed to the stack of rifles. 'Can I handle one?'

In response, he passed her a pair of latex gloves.

If someone had presented Lillico with a weapon like this, he'd have struggled to remember what end to hold, whereas Shona Fallon upended the thing and had it stripped down to its main parts in less time than it had taken her to squeeze into her gloves. 'Interesting,' she said.

'What are you seeing?'

'It's in good nick. Very serviceable with a wee bit of work. But the damn thing is smothered in grease. I mean, I know the humidity in here must be off the scale, but normally an airtight gun case and a few packs of silica gel would keep a gun rust-free in transit.'

'What are you inferring?'

'Looks like they're in long-term storage. We'll need to check the serial numbers to get the date of manufacture, but they might have been here for ages.'

Lillico nodded. 'Next obvious question is, who are they for?'

Fallon snorted. 'Well, thanks to the multicoloured fairground you guys are running on the cliff top, we'll probably never know.'

'Beg your pardon?'

'If you'd been a bit more delicate about this, we could have put the whole stash under surveillance and caught whoever picked it up.'

'And you reckon it's too late for that?'

Fallon turned to scowl at him. 'I think the big blue flashing sign yelling "we found your feckin' guns" might just tip them off. And you'll have chased away the sentry.'

'Sentry?'

She rolled her eyes. 'You sure it's not too late to get proper counter-terrorism in here? All this playing catch-me-up is gonna be a drag.'

Lillico pointed to his right. 'Weird cave next door, remember?'

'The sentry,' she continued, 'is someone deployed to guard a weapons cache between delivery and collection. A new arrival in the neighbourhood. An artist here for the summer. I dunno. Just somebody hanging around that the locals haven't seen before.'

'Thanks. I'll get straight on that.'

'As for who ordered these guns, that's anybody's guess. With all this talk about a referendum, it's fair to say tensions are high on the Emerald Isle.'

He watched her rapidly reassemble the gun and strip off the gloves. 'Now you've seen it *in situ*, are you okay if we shift this lot to our secure unit at Stranraer?'

She turned to go. 'Yes please.'

'While we're here,' said Lillico, diplomatically. 'Did you want to see the fairies?'

'Did they die of gunshot wounds?'

Lillico wasn't sure if this was a trick question. 'No.'

'Any additional weaponry, or suggestions the people responsible used the other caves?'

'None.'

She pointed at *Alpha* cavern. 'Then there's enough trouble right there, DI Lillico. I'm off to make a few calls. Find out if any of our known faces have lost a stash of guns. I'll see you in Stranraer tomorrow.'

Chapter 3

Chief Superintendent Macfarlane didn't like waiting. He was a rare visitor to Holyrood, the seat of Scotland's devolved parliament. That said, his face was sufficiently recognisable that at least a dozen people nodded in his direction before Canmore's aide came to collect him.

Entering a room lined with pale oak, the space had an old-fashioned flavour compared to the rest of the modern building. Bookcases packed with leather-bound volumes covered both gable walls, with space on one side for a drinks' cabinet. On the other wall was a framed photo of Canmore shaking hands with his father, Connal Canmore, who stood draped in the Saltire, Scotland's national flag. The man himself sat behind a large oak desk, busy writing something before he looked up to greet his guest. Macfarlane felt gratified when Canmore got out of his chair and approached for a robust handshake.

'Angus, thanks for making time at the end of a busy day.'

'Always happy to talk, Roddy. You know that.'

Canmore pointed to his desk and bid Macfarlane to take a seat. 'Family all well?'

'Aye, all grown up and away. Living south of the border these days; all three of them.'

'That must be difficult for Susan.'

'Aye. It's the grandchildren she misses most. Such a pity they're not closer to Edinburgh.'

'It's a problem, I agree. Scotland educates these fine young people before England steals them to work in London or Manchester or wherever. Good families like yours, stretched apart because there aren't equitable opportunities in Scotland. That's something we need to change; would you agree, Angus?'

'One of a host of things,' said Macfarlane.

'You and I have spoken about these issues before,' said Canmore, returning to his seat. 'That for the sake of our nation, we might someday invigorate the pace of change.'

'We've chatted over a whisky or two at your *New Scotland* fundraisers,' agreed Macfarlane.

'I wonder if you might join me in taking that conversation to the next level?'

'I might.' Macfarlane stopped to glance around the room. 'However, I'm bound to ask, is this a location where I can speak frankly?'

'You mean, is my room bugged?'

Macfarlane tilted his head but said nothing.

'My security chief, Steven Blaine, scans the room three times a week. We can talk freely here.'

'Alright then. Go ahead. What are you proposing?'

'First things first, Angus. As the working day is well spent, will you join me in a malt?'

'That would be very pleasant.'

Canmore got up and moved across to the oak cabinet, which he opened to produce two cutglass tumblers and a whisky decanter. Carrying these to his desk, the politician's face became troubled. 'You recall I was Justice Secretary when we first met?'

'I do. And I've always appreciated your support for my career.'

'My three years in that role, on top of my decade in legal practice taught me a great deal about the Scottish constitution.' He nodded soberly. 'I understand how it evolved and how it can be reshaped once our union with England is finally extinguished.'

'And in the future, sir, you'll make a fine First Minister,' said Macfarlane, accepting the generous malt with a smile.

'Now, we're both practical men, Angus. We've both cut a few corners in our time to serve the interests of this great country.' Canmore peered into his glass of molten amber. 'You know enough about how I operate to ruin me, and I think it's fair to say, I hold the same power over you.'

Macfarlane nodded, after a pause, but said nothing.

'And while some men would allow that knowledge to corrode their relationship, I find I trust you more than anyone else in the police service.'

'And that's mutual, Roddy. Otherwise, we wouldn't be where we are today.'

Canmore nodded and seemed satisfied to carry on. 'Ever since I felt compelled to launch *New Scotland*, I've dedicated myself to that single cause and now, I believe, I've discovered a path to Scotland's independence.'

'I'm listening.'

Canmore smiled darkly into his glass. 'From time to time, you'll notice that the Westminster government lets us down.'

Macfarlane snorted before he could stop himself. 'There's an understatement!'

'And thus, it is predictable, it will do so again.' Canmore clenched his fist. 'What I'm proposing is that on the next occasion, we take the resulting wave of anger amongst the Scottish public, and weaponise it.'

Macfarlane sipped but said nothing.

'For some time, I've been working at the margins of Scottish society. You know; building a network amongst those most disadvantaged by the current national arrangements.'

'You're a man of the people, Roddy. Whether they're wearing a Ranger's top or a Celtic, I know there are men in this country looking up to you.'

'And I've found heroes among that cohort who'll take the necessary risks to achieve our nationhood.'

'What kind of risks?'

'I'm going to use Westminster's antics to rally our kinsmen. We'll amplify their anger, so they don't just sit at home and grumble.' Canmore tapped the table with his knuckles. 'I'm going to arouse a war cry across our towns and cities.'

'You're talking about demonstrations?'

Canmore's expression suggested Macfarlane hadn't grasped the full ambition of the man's strategy. 'Did you know we could render this country ungovernable by controlling nineteen key facilities? Food distribution centres, fuel depots, mainstream media, certain … military assets. I could go on, but suffice to say, I want to see the men angry with Westminster's failures become organised. Rather than just get bevvied and hurl a few bricks through the window of their local M&S, we will form a militia with purpose.'

Macfarlane's grasp of the proposal suddenly flared. 'But the police would …'

'What would the police do, Angus?' Canmore tilted his glass at Macfarlane and didn't wait long enough to hear his reply. 'They'd do what their senior officers told them to do.'

Macfarlane studied his whisky for a long moment, letting his mind imagine how Canmore's tactics might play out. 'What you're proposing would be a dangerous moment, Roddy. The public would demand protection.'

'And rightly so. Which is exactly what you should provide, deploying your brave officers where the public most needs to feel safe. Outside their schools, shopping centres and civic buildings.'

'You mean, non-strategic locations, while this militia you're enlisting tightens its grip on key locations?'

'And all the while their numbers grow as people rally to our cause. Alba gu bràth, Angus. *Scotland forever*. I ask you now, will you join me?'

'You're ready to do this?'

'I've had face-to-face conversations with men I can trust. I'm only giving each of them a tiny part of the picture, but I'm confident I can navigate the path ahead.'

'And my role would be what, exactly?'

'I don't need you to lead from the front, Angus. You're a general rather than a foot soldier, and in that vein, I'll need you to deliver tactical paralysis when the time comes.'

'Misdirect resources,' Macfarlane concluded. 'Become grit in the machine.'

'And be seen to protect the public. Our cause will be poorly served if our police force isn't doing its utmost.' Canmore took another sip. 'And to that end, they might obstruct the British Army if it mounted a counter-offensive.'

'But in a fight,' Macfarlane spluttered. 'We'd never match them.'

Canmore's shake of the head was barely perceptible. 'We don't need to engage them with violence. We'll win at the school gate, in the office canteen, and in every dark recess of social media. The only war we need to win irrevocably is the battle for public opinion.'

'To triumph in another referendum?'

'No, Angus. We'll make our enemies stink so badly that independence will become the only rational response to their deceit.'

Macfarlane considered this. 'And my reward for the considerable risks I'd be undertaking?'

Canmore smiled indulgently. 'Scotland's Parliament will need a second chamber to guide the hand of the legislators who will shape our future. I imagine we'll appoint a senate from a cohort of the nation's most upstanding citizens.' He paused and leaned across the desk to touch Macfarlane's arm. 'Angus. I sincerely hope that you'll answer the call when it comes.'

Macfarlane nodded with satisfaction. 'It would be my honour.'

'Excellent.' Canmore got up from his desk and moved to top up their drinks. 'I value your support immensely, Angus. And if we've agreed our partnership, can you help me with something else?'

'Just ask, Roddy.'

'Two years ago, a burglar stole an early draft of our plans from my home office. The data was on an encrypted USB stick, but as the thief cracked the best security money can buy, I suspect they might eventually access the data.'

'I've not heard any reports, in either public or unofficial channels.'

'Likewise,' said Canmore. 'And I'm hoping the data stick was destroyed during an operation I mounted to retrieve it. Unfortunately, the patriot I tasked with its recovery was found dead in the sea close to Peterhead, so I can't know for sure if he was successful.'

'Dead? Do you mean, murdered?'

'One of your own divisions investigated his disappearance. *Special Investigations*, or something like that.'

'DCI Wiley and DI Lillico,' sighed Macfarlane, shaking his head. 'If I'd known the victim was so important to you, sir, I'd have deployed a more disciplined team.'

Canmore waved away the apology. 'The Fiscal recorded his death as an accident. I'm one of only two people aware of my operative's mission that day.'

'Do you know who killed him?'

Canmore reached into a desk drawer for his mobile. Unlocking the screen, he tabbed to a photo. 'This girl, Lorna Cheyne. The one who broke into my home and took my data stick.'

Macfarlane looked at the image of the pretty, willowy young woman. 'She doesn't look like she could hurt a flea.'

'Appearances, Angus. I suspect she's a highly trained operative.'

'Trained by whom?'

'If you'd asked me two years ago, I'd have guessed she worked for Britain's domestic security services. But during her time in prison, this person was a regular visitor.' Canmore swiped his phone screen to reveal a woman with appealing dark brown eyes and faintly Middle Eastern appearance.

'Who's that?'

'Adina Mofaz. Believed to be a Mossad operative in deep cover. She lives and works in plain sight and probably doesn't know we're aware of her.'

'Good grief, Roddy. What would the Israelis want with Scotland?'

'Mofaz associates with another man I've crossed swords with: Gillan McArdle, a journalist operating out of Dundee. A few years ago, they were both involved in a plot to discredit Scotland's *Stone of Destiny*. I faced down their plans during my time as justice minister, however they might attempt another disruption.'

Macfarlane remembered the incident as it splashed over the media for a couple of days. 'What is their objective?'

Canmore shrugged. 'To keep us on the back foot? Muddying the issue of independence so that it remains a festering sore? Preventing both countries gaining from a clean break? Honestly, it might be far more sinister than that.'

'And you think these people are a threat to us?'

'The journalist's a fool, but Cheyne and Mofaz might manipulate McArdle to use him against us.'

'I see. And what would you like me to do?'

'Cheyne has been serving time for her invasion of my home and others. She'll be released next Monday.'

'This woman is in prison? Surely that's given you ample opportunity to … address your concerns about her?'

'I tried. However, her skillset made her untouchable. I'll have new opportunities when she's out of prison.'

'To intercept her,' mused Macfarlane. 'Make another attempt to recover your data.'

'Yes. And observe who else she associates with. If she's part of a bigger cell, then we'll have the opportunity to find the weakest links.'

'Let me investigate. I'll alert you to any opportunity to question her.'

'You're certain you can do that without drawing attention to yourself?'

'Following this conversation, I'll be selecting a few men I can trust. Men who'll be proud to serve our cause in whatever way you see fit.' Macfarlane thought for a second and decided if he'd made this pact, he might as well double down. 'Was there anything else I can help you with, sir?'

Canmore looked down at his desk for a second. 'There is an emerging situation … but I've my very best man working on it.'

Macfarlane nodded. 'Don't hesitate to reach out to me if you need additional resources.'

'I'll do that.' Canmore laboured to his feet and extended his meaty right hand across the table. 'It'll be a pleasure serving with you, Senator.'

Chapter 4

Carlisle, Cumbria
21st December 1745

Dearest Mother,

With fullest pride and jubilation, I write with gratitude for urging our family upon this journey. When the call came to rally to the Prince, thou didst see the hesitation in mine eyes. And if thou hadst not pressed a single white rose into mine hands, I doubt courage would have swelled within my breast. "For the Prince," thou didst urge me as thou gavest the flower to me. "And to recover our good name and our lands so cruelly stolen." Rightly said, Mother, and I thank thee for illuminating these valiant ambitions for which we now fight.

It hath been four weeks since we marched to join the Prince, and I assumed we would journey southward. In truth, I expected by now to write to thee from London, reporting the city's fall and that England was once more in the arms of our Holy Father, under the honourable governance of a Catholic Stuart king. Instead, the Prince's army paused at Derby until the order came to withdraw north. The Manchester men were still in good spirits, expecting observant Catholics and Episcopalians to rally to us. But alas, that did not occur. If anything, our numbers dwindled with every mile trudged through the cold rain. Damn those deserters! They leave more gold and glory to those of us who remain steadfast!

At the end of our long march north, we procured a sudden victory. One week ago, under the brooding presence of our guns, Carlisle fell to the Prince without a single Jacobite casualty. We marched into the city and awaited orders to press south again. Instead, we received news of a large government army approaching, and the Prince, in his wisdom, hath decided the coming battle must be fought in Scotland. The bulk of the Manchester men, under Father's leadership, will remain here to defend the town. We pleaded with him to be steadfast by his side, however, due to our battlefield training, he ordered Richard and I to travel north with artillery attached to an Irish unit.

We embraced Father and assured him of our swift reunion, as the tide must turn, and the justice of our cause is heard in Heaven's highest court. Then our lands will be returned to us, and those cottars and millers' daughters who snub their noses at thee will curtsey once again.

I shall write again soon with better news.

Thy son,

Francis Towneley.

Chapter 5

While the police progressed whatever it was they were doing behind the blue tarpaulin in *Alpha* cavern, Gill drove to Portpatrick to find accommodation. Knowing it would be the following afternoon before he could return to the caves, he filled the remaining hours of his day working on an article for issue sixty-two. In the evening, he wandered the seaside town, chatting with Salina on his phone. Josh was already sleeping, so Salina entertained Gill with news of their son's antics.

The next morning, with more time to kill, he drove along the coast to Whithorn. This pretty market town with its wide high street and stone houses looked faded now, but back in the fourth century, an ancient saint had made this the very first Christian settlement in Scotland. It had been on Gill's "to visit" list for a long time, and he roamed the grounds of the old Priory with its ruined church and reconstructed roundhouse seeking ideas for a story. What would it have been like, he wondered, to bring the new faith to the shores of a land already saturated with older religions? Had St Ninian brought God's love, or a sharp sword to persuade the locals to give the new faith a try? Looking at the strategic location of the old Priory, Gill rather feared it was the latter. And had the old faiths crumbled during this onslaught, or had they influenced the customs, if not the core beliefs, of embryonic Celtic Christianity?

During a short downpour, while Gill sheltered in the vast reconstructed roundhouse, he speculated on what was ahead of him in the Wigtownshire sea cave. The wall art was fascinating but it was the human remains that stoked Gill's curiosity. He couldn't remember any Scottish discoveries which had included the remains of diminutive humans. Musing on this he realised the obvious parallels with an endemic Celtic myth.

At lunchtime, Lillico texted permission to return. They arranged to meet in Port Logan, however while he was still enroute, a text came in changing the meeting to the caves. There were fewer police vans than yesterday, although a mud-stained SUV announcing '*Caledonia Cave Rescue Team*' dominated the limited parking space.

Making his way down to the cave entrance, Gill found Lillico in conversation with the duty officer and Murray McGovern dressed in what looked like climbing gear.

'Do I need to sign in?' Gill asked.

'Aye,' said Lillico. 'We're keeping a daytime guard here for a couple of days, but the forensics work has finished.'

Gill nodded. To his eyes, Lillico looked stressed. 'You doing okay?'

Lillico dropped his hands into his pockets. 'Busy.'

Gill tilted his head at the caves. 'With whatever you found in there?'

'Aye, plus my thing in Kelso. It's all go just now.'

'Not seen you on the news. I take it your Borders enquiries are still ongoing?'

Lillico turned to face the sea. 'I doubt what I'm working on will ever be in the news.'

Gill felt a twinge of curiosity. 'Anything you can share?'

'Nope.'

He delivered a shallow shrug. 'Doesn't hurt to ask. And you're all finished on this site?'

'Apart from *Alpha* cavern, It's all yours.'

'You're not staying on to investigate the human remains?'

'I did an initial report for the Fiscal. Given the age of the remains, he's no interest in starting any formal proceedings. It'll be like Killiekrankie. We've recorded the bones, so after today, I've no ongoing involvement.'

'What about the wee girl, Annie Wallace?'

'I'm assisting the local team due to her proximity to *Alpha* cavern. She's still not talking, but from the context, her situation looks like an accident.'

Gill turned to extend a hand toward the other guy. 'Good to see you again, Murray.'

'Up until now, Murray has been on our payroll,' said Lillico, 'though today is his last day. If you're planning to work in the caves, and you want Murray to assist, you guys will have to come to a private arrangement.'

Gill took his first proper look at the man. Muscular and just a whisker more than five feet, his frame was powerful and yet compact, similar perhaps to the creatures Gill hoped to find in the caves. With calculating blue eyes, Murray almost crushed Gill's hand when he shook it.

'And good to meet you again, Gill.' Murray's accent was hard to place. Edinburgh or Perthshire, Gill reckoned. Either way, he'd been to a posh school. He looked Gill up and down. 'DI Lillico here was telling me you guys have worked together before.'

Gill made sure his face gave nothing away. 'Aye. Our paths have crossed.'

Lillico looked at his watch. 'I'm going to leave you to chat. I've got a briefing in Stranraer.'

Murray compressed the strip of police "No entry" tape with his foot and jerked his head at Gill. 'Let's go inside.'

Switching on his torch, Gill took a deep breath and followed Murray through the crevasse leading to *Bravo* cavern and from there through the narrow gap into *Charlie* cavern. A few minutes later, they were standing in the dimly lit room where they'd found human remains.

'Walk me through what you'd like to achieve here, Gill?'

'Did Lillico show you the bodies?'

'Briefly, before they were moved. Adult male. Adult female. Believed to have perished hundreds of years ago after the original cave entrance collapsed.'

'Yes. Based on the quality and quantity of cave art, this place seemed to be their settled home and not just an emergency hideaway.'

Murray nodded. 'It was a long time ago. Some poor folk had to make do.'

'Quite simply, I'd like to search for clues to reveal who they were and why they were living in these caves.'

Murray nodded. 'Sounds like a reasonable objective.'

'Can I ask you, as someone who spends their working life in places like this, what you observe when you look around this cave?'

Murray pointed in the direction they'd come. 'Well firstly, the access route we're using didn't exist until very recently. You can see the sheared rock is nice and fresh. I'd imagine it was the same event that opened the ceiling cavity that wee Annie fell through.'

'You're sure it's safe right now?' asked Gill.

'No way of knowing for sure. But rocks have their ways of speaking to you if they're heading towards a break. They creak and groan and disgorge small bits of debris.' He looked around. 'Everything here seems solid.'

'Okay, so you were saying yesterday there might be a route into another cavern. That begs the question, how did our deceased family end up in here?'

'Been considering that.' Murray walked over to a rock face. 'When you think about folk getting trapped in caves, the Hollywood trope is for a bunch of wee rocks to tumble down from nowhere and obscure the entrance. But what happens in real life is the roof collapses, obliterating everything. I think that's what happened here. Then skip forward to a week ago when the latest erosion opened a new access point.'

'Is there any way of knowing if a wider cave system lies beyond this cavern?'

'I'd recommend ground-penetrating radar. See if we can detect cavities beyond this one.'

'And we still can't tell how the family got in and out of this cave?'

'There's the clue I mentioned yesterday,' said Murray, walking over to the pool where ripples lapped against rocks at the seaward side of the cave. 'This is salt water. And while I've been working in here these past couple of days, it's been rising and falling. Meaning it's tidal and still connected to the sea.'

Gill stepped over to the deep, dark pool of green water. 'They moved in and out through there?'

'There are signs of a passageway, but it's full of stones pushed in by the sea.'

'Could you investigate?'

'Not on my own. I'd need to bring in two other guys. Help move the debris and cover the safety aspect.'

'I understand.'

'And that might only be the start of it. If you find further caverns beyond, we could be poking about in there for weeks.'

'How much are we talking?'

'I'd need to cost out the logistics based on several potential scenarios. If you give me your contact details, I'll mail you.'

'Sounds like it'll be expensive,' said Gill.

Murray pointed at the dark pool. 'I'd recommend three days to start. Get these stones shifted and confirm if there's another cavern to explore.'

'Okay,' said Gill. 'Send me your best price and I'll chat with my boss.'

Chapter 6

Later that afternoon, Lillico followed the sensibly flat heels of DI Fallon into Stranraer Police Station. Overlooking the concrete wasteland of an abandoned ferry terminal, the building resembled a run-down primary school in the middle of the summer break. After they'd signed in, the local detective sergeant led them to a brick corridor at the back of the building housing four cells. The doors to three were open, while the fourth was shut but unguarded.

'These days, the station isn't manned 24-7,' DS Dewar explained while he unlocked the closed cell. 'A lot of our capabilities are gradually being transferred to Dumfries.'

'Wonderful,' said Fallon, looking around the cramped room, stacked high with rifle boxes. 'I could enter this building in thirty seconds by swinging a brick at a rear window, then have at the cell door with a power tool in about two minutes. If you boys want to keep this lot safe, then you need to shift it to a properly secured unit.'

Lillico nodded at Dewar, then back at Fallon. 'Right after our meeting, I'll make a call.'

'You do that. And while we're talking about security, I'd say anyone working a terrorist case like this should carry a firearm. Ask your superiors about that while you're at it.'

Lillico turned around and led the group through several twists and turns until they reached the situation room. 'I'll organise an armed response team when these weapons are moved.'

'And afterwards?'

Lillico levelled his voice. 'This isn't Ireland, DI Fallon. Officers manning our day-to-day operations don't carry guns.'

'Suit yourselves,' she said. 'But as I'm authorised to carry a firearm, I'll not be relinquishing my weapon. You okay with that, Detective?'

'You must follow your instinct.'

Fallon nodded at the sparsely populated room. 'When does the rest of the team get here?'

The two uniformed constables, Lafferty and Hart, turned to look at each other while Lillico just winced. 'Welcome to Scotland, DI Fallon. This is it for now. Apart from DS Dewar who's gone to sort us out some coffee.'

Fallon shook her head and turned to scrub some football results off the whiteboard before rummaging for a marker pen that actually worked. By the time she turned around, Dewar was passing out their drinks. 'Right. What do we know about this case?' she barked.

'Branding on the weapons, boss,' said PC Hart. 'Plus, the munitions boxes.'

'Great. And what does that tell us?'

'I put out an urgent email to the manufacturer last night,' said Dewar. 'Those guns saw ten years service in the US Army before the manufacturer took them back as part of an equipment upgrade. They were warehoused for one year before their acquisition by a reputable dealer in South Africa.'

'I admire your out-of-hours working, Sergeant, but can anyone spot the flaw in that last statement?'

The room was silent for a few moments until Lillico took her drift. 'You don't think there are any reputable gun dealers in South Africa?'

'For the sake of argument, let's say the South African dealer places the guns on the international black market. By some route we've still got to determine, they find their way to sunny Scotland along with a meagre amount of ammunition. What does that tell us?'

'The main dump of ammo is still to follow?' asked Hart.

'The shooters already have plenty of bullets,' suggested Lafferty.

Dewar spoke between sips of his coffee. 'That part of the consignment was lost or seized elsewhere?'

'All fair observations,' said Fallon. 'If I planned to fight a war with these guns, I'd want a crate of ammo per rifle. We have just over a metric tonne, which is basically two full magazines per gun. That isn't a lot for an automatic rifle, even in burst mode.'

Lillico nodded. 'Most likely, the ammunition is being stored separately or is still enroute. Meaning, we need to be watching for it.'

'Now ask me the next obvious question,' Fallon prodded.

'Who were the guns for?' asked Hart.

'That is indeed the million-dollar question,' said Fallon. 'Any ideas?'

'Organised crime?' asked Lafferty.

'Wrong type of weapon. Too big and too flashy. Other ideas?'

'Gangs?'

'Give me strength,' she muttered.

Lillico cleared his throat. 'I guess the reason Edinburgh called for a counter-terrorism officer from Northern Ireland is because they believe the guns were destined for the province.'

'Thought that was all done with?' said Lafferty.

'Never,' exclaimed DS Dewar. 'Orange and Green will still be fighting come the end of the world.'

'What's your assessment?' Lillico asked Fallon.

Fallon looked down at her feet for a few moments. 'Politically, the current direction of travel in Ireland is for an island-wide referendum on reunification. Whether that leads to a united Ireland, or an entrenchment of the status quo is anyone's guess. But if the process loosens Northern Ireland's links to the UK, then we might see Loyalist paramilitaries preparing to fight against a Nationalist government in Dublin.'

'What kind of groups?' asked Lafferty.

Fallon shrugged. 'Loyalist Defence Force. Loyalist Volunteer Force, UDA. There are a bunch. For the uninitiated,' she said, frowning at PC Hart's fresh face, 'the Ulster Nationalists fought the British under the banner of outlawed republican groups like the IRA. Notionally, they're Catholic while the Loyalist groups that sprang up to resist them support British rule and its monarchy. Those guys on the whole subscribe to Protestantism, though I doubt many go to church. And the thing is, this latter alliance sees Scotland as safe territory. They've got family and cultural connections here. If this was a weapons stash for a republican outfit, I'd have expected it to come through the south of Ireland.'

'But why bring guns from Africa and stockpile them here instead of Ireland?' asked Hart.

'The guns have lots and lots of grease,' said Fallon. 'Which suggests they're in deep storage as a doomsday arms dump.'

Lillico shifted in his chair. 'Sounds macabre.'

'The Loyalists have done this in the past; built weapons stores for deployment in the event of closer relations between Dublin and Belfast.'

Dewar, as the oldest person in the room, seemed to doubt this. 'When was that, 'cause I don't recall anything?'

'There was a flashpoint in late 1985. A network of Loyalist organisations formed something called *The Ulster Clubs*. These groups rapidly went underground. Their motto was, "Hope for the best and prepare for the worst."'

'Long time ago,' observed Lillico.

'Aye,' said Fallon, darkly. 'It was. But in the circumstances, this arms dump might be evidence they're replacing their kit.'

Dewar lifted and dropped his shoulders, seeming to accept her explanation.

Fallon printed the word, "Loyalists?" on the whiteboard and turned back to face the team. 'Anything back from forensics yet?'

Dewar opened a report on his tablet. 'The forensics guys examined everything before it left the cave. Very few fingerprints on the outer packaging. Looks like they were wearing gloves. And if these guns have already passed through many hands, it's unlikely we'll get a hit.'

'Agreed,' said Fallon. 'Which means we'll have to get our lucky break another way. DI Lillico, have you had a chance to go hunting for our sentry yet?'

Lillico nodded at Lafferty and Hart. 'It's a confined area, so these two fine officers are going house to house this afternoon, starting at Clanyard Bay.'

'Gather photos if you can. Look for dashcam footage and images captured by internet-capable doorbells. And when you encounter holiday accommodation, get the names of recent guests so we can access their social media profiles. Be absolutely certain that anyone deployed to keep an eye on this weapons stash wouldn't have been using their real name. That means we need images that I can send back to Belfast and scan against lists of known faces.'

The others glanced at each other. 'We can gather names and details,' said Hart. 'But if we have to do all the desk work to flesh out the contacts, that'll really slow us down.'

Fallon brushed at a mark on her trousers. 'Then your superiors need to find a bigger team.'

'*Special Investigations* has desk researchers based in Bathgate,' said Lillico. 'If you give me details for a liaison officer in Belfast, my team can do the donkey work.'

'Good.' Fallon looked around the room and made a chivvying motion. 'Come on. What else should we be considering?'

'All those boxes of guns,' said Hart. 'I assume they arrived by boat?'

'Can think of no other reason to store them in a remote sea cave. Look at it from the courier's perspective. You deliver by boat, and later, you extract by boat. Means there's no chance of someone intercepting the weapons during a random vehicle check.'

Hart nodded. 'So, my next question is, how long would it take to shift that lot from a boat to the cave?'

'Good point. Let's look at ship movements over the last year. What vessels were in the area and lingered enough to deploy a rib for at least two hours?'

'Agree with your logic that the guns arrived by boat,' said Dewar. 'But we should check other routes too, like if there were any large vehicles seen in the area.'

'And there's a bunch of disused airfields around here,' added Lafferty. 'I'll check if anyone has seen unusual activity.'

'Good ideas, guys, but keep them coming. For example, did anyone look at the serial numbers on the guns?'

The Stranraer team glanced nervously at each other while no one volunteered a response.

'Your forensics people spent three hours yesterday, faithfully recording all those numbers, and no one thought to look?'

Again, she was met with obstinate silence.

'They flow in perfect sequence, apart from one gap near the bottom of the list where we skip twelve numbers. What might that tell us?'

'Six to a case, so maybe two cases got dropped in the sea?' said Lillico.

'Perhaps,' said Fallon. 'Or maybe they were pilfered, or …'

'They got separated from the main batch,' said Dewar, catching her drift.

'Exactly. Meaning they might be in circulation. So, be alert for them turning up.'

The meeting rattled on for a few minutes with Fallon prodding them to think beyond their usual range of rural crimes. When everyone had an action list that was as long as their arms, Fallon dismissed them.

'You're hard on them,' said Lillico, stepping up to the whiteboard.

'On who?'

'These local guys. At times you bordered on condescending.'

'Oh, the poor dears,' Fallon mocked. 'Didn't realise the Scots were so thin-skinned.'

'Believe me when I say, I don't give a grouse turd for what you think of us. But these other officers attend domestic callouts and traffic accidents for a living. They've not done counter-terrorism before, and you'll achieve more if you coach them.'

Fallon seemed to think about this for a few moments, then leaned close enough to Lillico for her breath to tickle his face. 'DI Lillico, have you ever seen the corpse of a man shot to death by an M16 rifle?'

Lillico closed his eyes and shook his head.

'Might not surprise you to know that I have, so spare me your team-building sentimentality. If I push these officers hard enough so they catch the intended recipients of these guns a few hours faster rather than by treating them all nicey-nicey, then that's just me doing my job.' He opened his eyes to find her glaring at him. 'If you've any problems with that, go phone your superiors and get me sent back to Ireland.'

Lillico nodded.

'Right. As the only armed officer in attendance, I'm away to guard those sodding guns with my life until you eejits find someone equipped to take them off my hands.'

She pushed past him on the way to the cells. 'Nice talk, by the way. Was there anything else?'

'Nope, that was everything. Besides, you've got a gun and I haven't.' He pulled out his mobile and wiggled it at her. 'I'll phone my boss. See if I can get us some armed gun-sitters.'

An hour later, Lillico was still in Stranraer checking the forensics data for anything else he might have missed when his phone rang. 'George. Thanks for returning my call.'

'What is it, Alex,' Wiley grumbled. 'Got fires burning and can't linger to chat.'

'Did you see the bulletin last night on the Wigtownshire arms cache?'

'I did.'

'Well, unfortunately, that's fallen in my lap. I'm going to need to beg some of Eliza's time if that's okay?'

'Fine with me.'

'And I have another logistical challenge.'

'You stay right where you are, Alex, while I rush down and mop your brow,' Wiley mocked. 'What do you want?'

'The long and short of it is, we have a van load of high-powered rifles stashed in the Stranraer clink and I need to move them to a secure location.'

Wiley took several seconds to respond. 'What's the problem with keeping them locally?'

'Security risk. We don't have the resources to protect them if the bad guys come back to fetch them.'

Again, Wiley was silent for a few moments. 'Might be tricky, Alex. I can think of a few good reasons why we'd leave them where they are.'

Lillico bit back his frustration. 'We have one armed officer who's a DI from Ulster. She's meant to be helping us work the case; not babysitting the gun stash.'

'I hear you, Alex,' Wiley growled. 'Give me an hour. I'll round up some officers I can trust.'

'George, what's the issue? This kind of weaponry should be in our highest-security lock-up.'

'Aye, maybe. But it might tie back to something I'm working on so I'd rather we kept this kind of firepower away from the central belt. Look, hold tight for a couple of hours, Alex. I'll find the right guys. An armed team I can deploy with you for several days. Just 'til things become clearer up here.'

Lillico hung up and wandered through to the rear of the station where Fallon was guarding the weapons. 'An armed response team from Bathgate will be with us in a couple of hours.'

'Great. Any word on when this lot moves to a more secure location?'

'Nope. For now, they'll be guarding the weapons on site which is clearly a sub-optimal arrangement.'

Fallon swore under her breath but said nothing.

Lillico tried to sound cheerful. 'At least you can get back to work tomorrow. What's your plan?'

'Should be obvious, DI Lillico,' she replied without lifting her head from her phone. 'I'm gonna sail back to Ireland to try and figure out who's ordered two pallets of heavy weaponry.'

'Okay then. Well, if you don't need company, I'm heading to my accommodation.'

'Sure. I guess it's well past your bedtime.'

Lillico glared at her but said nothing.

'Okay, sorry. That wasn't fair,' she mumbled. 'It's just ...'

'Just what?' growled Lillico.

Fallon thumbed over her shoulder at the locked cell. 'I thought Northern Ireland was finished with all this crap. Brings back unhappy memories, so it does.'

Lillico turned to go. 'Let's catch the bad guys, DI Fallon. Then we can all sleep a little easier in our beds.'

'As long as your armed response team shows up, I'll be on an early ferry. I'll start making enquiries and catch up with you later in the week.'

Chapter 7

'You look knackered,' murmured Cassy as the team gathered around the conference room table to make their final changes to issue sixty. 'The wee one still keeping you up at night?'

'Long drive back from Wigtownshire. Didn't get home until after eleven, and this morning I was up again at five.'

'And all courtesy of Alex Lillico?' said Mhairi. 'I thought you didn't do police jobs anymore?'

'This isn't part of a criminal investigation. Rather it was an incidental find that might offer us an interesting archaeological site in an old sea cave.'

Cassy arched her eyebrows at Gill. 'Sea monsters? Another gigantic eel?'

He shook his head. 'Basically, the cave contained the bodies of a primitive family.'

'We talking stone age?' asked Craig.

'Not exactly.' Gill pulled out his phone and tabbed to a photo. 'Based on some of the items found in the cave, we're estimating the remains are about three hundred years old.' He swallowed. 'But that wasn't what made it interesting. The bones indicate the people were all quite … small.'

'How small?'

'About a metre.'

'Kiddies?' barked Larry.

'No. These were very short adults.'

Cassy winced. 'I'm not following.'

Gill rubbed the back of his head. 'You guys aren't going to like this one.'

Cassy screwed up a piece of paper and threw it at him. 'Honestly, once we got past alien bones, I stopped being surprised.'

Gill shifted in his chair. 'There is one ubiquitous myth that we haven't covered in our media. It's prevalent across the whole of Scotland and especially the west.'

Larry nudged Cassy. 'If yon fella beats aroon this bush any mare, am gonna pick up the phone and report him tae the royal society fir the prevention o' cruelty tae bushes.'

Gill's hands flashed up. 'Okay, we've got potential proof that the Fae existed.'

Cassy's mouth gaped open. 'What?'

'The Wigtownshire sea cave I visited holds the first tantalising evidence for diminutive humans.'

Larry laughed. 'You're huntin' fir fairies now?'

Craig held up a hand. 'Hold the bus. Are we talking about mythical fairies or fabled ferries?'

Cassy worked to keep a straight face. 'Speaking as an islander, I have more faith in fairies than this county's ability to build car ferries.'

Gill ignored their banter. 'Fairy isn't a helpful word. It conjures up images of pocket-sized women with wings. But yes, *Fae. Guid Folk, Fair folk*, the *Little People* – these are all descriptions for a cultural dimension in Scottish folklore that's never been rationally understood.'

Cassy's shaking head morphed into a businesslike nod. 'And this cave; what facts were you able to glean?'

'A rockfall recently exposed a series of linked caverns and the police got involved because of the human remains. Since then, I've spoken to an experienced speleologist, and he suspects there's a blocked passageway leading to a more extensive cave system beyond the initial search zone.'

'Will the police be opening that up?'

Gill shrugged. 'They've no particular reason to. The local Fiscal has had sight of the bones in the morgue so unless there's evidence of foul play, they're done with it.'

'But you're still interested,' added Craig.

Gill looked around the faces. 'Well, think about it. A quick web search demonstrates Wigtownshire has a huge amount of Fae folklore. *Mys.Scot* now has exclusive access to excavate in the cave system, so we might uncover a rational basis to explain the myth.'

'Okay,' said Cassy. 'Still listening.'

'These caves might help us interpret Fae mythology and I'm going to give this a few days of my time.'

Cassy nodded at Larry. 'You did a story about the fairies of Glenshee about a year ago. Did you ever get the sense there was more to it than wishful thinking?'

'Naw, Cass. The story wuz a nice wee piece, but it wuz aw bollocks.'

'Did you talk to any experts?' asked Gill.

Larry thought for a moment. 'There was a fella based near Uig on Skye. Dinnae recall his name. Had a lang chat wi him on the phone. Dead passionate about fairies but the laddie was twa ghaists short o' a Christmas carol.'

'Okay. Could you dig out your notes and send them to Mhairi?' Gill turned sheepishly to Mhairi. 'Could you work your usual magic and see if you can uncover any solid data on the topic. Or find me an expert who can?'

Mhairi straightened her glasses and tossed her long brown hair behind her. 'I have a friend,' she began. 'She was a classmate when I was at uni.'

'Do you think she'd know anything about the Fae?' asked Gill, suddenly more optimistic about the task ahead of him.

'No,' sniffed Mhairi. 'She lives in London in a smart flat and works for the British Museum, where she leverages her expertise translating Sumerian cuneiform on ancient clay tablets into English. Meanwhile, I get to live in Dundee with my parents, scraping Google for fairy myths. I'm just wondering where I went wrong, really.'

Cassy leaned over and patted Mhairi's hand. 'But you play in Scotland's favourite ceilidh band. Your pal can't touch you for that.'

'Scotland's *favourite* ceilidh band?' Mhairi retorted.

Cassy's shoulders flinched. 'Okay. Broughty Ferry's favourite ceilidh band.'

'Hang on,' said Craig, lifting a hand. 'Gill, are you sayin' you're gonna be creeping around a crumbling sequence of sea caves?'

'Mebbe.'

'Okay.'

'What, Craig?'

'Just thinkin' you might want to make sure your life insurance is tickety boo.'

'Aye, laddie,' said Larry, suddenly serious. 'And dinnae breath a wurd tae the cat mag.'

'There,' said Mhairi, an hour later, laying a scrap of paper down on Gill's desk.

He looked up. 'What's this?'

'Telephone number and web address for a guy called Rory Carmichael. He runs a fairy trail in Wigtown. And that makes him the closest thing to an expert as you're going to get in the far southwest.'

'Wigtown's only thirty miles from our cave, so that's do-able.' Gill tapped the paper with his knuckles. 'But I've got to ask, is this guy serious?'

Mhairi glanced at the ceiling and jiggled her shoulders. 'He runs a cutesy forest trail full of artificial fairy houses, so that's not encouraging. On the other hand, his blog has oodles of well-written articles. It could be worth you having a chat.'

Gill watched Mhairi turn and walk back to her desk. 'Was that it?' he called after her.

'Was that what?'

'Your sum research on the Fae?'

'I'm really quite busy, Gill,' she said, sitting down. 'If you discover a fairy civilization that recorded its history on cuneiform tablets, then I'll jump back in.'

Heading home from work that afternoon, Gill felt chastened by the team's scepticism. Then again, no one had laughed out loud, so he sensed they'd get behind him if the story took shape. Leaving the office under a downpour, he dashed up Crichton Street and joined the main thoroughfare with its cluster of city centre bus shelters. He was about to trot passed them when he spotted a familiar figure dressed all in black. Frankie had been one of the very first candidates for the Read*Scot* literacy charity Gill managed with Rosemary Solomon, and over the course of a dozen sessions, he'd got to know the girl quite well. And at this moment, even though she sat hunched over her phone and hadn't seen him, Gill decided it was the right thing to stop and talk to her.

'Hey, Frankie. How's it going?'

The girl looked up and Gill noticed she'd put on a bit of weight since he'd last seen her. 'Oh, hi.' She shrugged. 'Auch, same old shite. How 'bout yourself?'

'Aye, busy. Darting here there and everywhere.' He studied her hang-dog expression for a few moments. 'You still kicking ass? Last time we spoke you were celebrating your first full year in a job.'

'Aye. Great while it lasted.'

'What happened?' he asked, gently.

'The buggers replaced the last of their manned checkouts with self-scanning. I tried to stay on as a shelf-stacker, but they could only offer me nights and that wasnae working for me.'

'I am sorry to hear that. Any joy finding something new?'

Frankie vaguely thumbed over her shoulder back at the city's main shopping centre. 'I was in there just now for an interview. A clothing retailer. But there were thirty girls begging for only two jobs. Based on the lassies doin' the interviews they'll probably go for skinny girls with fake tan and blonde frae a bottle.'

'Aye, the job market is tough at the moment. Are you keeping Read*Scot* updated with your details? Sometimes employers reach out to us looking for apprentices or the like.'

'Aye. Judy has my number.'

'Great. And have you considered going back to college for further training?'

'Nae cash, Gill. My mum and dad made it clear I need to be earning.'

Gill nodded his understanding while he thought desperately how he might help the girl. 'Listen, Read*Scot* is having its first national conference at the end of September. We've a stack of extra work to get ready for it. Would you mind if I gave Judy your name? I know she's looking for some extra help.'

'Here in Dundee?'

'The conference is in Edinburgh, at Rosemary Solomon's insistence, but most of the extra work will happen in our office here in town.'

Frankie's face brightened. 'Sounds great!'

'I mean, it'll be temporary, but it'll keep you ticking over while you find something permanent.'

'Thank you, Gill.' She leaned in to give him a clumsy embrace. 'Thank you so much.'

They chatted back and forth for a few moments until the arrival of Frankie's bus interrupted them. With a shy wave, she hopped on board and was gone.

Before he did anything else, he called Judy and left her a voicemail. One way or another he needed her to find eight weeks of constructive work for Frankie, and he hoped his spontaneous employment offer wouldn't ruffle any feathers.

Walking in search of his own bus, the sadness of the encounter weighed on him. Frankie had worked hard in her final year of college to lift her reading ability to something approaching average. But, when her education drew to a close, she'd discovered how unskilled she appeared when compared to many of her peers. And it was tough for any young person coming onto the job market during a period of intense technological change. As businesses fought to remain competitive, the rising power of machines was eating low-skilled jobs like Frankie's.

'Let me get this straight,' said Tony the following morning. 'This quote is to investigate a rockpool in a cave?'

'I know it looks like a large number, Tony. But it's a modest price to unlock what might become our biggest story this year.'

'What kind of story?'

'That a primitive, cave-dwelling society persisted in Scotland until the late eighteenth century,' said Gill, enthusiastically. 'We're talking cave paintings, homemade tools and clothes, subsistence living. Tony, you're the one who always sees the human angle in the history we uncover. Whether these folk were just outrageously poor, or whether they lived like this by choice, there must be a story here.'

'Agreed, Gill. But this quote is to explore one hole in a single cave. If you're right and there was some kind of community living in those cliffs, then this could be the first invoice in a very expensive dig.'

'If we find anything significant, it's likely we'd headline the story, then pass responsibility for the site to one of the national bodies. And they in turn might fund us to carry on.'

'And who owns the land you're working on?'

'It's a toss-up between the Crown Estates who own the seabed right up to the high tide mark, and the local dairy farmer who owns the fields above the cliffs. I've already spoken to him, and he's emailed to give his permission.'

'And you're sure this story has potential?'

'Even if we find nothing beyond what we've uncovered already, it's still enough to build an entire issue around. And I don't think we can report on that and just shrug our shoulders and say the physical challenges blocked any further investigation.'

Tony contemplated Gill's point of view. 'Okay. I agree it's not an extraordinary sum. I'm looking at it and wishing I earned what these guys charge every day.' He stopped to wave the piece of paper in the air. 'If I say yes, when do you think you'd start?'

'Murray McGovern says he needs a week to ten day's notice between us accepting his quote and commencing an excavation in the cave.'

'Meaning, it might generate material you could slot into issue sixty-one?'

'That's right.' Gill chanced a glance at Cassy. 'You're okay if we press ahead?'

'I am.' Tony pressed Murray's quote back into Gill's hand. 'But don't bring me any more of these unless it's a rock-solid story.'

'Was that a pun, boss?' Gill grinned. 'Cassy, did Tony just make a joke?'

Tony pointed at his door. 'Away you go, Gill, and dig me up a story.'

Chapter 8

Roddy Canmore heeled his office door closed and tossed his slim briefcase onto his desk. Then he reached into a locked drawer for a burner phone, snapping it out of its wrapper before tapping in a number.

'DCI Macfarlane.'

'Senator, I'm returning your message. Is this line secure?'

Macfarlane seemed to take a second to register the identity of the caller. 'It is, sir. Absolutely.'

'Good. I'm hoping you have an update on Lorna Cheyne?'

'I'm making progress. I know she'll be released next week, and I've confirmed she'll be living at her old home address.'

'Do you know if she's made any plans? Job applications, that kind of thing?'

'During her exit, interview she claimed she'll be working online. Something to do with the home security where she worked before.'

'Meaning she can start robbing more innocent people?'

'We'll be keeping an eye on her, sir.'

'Well, I want to send her a visitor. Be alert for my message, and when I send word, make sure your people stay well away from her for a couple of hours.'

He heard Macfarlane swallow while he processed the implications of Roddy's command. 'I'll see to it.'

'And you offered your help on my other emerging situation. My top man thinks it's time to bring your resources to bear.'

'Go ahead.'

'It's delicate, Angus. We're going to need your most trusted team.'

Chapter 9

*Stirling,
31st January 1746*

Dearest Mother,

Whilst near a postal carriage I seize this opportunity to convey our news. Firstly, let me assure thee that Father is well. Reports from Carlisle confirm the city's surrender to Cumberland was essential to spare it from destruction, thus his bravery in conceding the town was a mercy to its citizens. Though he is now a prisoner of the antichrist, King George II, that man is, I remind thee, an English gentleman and Father can expect forbearance, as can all our heroes.

I am glad to report successes from Scotland. Richard and I captained a small artillery unit that made short work of government forces at Falkirk last week. We now turn our attention to Stirling Castle, earnestly desiring its capitulation before Cumberland and his forces reach us. There are reports he hath taken Edinburgh and may soon move up the Forth. But the Mother of Heaven is on our side, and our victory will come as surely as the flowers in spring.

The Irish soldiers we march with are an uncouth lot, slow to cross themselves before battle and disposed to curse the Prince who pays for their loyalty. The Scots too are rough and unwashed, though many are godly. But I find myself yearning for the French soldiers, due to arrive any day now. I am sure there will be familiar faces amongst these brave comrades. Richard, for his part, prefers the Highlanders. He wishes me to tell thee he is learning to play the bagpipes, a most dreadful racket even in the hands of an expert!

We expect to journey south again soon once help arrives from the continent. By then, I hope to greet thee in person with a holy kiss.

Thy son,

Francis Towneley.

Chapter 10

With a week before the exploratory dig, Gill kept busy with work and family. Issue sixty was in good shape though the following one still needed a tonne of work, so between long hours at his desk and the early shift with Josh, he didn't have much spare time. And yet, there was one appointment he'd ring-fenced in his diary, and it bristled with peril.

'You're nervous,' said Salina that Saturday morning before he left for Edinburgh.

'My first time on a horse,' said Gill, with forced brightness.

'I get that, but are you going to do that other thing?'

'What other thing, my love?'

Salina picked up Josh and used the child's feet to playfully dig Gill in the ribs. 'The Doug thing.'

Gill made growling noises while he pretended to eat Josh's toes. 'If the opportunity comes up.'

'Oh, sure,' said Salina, over the top of Josh's giggling. 'I can imagine how that goes. "Hey, Doug, while we're chatting, are you aware one of my best pals is clairvoyant, and I'm sorry to tell you, but she's read your mail?"'

'I'll find a way to slip it into conversation,' said Gill.

And so, he felt nervous when he pulled up at a bus stop near Edinburgh airport and waited for his passenger to jump in. Adina's husband, Douglas Baird, was a tall, rangy man with a kind face and an academic air. After a few morning pleasantries, he gave Gill directions for his daughters' riding school near Livingston. The girls' lesson was later in the morning and Adina would bring them out in the family Tesla. Keen to encourage, he'd offered to tag along to Gill's first equestrian encounter. Driving out of the city, the two men chatted rugby for a few minutes and scratched around topics of conversation the way men do when they don't know each other well.

'This horse-riding thing,' asked Douglas. 'Has Adina put you up to it?'

'Aye.'

Douglas nodded. 'It's simply she didn't say why.'

'Complicated,' said Gill. 'Suffice to say we both felt the ability to ride a horse is a worthy life skill.'

Douglas thought about this for a second. 'Just for disclosure, she's told me about this armour thing you're both involved in.' He wiggled an uncertain finger at Gill. 'And she claims that you personally carry some kind of magical sword?'

'Okay. I see we're rapidly moving past sports and weather, Doug. You sure you want to get so intimate on a Saturday morning?'

'If you don't want to talk about it, I won't press you.'

'Actually, I'm glad she told you. Husbands and wives should be open about this kind of thing.' Gill threw him a smile. 'How do you feel about it?'

Douglas released a long slow breath. 'My faith has never got beyond a fundamental certainty about the existence of good and evil. I've never felt the urge to think anymore about it. To be honest, I find it rather unsettling to imagine angels driving around on motorbikes in their mission to direct humanity.'

'Trust me. I hear you,' said Gill, under his breath. 'I fully understand if it makes you uncomfortable.'

'On the contrary, I'm fascinated. Can you show me now?'

Gill flashed him a smile. 'Unfortunately, it doesn't work like that.'

Douglas tilted his head as an acknowledgement and Gill decided to steer the conversation. 'Tell me, how did you and Adina meet?'

'University College London. She was doing a postdoc in Persian Studies, and I was a year from finishing a PhD in British history.'

'Oh, aye. What period?'

'How the Jacobite rebellions shaped the first two decades of the unified parliament.' He paused to indicate where Gill should take a left. 'I met Adina at a staff reception a few months after she started.'

'And somewhere along the line, you moved to Edinburgh.'

'Yes. Scotland's National Museum headhunted Adina and I furthered my research by taking a teaching job at the University of Edinburgh.'

'Wonderful opportunity,' observed Gill.

'Yes. It all came about quite suddenly.'

'Almost like … a coincidence,' said Gill.

Douglas looked away. 'I guess.'

It was Gill's turn to suck in a deep breath because it was now or never. 'And she's never figured out you were working for MI5?'

'I beg your pardon?'

'Sorry, Doug. I thought we were being straight with each other?'

'Honestly, Gill. I have no idea what you're talking about.'

'That's fine. I'm sure they tell you to say that. But this information has been a burden to me, and I haven't had a better moment than this to get it off my chest.'

Douglas laughed. 'What? Sure, I'm just a boring academic. I can't imagine why you'd even suggest such a thing.'

Gill sighed. 'You'll recall the wee gathering for the Armour Group that Adina hosted in your home a couple of months back. Apart from Lorna who was still in the clink, I recall you met the rest of our team?'

'I did.'

'And in the course of that little gathering, you shook hands with Ailsa.'

'I would've greeted everyone who came that day …' Doug said, his face abruptly catching Gill's implication. 'Ah, damnit.'

'It's not consistent, but sometimes, Ailsa can see stuff just with a handshake.'

Douglas turned away. 'Adina hinted at that.'

'So, tell me, Doug. What is with you and MI5?'

Douglas was quiet for a few moments. 'I couldn't possibly comment.'

'Adina thinks you don't know about her.'

'About what?'

'Her past. The people she used to work for.'

'That's for the best.'

'Like I say,' said Gill. 'Husbands and wives should tell each other these kinds of things.'

'I love her. I don't want her to feel I've been dishonest with her.'

Gill shrugged. 'She's got broad shoulders. And in her line of work, do you think she'd be surprised?'

Doug's gaze hardened. 'Are you going to rat me out?'

'No. But I'm being honest with you by telling you I'm aware. And maybe, if I was in your shoes, I'd value the chance to talk about it.'

Doug left a lengthy pause. 'I didn't get much formal training. I was what's called an "asset" rather than a trained operative. My instructions were to befriend her and report her movements. That's all.'

'And then you fell in love with her?'

Douglas wiped a hand across his mouth. 'I couldn't carry on, doing what they wanted. So, my handler explained, that in the circumstances, my brief tenure with the security services was over. During a difficult evening in the bowels of Edinburgh Castle, he reminded me I'd signed the official secrets act, and I should say nothing to anybody.' He turned to peer at Gill. 'Even to guys with magical swords.'

Gill raised his left hand. 'Personally, I think you should tell Adina. Either way, your secret is safe with me.'

Douglas turned to fully face Gill. 'And what's your secret, Gill?'

'Do I have a secret?'

'Adina is wary of you. And I think all this matey stuff between you guys is a bit of a ruse.'

Gill said nothing.

'Yes,' murmured Douglas. 'The more I look at you, the more certain I am that you're hiding something.'

Gill slowed down to turn into the riding centre. 'The Armour Group is steering into choppy waters, Doug. You tell Adina what she needs to know about MI5, then I'll I give her permission to tell you about Finlaggan.'

'Finlaggan? As on Islay?'

'Aye. When you two have sorted out who knows what about each other, she'll explain what I mean.'

As Adina delivered her girls to their riding lessons, Gill's session was just ending. The man himself was bent at the waist, rubbing mud off his trousers and groaning before he stood up.

'Well? How did it go?' she demanded.

Douglas stood with his arms folded and gave the merest shake of his head. 'I think it's safe to say, he's not a natural.'

'The damn creature always seemed to be bouncing up while I was bouncing down.' Gill rubbed his inner thigh. 'I hurt in places I didn't know existed.'

'And I thought you were the action man,' she said, with her amusement feeding off her husband's thinly restrained glee.

'I don't think he was listening when the instructor explained how to get a horse to speed up and slow down.'

'I was in blind terror,' Gill protested. 'If I didn't want to be catapulted into space, gripping my legs around the ribs of the beast felt like the right thing to do.'

'Thank goodness she knew to stop at the fence, otherwise, the pair of you would be running yet.'

'Aye,' mumbled Gill, rubbing his shoulder. 'Pure dead brilliant.'

'Which horse was he on?' Adina asked Douglas.

'The one our girls like. The mid-size cob called *Pebbles*.'

'From where I was sitting, she was a fire-breathing, journalist-eating, warhorse.'

Douglas sniggered again, then reached to shake Gill's hand. 'I'll think on what we talked about.'

'Thank you.'

'And I'll see you at the same time tomorrow?'

'Och, I don't want to drag you out. I can come and suffer on my own.'

'Wouldn't miss it,' said Douglas, dryly. 'Haven't laughed so much in ages.'

Chapter 11

Two days after his second riding lesson, Gill's body still ached while he stood side by side with Ailsa. They were leaning against his battered VW Passat and staring at the oat-coloured brickwork of HMP Stirling. With its high mesh fences and soccer pitch, Gill thought it looked more like a school than a prison. Designed like a campus college, the only notable security was the entrance gate with its bars and cameras.

'Excited?' he asked.

Ailsa nodded. 'You?'

'Waited a long time for this.'

'The whole gang together at last,' said Ailsa.

They stood, with their arms lightly folded, with only a short delay before Lorna came striding across the carpark towards them. Gill's first impression was that she looked younger than he remembered from their encounters two years before. Her straight, straw-blonde hair was neatly brushed and cut to shoulder length. In her long, flowing limbs, Gill observed strength.

'Looking good, my darling,' said Ailsa, pushing off the car to greet her friend. They clung in a tight embrace for a long moment before Ailsa released her and nodded at Gill. 'And you two have met.'

'Hi, Gill,' said Lorna, offering him her hand. 'Sorry about the whole almost incinerating you, thing.'

Gill squeezed her hand in both of his. 'No problem. And thank you for the ... you know ... five second's grace.'

Lorna looked at her feet, embarrassed, then up at Ailsa. 'What's the plan?'

'We're meeting the rest of our crew in Glasgow. We'll grab some food together, then everyone who wants to can stay overnight at my hostel.'

'Tomorrow,' said Gill. 'I'll take you back to Portsoy. Unless you have alternative plans?'

'Thanks. That would be great.'

Gill opened his boot and Lorna tossed in her prison-issue holdall. Then with a sigh, she turned to the main prison block and raised her right fist in a long, silent salute. In response, from a dozen windows, hands, towels or blankets waved back.

'They're gonna miss you,' Ailsa observed.

Lorna nodded soberly. 'It's weird, but those were the best two years of my life.'

'No way!'

'Yes, way.'

'Ach, girl. You haven't seen anything yet.'

Arriving in Finnieston an hour later, Gill parked up and followed Ailsa and Lorna into the hostel. A quick check with reception confirmed the others were already gathered. Gill caught Ailsa looking nervously at Lorna. Perhaps she worried that prison would have diminished her friend, but when Gill sneaked glances at Lorna, the woman looked centred and peaceful.

'I've arranged for us to use the staff lounge for an hour,' said Ailsa. 'Give us a bit of privacy while we make our introductions.'

Lorna smiled. 'Great.'

Ailsa turned for the stairs. 'Then, if we're all playing nicely, we can go grab a bite.'

Gill followed on their heels, wondering what the next few minutes would bring. Walking into the lounge, Adina saw Lorna first and sprang to greet her. They shared a ferocious clutch for a few seconds before Adina turned to make introductions.

'This is Charlie.'

Charlie got to his feet, and unsmiling, took Lorna's hands and stooped to gently kiss them.

'And this is Rosemary Solomon. She is mother hen to us all.'

Solomon brushed away Charlie's helpfully outstretched hand while she struggled to her feet. She too, took both of Lorna's hands and pulled them to her cheeks. 'My dear, it is so good to finally meet you.'

'And …' Adina paused. 'I think you know Detective Inspector Lillico.'

Lillico got to his feet but didn't immediately move towards Lorna. Instead, he tugged the ends of his jacket and took a deep breath. A few seconds later, it was Lorna who walked over to him. 'Good to see you again, Inspector.'

'And you,' said Lillico. Taking her hand, he lightly shook it, then appeared to release his grip; surprise flowing across his face as Lorna gripped him tight. 'How … was your time in prison?' he asked in a conversational tone.

'Good,' said Lorna. 'Got lots of practise.'

Lillico didn't seem to know what she was implying. 'Football? Table tennis?'

'Bringing messages,' said Lorna. 'You know, with me being the *Message-bringer*, and all.'

Gill could see Lillico's face redden and wasn't sure he liked the direction of this conversation. But Lorna finally released Lillico and moved back to Ailsa's side.

After a long moment of mutual shuffling, Lorna peered around the group. 'Okay, so are you guys gonna show me or what?'

Solomon blinked twice. 'Show you?' she asked.

'The armour. I wanna check I'm running with the right crew.'

Solomon smiled dryly. 'My dear, these are not toys that the Armour Group parades at will.'

Lorna's head tilted to one side. 'But they can all do it, right?'

Solomon bathed Lorna in a stern stare and was just about to speak when they were all distracted by a metallic tapping sound to her left. Turning, they found the bulk of Charlie's body hidden behind a curved rectangular shield, the colour of shimmering mother of pearl.

'Bloody hell, Charlie,' gasped Ailsa, dashing to pull curtains that would screen the room from people passing up and down the corridor. When she returned, breathing heavily, her chest was covered by vibrant armour throwing off light forcing the others cover their eyes.

'Hey, dial that down, sister,' groaned Adina, her crystal helmet materialising over her head, neck and face.

Gill was next. The weight of his sword had increased over the previous moments while he reacted to the tension in the room. He drew his blade slowly and rested the tip on the floor while he gripped the hilt with both hands.

Lorna nodded, then turned to Lillico. 'Just you left.'

'Call me old-fashioned,' said Lillico, 'but I think this a situation where the lady should go first.'

Lorna laughed at this reference. 'Yeah. *Lady K* would have liked that.'

'May God rest her soul,' said Lillico, quietly.

Lorna gave a little jiggle, like she was warming up for a match. 'Gimme a second. Haven't done this in a while.' The others watched while she took a few theatrical breaths, then pointed at her feet. When nothing happened, she smiled nervously and tried hopping a few times, and again, pointing at her feet as if she was a compere introducing a cabaret act. As before, nothing changed.

'Definitely out of practise,' said Lorna, with a shake of her head. 'Maybe they just don't want to play today.'

Lillico took a step towards her, allowing the folds of his jacket to fall open revealing a shimmering crystal belt covering his waist and groin. Studying the man's expression, Gill could see the doubt in his eyes.

'No pressure, but try again,' he murmured.

'You know I can disappear,' protested Lorna. 'I mean, you've seen me do that, right?'

'Yes, but I've never seen your shoes,' said Lillico, slowly. 'And you know, just checking I'm running with the right crew.'

Lorna nodded at the gentle rebuke, then pirouetted on her toes and rotated through a circle. 'It's like Solomon says,' she quipped. 'This isn't a party trick I can do at will.'

Lillico took another step towards her, and Gill could see his doubt hardening into an accusation. He pointed at Lorna and … she disappeared.

Lillico stood transfixed while around him, the others burst out laughing, then started to clap.

'What just happened?' Lillico demanded.

Gill meanwhile could see the punchline coming and started pointing at Lillico's head.

'Boo,' yelled Lorna from where she'd jumped right behind Lillico.

Lillico flinched to one side, twisting to see Lorna leaning over him, delight plastered all over her face.

Flexing his fingers, he shook the tension from his limbs and let his arms slump. 'Okay. You got me.'

Lorna sidled up beside him, clearly delighted her trick had gone so well. She gave him a slight sideways jolt with her hip. 'Don't worry about me, Alex. I'm the real deal.' And walking into the centre of the room she did a little twirl. Peering at her feet, Gill observed her shoes resembled leather sandals, with loops going over her toes and feet, rising to wrap around her ankles. Like the other armour, it shimmered with colours between silver and pearl, though in Lorna's expression, the material was entirely flexible. Suddenly shy in the face of all the attention, she ducked between Ailsa and Adina before sliding her arms around their waists.

Adina patted Lorna's hand and threw Lillico a sympathetic smile. Then, over the next few moments, everyone's eyes fell on Solomon.

'Well,' said Solomon. 'I am delighted to observe, the Armour Group is now complete.'

After the awkwardness of their introductions, Alex Lillico enjoyed the evening, feasting on a spread of vegetarian and chicken dishes Ailsa had pre-ordered from her favourite Indian restaurant. Relishing the cardamom, coriander and cumin, he worked to soften his posture with Lorna, asking about her future work plans and for redecorating her home. Watching her chatting to Gill, he chided himself for his attraction to unattainable women. Eliza Hemmings had recently announced her engagement to her long-term partner, and Cassy Tullen remained utterly absorbed in the troubled life of her teenage son. And now, here he was, feeling like a shy schoolboy around a woman who'd masqueraded as a ghost to conduct a series of audacious thefts. In the process, she had terrified the few witnesses to her crimes and implicated her best friend in her criminality. Yes, he found Lorna appealing but at the same time, she was as unknowable as a deep dark pool.

Later, as the meal ended, he declined the offer of a night in Ailsa's hostel and left Glasgow to drive towards Bathgate. First thing tomorrow he'd a meeting with Eliza Hemmings to review the data gathered in Wigtownshire before heading back to Stranraer by lunchtime. The fact that he had another back-burner case over in the Borders was a distraction burdening his mental space to the maximum. So, with his eyes firmly on the road, he started the long drive home, determined at least to get a few hours in bed.

There was a puff of air beside him, as if the car's air-con unit had switched briefly on and off.

'Hi,' said Lorna, quietly from the passenger seat.

Lillico flinched in shock, sending his car veering halfway across the adjacent lane. 'How do you do that?' he shouted. 'You just … just jumped into a moving car!'

'The inertia is a bit weird,' said Lorna, giving a deft little shrug. 'But it's easy when I can see where I'm jumping to.'

Lillico gesticulated at the featureless motorway. 'See what?'

'I just pictured your face,' said Lorna. 'It's quite a nice face, though you could do with being a bit more smiley.'

'So, you thought you'd drop in for a chat?'

'No. This is business.'

'What kind of business?'

'In prison, someone tried to kill me. Actually, several someones.'

'And yet, here you are.'

Lorna looked away. 'I've learned how to make friends.'

'Friends?'

'There's a girl in there from Kilmarnock. Honestly, the lassie has fists the size of melons.'

'I'm sorry for your trouble,' said Lillico, fixing his eyes back on the carriageway. 'Your assailants; any idea who put them up to it?'

'No proof, but most likely the same esteemed politician who tried to kill me and my friend, Katie.' Lorna left a pause, perhaps wondering how much to say. 'I took something from him, and I think he's trying to get it back.'

'What did you take?'

'What it is and where it is now isn't important. I'm only here because I'm reporting a crime, Detective.'

Lillico grunted. 'If you'd like to pop into Bathgate tomorrow morning, I'll take a full statement from you.'

Lorna calmly shook her head. 'This isn't a formal matter. I can look after myself. It's the rest of the Armour Group I'm worried about. I told the others earlier, but you'd dashed off without saying goodbye.'

'Sorry. I've got an early start tomorrow.' He turned to smile apologetically to her. 'Are you looking forward to going home?'

Her shoulders dipped into a shallow shrug. 'Yes and no. It'll be weird without Gran. And I've no idea how people will treat me.'

'You'll have lots of friends who'll be glad to see you.'

Lorna took a few seconds to respond. 'Maybe.'

Lillico caught a little sadness in her voice. He glanced at her and remembered his first impressions of Lorna, with her pale blue eyes and long elegant limbs.

'Next weekend, Ailsa has offered to come and help me freshen up the house.' She turned to look at him. 'It sounds like the whole gang will be there. Do you think you'll be able to come?'

Lillico thought about this. 'Nothing social in my diary, so unless something blows up at work, I'll be there.'

'That would be great. Help me get to know you.'

'I'll do my best.'

'Take care, Alex.' And with that, Lorna jumped away.

Chapter 12

Eliza Hemmings was having a dull week. Although her workstation sat with others in Bathgate's civilian research cluster, she worked full-time these days for the *Special Investigations* team. And as much as she liked Alex Lillico, the guy wasn't afraid to ask her to go the extra mile. To process the images gathered in Stranraer's house-to-house enquiries, she had to take blurry, sideways photos from doorbells and smartphones and drop them into image manipulation software, producing cleaned-up, forward-facing views. And that's if they had an image at all. Many of the holiday home bookings had no locally captured photos attached, so she had to take contact details and dive into social media to find a picture. The final stage in her hunt was to take each captured image and run it against a wide net of potential suspects as identified by Shona Fallon. It was a relief, when two days in, she got a hit.

'Sorry, late finish last night in Glasgow,' said Lillico from his car when he picked up her call. 'With you shortly.'

'No need to come in. I've got a hot lead for you on your Stranraer investigation.'

Lillico sounded interested. 'Okay.'

'I've been trawling the images gathered in your door-to-door work and cross-matching them with Shona Fallon's files. There's one image in both datasets, a guy by the name of Iain Lynch,' said Eliza. 'Son of a UDA paramilitary. Iain is on file as a "person of interest." His father is a little more hardcore having done time in the 80s for attempting a hit on a Nationalist politician.'

'And where have we seen him?' asked Lillico.

'Your uniform guys crossed Lynch's path at Port Logan, in a caravan site. Just north of the weapons cache.'

'Eliza, this is excellent. Does this guy have any kind of criminal record?'

'No convictions. The PSNI interviewed him in 2015 after a social media outburst when he bragged, and I quote, "he'd bury the *Provos* under guns."'

'Sounds like a lovely chap. I'll radio ahead and we'll get right on it.'

It took three hours for Lillico to drive down to Portpatrick and rendezvous with two uniformed officers before driving down to Port Logan. This tiny hamlet comprised a row of white cottages facing the sea across a sandy beach. An old stone harbour, little more than a jetty topped with a lighthouse, marked the end of the town and beyond it, a potholed track led to a mown area dotted with tired static caravans. An old man carrying a black refuse sack appeared at the door of a toilet block and gaped at the arrival of two police cars.

'You've a guest here,' said Lillico, stepping out of his vehicle and presenting his warrant card. 'Iain Lynch. Can you tell me which van he's in?'

The old man stared back at him. 'Nobody here with that name.'

Lillico held up an image on his phone. 'How about this guy?'

The old man stumbled forward a few steps and directed a shaking forefinger further down the field. 'Gerry Wright. He's in number four. Though I've not seen him for a couple of days.'

Lillico nodded at the two officers to go and try the van, before turning back to the janitor. 'Gerry's real name is Iain Lynch. Do you have a key to his van?'

'What's this all about?'

'Just need to have a word with Mr Lynch.'

The old man's watery blue eyes peered in the direction of Lynch's caravan then back at Lillico. 'Do you have a warrant, son?'

'Really?' said Lillico, not hiding his exasperation. 'I can organise that. What's your name, sir?'

'Reggie McCabe.'

'You're the manager here?'

'Owner, manager and chief toilet scrubber.'

'Well, Mr McCabe, we can sit in my car and start filling out the paperwork. Of course, I'll need you to stay right beside me while we complete all the forms. Might take a couple of hours so, if you want to go down that route, I'll need to sling some "Police – No entry" tape around the whole site. Then we'll need to wait for authorisation from the local sheriff. That could take days, so in the meantime, to keep my team busy, I'll run a full health and safety inspection. Goodness knows what we might find. The whole thing could be quite troublesome. All being well, we'd have you up and running again by the end of the summer.'

The old man scowled. 'You only needed to ask nicely.'

'Top priority investigation, Mr McCabe. As one of my colleagues reminded me recently, we don't have time for nice.'

Reggie started to stumble away. 'I'll fetch the key.'

Lillico drew his hands to his hips and bit back against an explosion of frustration. A string of perplexing crimes across the Borders had filled his last twelve months and now he felt drained. He still despised bullying tactics, and he hated the prospect he'd become like George Wiley; cutting corners left and right to make the job a little easier. But then, he didn't enjoy needless obstructions to his work. If people like Reggie demanded to play by the book, that could cut both ways.

'No one here, boss,' said PC Lafferty five minutes later as Lillico arrived at van four with the park owner in tow.

'Mr McCabe. Would you voluntarily allow us to have a quick look inside so we can be sure Iain hasn't fallen and hurt himself?'

'Be my guest,' he grunted.

Officer Lafferty unlocked the door, and calling ahead, moved inside. Followed by PC Hart, their search took less than a minute. 'Nobody here, boss. Looks like they've taken their stuff and done a runner.'

'What?' said Reggie. 'But he's booked until mid-July'

'It appears he's left early. Did he say where he was from?'

'Said he was from London.'

'Did he sound like he was from London?'

Reggie thought. 'No. He was an Irish fella.'

'And did he tell you what he was doing here for the past few weeks?'

'Bird Watching,' Reggie shot back. 'Dead keen he was. Out mornings and evenings, away with his binoculars.'

'Where did he do that? I imagine there are a lot of different habitats around here if you're happy to drive for a couple of miles.'

Reggie shook his head. 'Said he liked the cliffs. He only ever walked south.'

'Towards Clanyard Bay?'

'Aye.'

'Thanks. I'm going to need you to lock the van again until we get a forensics team down here.'

'But you said …'

'We'll get the paperwork done and be out of your hair as quick as we can. In the meantime, can you take PC Lafferty and show him Mr Lynch's booking. I want to glean his address, contact details, car reg. Anything at all.'

Lillico watched them walk away and nodded at Hart to guard the van. Then he dialled Shona Fallon. 'Got a contender for that sentry we were discussing.'

'Excellent. Do you have a name for me?'

Lillico gave her what he had.

'Never heard of him. Don't suppose you have him in custody?'

Lillico sighed. 'Initial reports say he bailed out four days ago.'

'No surprises there. Still, this is fast work. I'll take those details and go rattle some cages.'

After Fallon hung up, Lillico felt unsettled. Leaving the uniform guys to do their thing, he took himself off and followed a narrow path through a waist-high thicket of summer ferns. Reaching a weathered park bench anchored in sandy soil, he took a deep breath of sea air before brushing off some debris and sitting down. On one level, he felt pleased with himself and his team. Solid policework had chased down a strong lead, and even Fallon sounded satisfied with their progress. Why then was he uneasy? Why was he struggling to pass off his treatment of Reggie as just another cost of efficient policing? He analysed his emotions for a few minutes then reluctantly admitted that his treatment of the man hadn't been fair. Taking a last deep breath of salty air, he stood up and reluctantly followed Reggie back to his office. It was a dingy, rubbish-strewn hovel that looked like the windowless storeroom at the back of the toilet block. Lafferty was still there, faithfully copying details from a paper register into his notebook.

'Mr McCabe. Could I have a word?'

Reggie's shoulders sagged and he followed Lillico back outside. 'What is it now, lad?'

'I want to apologise for my tactics earlier. What I said wasn't strictly true and I bullied you to get your urgent compliance. Based on the Police Scotland code of conduct, you have a reasonable basis for a complaint against me. If you'd like to proceed with a complaint, I will of course …'

'Wait, Detective, wait,' said Reggie, raising his right hand. 'It sounds to me like you're on the trail of a bad one. Let's get this done and then we can both get on with our days.'

Lillico saw sincerity in Reggie's eyes and nodded his thanks. 'Well, I apologise again. In my line of work, nothing matters more than the truth.'

Reggie nodded an acknowledgement and turned back towards the office, leaving Lillico to hitch his thumbs into his belt and ponder what came next. Grasping another thought flitting around his slightly less cluttered brain, he followed Reggie back into the office. 'Have any other guests recently left with little or no warning?'

'Aye. Lynch is the second this week.'

'Who was the other, if you don't mind me asking?'

Reggie leaned over the ledger. 'Chap called Stevie Blaine.'

'Would you have an image for him? The same way you did for Lynch.'

Reggie winked at Lillico. 'You gonna give me the same wee song and dance about getting a warrant for that information?'

Lillico smiled and stared at his feet for a few moments. 'I'll just appeal to your good nature, if that's okay. Then I'll get out of your hair as quickly as possible.'

Reggie seemed satisfied. 'Sure. I have an old CCTV system at the gate. Use it to deter fly-tippers. Gimme a second and I'll pull up an image of the guy.'

'Stevie Blaine,' Eliza repeated over a poor connection ninety minutes later. 'He's on our database due to a GBH conviction a few years back. These days he runs personal security for the leader of *New Scotland*.'

'You are joking?' Lillico said, covering one ear with his hand.

'Not joking. However, Blaine is not the guy in the images you sent.'

'Okay.'

'That particular big fellow has no criminal record to speak of, although we charged him a few years back for financial crimes while he worked for Aberdeen City Council.'

'And his name?'

'Billy Whyte. These days he's a local councillor for *New Scotland* in one of the Aberdeen constituencies. Oh, and he's a keen birdwatcher. His name and image pop up in a bunch of blogs.'

Lillico was silent for a few moments.

'Alex. Are you still there?'

'Yeah, I am. Just wondering why Billy Whyte would be pretending to be Roddy Canmore's bodyguard?'

'Hardly a coincidence he was holidaying two doors down from a terrorist suspect.'

Lillico chewed on this for a few moments. 'Does it suggest there's a Scottish connection to the guns?'

'I'll leave that question to you, Alex.' She tapped her keyboard a few times. 'Did you want me to keep processing images from Wigtownshire?'

'Please. But put a lower priority on the rest as it looks like one of these guys will have been minding the cache.'

'Sure.'

'Instead, can you start looking at ship movements? I need to know if any vessel lingered close to Clanyard Bay over the last few months.'

'Are we talking fishing boats or container ships?'

'Any vessel capable of carrying several tonnes of cargo and sitting still long enough to deploy a small boat to carry weapons to the shore.'

Eliza thought for a few moments. 'Yeah, I can do that. Ships must broadcast location data, so I'll figure out how to source that.'

'Thank you, Eliza. As ever, you're amazing.'

Chapter 13

Perth,
30th March 1746

Dearest Mother,

With great sadness, I must bring thee grievous news. Today I heard a trustworthy report that Father was executed along with the other officers of the Manchester regiment in the early days of March. This bulletin was too miserable for me to believe at first. Then, the Prince in his kind munificence, granted me an audience with our spy from London who carried this lament. This godly rogue assures me he saw Father die but begs thee to know thy husband did not suffer.

There is a change in the air here. No soldiers yet from France, though come they must. Meanwhile, new units arrive daily from the north as the Prince masses his army to take on Cumberland at Aberdeen. The news of these traitorous executions in London hath put fire in our bellies. We are eager to be at them, and when we have ground Cumberland's men into hasty Highland graves, we will surge south to victory.

Thy son, and companion in thy grief,
Francis Towneley.

Chapter 14

Lorna felt strange being back in her hometown. At first, she kept her head down, believing irrationally that everyone would know she'd been in prison and would judge her for it. But after a few days passed she realised that if anyone knew how she'd spent that last two years, they weren't mentioning it. Even when some familiar faces stopped to talk to her, they assumed she'd just been out of town for a while, which Lorna confirmed with a nod, as broadly it was true. And though she felt safer out and about, it was her third day at home before she finally mustered the courage to walk in the direction of the harbour.

Striding downhill towards the ancient stone port, with more courage in her feet than her heart, the first thing she noticed was *The Maltings* was still there, though during the years of her confinement, it had become *The Harbour Café*. This plus small changes to the décor suggested the previous owners, Lyle and Angie Caldwell, had finally thrown in the towel. She took a seat at the far end of the terrace that had once been her personal domain and waited for the server to notice her. When he finally pitched up, the acne-faced lad wasn't someone she recognised. She ordered a coffee and took tentative steps towards the question she was gagging to ask.

'You new here?'

He shrugged. 'This is my second season. Kinda makes me an old hand.'

'Used to work here myself,' said Lorna, trying to keep a conversational tone. 'Couple of years back.'

The lad thought for a moment. 'Not sure there's anybody left from that era. It's before my time.'

'I see the Caldwells have moved on.'

'Oh, they still own the building. But they've leased out the café and turned the house into an Airbnb.'

Lorna nodded. That won't have been popular with the locals. Lyle and Angie's last curse on a community they never learned to embrace.

The lad took her silence as the opportunity to move. 'I'll get your coffee.'

As suspected, her drink took more than a few minutes to arrive. Determined to face down this particular demon, Lorna sat back and rested her feet on the spindle of a nearby chair. For old times' sake, she'd been tempted to ask the lad for a vegan nut slice because underneath her nerves she was hungry. Instead, she closed her eyes and tried to enjoy the sunlight and the heat reflecting back on her from the old walls.

'Well, look what the cat dragged in,' said a voice beside her, as someone slapped down her coffee. Lorna opened her eyes to find Katie, dressed in kitchen garb, plus her trademark harlequin boots.

'Oh,' said Lorna. 'Didn't think you still worked here.'

'Work here?' barked Katie, yanking out the chair where Lorna was resting her feet and plonking herself down. 'I run this joint.'

'Really?'

'Remember Marco, the ecowarrior boyfriend?'

'Smouldering Italian eyes,' remembered Lorna.

Katie swung her left hand into view where a row of tightly packed diamonds caught the sunlight. 'Well, we're officially an item now. And it turns out his lofty planet-hugging credentials are bankrolled by his industrialist daddy.'

'Oh, that must have hurt.'

Katie sniffed and rubbed her nose. 'I forgave him when Daddy put up the cash for the lease here. I've got two years to make a go of it.'

'Like it,' said Lorna, looking around and nodding. 'Busy.'

'Considered switching it to a bistro, but coffee and cake is where the margin is.'

'And you're doing well?'

'You know, usual gig. Dead in the winter. Hootchin' in the summer.'

'Glad to hear that. You hiring by any chance?'

'Full roster just now,' Katie shot back.

'Aye well. My probation officer says I should avoid customer service roles. My waitressing days are probably behind me.'

Katie lounged back in her chair and propped her boots against the table, spilling some of Lorna's coffee in the process. 'So, how was it?'

'How was what?'

'Your time inside.'

Lorna peered at her old friend for a long moment. 'It changed me.'

'How?'

'Made me more compassionate,' She dipped her shoulders up and down. 'Toughened me too.'

Katie snorted. 'You? Tough?'

'Hard as nails,' Lorna replied in her sweetest voice.

'Oh yeah. Like how?'

Lorna sat up a little and pushed her shoulders forward before wiping all emotion from her face. 'Let me give you an example, bitch. You're either gonna get your boots outta my personal space, or you can lay right there and watch me break your ankles.'

Katie gave a belly laugh, unwinding her long legs and tucking them back under the table. 'And did you get to ... you know ... do your thing?'

'A couple of times. Just 'til Gran died.'

Katie nodded. 'Sorry, I didn't come to her funeral. I still hated you.'

'You'd every right to. And honestly, I'm so glad you didn't me see that day. I was a mess, and that was just the crappy prison clothes they gave me.'

Katie nodded and acknowledged the acne-faced lad's gestures that she was needed back in the kitchen. 'What's next for you?'

'I'm going self-employed. I'm starting a web security business.'

Katie looked scandalised. 'You! With your criminal record?'

'Aye,' Lorna protested. 'Who better to evaluate security systems than a successful thief?'

'Might be more lucrative to go back to your life of crime.'

'It was never about the money, Katie.'

Katie nodded, pausing to scratch at something on the tabletop. 'That twat, Nick Babel. You really showed him.'

'I'm not proud that I took revenge on him.'

'But I was glad you got him,' said Katie. 'Though I didn't hear about what you'd done until later.' She finished picking at the table. 'I woulda liked a bit of that action myself.'

Lorna stared at Katie's hands. 'Yeah. Getting him tasted sweet at the time.'

Katie rose to her feet and stood with her shoulders squared to Lorna.

Lorna followed her lead and drew herself to standing, her face close to Katie's. 'It's good to see you again.'

'Is it?' Katie shot back.

'I've missed you every day.'

'Oh, really?'

'Yes.'

'You know I'm still mad at you?'

'You can be mad at me but still love me a bit.'

Katie turned away and scowled into the far distance. 'These days I don't finish until six.'

'Overnight at mine?'

'You thinkin' of gettin' wasted?'

Lorna shrugged. 'I haven't had a drink in two years. It'll be a cheap night.'

Katie clenched her fists by her sides for a few moments while she pondered Lorna's proposal. Then she turned around and hugged Lorna until she thought her ribs might break.

Friday morning saw Gill and Cassy in the conference room with printed proofs of the latest magazine issue lying around in neat piles while they both carried out their respective checks.

'Do you ever get tired of doing this?' asked Gill, as he signed another sheet.

'What do you mean?' asked Cassy without looking up.

'I mean, issue sixty. That's five years we've been doing this.'

'Bit late if you wanna make a splash about it. "Fifth birthday collectors edition" or something like that.'

'No. I'm thinking more on a personal level. You know; we do our work, we write it up, slam it in the magazine and jump back on the hamster wheel for another month.'

Cassy gave the slightest shake of her head. 'It's just work, Gill. And we're good at it. And we'll keep on being good at it as long as we don't let our guard down.'

'I guess.'

'Which is why I'm worried about this Wigtownshire story.'

Gill paused his reading and tossed the sheet back on the table. 'What's bothering you?'

Cassy looked up to meet his gaze. 'Please don't tell me you expect to find fairies in that cave next week.'

He couldn't quite suppress a wry smile. 'If I did, would that be a problem, Cass?'

'Come on, Gill. You once told me you believe in magic. Do you really think that cave will contain wings, and wands and jars of fossilised pixie dust?'

He thought about this for a second. 'Nope. I guess I'll be happy if I simply achieve some insights into the lives of the two diminutive people we found.'

'Okay, let's talk about them for a second. So far you have the bodies of two deceased adults who are significantly shorter than average. Why are you even considering these poor people were Fae?'

'I dunno. I guess it was where my brain went first. Lillico thought so too if you ask him.'

'Just don't stretch the facts too far for the sake of conjuring a story.'

He gave her a solemn nod. 'I never do, and I won't this time either.'

'Good, I'll hold you to that,' said Cassy, flashing a smile and adding her signature with a flourish to the final sheet. 'Now we've got that sorted. What are your plans for this weekend?'

Gill rubbed his chin while he thought about this. 'I'm heading up north first thing tomorrow to see a few friends.'

'Oh, yes. Forest walks and boozy evenings?'

'Aye, a bit of that. But mainly we're helping a pal fix up her house.'

Chapter 15

He could have delegated the task to local officers, however Lillico wanted to interview Billy Whyte in person. The long miles from southern Scotland to Aberdeenshire on that Friday morning would have been a burden, had it not been for the fact he'd already accepted Lorna's invitation to join the rest of the group in Portsoy the following day. In response to his request, uniformed officers called on Billy Whyte shortly after dawn, summoning the man to spend several hours inside Kittybrewster Police Station while Lillico drove up to meet him. When Lillico arrived, he was surprised to see Billy hadn't called in a solicitor.

'Mind if I record this?' asked Lillico as he sat opposite the bulky figure of Whyte. 'I mean, you're not under caution or anything, but it will save me writing a transcript.'

'Suit yourself. What's this about anyway?'

'You were in Port Logan recently. Staying in a caravan for … nine days,' said Lillico, referring to his notes.

Whyte nodded calmly. 'I was.'

'Can I ask what you were doing during that time?'

'Bird watching.'

'Yep, I gather it's great birding around there. Spot anything nice?'

Whyte shrugged. 'Same ol' stuff. Though it was nice to get out amongst nature for a few days.'

Lillico nodded at his notes. 'Can I ask why you registered at the park under a false name?'

'Is that a problem, Detective? I mean, it's not like I was making a passport application.'

'Please, just answer the question, Billy.'

Whyte shifted uncomfortably. 'I was there with a woman. Taking an assumed name was her idea of a laugh. Like booking into a hotel as Mr and Mrs Smith.'

Lillico held his hands out and beckoned for more information.

'She's married,' Whyte protested. 'Just a lass I met on the birding circuit. We were trying to be discreet.'

'And you chose the name, Stevie Blaine?'

'Aye, well, in the heat of the moment, Stevie's was the first name that dropped into my head.'

'Do you know Mr Blaine personally?'

Whyte puffed his cheeks. 'Not personally, but I've met him at conferences and the like. Operates personal security for Rodderick Canmore. But you probably know that.'

'I do.'

'Look. Maybe it seems a bit daft to borrow Stevie's name, but there's no crime here.' Whyte leaned forward and laid an arm on the table between them. 'You've had me cooling my heels in here all morning and that's all you wanted to ask me?'

Lillico swung his laptop screen to show Whyte a photo. 'While you were having a tryst in Port Logan caravan park, this man was staying in a nearby van. Do you know him?'

Whyte flashed a momentary glance at the screen then turned his condescending gaze back on Lillico. 'Never seen him afore. Who is he?'

'A person of interest in our enquiries. You sure you haven't spoken to him?' Lillico prodded. 'He's a birder like you. You might have seen him on the cliffs near the park, or above Clanyard Bay.'

'The thing about birders,' said Whyte, flopping his wrist dismissively at the screen. 'We're all wrapped up in camo gear and the one thing we have in common when we're birding is that we don't talk much.'

'Ever hear of an Iain Lynch?'

'Nope.'

'And this lady friend of yours ... can you share a name?' Lillico retrieved his laptop. 'Might help corroborate your story.'

Whyte smiled down at the table. 'Unless you're planning to charge me, I don't feel minded to divulge that information.'

'It's just that when I asked the park manager, he said you'd booked under a single name. Said he didn't see any women in the vicinity of your van all week.'

Whyte smirked. 'What can I say, Detective. We were indoors a lot.'

As the Armour Group mustered at Lorna's house on Saturday morning, everyone looked to Ailsa to take the lead. Keen to help her friend, she had billed the gathering as a team-building weekend. Stale from two year's neglect, the old stone house needed thorough cleaning and a bevvy of small repairs. In the event, they found that Lorna had used the week since her release to do a lot of the smaller jobs herself. When they arrived that Saturday morning, they found Lorna had even managed to stack the furniture in two rooms, allowing Gill and Charlie to start painting straight away. Lillico put his hand up to repair the exterior window frames, while Ailsa held the ladder for Lorna while she worked to replace two fallen tiles.

'You sure you don't want me to do the high-up work?' Ailsa called up to her.

Lorna grunted with effort while she forced the heavy slate tile into a row beside its neighbours. 'I'm the one ... with the emergency crystal parachute ... remember?'

'I hear you,' said Ailsa, her attention drifting to the nearby open window. Between watching Lorna and holding the ladder straight, she was trying to keep track of a long, exaggerated story about how Charlie had once risked arrest by attempting to steal wind turbine components from Dundee docks. But between Charlie's thick accent and Gill's laughter, she lost track around the point when Charlie realised he wasn't going to fit a sixty-metre turbine blade into the back of a van.

The day proceeded at a pace and Ailsa switched to painting the inside of the window frames while Lillico continued to toil outside. To relieve her boredom, she made faces at him through the glass while he ignored her. Ultimately, she was delighted when she finally baited a response from him. Sticking his tongue out at her, he turned and found Solomon giving him a matronly stare.

They cooked together later, Adina blowing everyone's socks off with a stunning Persian bean and lamb stew she'd loaded with spinach, fenugreek, and parsley. Afterwards, as they relaxed in her tiny lounge, Lorna lit her woodburning stove and opened two bottles of wine.

'We shuid hae dane this years ago,' said Charlie while he sprawled in front of the fire. He'd chosen to stay off the wine but was enjoying the flames licking at the inside of the glass.

'Aye,' said Gill. 'Good craic.'

'Ooh, any volunteers to help me wallpaper the back bedroom tomorrow?' asked Lorna.

'I'll do it,' said Adina.

Lorna stretched across the gap between two chairs and tapped Lillico's hand. 'You wanna help?'

'Sorry. I'll be finishing the exterior frames until early afternoon, and then I'll need to shoot off.'

'So soon?'

'Work, I'm afraid. Come Monday morning I need to be at the opposite end of the country.'

They murmured a few job swaps back and forward and quickly arrived at a consensus of what they'd like to achieve in the remaining time. That was the moment Ailsa noticed that Solomon was rather quiet. She reached out and caught the old woman's attention. 'Hey, Solie. What're you thinking?'

'Tomorrow, we should make time to hear Aura,' said Solomon, quietly. 'Perhaps sit by the harbour before things get busy.'

There were murmurs of agreement.

But Ailsa sensed her old friend wasn't finished yet. 'Solie?' As Solomon turned to face her, Ailsa noticed her mentor had tears in her eyes. 'What's wrong, Solie?' Immediately, the room hushed.

'Oh, I'm sorry to throw a dampener on what's been a lovely day,' said Solomon, briskly wiping her face. 'But I'm afraid I have an announcement to make.'

Ailsa swallowed and wondered what was coming next.

'Although I always feel very youthful around this wonderful group of people, I have to face the fact that I am seventy-four next week.'

'Spring chicken, lass,' murmured Charlie.

'Yes, but I have less energy with every passing week, and I feel I should prioritise my remaining strength on an area where I can have most impact.' She looked around the faces. 'As Chairman of the Read*Scot* charity I started with Gill three years ago, I find that I'm able to do something every day that either blesses the life of a child or equips my successor to replace me when I step down.'

'Aye,' said Gill. 'But not for a while yet.'

'Agreed,' said Solomon. 'And yet I find I must trim my workload, which brings me to the Armour Group.'

'Nae, Solie,' whispered Charlie, seeing what was coming.

'Look around you,' she said. 'You're a tight-knit, high-functioning group of gifted people. You shouldn't really be friends and yet you are. As a group, you're in better shape now than you've ever been, and I know you'll face whatever's coming at you with fortitude.' She stopped to shake her head. 'You don't actually need me anymore, and for that reason, I'm stepping back.'

'You're the glue that holds us all together,' said Adina.

'Am I? Or was I the scaffolding you needed during the construction phase, which now needs to be pulled away?'

Ailsa could see Gill looked devastated. As their mentor, no one had relied on Solomon more than him. 'We'd be nowhere without you, Solie,' he said.

'At one time. But I'm not actually one of you.' She stopped to wipe away another troublesome tear and force power back into her voice. '*The Book* lists six pieces of armour. My role, as I see it, was to draw that out in each of you. To guide you. And now I must leave you to grow towards whatever comes next.'

'If I may be so bold,' said Gill. 'There are actually seven pieces of armour.'

'Oops,' Ailsa found herself saying. 'The scientist can't count.'

Gill counted on his fingers. 'Shield, sword, helmet and belt. That's four. Then breastplate and finally shoes, making six.' He held out his hands in a "come on" gesture.

'Sorry, Gill,' said Lillico. 'Just not getting you.'

'Pity's sake,' said Gill, closing his eyes for a second. 'I can see why they gave me the sword.' He pointed around the room. 'All those pieces of armour, and at the end they're held together by a seventh piece. And maybe it hasn't manifested yet, but I think there's one piece of the armour still to come.'

Ailsa and the others stared blankly back at him.

Frustrated, Gill got to his feet. 'If it's not obvious to you, I'm not going to spell it out.' He brushed Solomon's shoulder on his way to the kitchen. 'Love you, Solie. But I don't think you're going anywhere.'

'It's time, Gill,' she replied quietly.

Gill pointed at his glass. 'I'm getting more wine. Anybody else want anything?'

Chapter 16

Lillico gathered himself to leave Portsoy on Sunday afternoon while the others were still working. Pleading pressure of work, he reminded them he'd an early meeting on Monday, though in all honesty, he was ready to escape. The individual members of the Armour Group were wonderful, and at the same time, maddening. Especially Lorna with her gentle teasing and her frustrating ability to suddenly materialise behind him. Worst of all was Solomon's news. Her temperament had dramatically improved in the hours following her announcement, even though it left everyone else feeling flat. The purpose of the Armour Group still wasn't clear, and in the light of that, Lillico felt concerned. The fragmented, contradictory, animated personalities in the group had been hard enough for Rosemary Solomon to manage. What they'd be like without her guiding hand wasn't something he wanted to imagine.

There was however one conversation he needed to have, and he took Gill aside before he left for Bathgate.

'How's it going in the caves?'

'My boss put up the funds for an exploratory dig. I'm back down there for three days, starting tomorrow,' said Gill, glancing at his watch. 'I've got a crazy early start, so I'd better hit the road shortly.'

Lillico tucked his thumbs in his belt and stared at the ground. 'If that's the case then I need to make you aware of an ongoing threat in that area.'

'Is this about whatever you found in *Alpha* cavern?'

'Yes. And I'm telling you about this as a friend, just in case you witness anything unusual.'

Gill nodded for Lillico to carry on.

'We found a cache of guns we believe links to an Ireland-based terror organisation. We haven't announced the discovery as we're chasing down some leads, but it's just possible those guys might come back, looking for their weapons.'

'I see.'

'And while there's no explicit threat, you should stay vigilant. If you see anything out of the ordinary, call me.'

'Is Murray aware?'

'Absolutely not. I'm breaking enough rules just by telling you.'

Gill grasped Lillico's arm. 'Thanks for letting me know. I'll keep my eyes open and alert you if I detect any threat.'

Lillico began his working week with an 8 am meeting with Eliza, who looked up and smiled as he approached her desk. 'I've been ploughing through the marine traffic data we identified.'

'Thanks. That was quick.'

'Oh, the chance to pull some weekend overtime. And it was the kind of data task I enjoy.'

'What search parameters did you use?'

'I looked for a vessel between ten and two hundred tonnes, lingering for two hours or more at coordinates well off the main sea route. In the end, it was a cinch.'

'Excellent. What have you got?'

'It's mainly small fishing boats working in those waters, however late on seventh of May, a pelagic trawler called *Argonaut* was in-bound towards Clanyard Bay. On route, its transponder went off for four hours. When the beacon illuminated again, it was moving up the North Channel away from Wigtownshire.'

'And it would have had time to make an extended stop near the bay?'

'I calculate it would have had at least two hours.'

'Pelagic trawler,' murmured Lillico. 'Those kinds of boats have massive fish holds and cranes.'

'I can send you a picture of it. It's got a long, covered deck, so there'd be enough space to hide a small RIB.'

'Brill. And do you know what the boat's home port is?'

'It's registered in Kilkeel, in Northern Ireland.'

'Excellent work, and the next question it prompts is this. Where was the *Argonaut* in the weeks prior to this incident?'

'It might take me a few days to access that data, but I'll get right on it.'

Lillico thanked her and returned to his desk to call Shona Fallon. 'Is it okay if I interrupt your Monday morning?'

Wherever she was, Fallon yawned. 'Well, it's not as if I'm laying around in the pub.'

Lillico decided to try humour. 'Really? You disappoint me. I thought heavy drinking was an integral part of PSNI culture?'

'Ha, bloody, ha, you cheeky Jock. I'm working my contacts here in the province to get some background on Iain Lynch.'

'How's he looking?'

He heard Fallon sniff on the other end of the line. 'He's been keeping out of trouble. Most of my contacts are surprised he might be active again.'

'Okay. You said that these guys are good at staying under the radar.'

'Most of them. Historically, Iain has a reputation as a brag, so if he was planning a big weapons import, then I'm surprised he's said nothing to nobody. What about the other guy, Billy Whyte? Did you track him down?'

'Aye. Interviewed him last Friday.'

'And?'

'He played it pretty straight. Claimed to have been tucked up in his van all week with a girlfriend. I didn't mention guns but asked him if he knew Iain Lynch and he claimed he didn't.'

'Why was he using an assumed name?'

'Says he was being discreet as the lassie is married.'

'Is there anything that connects him to Lynch?'

'Nothing I can find. I'll have my researcher dig around a bit, but it looks like Lynch is the guy we need to focus on.'

'I'd agree. For Lynch to be lingering in a remote caravan park, less than two miles from a gun stash, can't be a coincidence.'

'I'll leave Lynch with you, if I may,' said Lillico. 'In the meantime, the reason for calling is that I have better news.'

'Please,' said Fallon. 'Do tell.'

'We have a lead on a boat.' Briefly, Lillico updated her on the *Argonaut*.

'Sounds like progress. Maybe Police Scotland isn't as crap as it's reputed to be. I think I'll stay in the province for a couple more days. And while I'm here, I'll try to catch this boat during a stopover in Kilkeel. Check out their body language when I ask them about a nighttime layover near a certain cliff-ringed bay.'

Lillico thought for a second. 'You sure you want to be as public as that?'

'We must assume the sentry witnessed the weapons cache being compromised. The terrorists will know we have their guns and will be covering their tracks.'

'It fits, though,' said Lillico. 'I'm not intimate with Ulster's regional politics, but I believe Kilkeel tilts more orange than green.'

'It does,' Fallon confirmed. 'And in a big trawler like the *Argonaut*, the Wigtownshire coastline is just a couple of hours away. Perfect place to store a big stash of Loyalist weapons.'

'Okay, Shona. Be careful and stay in touch.'

At the same time as Lillico was updating Fallon, Gill was arriving at the caves for the planned three-day dig. The police tape was gone and replaced by a sign declaring, "Dangerous caves – safety survey in progress – NO ENTRY." A small petrol generator puttered away to itself, and a cable ran back into the cave mouth that was now strung with electric lighting. As Gill followed the cable, he met a burly, bearded young man coming the other way, carrying a plastic basket loaded with stones.

'Who the hell are you?' asked the man as they brushed shoulders in the narrow space.

'Gill McArdle,' he replied as the pair stopped and looked each other over. 'I'm the archaeologist.'

The man nodded, thoughtfully. 'Ah ken your face from the news. Some crap about the *Stone of Destiny* being faked.'

'Those stories weren't made up,' said Gill with as much humour as he could muster. 'When you look at the physical evidence …'

'Whatever,' interrupted the man as he carried on walking. 'Murray is expecting you.'

Gill watched him go, then brushed off the testy encounter before following the cable towards *Charlie* Cavern. Arriving in a pool of abundant light, Gill found the place less foreboding than his previous visit.

'You guys don't hang about,' he said to Murray's bent back.

Murray looked up from where he was bundling stones into another plastic basket. 'Oh, hi, Gill. We came up last night. Wanted to make a quick start.'

Gill looked around. Even with the harsh lighting, the further reaches of the cave were splashed with shadow. 'Thanks for fencing off the top end. I'm planning to sift for any useful fragments.'

'Not a problem. I've worked with a few archaeologists over the years. When you've found yourself on the wrong side of a bollocking, you learn to be careful where you place your feet.'

'Ah. Sorry about that. People like me stumble into places overlooked for centuries and suddenly get very precious about them.'

'I've got two lads working with me,' said Murray. 'Donnie's working in the pool, and you'll have passed Joey on the way in.'

'We met,' Gill confirmed.

Right on queue, Joey reappeared with his empty basket. After an icy nod to Gill, he turned his attention to the water. 'Bro, do you want me to take a turn in the pool?'

'Please. Gettin' a bit Baltic in here.'

Murray made hasty introductions, then once Donnie was clear of the water, he pointed at the gently undulating surface. 'You can see the push/pull from the waves now. Means the debris we're clearing is opening a channel to the sea.'

'Is that wise?' asked Gill.

'Kinda tests our hypothesis about the pool being the original gateway to this little hidey-hole. Maybe we'll find a passage to another cavern and maybe we won't.'

'You okay if I start working behind you?'

'Sure. Do you have enough light up there?'

'Aye. I brought my own lamp.'

'Grand,' said Murray. 'We'll be breaking every couple of hours for a hot drinks and a bite so don't be shy. Just muck in and join us.'

'Thanks. I will.'

By the end of the working day, Gill had finished sifting through dust and gravel where the human remains had been found. A few final scraps of bone, plus fragments of simple pottery were his only finds on what had been a quiet day. Meanwhile, Murray's team had worked tirelessly to clear the pool of debris. Just before they packed up for the day, Murray called Gill over to join the others. The combination of the outgoing tide and the drainage pump had emptied the pool of water and now only a muddy puddle remained.

'Here's the way I see it,' said Murray, beckoning Gill to join him in the rocky pit. 'If you look at where the water is draining away, it indicates the sea is roughly in that direction. If we wanted to, I suspect we could dig on until we met open water. But that would only make it easier for the tide to come and go and there's another feature I want to concentrate on.' He pointed to a fissure in the rock that Gill hadn't seen before as it had lain submerged in the pool. The route was still blocked for now, but Gill could see that with more digging, an adult could slide through, assuming they didn't mind crawling at an angle. It was Murray's intention the next day to press on and get a sense of how deep this cavity ran.

'Interesting,' said Gill. 'If our deceased troglodytes had an annexe, this is where it would lie.'

'Aye. And unless it's jammed with big rocks, we'll clear three to five metres of that tomorrow.'

Gill nodded. He was in awe of Murray's work ethic. 'Looking forward to it already.'

The group made ready to leave. 'You guys staying locally?' Gill asked.

'A cheap wee holiday house in Port Logan. How about yourself?'

'B&B in Portpatrick. It's a bit further to drive, but at least it's got a few pubs.'

Joey brushed close to Gill's face as he moved towards the exit. 'Well, it is midsummer's night, pal. I'd imagine once you've had a few bevvies, you can strip to your undies and go dance round a stone circle or something.'

Gill turned to stare at Murry and gestured at Joey's retreating back as if to say, 'What's with him?'

Murray leaned close to Gill's ear. 'I hire these guys for their muscles, not their polite manners. Joey's a hard worker, but if he gets on your nerves, I'll tell him to behave.'

Chapter 17

After a leisurely drive back from Portsoy in Charlie's company, it was almost Monday teatime before Rosemary Solomon slid a worn brass key into the lock of her pretty little cottage in Dundee's Dalkeith Road. When her parents died young, she'd used her inheritance to buy what she considered at the time to be a rundown bungalow at a grossly inflated price. But years of care and steady refurbishment had polished it into a gem of a house, and it had been her home for forty years.

She'd never married. Not that she didn't like men; just never met the right one. Always hoping and waiting for him to come along, though he never did. While that had been a sadness for her, it wasn't as if her house had been a quiet retreat for all those years. Church pals, work colleagues, and neighbours. There'd been no end to the coffee drunk and bottles of good red wine shared amongst friends. Solomon had laughed in this house until her sides ached. And cried until she was certain she would die of dehydration. Her house was a sanctuary; a place where friends could drop in and expect a welcome, or accept a rain check if she was immediately busy. And gradually over the years, a special group of people had risen to prominence in her life. Like her, their lives focused on one intent - to adore their Creator and watch for signs he was at work in Scotland.

Then came the Armour Group.

At first, she'd been reluctant to talk about this new dimension in her life; preferring to hope it would fade away. Over the last five years, and against her expectations, the group had grown and rallied. Now her few most cherished visitors were trusted to hear her hopes and fears for this emerging group of extraordinary young people.

She and Charlie had stayed on an extra night in Portsoy, partly because she wanted to meet Lorna properly, and partly because she didn't want to leave ahead of the others as that would have underscored her withdrawal from the group. She'd realised it would be a tough moment. As a teacher for decades, she'd known the pain that came from prising off the affections of children graduating from her care. Flying away to jobs or into the university and college systems, it was hard for them at first. But as she'd always said, "I can't go where you're going. So, with fond memories and my every blessing, go be the best that you can be." And she believed it was the same for the Armour Group. For them to fly towards their destiny, they needed to leave her behind. And honestly, she'd expected to feel relief; a degree of closure that this unexpected, uninvited dimension of her life was coming to an end. But she didn't feel like that today. In truth, as she pushed open the door and stood alone on her porch, she suddenly felt bereft.

She hung her coat in the hall and tossed her keys on the vestibule dresser and immediately she could smell baking. Her first thought was that she'd left scones in the oven before she'd departed for Portsoy, but quickly reminded herself she'd be arriving to smoke, rather than the warm buttery, treacly smell that now caressed her tastebuds. It must be a friend then. Knowing the spot where she stashed a spare key, someone must have let herself in to warm up the old cottage with baking.

'Hello,' she called.

To no answer.

'Maggie, is that you?'

Still no answer; just the sound of the kettle coming to the boil and the gush of hot water being poured on teabags, and immediately, Solomon's skin began to prickle.

'Who's there?' she demanded loudly, fishing out her phone and tabbing to Charlie's number. If she was being invaded, Charlie was the man who would run to her aid.

Step by careful step, Solomon crept down the hall. Glancing to her left she saw the wood burner had been lit, and the coffee table was set with cups and plates. Whoever the hell this was, they'd damn well made themselves at home. Refusing to surrender to fear, she plucked a golf umbrella from its stand and strode into the kitchen to face down her intruder.

An immense man stood hunched over her stove, sliding a cake from the oven, emitting a tiny gasp of pain while he levered his creation onto the rack beside a batch of scones. Dressed from head to foot in biker leathers, he had a single long sword slung across his back. Bizarrely, he wore the *Garden Birds of the UK* apron she normally used for baking. She'd never met this individual, but aside from the apron, six people she knew had perfectly described him.

'Raphael?' Solomon spluttered.

He turned to smile at her, as if aware of her presence for the first time.

'Apologies. I've used the last of your almonds.'

Solomon swallowed. 'What are you baking?'

'Tarta de Santiago,' said Raphael with a flourish.

Solomon released a jerky nod. 'An old Spanish recipe.'

'Yes. I was stationed there for a long time. It became a favourite.'

'A long time?'

'A very long time.' He stood up straight and spread his arms wide. 'But now I serve in this wonderful land with its lochs and mountains.' Raphael bobbed his head from side to side. 'But the shortbreads and the clootie dumplings … not everything is to my taste.'

Solomon slumped against the door frame. 'I'm surprised you eat at all.'

Raphael grinned. 'On occasions.'

Solomon shook her head. 'Are you really here? Something in my tired old mind makes me wonder if I'm imagining you.'

'Oh, I am here alright. Approaching the culmination of my mission.' He reached to grasp the cake tin, but his hands sprang back in pain, sending him muttering to the sink to run his fingers under cold water. 'Though it appears, my kitchen skills are rusty.'

'Have these,' said Solomon, keeping her distance while passing him oven gloves.

He nodded gratefully and a few seconds later, he slid the cake onto a serving plate and picked up the teapot. 'Can we retire to your sitting room? We have much to discuss.'

Solomon turned around and with a wary glance over her shoulder, walked towards her front room and sank nervously onto the sofa. Raphael followed, gingerly laying down the afternoon tea and casting aside the apron.

He moved to pour the tea. 'How was your trip to Portsoy?'

Solomon took the cup from him. 'Oh, you're just going to leap in? Don't you fellows have a standard script you need to run through first … I bring you good tidings … don't be scared … etc etc?'

'Rosemary Solomon isn't scared of angels,' Raphael retorted. 'But we have precisely twenty-eight minutes and ten seconds until we are interrupted so I'd like to press on.'

'Okay. And I presume this isn't a social call?'

Raphael grinned at her over his teacup, the sleek bone china nestling like a toy in the angel's gigantic hand. 'You're right of course. Though I must say, it's a privilege to finally meet you.'

She swallowed a first mouthful of tea. 'I think the honour is all mine.'

Raphael gently shook his head. 'As a heavenly being, I do not have to struggle with doubt. Indeed, the only thing that can undo me is my choice to remain obedient, whereas humans must navigate both these challenges. In this land, and amongst your generation, you are a titan of the faith.' He closed his eyes momentarily. 'The mountains you have moved …'

'I'm glad you feel like that,' Solomon sniffed. 'From a human perspective, you're never quite sure how you're getting on.'

'And the longevity of your deeds,' Raphael continued. 'Read*Scot* embodies the Nazarene's heart for young people. And your efforts with the Armour Group continue to prepare them for what must come.'

Solomon pecked at her tea. 'I make encouraging noises, but they're still a mess. I'm sure you know that.'

Raphael raised an eyebrow. 'And now you've abandoned them?'

Solomon looked away. 'Not the word I'd use. I think it's fairer to say, they've outrun me. I cannot go where they are going and so I risk holding them back.'

'And if they're still a mess, why do you think that is?'

'They can play nice, but there's still tension in their ranks. And the mission that would force them together isn't clear.'

Raphael gave her a brief serious glance before he turned to cutting the cake. 'The mission will soon be apparent. Meanwhile, their division is something we need to address.'

'Well, on you go then, Raphael because I'm exhausted. I've mothered them through years of uncertainty, and nurtured their gifts, even when frankly, they've put those skills to dubious uses. And now, I'm worn out. I have nothing more to give them.'

Raphael laughed quietly to himself. 'Is that right?'

'Absolutely! And the armour they hold makes no sense. One has a sword, and another has a shield. Yet another has a helmet or a belt.' She rattled her cup from her saucer as she took another sip. 'I suspect, once upon a time, all those items were meant to be worn together.'

'Good observation. Now talk to me about your role in the Armour Group.'

Solomon laid down the cup and splayed out her hands. 'I was a facilitator. And a nurse. I prayed for them continuously and encouraged them whenever I could.'

'You prayed continuously,' Raphael repeated. 'And you'll continue to do that?'

Solomon thought about this for a second. 'I'll ask the Creator to help them, yes, because they need all the help they can get. But in practical terms, I'm not sure there's more I can do.'

'Then let me explain by giving you this,' he said, reaching to the floor to gather up a plastic bag Solomon hadn't noticed before. Warily, she looked inside, then back at his face where she held his gaze for a long moment. 'I've got an unfamiliar man in my house offering me underwear?' she said incredulously.

Raphael scratched the back of his neck. 'Apologies. I've had to improvise. Let's call them the *undergarments-of-togetherness.*'

'The what?'

Raphael shook his head. 'The passage in *The Book* alludes to seven pieces of armour, not six. Very many people omit the most important part, while you, Rosemary Solomon, do not.'

'A seventh piece,' said Solomon, remembering Gill's comments. She pulled the drab grey leggings and top from their packaging and laid them across her knees, then peered up at him, confusion all over her face.

'It's a metaphor,' Raphael continued. 'The armour never reaches its full potential unless the wearer seeks the Creator's will. Without that connection, soldier to king, king to soldier, the armour sections are simply disconnected pieces of metal.' He nodded at the thin, elasticated cotton garments. 'Try them on. You'll see what I mean.'

Solomon continued to stare at Raphael, eyes blinking.

'Sorry,' he said. 'I'll give you some space.' He gathered up his teacup and walked out of the room.

After a moment of frozen indecision, Solomon changed quickly, stripping off her travelling clothes and tugging on the gifted undergarments, eager to hide her embarrassment from Raphael who was noisily clearing up in the kitchen. She glanced in the mirror hung over the fireplace, cautiously hiding her ageing body from Raphael's gaze. She pulled the top part down over her midriff and smoothed out the fabric as best she could. Then she stared down at herself, surprised by how comfortable the fabric felt against her skin. Tugging the last fold into place, she noticed something strange. The grey cotton began to glisten, and then it began to grow, extending out to the ends of her limbs, up her throat and neck, and down to the ends of her toes. Then things turned really weird. She could see it with her eyes, but she had to stare back at the mirror to confirm it.

'Raphael,' she called as the garment started to harden around her waist.

But Raphael was whistling in the kitchen, intertwining a melody with something sung gently in Spanish.

And the garment wasn't finished yet. From every part of the shimmering cotton, crystal began to form, spilling up and over her body.

'Raphael!'

His head popped around the door. 'You can see it now?'

As the crystal reached her chest and her neck. Solomon had to suppress a gagging sensation as it swept up over her mouth and around her head. She could still breathe, though her vision became obscured, and she rushed to push back the visor that had materialised across her face. For a brief second, she staggered under the weight of the armour. This clumsy step forward allowed the pieces to connect, supporting her and responding to her movements.

'Looks good on you,' observed Raphael from the doorway.

Solomon ran her gloved hands down the tailored crystal armour that now encased her body. Studying herself again in the mirror over the fireplace, she observed the same pearlescent metal the others wore, with one notable difference. Hers was worn at the joins. And although burnished to a glistening finish, the shield, breastplate and helmet carried the scars of battle.

'Sorry about the scratches,' said Raphael. 'But it's had a lot of service over the years.'

'It's second-hand?'

Raphael chuckled, then stepped into the room to gather a sword from behind the sofa where he'd been sitting. Holding it so that the blade hung vertically, the tip pointing at the floor, he studied the intricate decorations on the hilt for a moment before thrusting the flat edge of the sword hilt, hard against her chest. And although her ears rang with the noise, the force of his blow didn't push her backwards.

'There's no such thing as second-hand armour, my dear.'

'But these scratches …'

'I would like to have said this sixty years ago,' whispered Raphael. 'But only today have I received permission.' He stood to attention and towered over her. 'Rosemary Solomon. Welcome to the Armour Group.'

Chapter 18

By mid-morning the following day, Gill was tiring of the caves. On the archaeological front, *Bravo* and *Charlie* caverns had already yielded their best secrets. Added to that, Murray's crew had found their way blocked by a single large stone and were using a power tool to carve it up into manageable pieces they could haul away. Needing to escape the noise and dust, Gill took himself back to his car for half an hour to check emails and call the office. When he returned, Murray and Joey had ditched their light working clothes and changed into full protection suits made of scuffed yellow plastic. He couldn't see Donnie, though he could hear him dropping stones in the basket somewhere out of sight.

'Joey opened a route to a cavity beyond that blockage,' said Murray. 'We're going to take a look.'

'What, all of you?' asked Gill.

'Donnie is staying here to act as our safety guy.'

Perhaps after hearing his name, Donnie emerged from the excavated slit in the rock and nodded at the water. 'Tide's coming in, boss. Let's not hang around in there.'

'Twenty minutes,' said Murray. 'Then we'll review.'

Joey gathered up a small yellow suitcase and a waterproof torch. Then he and Murray stepped through the shallow pool, before dipping into the newly excavated passage and disappearing from sight.

'The new cavern,' said Gill. 'Could you see much from where you were standing?'

Donnie shook his head. 'Just a big black space. Good sign though. Suggests a deep cave.' He busied himself unpacking an identical yellow case. Unwrapping a wire, he dipped an electrode into the pool and connected the wire to the device. Then he switched it on and set about adjusting the controls, working to reduce hissing and buzzing interfering with the connection.

'Hey, Don. Radio check,' came Joey's voice.

'Loud and clear, bro. How's it looking?'

'Got a rubble-strewn corridor. Two metres wide and elevating at fifteen degrees. Seems to connect to a higher chamber eight metres to the northeast.'

'Righto. Proceed with caution.'

Donnie replaced the mic and checked his watch.

'That thing works through rock?' asked Gill.

Donnie looked up and grunted. 'Yeah, regular mobiles don't work down here. The system we're using employs rock and water to carry low-frequency waves.'

'And you're using the water?'

'Aye. Joey will be tapping his electrode into the dirt or into a rock fissure to make good the connection on his side.'

'And it works over long distances?'

Donnie jiggled his head. 'Depends if there's any interference, but it's generally solid over several hundreds of metres.'

A crackle on the radio interrupted them. 'Stepping into a chamber,' said Joey. 'Bloody hell, it's massive. Thirty metres by twenty under a cascading roof. Talk again in two.'

'Acknowledged.'

The radio went silent again.

'You guys ever get nervous doing this?'

Donnie didn't look up but shook his head. 'Been doing it since I could walk. My dad and Murray are pals. They did a lot of amateur caving before Murray started his business. Personally, I never thought about doing anything else.'

'But you must have had a few scares?'

'Nah. You do this long enough and you learn to recognise when a cave isn't solid. Your safety becomes instinctive if you know what I mean.'

'Yes, I do.'

'Mind you, there was this one time …' Donnie was interrupted by Murray coming on the line.

'Right. We're in the centre of what we're calling *Delta* cavern. We're seeing several natural branches going off north and east, plus a few more that look man-made.'

Gill beckoned to Donnie to pass him the mic. 'What are you seeing?'

The line crackled for a few seconds. 'There are dozens of wee alcoves. The softer layers of rock are almost a honeycomb.'

Gill swallowed. 'If you've time, can you check for any signs of habitation?'

'I'm grabbing a few photos. Don't know what this place is, but I've never seen anything like it before.'

Gill was intrigued by the thought of what lay in the newly discovered cavern. But today's window to explore had passed as the incoming tide pushed water into the pool faster than the pump could remove it. Taking control of the situation,

Murray evacuated *Delta* cavern and left his lads to tidy away the gear while he took Gill outside and displayed the photos he'd taken.

'You've got alcoves here and here,' he said, pointing at indentations in the rock. 'And this central area is worn smooth. I'd say it's been intensely trafficked at some point.'

'Couldn't that be water erosion?' asked Gill.

'No, because if it was, I'd see equivalent smoothing on these vertical surfaces.'

'What about artefacts?'

'I didn't want to touch anything, but there's debris in the alcoves. Maybe timber or fabrics that have rotted away. And take a look at these.' He handed the phone to Gill so he could tab through a series of shots.

Gill stared open-mouthed while he reviewed images of fired clay, metal pots, and bottles. Corroded spoons, axes and green-stained copper pots. Alongside these were pieces of rusty steel of uncertain application. 'It looks like an underground village,' he murmured.

'I was getting that feeling,' said Murray. 'This afternoon, we'll get the radar machine onto the clifftops and see if we can chart these caverns from above.'

'I've used ground-penetrating radar', said Gill. 'I doubt it will be able to look that far underground.'

Murray tapped him on the shoulder. 'You haven't seen our piece of kit. If you've got an auntie in Australia, I could probably tell you what she's having for breakfast.'

After a bite of lunch, the team set to mapping the cavern system. Compared to the small radar machines Gill had used, Murray's kit was a high-powered device similar to a ride-on lawnmower. Joey drove the appliance while Donnie walked ahead of him checking the ground. Murray meanwhile was gathering information from the radar as it beamed data to his tablet.

'As long as you've got solid rock with low conductivity, we can get down to forty-five metres, which allows us to see these fissures in the rock,' said Murray, drawing his finger across the screen. 'This is *Charlie* cavern, and here's the new *Delta*. Joey's starting to do multiple passes over it now.'

'I'm amazed you can interpret this,' said Gill, looking at all the criss-crossed lines.

'This is just a partial representation of the data. When we get back to base this evening, I'll load it up onto a powerful laptop and create a nice multicoloured 3D representation of the caverns.'

Gill shook his head. 'You guys have achieved so much in two days.'

'Ah, well. Tomorrow is the main event.'

'What are you proposing?'

'If you're willing Gill, I'm going to take you into *Delta* cavern for ten hours.'

Leaving the crew to continue their survey, Gill decided to explore the fields above the cave. Murray's scans would hint at what lay beneath their feet, but Gill wanted to see the wider context of where the caves lay within this coastline. In many senses, this land was like other coastal regions of Scotland. Good grazing pastures rolled over mini hills called drumlins, formed by sediment laid down by retreating glaciers tens of thousands of years before. Below these fields lay the almost vertical cliffs, tapering to the coastal strip of exposed rock where the sea continued its relentless erosion of the British Isles. Following a northbound path from Clanyard farm, he walked half a mile towards Port Logan and Portpatrick, looking for a vantage point where he could gaze back on the cave entrance and study the landscape around it.

Climbing over a locked gate, he tiptoed through a field of cows and made his way towards the cliff edge. He'd observed that Wigtownshire was full of cows. The land wasn't fertile enough for intensive cereal production, but the grass grew fast and green, feeding the tens of thousands of Belted Galloways. Dark chocolate brown, with a wide creamy stripe around their midriff, they were the region's most successful local breed. This particular field extended over several small hillocks and Gill estimated there were up to a hundred of young "Belties," grazing along its length. Reaching a fence line, he estimated he was in a perfect position to look down on the cave. To see it, however, he'd have to break the cardinal rule of Scottish rambling, by climbing over the barbed wire fence that stopped the cows getting too close to the edge. He looked over his shoulder to check he wasn't being observed, then, certain he was alone, he hopped up and over the wire, before dropping down on his belly and creeping to the cliff edge.

From above, like giant teeth emerging from a grassy gum, he studied the rocks around the sea cave where they met the softer ground. At the margins, a narrow sheep path wove its way through the grass. The cave entrance itself was obscured, but looking at the land, he visualised the cave's location inside a small promontory within Clanyard Bay. Formed by long fingers of rock reaching down into the sea, this feature was particularly exposed to erosion and the glint of fresh grey granite revealed where a giant piece of stone had calved away from the rock face and slid several metres towards the sea. This movement had strained the land, opening cavities in the soil above the fallen rock, some of which had devoured sections of the little informal path. And it was into one of these cavities young Annie had fallen.

Gill took a few photos to jog his memory later and satisfied himself he knew roughly where the caverns lay beneath the land. Tucking his camera away, he turned around to leave and got a shock. While he'd focused is attention on the shore, two dozen of the young "Belties" had stealthily crept up to the fence line. And more were coming all the time, the late-comers running heavily over the ground like overweight racehorses in their rush to join in whatever curiosity had attracted their kin. Stuck on the cliffside of the fence, Gill made authoritative shooing sounds and waved at the animals to disperse. This had the opposite effect as they pressed forward, leaning their muzzles over the wire and snorting in his direction. Determined to escape his confinement, he did his best to mount the fence, and for a brief moment, swung one leg back over the mesh forcing the animals to flinch away. But before he could transfer his balance to his right leg, they surged forward again, pushing him back off the fence and catching his inner thigh on the barbed wire.

'Shit,' he muttered, rubbing his gashed leg, and lamenting the slash in a decent pair of walking trousers. Worse still, he was now shrouded in the thousands of flies that attended the animals; and he batted them away while he considered what to do. When no obvious solution presented itself he spent the next thirty minutes, trying to summon the courage to phone Murray and ask for assistance.

Then, unexpectedly, the animals started to move.

'Hey, hey, hey,' said a calm voice, as a figure approached with a walking stick in hand, gently and assuredly shooing the animals to move along.

'If you're the farmer, I'm really sorry about climbing over your fence,' said Gill.

'I'm not the farmer,' said the man in a soft American accent. 'Just out for a walk.' Dressed in green tweeds, with a V-shaped beard and pencil moustache, what most caught Gill's eye was the man's angular green cap. This headgear was distinctly unfashionable and to add insult to injury, it had a pheasant's tail garnishing its rim.

'Well, farmer or not, you seem to know your way around cows,' said Gill.

'Slow and steady is the trick. Don't run towards them or run away. And if they charge at you, just stand still, then step to one side at the last minute.'

'I see. Thank you.'

The man saw Gill safely over the fence and with occasional backward glances, they walked in silence until Gill was back on the main path.

'Where you headed?' asked the man in the jaunty hat.

'Clanyard. How about you?'

'Port Logan.' He nodded and smiled. 'Guess I'll see you around.'

'Thanks again,' said Gill, and meaning it. 'And I'll keep to the right side of the fence from now on.'

A little embarrassed by his mugging by a herd of frisky cows, Gill texted Murray to say he was heading back to Portpatrick for the evening but that he agreed with Murray's recommendation to spend tomorrow in *Delta* Cavern. Having made this commitment, he decided a beer might help calm his nerves.

Arriving back in town, he parked up at his B&B and spent the next hour wandering around the harbour area while chatting with Salina. Together, they collaborated to entertain Josh over the video call, laughing when the toddler kept dashing off in the hope that Gill would chase him. Portpatrick was like many other old fishing villages in that it clung to steep, sloping land where all roads led to the harbour. Dotted with a mixture of pleasure craft and small commercial boats, the three natural basins forming the harbour were the focus of the town's past and present industry. In the old days, local lairds imported cattle from Ireland, ranching them in the local countryside until buyers in the south were ready to take delivery. These days, the emphasis was on tourism, with a clutch of old and new hotels ringing the shore, all under the gaze of a clifftop edifice called the Portpatrick Hotel. With the brooding presence of a Victorian hospital, Gill observed the venue looked like a setting for an Agatha Christie novel.

Standing astride one of the concrete walls slung between a series of natural basalt islands, Gill chatted with his family and did his best to hold Josh's fascination while he showed him guillemots diving and hunting in the clear water. Then when Sal and Josh headed for bed, Gill looked for the best place to enjoy a beer. Slipping into the Crown Hotel, he ordered a cask ale and found himself a table near the window. Opening the emails on his phone, he started catching up on correspondence until he was distracted by a wild-haired lady trying to get service at the bar. In her late sixties or early seventies, she demanded a rum and coke, and it was a fair assumption it wasn't her first.

'Last one, Joannie,' he heard the barman say. 'Then it's home time for you.'

Joannie grumbled and fished for coins so she could pay for her drink. Gill tried not to eavesdrop and concentrated on a long email from Cassy.

'Oo are you, then?' asked the wild haired lady, yanking out a chair and sitting down opposite Gill.

Gill felt his shoulders sag a little. 'A visitor,' he said, diplomatically. 'I'm in the area for work.'

'You the one building them new houses?'

'No. I'm an archaeologist.'

'An archie what?'

'I dig up old things. Stuff that will enhance our understanding of the past.'

'Plenty of old things around here,' the woman grunted. 'You could start with my Harold. He's old and buried plenty deep.'

Gill assumed she was attempting humour and smiled.

'Where you workin' then?'

'Way down the peninsula,' said Gill. 'You won't have heard of it.'

'Tell me, Archie-thingey.'

He sighed. 'Clanyard Bay. It's beyond Port Logan.'

'Where young Annie was found,' the woman observed.

'That's right.'

The woman gave her head an irritated little shake. 'They never should hae taken her outta that cave.'

Gill couldn't quite believe his ears. 'I beg your pardon?'

The woman glanced darkly around the bar, then spoke to Gill in a low voice. 'The *Guid Folk* took that girl. It's aye bad luck to interfere with their work.'

'She was a wee girl, lost down a hole,' Gill protested quietly. 'It was a miracle they found her when they did.'

'Joannie,' called the barman, angrily twisting a glass in a cloth. 'Enough of your nonsense. Away home now.'

'Am sayin' nothin', Kenny,' she protested over her shoulder.

'And anyway, your taxi is here,' he said, nodding at a man in a red rain jacket who'd just put his head around the door.

Angrily, she knocked back her drink in a single gulp. Then scraping back her chair, she scowled at the barman. 'I'll put a hex on you, ya snitch.'

'Lovely to see you too, Joannie,' he shot back.

The man in the red coat caught her arm and steered her out of the bar. Immediately, the atmosphere in the room changed for the better.

'Sorry, about that, pal,' said the man. 'Had her troubles lately. She's not normally that bad.'

'No problem,' said Gill, forcing a smile and turning once again to Cassy's voluminous email.

Chapter 19

Gill stood in a protective suit and breathed deeply. The thing was bulky with numerous pockets filled with emergency gear. Even though he'd been assured the cavern was safe, he felt extremely nervous.

'You sure you want to do this?' asked Murray, fussing around Gill's suit, ensuring that the pockets were closed and the Velcro flaps pressed down.

'Not really,' said Gill. 'But it's the obvious next step. I've got the knowledge to interpret what you guys found yesterday.'

'I mean, you're the client. No one will complain if you decide you want us to record everything on video.'

'I'm good, Murray. And it'll be far easier to see it first hand.'

'Okay. Donnie is our external safety guy today as Joey has first-hand knowledge of *Delta* cavern. Don, can you walk us through the risk assessment?'

Donnie swiped his forefinger across his tablet screen. 'It's 10 am now and we're approaching low tide. You can enter or exit the cavern until 1 pm, before rising water levels fill our access route. You can exit the cavern at 7 pm once the tide recedes again, so that is the scheduled end point for this expedition.' He looked up. 'Okay so far?'

Gill nodded.

'Weather forecast is good so we're not expecting external wind or rain to impact you for the duration of the expedition.'

'Great.'

'An initial inspection of the *Delta* cavern suggests it is a stable environment. However, numerous side passages exist, and these remain to be explored.'

Murray cut in. 'The point is, Gill. Don't wander. You check out the main gallery while I start inspecting the radials. We'll touch base every half hour and I'll tell you what bits you're free to explore.'

'Radio checks are set at once an hour, on the hour,' said Donnie. 'Everyone happy with that?'

Gill followed Murray's lead and nodded.

'Finally,' said Donnie. 'Your suit contains water bottles, six hours of emergency oxygen and a basic first aid kit. Gill, can you confirm you know where these are, just in case you and Murray were separated?'

Gill tapped various pockets and listed the contents. 'Confirmed.'

Murray held his palm out to Gill. 'From an archaeological standpoint, is there anything you want to tell me?'

'Take lots of photos,' said Gill. 'But as far as you can, don't touch anything.'

'Okay, then.' Murray tapped Gill on the arm. 'Good to go?'

'Feel like an astronaut,' said Gill, tightening his hard hat. 'But, yeah. Ready for anything.'

Murray smiled. 'Joey, you take point, and Gill, you follow me.'

Stepping down into Murray's wake, Gill was soon waist-deep in seawater. Mercifully, the suit was well sealed and although he felt the cold press of the water, no dampness reached his inner layers. Checking he'd aligned his head torch, he followed Murray around the rock buttress, then leaned into an angle to enter the narrow tunnel. With stone walls pressing close to his left and right he had a moment of giddiness when his claustrophobia squeezed his rational mind. A childhood memory of getting stuck in a road culvert, plus his more recent experiences under a sandstone slab in Orkney, crowded his thinking in moments like this. But the journey between the two caverns only lasted for a few minutes and soon he was standing up straight, looking at a gradual climb up a rock-strewn tunnel towards *Delta* cavern.

His guides didn't speak but kept walking slowly until they stood side by side on the lip of a bowl-shaped room, with their headlamps sweeping across the walls. Gill looked around and gasped.

'Welcome to Neverland,' said Murray.

'I'm off to explore,' Joey announced, his head torch bobbing away in the dark. Gill meanwhile illuminated his torch beam and swung it around *Delta* cavern. 'What do you make of the geology down here?' he asked.

'Kind of a weird mix,' said Murray. 'On the south wall, we have the edge of a granite intrusion. That looks quite weathered to me and I suspect it was exposed to the sea at one point.'

'And the sloping roof?'

'The north wall and the bulk of the inhabited caverns are formed from sedimentary rocks. Something called turbidite. Looks like the sea undercut this softer material aeons ago to create a cave which has subsequently collapsed, producing this sloping roof.'

'Creating a gallery behind this slumped material,' murmured Gill while he swung his torch beam through a slow three hundred and sixty degrees. From this position, some of the sections of the cavern were too deep for his light to penetrate. 'And all these wee channels?'

'That's where first the sea, and later the inhabitants of this place, excavated soft layers of turbidite from between the harder layers.'

'You think people dug those out?'

'I'll show you in a second. There are tool marks in the walls.' Murray glanced at Gill. 'Now you've had a cursory introduction, how do you want to play this?'

Gill released a pent-up breath. 'Even with twelve hours, we'll only manage a brief survey. I'm gonna need to come back with a bigger crew.'

'No problem. We can run a lighting cable through from *Bravo* cavern. You might want to think about where you'll establish an HQ.'

'Yeah. We can talk about that as we go.' He turned to face Murray. 'Your photos showed some remarkable finds. Can we see those first?'

'Sure. Follow me.'

'This is another one with lots of pots and pans,' said Murray twenty minutes later while he indicated a dark recess in the rock. 'It's like the last one I showed you. Situated higher in the gallery and one of the better locations. Deeper and dryer than some of the lower down niches.'

'Kinda suggests there was a social hierarchy,' observed Gill, gently picking up one of the household items and studying its vintage. 'This stuff looks to be seventeenth or eighteenth century.'

'How do you think they got here?'

'Pretty worn. I'd guess these items were other people's discards.'

Murray touched his shoulder. 'Get a grip of yourself for the next one. I didn't take any photos of this alcove 'cause it's a bit disturbing.'

Nervously, Gill followed Murray along a ledge until they reached another of the higher chambers. In this one, he immediately spotted the skeletal remains of two people.

'In these damp conditions, they're pretty far gone. Especially the kid.'

Gill shook his head. 'That's not a kid.'

'You think it's another dwarf?'

'Look at the pelvis. I mean, yes, she's tiny, and an expert might contradict me, but I'd say she was an adult.'

'That's weird.'

'The first ones we found were small too, but not as small as this.'

'The other one was a big fella. I'd say six feet.' Murray pointed at the blackened remains of some fine wooden pipes draped in the rotted remains of old cloth. 'Any idea what those are?'

'Seen those once before during the exhumation of a seventeenth century graveyard. Unless I'm mistaken, those are bagpipes.'

Murray glanced around at the confines of the rock cavern. 'That would be a devilish noise in a place like this.'

'I guess,' said Gill, glancing at his watch. 'How much more do you have to show me?'

'We've covered the stuff that Joey and I saw, though there are other sections we should look at if you have the stomach for more.'

Over the next hour, Gill and Murray slithered over damp rocks along a twisty channel they christened *Echo* cavern. They lingered by carvings on some of the smoother rocks and although they were hard to make out, Gill thought he could see words and names in English. There was a draught here, with fresh air blowing into their faces and tempting them ever forward. But half an hour in, Murray reported the signal on their safety radio was getting weak and he'd decided against going any deeper. Returning to *Delta* cavern, they found Joey waiting for them.

'No signs of further habitation beyond *Echo* cavern,' reported Joey. 'However, I've found one small cavern you guys should see.'

He led them down a side passage that progressively narrowed, and for a short time, Gill thought they were approaching a dead end. But at the last moment, the passage widened into a bowl-shaped room where football-sized holes pitted the walls. Each cavity was loaded with blackened debris and a two-metre-long smooth slab dominated the centre of the room.

'Stinks in there,' observed Joey without going any further. 'Welcome to *Foxtrot*.'

'Aye,' said Gill. 'Do you recognise the smell?'

'Hate the stink of old bones,' Murray retorted. 'Two minutes, Gill, then we're outta here. You go and have a poke about if you want. We're gonna sit this one out.'

Chapter 20

Aberfeldy,
19th April 1746

Dearest Mother,

Woe upon all of us who are faithful and good. Gird thyself, Mother, for in these desperate moments I must alert thee to calamity. Three days ago, I left my brother Richard dead upon the field at Culloden. He died valiantly amongst hoards of Highland lads and this pitiful tragedy happened thus. Before battle had properly been joined, our guns were targeted by Cumberland's long shots. Twice or thrice, we exchanged fire until the forsaken moment when our 13-pounder was struck while Richard was reloading. He lived long enough to tell me of his love for thee and to press into my hands the pipes he hath carried across his back these past months. I shall bring them to thee, daubed with his most honourable blood.

I shall not recount the battle's tale, as it was a ramshackle affair. The Irish were deployed to engage Cumberland before he reached Culloden. But they and many of the two thousand men sent on that urgent mission never returned to the battlefield. It was left to the Highlanders to win the day, and in that brave endeavour, they failed, dying in droves upon bad, wet ground. I mingled with the survivors as they rallied at Ruthven Barracks, but then the order came to disperse. The Prince, it appeared, had fled.

I shall not divulge my anticipated route back to thee in case this letter be intercepted by our enemies who are all around. Suffice to say, I shall throw myself upon the mercy of those good houses in Southern Scotland who are pledged to our cause. They can assist me on my return to Burnley, though I shall linger with thee only for a few days, then make haste to France where we shall prepare for the next and surely victorious effort to win back our land.

Thy grieving son,
Francis Towneley.

Chapter 21

Working from his B&B, Gill began his new day with a long call with Cassy including a brief injection from Tony. After hasty assurances that he would attend the publisher's meeting the following day, they focused on the Wigtownshire dig. Having had a few hours to consider the previous day's finds, Gill was now bursting with excitement. He described everything he'd seen in as much detail as Tony could tolerate, then explained what they'd achieve if the newly discovered caverns were thoroughly explored. After some back and forth, their collective enthusiasm for an archaeological investigation rose dramatically. And with the cave system now accessible at low tides, the race was on to collect artefacts and record the scene before curious visitors started to erode its history. Aside from booking Murray's crew for at least another week, Gill would need a dig team, and a university willing to process the finds. Raising these resources would be Cassy's focus for the rest of the day.

With the cavern offering Gill some serious story potential, one question now consumed him. Who were the diminutive cave dwellers of Clanyard Bay? He needed ideas and context, so it was time to talk to anyone who might usefully have an opinion, including the local expert discovered by Mhairi.

When Gill arrived in the rustic car park of the *Wigtown Fairy Trail* early that afternoon, all his enthusiasm for this research fluttered away. From the safety of his car, he could see across an acre of muddy woodland, peppered with tiny, brightly painted houses, all contrived from tree stumps and plywood, with the few living trees adorned by tiny doors and mailboxes. Gill watched a gaggle of little girls in frilly dresses and gossamer wings, dancing around from house to house, squeaking and pointing and bestowing flourishes with pink sparkly wands. At that moment, one of the adult chaperones looked at him. A man of about Gill's age glumly made eye contact, then looked away. And that's when Gill realised, if he hadn't already committed to meet the proprietor, he'd have quietly turned around and driven away.

Rory Carmichael had sounded eminently reasonable when Gill had spoken to him the previous day. Unassuming, and not especially curious about why Gill was visiting, he'd suggested 3 pm for their meet-up. Looking at the kids dancing in the forest, the birthday party preceding Gill's scheduled visit was evidently running late. Resigned to his fate, he picked up his phone and spent the next hour dealing with correspondence.

A little while later, there was a flood of excited children splashing across the car park and loading into SUVs. When the partygoers drove away, it was time for Gill to check the lie of the land. He got out and tip-toed through the puddles to the entrance of the "fairy castle." In reality, this was an ageing garden shed, garnished with makeshift wooden turrets. The door was open, but the till and gift shop were unmanned, so he proceeded through the room and out to an area of raised decking. A man in his mid to late sixties was sitting on a wooden chair with his eyes closed. He had short silver hair and a thick but neatly trimmed angular beard. On the table beside him lay a jaunty green cap, topped with a dusky red feather, and Gill realised he'd met the man before.

He cleared his throat. 'Rory Carmichael?'

The man's dark brown eyes flashed open and found Gill's face. 'When we spoke on the phone, I wondered if it might be you,' he said with a soft American accent. 'My new friend, the cow-whisperer.'

Gill McArdle,' he replied, offering Carmichael his hand.

The older man gripped it. 'Apologies I'm running late. Got a late party booking. And as I'm sure you'll agree, the paying public must come first.'

'If it's inconvenient, I can …'

'Oh no, all finished now, thank goodness. Please pull up a chair and we can talk. Can I get you a cup of tea? Something stronger?'

'No, thank you,' said Gill, perching on the end of a long wooden bench. 'And I'll try not to take up too much of your time.'

Rory waved a hand vaguely in Gill's direction. 'No problem. If you haven't brought a carload of squealing eight-year-olds, you can have as much time as you want.'

'When we spoke earlier, I mentioned that I edit a magazine. We report on Scottish myths and mysteries, especially anything with a cryptozoological angle.'

'Sure, I've heard of you, Mr McArdle. And I'm curious about whatever brought you to Clanyard Bay.'

'I'm doing an archaeological dig down there. I'm trying to understand the local legends so I can interpret our findings.'

'Oh, aye? And what have you found?'

'You might be aware there's an on-going police investigation around the disappearance of Annie Wallace.'

Gill gave Rory a self-conscious smile. 'So, I'm afraid I'm not at liberty to talk about the details just now. But suffice to say, I'm considering a feature on Celtic Fae.'

'Are you now?'

'And when we did a trawl of Scottish-based experts with something approaching an objective opinion on the subject, your name came up.'

Rory closed his eyes again and grinned. 'And here you are, preparing to immerse yourself in fairy lore.'

'I'll definitely listen to the legends,' Gill admitted. 'Though I take a pragmatic approach to my research.'

'You might struggle then,' said Rory with a melancholic smile. 'Any rational discussion of fairies has more to do with culture than science.'

Gill found himself agreeing.

Rory slapped his chair and stood up. 'To begin our discussion, why don't I give you the grand tour?'

'Tour?'

Rory jerked his head in the direction of the woods. 'Come on. Come and see my trail.'

Reluctantly, Gill got to his feet.

'Oh, don't be like that.' Carmichael jerked his chin at the nearest grotesque and colourful little house. 'To understand how the story of the Fae began, you need to see how it ends.' He picked up his pointy green hat and donned it before stepping down onto a path carpeted with damp woodchip. Gill fell into step beside him and made polite conversation for two minutes.

Arriving at the centre of the fairy village, Rory nodded at a cluster of doll's house style buildings. 'It's hateful, isn't it?'

Gill rubbed the back of his neck. 'But this is your business, right?'

'Aye but look at this trash! It's the moral equivalent of taking those wonderful waterhorses you discovered, then breeding them down to the size of pit ponies. The final insult would be to sprinkle them with glitter and sell them to a circus.'

Gill admitted that Carmichael's analogy seemed reasonable. 'Why do you do it then?'

Rory smiled. 'I know a lot about the Fae, and my blogs are well enough written, but they don't generate much income. This park seems to be the only way I can monetise my knowledge.'

'Doing kids' birthday parties?'

'And I run occasional seminars. A lot of folks come to Wigtown for the various book festivals, and on those weeks, this place goes like a fair.'

Expecting to smell whisky on Rory's breath, Gill instead caught the whiff of a long personal story and decided to keep his host on track. 'You say this is where fairy lore ends?'

'Yes.' Rory wiggled a finger at the little houses. 'When you think of fairies, what springs to mind, Gill?'

Gill screwed up his face for a moment. 'Something small and feminine. Gossamer wings, and a wand.'

'Tinkerbell,' Rory snorted. 'Walt Disney changed our understanding of fairies forever when he transferred Peter Pan from the book to the big screen.'

'I suppose we can lay that at JM Barrie's door as he wrote the story.'

Carmichael nodded. 'Are you aware Barrie used to live around here?'

Gill shook his head.

'Just down the road in Dumfries during his late teens. Rumour has it he learned about the Fae while he journeyed around Wigtownshire.'

'It sounds like you're not a fan of his work?'

'On the contrary, his book is excellent, once you get your head around his old-fashioned humour. And his writing is a great deal darker than the film Disney based on it. In the book, Peter is careless, carefree and a narcissist. A caricature of Fae mythology boiled down to the simple catalogue of rights and wrongs that epitomise a Victorian children's book.'

'Hence the tiny houses,' Gill concluded.

'Yes. He took a Scottish myth about the *Little People* or the *Guid Folk*, or whatever, and morphed their race into impossibly tiny humans. His work changed public perception forever.' Carmichael waved a hand at the toy-sized dwellings. 'Which is why we have this aberration rather than a more objective discussion of the topic.'

'Did you build all this yourself?' asked Gill.

Rory shook his head. 'There are some clubs in town. Men's sheds and other makers. They build what they want and install them for me. It's all free to me if I make occasional donations to their clubs.'

'Good arrangement.'

'Aye.' He turned to face Gill. 'But this isn't the Fae, Gill. It's simply an echo from an old film, based on an even older book, framed from scraps of Scottish fairy lore.' He plucked off his hat and thrust it angrily at the model village. 'Whatever the Fae were, they weren't this.'

Gill nodded. In many ways, he found this reassuring. 'And what, in your opinion, is the basis for the Fae mythology?'

'Haven't you checked out my website?' Rory shot back.

'I've an office-based researcher,' confessed Gill. 'She's going to write me a summary.'

'I could give you a verbal synopsis,' said Rory, looking at his watch. 'For some modest compensation.'

Gill nodded thoughtfully to buy himself some time. He hadn't talked to Tony about a budget for this trip, so his expenses were limited to bed and board. 'What kind of compensation were you thinking of?'

'Are you staying in Wigtown tonight or heading back to Dundee?'

'I'm staying at the Bladnoch Inn, then shooting off first thing.'

'Perfect. How about I join you there for supper and a couple of drinks.' He nodded back at the fairy castle. 'And twenty pounds in the till to keep my craftsmen encouraged.'

Gill chewed on this only briefly. Rory was eccentric but self aware, and he seemed to know his topic. 'Okay. That's a deal.'

'The hat,' said Gill as they drew up alongside the riverside inn. 'I take it's a reference to Peter Pan?'

'Yes,' said Carmichael. 'Though I suspect Barrie acquired it from Robin Hood.'

'And you're Canadian?' Gill probed.

'You've got a good ear. I'm from Nova Scotia.'

'What brought you to Scotland?'

'Came here on a road trip during my student years. Hung around awhile researching my family's eighteenth-century roots in Kirriemuir. Went back and forth for a few years, then eventually got a steady job in Wigtownshire.'

'Cool. What did you do?'

'I was a Baptist minister,' said Rory, flatly. 'But I got outta that game ten years ago.'

'And now you sell fairytales.'

'Because I find myself sympathetic towards the Fae,' said Rory, stopping outside the door of the old pub. 'And ever since Annie Wallace fell into that sea cave, I think you're developing a taste for the subject.'

'Just curious,' said Gill.

Carmichael spread out his hands. 'And why wouldn't you be? A little girl disappears and suddenly rumours abound about evil fairies being back in business.'

Gill's response wasn't as fast as it needed to be. 'I think that explanation is unlikely.'

'This is wonderful,' Carmichael enthused. 'A high-powered investigative journalist breezes into town bribing an old *Bluenoser* with beer in exchange for his knowledge of the Fae.'

Gill smiled. 'I don't know about "high-powered." I've spent three days in those caves and my body feels like I've been tossed out of a moving car.'

'You'll need an ale then.' He held the door open. 'Shall we?'

'Let's,' said Gill.

An hour later, Carmichael pushed back his plate. 'That was excellent as usual. Time for me to pay my tab.'

Gill had enjoyed the man's company and now he waved a hand. 'I'm not going to twist your arm, Rory. Only talk if you want to.'

'It's my specialist subject, Gill. My passion.' Carmichael tapped the table with his knuckles. 'Let's go back to JM Barrie and Peter Pan for a second.'

Gill took a swig of beer. 'Sure. What's your angle?'

'For a start, I referenced the darkness in Barrie's writing you don't see in the film. In the book, Tinkerbell is a gossamer-winged fairy who's in love with Peter. When she realises she's lost his heart to Wendy, she becomes vengeful.'

'The Fae do have that reputation,' said Gill.

'Oh, aye. They're tiny. Mischievous. They can curdle milk, sicken cattle, and lead weary travellers into bogs.' Rory stopped to take a sip of his pint. 'In short, we demonised them. And the worst part of their legend alleges they stole children.'

Gill stared at him, wondering how much, if any, humour there was in that last remark.

'Or at least,' Carmichael continued, 'that's what they're saying in Portpatrick.'

'I think the Fae abducting children is more of an eighteenth-century idea than twenty-first.'

Rory looked away. 'Okay, let's explore that hypothesis. If we assume they do exist, would you say the Fae are cruel or kind?'

Gill pondered this for a moment. 'If we're speaking hypothetically, I'd say they're capable of both. But I suspect they see themselves as very different to us so they might be dispassionate towards our pleasure or anguish.' He sipped his beer. 'What do you think?'

'I imagine they're closely connected to nature. They'll be guardians of their habitat, be they dwellers of the woodland, waterways or sea.'

'And what about poor Annie Wallace?' Gill sat forward in his chair and lowered his voice. 'Do you really think there's even a grain of truth in the suggestion the Fae had a part in Annie's disappearance?'

Rory smiled. 'For that to be true, you'd have to believe fairies exist. And isn't that a stretch?'

Gill sat back puzzled. He'd met people like Carmichael before. He thought about Sandy Brightman, spending her adult life looking for a monster in Loch Ness that, in her heart of hearts, she didn't believe existed. 'You're devoting your life to Fae folklore, and yet you don't believe in them?'

Carmichael took another sip. 'Oh, I believe in them alright. But clearly, I'm not buying into the Hollywood caricature.'

'What are they then?'

Rory pulled a wry smile. 'You're asking to hear my innermost secrets there, my new friend. Why don't we save that juicy question until you've formed your own opinion on the subject?'

'Okay,' said Gill, trying a different tack. 'You're local. What can you tell me about folklore on the Portpatrick peninsula?'

'This part of Wigtownshire has always been an isolated community where old traditions died late. I can tell you that faith in fairies started to disappear in Scotland during the late eighteenth century after the clearances. But around here? One hundred years later, there were still workmen refusing to widen roads if they feared they were encroaching on fairy territory.'

'I see.'

'And the peninsula has perfect geology for it.'

'What do you mean?'

'The whole area is riven with sea caves, just like the one where they found that wee girl.' He tilted his glass at Gill. 'Ask your researcher to go hunting for that topic. Look for Clanyard Bay in particular.'

'Thank you. I will.'

'That whole area is steeped in fairy myth,' Carmichael observed. 'Which is partly why I was visiting Clanyard the day you met me.'

'Looking for a Fae connection to Annie Wallace?'

'Studying the context, Gill. Near Clanyard is a spot called the *Cove of the Grennan*. Sailors used to throw bread ashore for the fairies to ensure a good voyage around the Mull. It's possible the cave at Clanyard Bay connects through a series of galleries all the way through to Luce Bay.'

'Perfect fairy territory?'

'Exactly. Ignore the cutesy wee houses dotted around my fairy trail. If they ever existed, fairies lived underground. Tolkien had it right when he caricatured them as Hobbits.'

'Are they considered to be Fae?'

'Fairies and Fae – unless you're a purist, those are both catchall descriptions for a host of myths from pixies to prowlies and elves to goblins.'

'And you're proposing they once existed in this area?' asked Gill.

'Again, I'll answer your question with a question of my own,' said Rory, swilling his beer. 'Isn't it possible they were once like the hares and the skylarks? An endemic species, driven to the margins and possible extinction by agricultural improvements. Their habitats ploughed over, and their place in the food chain disrupted by modernisation.'

'Hares and skylarks are benign to humans. At best, fairies were always treated with suspicion.'

'Ah,' said Rory, raising a forefinger. 'And the question that follows from that is, why? Why were we so scared of them if they were so like us?'

'Maybe our predecessors feared them in the same way modern humanity is both fascinated by, and scared of, the possibility of an alien species.'

Carmichael nodded. 'I like that comparison. They're like us, but they're not us. Which is perhaps why the church where I served loathed the suggestion of their existence.'

Gill considered this. 'I know Celtic Christianity tried to rub along with indigenous belief, while the Roman church and all expressions that followed it sought to crush faith systems that conflicted with their own.'

'Indeed. And depending on where your research leads, you might eventually understand why that saddens me.'

'Ignore me if this is a personal question, but is this the reason you left the ministry?'

Carmichael looked down at his drink and smiled. 'I made some observations about local church history that turned out to be very unpopular. Then the church did what it always does when confronted with historic crimes; they buried the evidence and moved swiftly to denial.'

Gill nodded sadly. 'That's what happens when the institution stops protecting the people in its care and only looks to self-preservation.'

'And it didn't do them any good in the long run,' said Carmichael. 'Scotland's old church denominations around here are all dead or dying. Maybe, if they'd admitted to some of these historic crimes, they'd be in better shape.'

'What particular crimes do you have in mind?' asked Gill.

'Let me simply suggest the church had a hand in creating the Fae, and then it persecuted them.'

Gill felt puzzled. 'You're jumping from saying fairies might have existed, to saying the church created them?'

Carmichael wiggled his nearly empty glass. 'Sorry. My convictions solidify when I've had a few drinks. And I get too lazy to qualify everything with ifs, buts and maybes.'

Gill smiled. 'Actually, I do that too.'

'And do you have faith, Gill? Your sadness for the church suggests you do.'

'I do, yes. But I've never found a church home that allowed me to explore it, so I engage in faith with a group of like-minded friends.'

Carmichael nodded. 'Probably for the best. I'm glad you have pals like that.'

'Would you like another beer?' asked Gill, thinking this conversation had longer to run.

Carmichael smiled and shook his head. 'I've a party on my fairy trail first thing in the morning, so I'd better head off. But let me ask you, what are you doing next to investigate Clanyard's Fae?'

'I'm going back to the caves,' said Gill, finishing off his beer. 'If I can get my boss to agree, I'm going to conduct a thorough archaeological dig.'

Carmichael nodded. 'Sounds like a logical next step. Afterwards, please swing by and let me know how you got on.'

Chapter 22

Gill left Portpatrick early on Friday morning to make it back to the office for midday. Tucked in the conference room with the *Mys.Scot* crew, he ran through the outcome of his three-day expedition in the Wigtownshire caves.

'Let me check if I've got this right,' said Cassy. 'We've moved on from having two tiny dead people to saying there's a whole village below ground. And once-upon-a-time, it was what? Inhabited by pixies?'

'Whatever word we choose for them, we have irrefutable evidence they were diminutive. One task at the next stage will be to work out why.'

'And you reckon this community existed for years?' asked Craig.

'Again, we'll need to check the bones. My bet is when we analyse the samples we'll prove there were multiple generations of related people.'

Cassy gave her head an irritated little shake. 'Oh, this is barmy, Gill. What would these people do for food? For light? How did they keep themselves warm?'

'All questions for the next dig,' said Gill. 'Assuming Tony signs off on it.'

'Actually, this story is starting to sound promising,' said Mhairi, inching a little closer to Gill. 'I think Tony will bite your hand off.'

'You didn't sound so enthusiastic when Gill first floated this idea,' Cassy huffed.

Mhairi threw Cassy a diplomatic smile. 'But now Gill has been inside the cave, I think this story has legs.'

'Then you can take the lead on this one,' sniffed Cassy. 'Frankly, I've got enough going on in the real world.'

Gill ignored Cassy's folded arms and nodded energetically. 'Which is why we need to research any established myths about this part of Scotland. Mhairi, I understood your initial reluctance on this, but we've got the basis of a story here and I need you to step up to the plate.'

Mhairi nodded. 'I'll build you a preliminary pack of facts and legends.'

'Thank you. Rory Carmichael said we should research Clanyard Bay in particular. Given it's our dig site, I'll take anything you can give me on that, no matter how tenuous.'

'I'll get you anything I can.'

'Cassy. We may need to rejig issues sixty-one through to sixty-three. This will be a developing story so we should start thinking about what material we could postpone.'

'Okay, you're the boss. But don't forget we've a fixed window to dig in Broughty Ferry next month.'

Gill gave her what he hoped was a reassuring smile. 'That one is yards from my front door. I'll be able to do it with one hand tied behind my back.'

'Sorry to be a bore,' said Craig. 'But as you have human remains in the caves, won't there be legal requirements to report those?'

'Already on it. Lillico isn't excited but as he was first on the scene, he's taken responsibility for reporting to the Fiscal.'

'Alex has been in these caves with you?' asked Cassy.

'Not the recently discovered ones. I've just sent him our photos so, he might decide to review the remains *in situ* before we move them.'

Cassy nodded her understanding. 'I spoke to someone over at Glasgow Uni. He's offered us a secure lab space for any artefacts you find but he absolutely refuses to handle human remains.'

'Not a problem. We'll have those sent to Lossuary.'

Cassy shivered. 'This is sounding more like Mhairi's gig with every passing breath.'

Mhairi nodded. 'Sure. I can support Gill onsite. As long as I don't need to go inside the cave.'

'Thanks. I'll take you up on that,' said Gill, before addressing the wider team. 'I'm going to be in and out of the office over the next few weeks. I'll keep sending you material so start drafting articles once we know what we've got.'

The meeting broke up with Cassy disappearing back to her desk without another word. Gill nodded at Mhairi. 'Looks like it's you and me taking this to Tony. Coming?'

'Fairies, Gill,' said Tony after Gill finished presenting a mocked-up magazine cover for *Mys..Scot*, issue sixty-one. 'Please tell me you're not being serious.'

'Hear me out, boss. I'm not proposing we've found humans the size of insects,' said Gill, doing his level best to sound reasonable. 'We'll be exploring the origins of Fae folklore in Scotland.'

'And this cave helps you, how?'

'Based on my initial assessment, we're going to find the remains of a once flourishing community. Maybe even something that survived through several generations.'

'Made more interesting by the fact that they were all shorter than the average six-year-old,' added Mhairi.

'And we have the data to prove this?'

'Police pathologists discovered two tiny skeletons after Annie Wallace's rescue, and I saw evidence for several more while I was in the cave system.'

Tony shivered. 'For once I'm glad I work an office job. I'll be fascinated to read about this but there's no way you could persuade me to visit those caverns.'

'And that's the massive appeal of this story, boss. Our readers get to see inside a whole mythical subculture, and they can do it from the comfort of their own homes.'

'Can you show me what you've got so far?'

Gill cracked open his laptop and let Tony tab through the images while Mhairi stood with her left hand draped over Gill's shoulder.

Tony gave a satisfied nod. 'It's hard to see the context in these images but the way you describe it sounds impressive. How do you see this playing out in the magazine?'

'Over two issues,' said Gill, moving a fraction to dislodge Mhairi's hand. 'If we go ahead with the timescales I'm proposing, then issue sixty-one would explain the discovery of the cave, its geology and local folklore. Issue sixty-two would focus more on the individual items we discover and flesh out the human aspects of the story. And there'll be follow-up articles in issues beyond that as we engage the scientific community with our findings.'

'And a ten-day dig costs the same as the exploratory excavation. How did he work that out?'

'Murray says it's less effort as we don't need to shift any rocks this time. The three guys will rotate between being the safety officer outside the cavern with two fulfilling an archaeologist's role while they're in the cave with me.'

'And Fiona's confirmed she's available?'

Gill bobbed his head. 'She's not bursting with excitement at the thought of working underground, but yes, she's up for it. There's not a tonne of space in there so with her supervising, she'd have me and Murray's team as her whole crew.'

'And when would you start?'

'A tidal pool protects the cave entrance, but that won't deter the more adventurous souls who hear about it, so I'm looking to do this quickly. The working plan is to start at the back end of next week.'

Tony switched his gaze to Mhairi. 'What do you think?'

'Looks great on paper, really.'

Tony nodded thoughtfully. 'I'd agree. Crack on, Gill. And best of luck.'

After the meeting, Gill held the door for Mhairi and pulled it behind them before he spoke. 'That was easier than I expected. Do you think the old fella is losing his touch?'

Mhairi shook her head. 'You brought him a sound proposal and he went for it. Simple.'

Gill jiggled his hands. 'I liked it better when he fought me on these things.'

'And you caught him on a Friday. Always easier to press him on a decision if it's the day of a publisher's meeting.'

'Yeah. I was going to ask you about that. I'm heading to Islay later this afternoon and I was wondering if you could stand in for me?'

'What? You're going way up north, just for the weekend?'

'Actually, Islay is southwest of Dundee. You just feel you're driving north because of the landscape.'

'Are you taking the family?'

'Aye. We've got some business we need to attend to.'

'Sounds ominous. Anything you want to talk about?'

Gill was unsure how to explain his three-day trip to the Western Isles. 'I've inherited some property.'

'Brilliant! A nice wee cottage in Bowmore?'

Gill shook his head. 'More remote than that. And from what little I've heard, it's a bit of a fixer-upper.'

She raised a hand in farewell. 'Have a great time, and I'll update you on Monday if anything significant happens at the meeting.'

'You got five minutes?' asked Gill a few minutes later after he'd packed his laptop ready for a quick exit.

'Business or personal?' asked Cassy without looking up from her computer.

'If I say personal, I guess you'll body swerve me?'

'You're bang on,' she said, flatly.

'Business then. My office, please. ASAP.'

She looked up. 'You don't have an office.'

'The V&A. We can do this in the time it takes us to walk there, buy a coffee and walk back again.'

Cassy snatched a glance at her watch. 'Walk quickly, yeah?'

'What's up?' he asked as soon as they were clear of the office building.

'Aside from my mum being sick? And the police giving Zack a formal caution for the second time this year? Life's a bed of roses, but you know all this already, Gill.'

'I do, and it's tough.'

'And Alex Lillico doesn't call as often as he used to. Did I tell you that?'

Gill bit his lip, then shook his head.

'I mean, I just don't have the headspace for a man. But it was nice when we chatted. Nice that he was interested.'

'His head is pretty full too, Cass. He doesn't talk about it but this thing in the Borders has run him ragged.'

'I get it.' Cassy slowed and touched her head against his shoulder. 'He shouldn't have to wait for me to get my shit together.'

'And you don't know what will happen, so don't give up.' He clapped his hands. 'Right, this is good, but keep going because I think there's more.'

She stole a glance at his face. 'This your "magic" inner voice speaking?'

'Actually, I think it's plain enough for everyone to see,' he said, reaching out and offering her his hand.

Cassy glared at it for a few seconds, then clasped it. 'I've had to go back for more counselling.'

He gave her arm a gentle tug. 'That's okay. You were abducted and traumatised on that mountain. Then a few months later, you watched your ex-partner being murdered. Honestly, Cass, I'd be more worried if you weren't in therapy.'

'And this whole cave exploration thing has set me on edge. I can't get over the thought you might die in there.'

Gill gave her his most encouraging smile. 'I can assure you; the plan is definitely to come home safely.'

'And if you're working with Mhairi, don't dare stay in the same hotel as her.'

'Beg your pardon?'

'She's like a mushy teenager around you these days.' Cassy pulled a face. '*Oh, Gill you're so clever! Oh, Gill, what a great idea for a four-page spread.*'

'What can I say? Mhairi likes to flirt with gorgeous men.'

'She does. What's worrying me is she's starting to flirt with the just-about-okay-looking ones, like you.'

'I'm her boss, Cass. Nothing's going to happen.'

Cassy glanced around. 'Says the man walking down Dundee high street in an intimate clutch with his office manager.'

Gill looked away. 'Says the man walking down the road trying to encourage his second-best friend in the whole wide world.'

'Hm. Let's hope none of Salina's pals see you.'

'Don't care if they do. Though Salina's pals are all posh and live in St Andrews so it's really unlikely.'

Just for a moment, Cassy smiled.

Gill gave her arm another tug. 'You haven't mentioned Larry yet.'

'What about him?'

'I saw the hash he made of the quarter-page ads this month. Honestly, I thought you were very restrained not to fire him.'

Cassy spun to face him. 'Can I do that?'

Gill coughed. 'Not without talking to me first. But he's been off his game a bit recently and you justifiably find that frustrating.'

And that comment lit the touch paper. For the rest of the five-minute walk to the museum coffee shop and for the ten minutes it took to walk back to the office, Gill listened as Cassy fumed about every person and every pressure in her life. As they were mounting the stairs back up to the second floor, she was smiling and laughing again.

'Do you think I'm a simple creature?' she asked, pausing outside the double doors.

'How do you mean?'

'Take me for a coffee. Pat my head. Let me have a wee rant to clear the air?'

Gill shrugged. 'You're a grown-up woman whose life is very full and very serious. You're entitled to have friends like me. You know, people who take a few minutes from time to time to listen to you processing your legitimate worries.'

Cassy thought about this for a few seconds, then yanked open the door for him. 'That was the correct answer. Now, away home and have a wonderful weekend.'

Chapter 23

After the four-hour drive from Dundee, followed by a bracing two-hour ferry sailing, it was well into the evening before they all converged on Islay and the rambling farmhouse they'd hired for the weekend. Adina's family arrived first so their girls could explore, while the rest of the Armour Group, plus Salina and Josh, took later sailings. To their collective surprise and delight, Solomon announced she would be joining them. This raised a few eyebrows when she didn't explain why she'd had this change of heart. But her presence made them feel more complete, whether she participated in the lairdship ceremony or not.

As the team started to gather, Ailsa oversaw the logistics while Adina offered to cook, with Douglas, Lorna and Lillico assisting. Solomon steered Charlie into the cavernous lounge and remembering perhaps he was the only member of the group with an arson conviction, she supervised him while he laid and lit a cosy log fire.

Slowed down by the need to feed Josh along the way, Gill and Salina were on a last ferry of the day and consequently, the last to arrive. Gill hauled gear in from the car while Salina laid their sleeping child in a travel cot. Hungry, and ready for a drink Gill finished his exertions and wandered down to the kitchen. Finding it empty, he was suddenly struck by how quiet it was in the house. Following the sound of the crackling fire, he stepped into the lounge and found Salina, stopped in her tracks and glaring across the room at Adina. He swallowed, remembering that this was the first time they'd met in person since Adina had abducted Salina at gunpoint, three years before. Salina stood with her arms by her sides, her hands twitching while her brain ran fight or flight simulations Gill could only imagine. Lillico and Charlie stood poised, ready to intervene.

Adina was last to see Salina, breaking off her conversation with Lorna and taking a cautious step backwards. Staring, wordlessly, at Salina, her crystal helmet manifested. And in this silent confrontation, the two women stood poised for several long seconds. Gill tensed, uncertain what to say, then coughed nervously as Adina suddenly took several long strides towards her former adversary. When the two women were a sword's length apart, Adina stopped and took off her helmet. Then she knelt with her head low and laid the weapon to one side.

'What I did to you was inexcusable,' she said, quietly.

Salina swallowed. 'Yeah, it was. But anyway, you're excused,' she said, extending a hand and hauling Adina to her feet. 'And thank you for saving my husband, you know, from time to time.'

'It's a regular gig. I'm getting used to it.'

As the pair continued to clench each other's hands, Gill could see the whites of their knuckles for several long seconds. Then they dropped the grip and clumsily embraced.

Ailsa came and stood beside them both. 'Maybe we should eat?'

After a meal of tapas, Spanish salads and lightly grilled meats, Salina excused herself to check on Josh while Charlie and Ailsa did the washing up. Solomon raised her eyebrows at Adina when Lorna and Lillico fell into yet another earnest conversation; arguing this time about reforms to the prison system intertwined with a heated debate about the best 80s band. With midnight fast approaching, the conversations flowed freely, and the plan had been to gather in the lounge again for a nightcap. But given the lateness of the hour, Solomon and some others started to drift off to bed. Gill was too wired from the long drive for immediate sleep, so he took himself outside to wander under a clear mid-summer sky.

Clutching a small whisky, purchased in haste from a nearby distillery, he took a long sniff of the bulb-shaped glass, enjoying the complex smoky aromas while he stared out over the landscape. To the south lay the glorious white sands of Machir Bay, while to the east was Loch Gorm, lying in a wide expanse of peat bog. From the grounds of the farmhouse, the loch looked like an undistinguished area of flooding, but it was this dark water, and its carefully stewarded peats that gave the island's famous whiskies their flavour. From this distance he could just make out several small islands dotted across the loch and in the dead centre he saw the Isle of Kilchoman. An island of mosses and heathers in a loch, resting in the middle of a bigger island, this inheritance had been a modest fortress compared to Finlaggan. In two days, following the requisite "feast" in his banqueting hall, it would all belong to him, plus all the responsibilities that implied.

'Feeling nervous?' said a voice behind him.

He turned to find Adina, strolling across the uneven ground.

'A little. I mean, I imagine it will be quite routine. We'll do some tidying up and when we've got enough space for a picnic, we'll have the ceremony. I doubt there'll be any fireworks.'

'Not about the practicalities, Gill. The fact that on Sunday, you'll finally be the Laird of Finlaggan, and then you'll just be one magic horse away from dismantling Scotland.'

'No plans to take it that far, Adina. I like Scotland the way it is.'

She stepped up beside him and peered at the distant loch. 'And I agree, Gill. But if this kill-switch exists, then it exists for a reason.'

Gill grunted a response but said nothing.

'Thanks for encouraging Douglas to tell me about his connections to MI5.'

Gill gave a single nod. 'I take it you already knew?'

'Of course.'

'And yet you continued your friendship with him?'

Adina turned her dark eyes away from Gill. 'He was bookish and cute. The British picked out the perfect man for me. Who was I to ignore a gift like that?'

'Even though he was reporting on your movements for several years?'

'Straight out of the spy's handbook, Gill. Make the other side think they know your every movement.'

Gill smiled. 'Yeah, I can imagine.' He took a moment to stare into the beautiful face of his friend. 'Was there anything else, Adina?'

She shook her natural curls out of her eyes. 'Why would there be anything else?'

'It's just that, every now and then, I feel you're holding back from me.'

Adina stared at her feet for a long moment, then lifted her eyes to meet his. 'If I was, would you trust my judgement?'

'Of course.'

She lifted a hand and squeezed his arm. 'Until tomorrow, then, and whatever it may bring.'

'Thank you.'

'And we'll talk, Gill. When the time is right.'

He wanted her to linger and divulge her secret, but he felt her grip fall away when she turned back for the house. 'Goodnight, Adina,' he sighed.

Ailsa's phone call to the local estate office during the previous week had secured the only boat on the loch available for rent. An open-topped skiff with an outboard motor, it was long and narrow with benches for three anglers to fish side by side. It was a stable little craft so the following morning, five members of the Armour Group set out for the isle with Ailsa at the helm.

The Isle of Kilchoman lay low in the water, with a low hump near its centre being the only hint of its earlier habitation. Gill had researched it, of course, and the records showed that at one time, the acre-sized island held a clutch of low stone buildings. Five hundred years of neglect however had seen much of this crumble into the loch. The rocky shoreline made it challenging to even set foot on the isle and they did a slow circuit until they found a westerly facing spot where a small beach had eroded into the old stonework. The group, minus Salina, Adina and their children, established a makeshift jetty before Ailsa returned to the shore to fetch Douglas and load the boat with tools and provisions. Half an hour later, when the skiff returned, Gill helped Ailsa pull it safely onto the gravel.

'How are things back at the house?' Gill asked.

'All good,' said Ailsa. 'Sal and Adina are playing nicely and are heading to the beach soon. Solomon plans to curl up at the farmhouse and read.'

'I so totally didn't see that coming between Sal and Adina last night.' Gill shook his head. 'Sometimes I'm an idiot.'

'Quite a lot of the time, actually,' smiled Ailsa. 'You have the emotional antenna of a worm.'

'Hey, easy,' said Gill, with a straight face. 'I'm the laird here and I could have you chucked off this rock.'

Ailsa tossed her mane of auburn hair and laughed. 'You're not laird until after tomorrow's ceremony. And besides, I'm the only one who knows how to work the boat.'

'Yeah. I guess.'

'Why's Solie even here?' Ailsa whispered. 'I'd have thought she'd have dodged this weekend.'

'Maybe she's having second thoughts.' Gill winked at Ailsa. 'Maybe she'll shake your hand and let you grab a sneaky download.'

'Ooh! That could be worth a shot.'

'Nah,' said Gill, gathering up an armful of tools. 'Solie always knows what's going to happen before it happens. She'd see you a mile away.'

Lillico, Lorna and Charlie arrived to chase away their speculation, and soon the group was ready to start work in earnest. Back in the old days, vegetable production would have consumed what little green space existed on the isle. But in this century, it was all heather. They set to cutting back the undergrowth with Charlie hacking a swathe through the jungle until his forearms bled. Gradually, the footprint of the old building began to emerge. By late afternoon they'd cleared a space around the thick walls of the old castle keep, plus all the internal floor space. While at one time, the roofless building must have stood twenty or even thirty feet high, today, only tiny portions were more than head height. Ferns jostled for light under a single stone arch until Charlie's petrol-powered cutter took them all down. As the sun began to dip, they stood sweaty and tired, surveying what they'd achieved. The forecast was fine for the next day, so they returned to the farmhouse. Tomorrow, if everything went to plan, they'd acknowledge Gill as the new Laird of Finlaggan, and place him two steps from the power to tear up Scotland.

With Sunday arriving fair, as per the forecast, Solomon announced she would stay in the old farmhouse while the others went out to Gill's island. In their mentor's absence, they designated Charlie as master of ceremonies, before helping Adina create a luxurious picnic of salads and elaborate sandwiches. And as soon as they were organised, Ailsa started ferrying everyone out to the isle. They'd included the children for the first time and Adina's girls went scampering amongst the ruins with their father while Salina led Josh by the hand and worked hard to let him explore in safety. When the agreed moment came, Charlie called everyone to attention. Self-consciously, the six members of the Armour Group came and stood in a circle while the other family members sat on the ruined walls and watched.

'What happens now?' asked Lillico after a long silence.

Charlie shook his head. 'Ah dinnae ken.'

Ailsa reached across and brushed his arm. 'The stipulation was simple. We raise a glass to the new laird, then we hit the picnic.'

'You're sure there's not more ritual to it?' asked Lillico.

'We asked and asked Aura for more direction, but this is all we've got,' said Ailsa.

'I've written a letter to the registry office which we can all sign,' said Adina. 'It confirms we've adhered to the conditions of the inheritance and legally adopts Gill as the Laird of Finlaggan.'

'Thanks,' said Gill, shaking his head. 'But I agree with Alex. Something doesn't feel right.'

'Whadja mean?' asked Lorna.

Gill shook his head. 'This feels like an empty ceremony. A box-ticking exercise. It seems utterly two-dimensional compared to everything else we're doing.'

'Listen,' said Ailsa. 'I'm starving. Laird or no laird, you've got two minutes before I hit the sandwiches.'

'I'm starting to feel it too,' said Lorna. 'Something's off.'

Gill caught a sudden glimpse of crystal armour and turned to Charlie whose face bristled with concern. 'What're you getting, Charlie?'

Charlie's shield fully manifested and he twisted to scan their perimeter. 'Thir's mair tae this than meets th' eye.'

They could all feel it now, and one by one, their armour dazzled under Islay's mid-summer sun.

'Anybody?' said Gill. 'Does anyone have a sense for what's happening?'

And for the first time, they all heard the distant engines of a powerful boat approaching the island.

Charlie sprang from the circle and leapt onto the highest section of the castle wall. 'Somebody's comin' richt taewards us.'

'Who?' asked Gill.

'A dinnae ken. A muckle black boat.' His alarmed face flashed back towards them. 'Ah think we need tae defend oorsels.'

The boat was getting closer and in response, each member of the group moved to either take cover or defend the children. Adina gathered her family under the stone arch for a few seconds, but then, with an exasperated sigh, she stepped back into the centre of the clearing. 'Oh, come on! We're playing at being soldiers now?'

'We've got our armour,' hissed Ailsa. 'We protect ourselves until we see what's coming.'

'No, but seriously,' Adina shouted.

'What's your point?' asked Lorna.

Adina looked angry now. 'You really want to know?'

'Yes.'

'Well, look at us!' She swung her arm around and pointed at them all in turn. 'We're a convicted thief, a reformed junkie and a jumped-up cop whose obsession with the truth makes him the poster boy for the blindingly bloody obvious. Led by an archaeologist of dubious professional standing who's never had a day's sword training in his life!'

Lillico pointed at her with the flat of his hand. 'And don't forget to include the retired double agent.'

'Aye, an' we're nae exactly th' Avengers, Charlie added.

'If you're proposing a change of tactics, Adina,' Gill called from where he sheltered Salina and Josh. 'Do it quickly.'

'My point,' said Adina, dropping her voice. 'Whatever is coming on that boat, I don't think we're ready.'

'Ready?' Ailsa asked.

'To defend ourselves. To know what to do if Gill ever declares *The Torn Isle*.' She lifted off her crystal helmet and held it by her side. 'Frankly, we're not ready for anything.'

Charlie was edging closer to the entrance and peering down on the water. 'We dinnae git tae be aye sorted oot.'

Below them, they could hear the engine throttle back, then a great woosh of water as its wake hit the island.

'What can you see, Charlie?' called Ailsa.

Charlie leant out. 'Twa fowk. Och man.'

'What?'

'Thir's somebody bustin' wi' armour. They're comin' onto th' island. Bit ah ken th' driver. Yon muckle angel fella, 'n' noo he's drivin' away.'

'Quickly,' shouted Douglas. 'Salina and the kids with me.' Helping Salina heave Josh up into her arms, he shepherded the children under the archway and away into the ruins.

Below their position, the engine roared again while Charlie scuttled back to the centre of the roofless hall and raised his shield. Ailsa stepped to his left flank and extended her breastplate while Gill moved to Charlie's right, sword drawn and poised. And in this position, they waited, listening to the metallic sounds of the warrior clambering over the stones, until finally, their head and shoulders appeared.

The figure that stood before them a few moments later was covered head to foot in crystal armour shimmering with technicolour pulses. A matching shield with a lion motif and a long sword slung from their belt. Seeing their defensive stance, the warrior paused a few steps from the wall.

Convinced this was no ordinary armour, Gill studied the new arrival. Noticing subtle matte lettering on the shield, he discerned the words, *Rex Gladio.*

'Who are ye?' shouted Charlie, thrusting his shield towards the interloper.

'Wait a second,' said Gill, shouldering his sword and stepping beyond Ailsa and Charlie. 'If you carry *Rex Gladio*, then you're with us, right?'

The armoured knight before him responded by relaxing and lifting their visor. Solomon's face appeared. 'Sorry to have caused such evident alarm. I'm hoping I haven't missed the picnic?'

'Solie!' shouted Charlie, shouldering his shield and stepping forward to embrace his mentor. 'Yer timin' is juist braw.'

'Oh, good,' she replied. 'Because I'm bringing news.'

Chapter 24

Fifteen minutes later, they were back again, standing in formation. Adina's girls still looked startled, pushing against their father's chest and under the protection of his arms. Josh meanwhile was carefree, sitting happily between Salina's feet, methodically plucking the flowerheads off a clump of heather. Gill paused to glance back at his son before answering Solomon's call to join her in the centre of the circle where he now faced her drawn sword.

'Should I kneel?' asked Gill.

'Let's agree not to kneel,' said Solomon. 'Except to the one who created us.'

'I was just wondering …'

'Gill, please don't overthink this. I've got instructions. Let me concentrate so I don't accidentally stab you.'

Lorna giggled nervously and turned to poke Lillico with her forefinger. When he didn't reciprocate her smile, she gently laid a hand on his shoulder.

Solomon took a deep breath, then solemnly, she raised her sword and used the flat of the blade to touch Gill's right shoulder, then twisted it counterclockwise so the same flat edge touched his left. 'There. That makes you the Laird of Finlaggan.'

'Was expecting a tiny bit more formality,' Ailsa grumbled. 'After the theatrical arrival on an angel-propelled motorboat.'

'Now,' said Solomon, ignoring her. 'This next part is important for us all.' She walked around the circle, making eye contact with everyone in turn. 'The days ahead aren't getting easier. If you are willing to follow wherever Aura leads, to run towards the fire rather than away from it, can you step forward, and on the count of three, I want you to touch my blade.'

Brief glances were exchanged, until one by one, they stepped within reaching distance of Solomon's sword.

'Ready?' she asked, lifting her weapon to the horizontal. 'One, two ...'

The touch of Solomon's sword sent Gill sprawling backwards as if jabbed with an electrical cable. Shaking his head to clear a moment of dizziness, he discovered he was lying on a carpet of damp heather. Above him, Islay's blue sky was gone, replaced by leaden low grey clouds. Feeling moisture seeping into his clothes, he sprang to his feet and looked around.

He was alone, standing a short distance from a stone circle. Seeing it, and casting a quick glance around the landscape, he recognised the setting as the Ring of Brodgar, on Orkney.

'What?' he whispered to himself when he saw a group of people walking away from him as they threaded their way back to some cars. At the rear of the group was a young boy he recognised as Noah Trevelyan, running to catch up with his mother. The events of this day in his past rushed back at him. The death of Noah's father, and Gill's entrapment in his friend's grave. His growing attachment to Salina Ahmed, running hand in hand with his terror she'd be crushed in one of her diving machines. And it was then that Gill understood, this was a place where he'd made decisions. Physically, or in a memory, he was back in the moment when he'd first accepted Raphael's sword. The weapon manifested now, and he drew it, slipping into a defensive posture until the significance of this moment became apparent. This was the place where he'd said 'yes' to the offer of a new way of living. He hadn't asked for it. He hadn't earned it, though it still threatened to cost him everyone and everything he held dear. And even now, if he'd the ability to change his mind, in the light of everything he'd witnessed, he'd still have accepted the sword and stepped behind the veil.

Behind him, someone giggled, and he spun around to find Aura, sitting on a rock. She was smiling, the Saphire blue of her eyes sparkling beneath the waves of long platinum-blonde hair.

'Majesty,' said Gill, dipping his gaze and sword tip towards the ground. And instantly, in a blur of motion, Aura moved behind him. He sensed her presence and felt her forefinger running down his right wrist and across his knuckles where he gripped the hilt.

'Oh, Gill, so much has changed,' she whispered. 'See how easily the blade rests in your hands.'

Gill knew what she meant, but stood silently, transfixed by her touch.

'And through your words and actions, you have made yourself a worthy *Sword-Bearer*.' She drew her fingers back up his hand. 'You accepted my gift, and now, if you are to survive the coming battle, you need to accept another.' Suddenly, she gripped his wrist. 'Do you know why we gave you the sword, Gill McArdle?'

Gill had thought about this over the intervening five years. He knew the sword was representative of *The Book*, a sprawling collection of writings from across the ages, recording the vast canvas of humanity's interaction with its Creator. It had been a puzzle to him at first, only yielding brief insights through the actions of individual characters. But the more he'd wrestled with it, the more he'd grasped the overarching themes. Polishing his understandings until they glistened like jewels, he'd finally perceived the great precision at the heart of *The Book*. For amongst the cogs of kings and nations, there was a rhythmic march of human history, ticking down to a moment when the Nazarene would inevitably come.

'Your academic mind,' Aura continued, 'meant you couldn't believe until you recognised my sovereignty within a coherent framework.'

'Divinity was so alien to me,' Gill stuttered.

'Until you saw the logically argued words in *The Book*, Gill, and understood how science and archaeology underpinned its claims, you could never believe.' She paused. 'For the others it is different and yet the same.'

'How so?'

'Alex Lillico sees the world in black and white. He gravitates towards truth-tellers and devotes his life to exposing liars. It's the compass he uses to steer his life. For Ailsa, her sense of good and evil is so strong she sustains an overpowering urge to do the right thing, resisting any compromise. And Adina comes from a different culture. Her knowledge of the Nazarene came at a high price, meaning she will never be dissuaded.'

'And Charlie? He's the one who started this.'

Aura smiled. 'Charlie's never been much for books. But when his addictions threatened to overwhelm him, he called out to me.'

'I think we all do that from time to time.'

'With Charlie, it's different. When he needs my help, he asks and never doubts that I'll be by his side.'

'And while some of us are self-conscious about our belief, Lorna isn't scared of anybody. She just says what needs said.'

Though he couldn't see her he could almost feel Aura's smile. 'Each of you rose to your gifts because we offered you the piece of the puzzle you'd most readily understand. But soon your individual powers will not be enough, so I have other gifts that will help you in the coming days.'

'What do you mean?'

'It's time for you to put on the rest of the armour, Gill. To wear certainty like Adina. To be a message-bringer like Lorna. Above all, to pick up your shield, so that like Charlie, you'll have faith to withstand what's to come.'

Gill's pause was barely a heartbeat in duration. 'I will.'

Aura's touch disappeared and when he spun around, she was gone. And on the rock where she'd first been sitting, lay six pieces of armour, crafted from the same shimmering crystal as his sword. He stepped over to examine them, setting out the sections and considering how to put them on.

The undergarment would have to go first. The fine, shimmering cotton was close-fitting, and he realised he'd need to strip to his underwear to pull it on. And while on the face of it, he was all alone on an Orcadian moor, he was mindful this was a vision, and some part of him wondered if, in another version of reality, the rest of the armour group might be standing around sniggering. But it was Aura's instruction, so it was the obvious way to proceed. With the undergarment snug around his body from his wrists to his ankles, he picked up the breastplate. He draped its shoulder coverings over his body and felt the crystal plate nestle against his chest, with straps threading themselves together until the pieces pulled snuggly against his torso. Then, he picked up the belt, buckling it on his right side as he'd seen Lillico do, and enjoying the synchronous movement between the belt and breastplate.

Next were the shoes. He just had to step into these, finding the leather-like material snaking up his legs until they overlapped the undergarment. His helmet differed from Adina's; with no front-facing visor, but with the addition of metallic flaps that came down over his ears. He pulled it on and found it was weighty and yet, comfortable. Next, he plucked up his sword and went to slide it into its shoulder scabbard. But the breastplate and shoulder pieces made it too high, so he grappled for a few moments until the scabbard found a new location on his belt, attaching on his left side, near his elbow. And finally, he picked up the shield, admiring the pearlescent shimmering motion in the metal as he felt its weight. Heavier than he expected, he judged it could stop a bullet. He stood for a moment, wondering what on earth he must look like, standing in all this gear. And in that self-conscious state, he suddenly found himself back on Islay.

Looking around the ruined stone hall, he saw every member of the group now glistened with completed armour. There were subtle differences. His sword was long, akin to a Scottish broad sword while the others carried short weapons, attached to their belts or thighs. Lillico's armour looked nimble while Charlie's was heavy-set and powerful. Lorna meanwhile looked lithe and lightly equipped in a material that looked closer to a chain mail. Adina however, looked uncomfortable, burdened under the weight of her equipment until she seemed to stagger forward a few paces allowing all her pieces to click into place. The alarm in her face alerted him that they'd all endured their own versions of his flashback to Orkney.

'Why did I have to go back there?' Adina gasped.

Ailsa moved to her side. 'I didn't enjoy my trip down memory lane either, but we're together now.'

'You okay?' Gill asked Lillico, seeing his shocked white face.

'My father …' Lillico began, before stopping and shaking his head. 'Never mind.'

Charlie had dropped into a squat and was sucking in air. He shook his head at Gill. 'Dark days, man. Dark, dark days.'

'They threatened to kill me if I didn't recant,' Adina stuttered. 'And the truth is, I would have obeyed if I could.' Adina collapsed into Ailsa's open arms. While they endured her uncharacteristic fragility, they remembered what their own journeys with Aura had cost them. One by one, they added themselves to the huddle, until Adina's silent tears ebbed away.

'Now you all wear the complete armour,' said Solomon, resolutely. 'You did not earn it and being honest, none of us are worthy of it. But it is Aura's gift to each of us while we prepare for the battle that's yet to come. My advice?' She paused to check they were hearing her. 'Wear it every day so you're ready when the time comes.'

To the sounds of Adina's muttered thanks, they all extricated themselves from the crush.

Solomon nodded at Lillico. 'Don't look so worried, Alex. Today the armour is visible to all, while most days it will sit privately within you. Your daily challenge, if you're going into a fight, don't leave home without it.'

Lillico nodded, but from the look on his face, Gill could see he was still processing the implications.

'Now,' said Solomon. 'Raphael wants to make you aware that *The Vigil* in Orkney is multiplying. It is already present here on Islay and is springing up throughout the Hebrides, and sporadically across the central belt. There's no logic to it so we can't predict what will happen next, except to grasp that in towns and cities and rural communities, others are gathering to hear Aura speak. Raphael tells me there will be seven thousand people in all.'

'To what end?' asked Lillico.

Ailsa sheathed her sword. 'I don't think that matters. The point is, they're with Aura and that means they're with us too.'

'It's my understanding,' said Gill, addressing Solomon. '*The Vigil* holds similar values to early Celtic spirituality. There's no denominational orthodoxy, so everyone's experience is unique. It's an expression of men and women taking responsibility for meeting their Creator for themselves.'

Solomon nodded. 'And I have no doubt they'll meet the Nazarene in unexpected places, and when you encounter these believers, don't be surprised to find armour bearers among their ranks.' She looked around their faces to make sure they understood.

'People like us?' asked Lorna.

'The growth in *The Vigil* implies the Armour Group is not destined to be a closed club. Beyond these first seven, I believe many others will accept Aura's gifted armour.'

Falling into silence, they were all distracted by happy sounds from Josh, cradled in Salina's arms. Beside her, Doug looked ashen-faced. 'As soon as somebody has a moment,' he whispered, 'I'd love to know what just happened?'

Adina wiped her face and strode to be beside him, showing her girls the new armour. Then gradually, after a few minutes of wonder, her weapons faded from view.

Ailsa's armour was the last to disappear. 'This has been really, really cool, but can I raise a technical point? I'm telling you; Gill isn't the laird until we've properly feasted.'

'Yes,' said Solomon. 'After all that excitement, let's eat.'

Dazzled by the events on the island and relieved that Solomon was now firmly part of the gang, everyone started to pack for home. The children played games around the old farmhouse while the adults snatched conversations about what had happened. Only Gill felt a desire to be on his own. Burdened with the thought of what might come next, he found himself back outside, standing on the spot where he could look across the shallow expanse of Loch Gorm.

'How're you doing?' asked Salina, arriving beside him, carrying Josh.

He turned and slipped an arm around her shoulder. 'Good, thank you.'

She leaned into him. 'Quite a day.'

'Aye,' he said, kissing her. 'Do you think all this spiritual armour will be hard to keep clean?'

She smiled and brushed his cheek with her forehead. 'What's coming, Gill?'

He pulled her against his body. 'Honestly, my love, my words would be empty speculation.'

Salina nodded and said nothing.

'Listen, I need to ask a favour. And it's fine to say no if you're not comfortable.'

Salina used his shoulder to push hair from her eyes. 'What do you need?'

'I've had a nudge from Aura that there's someone I need to see. I'd need the car, so how would you feel about travelling back with one of the others?'

Salina considered his request. 'Who, Gill? And where are you going?'

'Let's just say, I need to swing by the Temple of the Isles, before catching up with two old friends.'

Salina leaned in and bit him sharply on the ear. 'Promise not to tear up Scotland without warning me first?'

'Och, that's sore. And yes, I promise.'

'Okay. Lillico came up here on his own and I'd trust his driving.'

Gill took Josh from her arms and hugged him. 'Thank you.'

'How long will you be away?'

'Just a couple of days. I'll let Cassy know I'm working remotely and should be back by midweek.'

She squeezed his hand. 'Okay, do it. But first, you're gonna help me move the car seat before you disappear on your adventures.'

Chapter 25

An hour later as Gill watched Lillico drive away bearing his precious cargo, he pulled out his phone and took a deep breath. This call was important, and it was long overdue.

'Rani,' said Gill as the number picked up. 'Gill McArdle here. Been a long time.'

'Gill,' gasped Rani Kumar's voice. 'So good to hear from you.'

'How are you?'

'I'm great. Better than great.'

'Wee bird tells me you're married.'

'I am, to someone I met professionally. A chap called Graham McGregor.'

'Didn't he help you set up the horse sanctuary?'

'He did. And better yet, he has a young daughter who needed a new mum.'

'Goodness. What's the story there?'

'Graham lost his first wife to breast cancer. Amy was just three when her mum died.'

'That's tragic.'

'It is. By all accounts, Amy's mum was a wonderful woman. But now I'm here for them both and they're here for me,' said Rani, her voice radiating happiness.

'What a whirlwind,' said Gill. 'I'm so pleased for you.'

'And how about you? What's been happening?'

Over the next few minutes, Gill updated her on his marriage to Salina, the arrival of their first child and briefly, how things were progressing on the magazine. Then he drew a breath and got down to business. 'Listen, I'm up on the Isle of Lewis this week on a personal errand. I'm wondering if I could pop in and say hi?'

'Absolutely. And it'll give you a chance to meet our boy. You remember MG1914?'

'I do,' said Gill. 'I take it he's still around?'

'All grown up and in his prime. He's a fine animal. I'm so glad he survived Minos Genetics.'

'Me too. Hey, I'll be in touch in the morning and check what time you're available.'

Gill took the night ferry to Harris, arriving in Tarbert after dark. It was too late to find accommodation, so he chose a discreet layby to pull over and grab a couple of hours sleep. He'd already decided that dawn was the best time to visit the old Callanish stone circle and do what he'd come here to do. The forecast was for rain later and besides, at 6 am, he was unlikely to be disturbed. He parked his car a short distance from the monument and walked up the approach road with his mind open to anything Aura might say.

On that sun-washed morning, it felt strange to be back here. The journey that had transformed his life had begun under the shadow cast by these stones and a fretful part of his brain wondered if this was where, someday, it might end. He pushed the dark thought from his mind and strode to the centre of the crudely cross-shaped monument. Its layout had always puzzled him. The cross was a familiar symbol, loaded with meaning and he had to remind himself that these stones had been raised two thousand years before the Nazarene had come and gone from the Earth. Was the shape a coincidence? People had hypothesised that the circle with its four avenues was designed as an astronomical observatory, but the truth was, nobody really knew the purpose of these stones.

He slowly paced clockwise around the monument, then paused before circling it in the opposite direction, trying to imagine what it would feel to do this for real, astride a waterhorse, announcing a declaration that cut Scotland in two. Without any inspiration prompting his brain, he stopped and found an exposed rock where he could sit. And there he sat for half an hour, staring out across the moor where he'd exposed the waterhorse bones five years before. That day had been a triumph and become a conduit for many good things in his life, and yet, the longer he sat, the more a heaviness settled upon him. Not the kind of blackness he'd experienced around Sariel. Rather, the thought a future moment could seem so hopeless declaring *The Torn Isle* became a good idea. He was musing on this unhappy puzzle when he heard the gentle huff of a leather jacket as a man sat down beside him. They sat in companionable silence for a few minutes and eventually, it was Gill who spoke.

'Will I really have to do it?'

'I don't know,' said Raphael, tugging at a grass stem`. 'That kind of foresight is not among my powers. But I'm glad you're prepared.'

'Not sure I'm there yet. Things would have to be pretty bad, Raph.'

Raphael leaned across and gave Gill's shoulder a gentle push. 'Things could be worse. Long ago, I was once the guardian of a general. He was tasked with leading an army around an enemy city for seven days while his people blew trumpets.' Raphael laughed. 'He moaned and groaned about being a man of action, though in the end, he still obeyed.'

'I remember,' said Gill, recalling the story. 'I named my son after him.'

'So you did,' said Raphael's smiling voice. 'Like you, he was trusted to do the right thing while a far bigger story played out around him.'

'He tore down a city. I might disrupt an entire nation.'

Raphael sucked an inward breath. 'Part of me is eager to see what will happen. The other half dreads what it will cost.'

Gill turned and looked at Raphael. 'If it happens, will you stand with me?'

Raphael nodded. 'We never go into battle alone, my friend.'

As Gill left the A858 near the hamlet of Dalbeg, the peace he'd experienced around Raphael suddenly evaporated. He pulled off the road and halted on the verge with his pulse racing. Below him, about a mile distant, a single boat bobbed in a sheltered bay. Between here and there was a smattering of farm buildings, and the first of these had a modern stable block with an exercise yard enclosed by a low wooden fence.

Of course, he knew why he was nervous. This was Rani's home and the base for her equestrian charity. Born out of remorse for her treatment of horses during the time she'd worked for an animal genetics firm, Rani had started the charity five years ago with her new husband. And among the ranks of wild and domesticated horses that passed through their hands was a small indigenous stallion with the designation, MG1914. Recognised by only four people, this animal was the only known candidate horse to display waterhorse latency. Like most of his ancestors, it was unlikely he'd ever undergo the metamorphosis, but just knowing he existed sent a shiver down Gill's spine. And the reasons for this visit? To say hello to an old friend, and to look MG1914 in the eye and contemplate what he found there.

With his engine idling, he spotted a woman striding across the exercise yard, with a little girl running in her wake.

'Oh, man up, McArdle,' he mumbled to himself. Rani spent her life around these animals, she'd know right away if anything about the horse had changed. He took a deep breath and shoved the car in gear, then drove slowly downhill to meet Rani and her family.

'Bru?' said Gill, a few minutes later.

'Yes', said Rani, sheepishly, throwing Gill an embarrassed smile.

'Let me get this straight. You have the last living, breathing waterhorse on the planet and you named him after a soft drink?'

'It's not like he's a racehorse, Gill. He doesn't need a fancy stable name. So, when Amy gave him that as a pet name, it kinda stuck.'

'May I ask why?'

'He loves the taste of Irn Bru,' cried Amy while she swung happily from Rani's arm.

'Brilliant,' said Gill, with a glint of humour. 'And on top of the waterhorse latency, you're feeding him sugar in a highly caffeinated drink?'

'We discovered it by accident so don't judge,' laughed Rani. 'He's had it like a couple of times. Mainly we give him boiled sweets with the same flavour.'

Gill cleared his throat. 'And is there any chance I could meet Bru, while I'm here?'

'Ah,' said Graham. 'Might be a problem with that.'

'The mares are in season,' said Rani. 'And Bru does like to get out amongst his kin and …'

'Make new friends,' Graham finished.

Gill looked from one to the other. 'So, what you're saying …'

'You can safely say Bru's doing his bit to make sure the waterhorse bloodline is preserved', said Rani.

'He'll be back later', said Amy. 'He always comes home at night.'

'He's a bit of a homebird,' said Graham. 'Likes his comforts.'

'After a busy day on the moors,' said Rani, scratching the back of her head. 'He probably needs a little feeding up.'

'Talking of which, come and have some lunch,' said Graham. 'Rani has told me lots about you, though I'd love to fill in some blanks.'

Revelling in the woman Rani had become, Gill enjoyed his time with the household. The couple were ten years older than Gill and carried a gentle love for each other that seems unique to those who find true companionship late in life.

'I stayed on the island until my solicitor dealt with the charges stemming from my time working for Minos,' Rani explained.

'You were banned from working with animals,' Gill recalled.

'Yes. When we got that overturned, I went back to London and sold my flat. And used the cash to buy this farm. Graham is a vet, and he helped me in a professional capacity to find a suitable piece of ground for an equestrian charity.'

'I'd recently been widowed,' Graham explained. 'In those days, Amy was still a pre-schooler, so I'd often take her on my farm visits, which is how this pair first met.'

'It was love at first sight,' said Rani, shaking her head.

'And I was the associated baggage,' winked Graham.

'It was the pair of you,' Rani protested. 'You guys were a joint ticket right from the off. Both so wounded and alone, and yet so wonderful together. I watched you care for each other and decided that if I even had a tiny amount of that love in my life, I'd be the happiest woman in the world.'

In response, Amy groaned and started mimicking icky kissing sounds.

'What age are you now?' asked Gill, turning to the girl.

'I'm eight,' Amy said, brightly.

'Going on eighteen,' said Rani, full of mock indignation.

Gill joined in their laughter and marvelled that almost impossibly, Rani looked younger now than when she'd worked for Minos Genetics. Basking in her new family, the love of a good man and the unexpected blessing of a healthy child.

'He's coming,' yelled Amy, dashing to the kitchen window with her arms flung wide. 'Come and meet him, Gill.'

Gill let Amy drag him by the hand and together they shuffled out to the sandy expanse of the exercise yard. A great grey horse was cantering over the moor towards the farm. In the wildest expression of freedom Gill had ever seen, it coasted over the fence and into the yard as if the boundary was no obstacle at all.

'Can't be', said Gill, staring at the animal. 'The Hebridean animals were all tiny.'

'They're typically one hundred and twenty centimetres at the shoulder,' said Rani. 'This fellow is one hundred and sixty, which makes him almost as big as your typical Clydesdale.'

'You're certain it's the same horse?' Gill spluttered.

Rani went back into the house and returned a minute later with the scanner they'd used to track the waterhorses back in the days of Minos Genetics. She fired it up and once the machine was live, she pointed it at Bru's neck and waited until it detected the I.D. chip planted in the horse's lower neck. 'RFID tag is 1914, Gill. This is our boy.'

'How's he so big?'

Rani shrugged. 'He's a wild animal. He's just a particularly lovely specimen.'

'I've been taking riding lessons,' said Gill, to no one in particular.

'Oh aye. Are you any good?'

He cleared his throat. 'My instructor thinks my horsemanship shows promise.'

'Is that so? How promising?'

'Apparently, it's a miracle I haven't broken anything yet. She thinks my bones are made of rubber.'

Amy's face broke into an eager smile. 'Gill could ride Bru!'

Rani placed a hand gently behind her daughter's head. 'Oh, darling. You know what he can be like.'

The little girl protested. 'But they should get to know each other.'

Gill cleared his throat. 'At this stage, I'm happy just to give him some hay … or a highly caffeinated boiled sweet.'

'Amy rides him all the time,' said Rani flatly.

Gill stared at his old friend, and he knew his eyes must blaze with incredulity. 'You put your precious eight-year-old on … that thing. Knowing what he is?'

'He's a horse, silly,' said Amy, scuttling off towards the tack room.

Rani leaned towards Gill. 'She doesn't properly understand about Bru. In all likelihood, he'll live his natural life, and Amy will never know there was anything different about him.'

'But Rani …'

'Maybe Amy is right, Gill. You should take him for a canter.' She turned around to check on Amy. 'And most days, he's quite lovely.'

Amy returned with a brown leather bridle. 'He'll let you use this if you ask nicely.'

Gill looked at the flimsy straps and towards the tack room. 'Okay. I'll give you a hand with the saddle.'

Rani shook her head. 'No saddle, Gill. The leather bridle is all he'll give you.'

'Really?'

'It stems from a rule we have with the feral horses. We don't think it's ethical to put a saddle on them, even if they seem relaxed around people.'

'But no saddle means no stirrups. How do I mount him?'

Rani pointed to four stone stairs that led to nowhere. 'You use our mounting block. Come on. Let's give it a go before you start thinking about it.'

But Gill was already thinking about it. Right at this moment he would rather have jumped off the May Isle rather than get close to this beast. Reluctantly, he took the riding hat proffered by Amy and watched Rani gently offer Bru the leather bit. The horse took this willingly, allowing Rani to slide the bridle up and over his ears, careful not to tangle his forelock while she fastened the various straps and buckles in place. Whispering reassurance, she led him to the mounting block where Amy stood patiently, waiting to show off her skills. And skilled she was, sliding gracefully onto the animal's back and slipping into a natural seated position.

He watched Rani lead Bru around two circuits of the exercise yard, while Amy sat lightly and confidently upon his back, her legs hugging his sides contentedly, and hands taking a loose grip on the reins near the buckle. The child's posture was excellent, and the motion of her body synchronised with the animal as first they walked, then slowly trotted around the yard. And when Rani bid him stop, Bru halted by the mounting block. Amy slid off and fetched Gill, taking him by the hand and dragging him up the four steps.

The steps met the horse where its front legs joined his body. Without a saddle to grasp, Gill gingerly took up some of the wiry, grey mane in his hand, steadying his left leg on the block and swinging his right, high over the horse's back. Bru puffed with impatience, but Gill held his nerve, bending his knees and pushing himself up and forward until he was able to sit up and find a comfortable seated posture.

'Well done,' laughed Rani. 'If you were going to fall off, that was probably the place.'

Gill gently tugged the right-hand side of the rein, and the horse took this as an instruction to move. He moved forward a few steps, then stopped to graze some hay.

'Give him a little nudge,' said Rani. 'And keep your heels down. It'll help your balance.'

'Come on,' said Gill with more authority than he felt, nudging the horse by flicking his pelvis forward. And obediently, the animal began to move.

'You're doing great,' cried Amy. Gill couldn't help noticing that Rani had placed her daughter safely on the other side of a fence.

He leaned over and patted the horse's neck. 'Good boy,' he murmured, trying to sound confident.

This interaction seemed to catch Bru's attention, and he stopped and turned to look at Gill with his right eye. Then he faced forward again and continued to complete the first circuit of the exercise yard. Gill would happily have stopped there, but Bru broke into a trot and Gill tried to coax him to slow down.

What happened next was probably a breakdown of communication. What Gill had intended as a gentle check of both reins to slow the animal was interpreted as a nudge to say, 'speed up.' The trot broke into a canter while the horse continued to ignore Gill's voice commands. At the far end of the yard, closest to the house, the animal slowed to a halt and gazed across the exercise area and onto the moor beyond.

'Aw, no,' he heard Amy say to her mum.

Rani too had seen some hidden danger and moved sharply in Gill's direction. But this only seemed to spur the animal into action. As Gill felt Bru's body tensing beneath him, he didn't have time to panic before Bru sprang into motion and bolted towards the fence.

Gill had been told in no uncertain terms, "Do not dig a horse in its ribs with your knees." The sensation was uncomfortable for the animal and liable to make it run or buck. But with no saddle to grip and as the metres between the horse and fence were devoured, terror flared in his chest, and he felt his knees disobey his training.

Bru cleared the fence like a show jumper, his forward momentum flowing into a continued gallop. Gill gave up shouting almost immediately and focused his efforts on staying mounted. Without a saddle, it was an uncomfortable ride, until the astonishing moment came when Gill's movements synchronised with the horse. By now, they were charging downhill towards the sea, gliding right to avoid a fence line and the steep slope beyond it. For a full minute, they sped along, and Gill was one with the animal, shouting with delight while the longest lengths of Bru's mane flowed into his face like a sensuous feeling of a long-haired girl. But the moment was very brief because Bru broke left to leap over a hazard, disconnecting Gill from his balance and sending him tumbling into the edge of a marsh.

He lay on his back, dazed and feeling the unpleasant sensation of cold water stepping into his clothes. Gradually he extended each limb to check if he'd broken anything. Mercifully, he was intact. And it appeared, no one had witnessed his fall. Even Bru had stopped about twenty metres away and now grazed the green grasses along the margins of the boggy ground. Patting himself down, Gill started to walk back to the house. By the time he reached the edge of Rani's property, she was leaning against the fence, with Amy standing two bars up so their heads were level. Bru meanwhile had come up behind him, nudging Gill's back with his head, like a schoolmaster reprimanding a run-away child.

'We're meant to be developing our teamwork,' muttered Gill over his shoulder at the horse, staggering for a few steps as the power of the animal propelled him forward. 'No, don't try and wiggle out of it. You've probably had too much caffeine today, you great mangy …'

'That went well,' Rani shouted across to him.

'Be honest,' said Gill. 'You knew he would do that.'

'He has this thing', said Rani. 'When he stops like that and looks at a faraway fence. It's like he's measuring his stride.' She giggled. 'I am sorry. I should have held onto the bridle.'

Gill leaned on the fence, still catching his breath, while Bru came up beside him. The horse swung his head towards him, bashing Gill sideways and forcing him to clamber untidily through the fence.

'Aw,' said Amy. 'I think he likes you.'

Chapter 26

On the same day as Gill was making new friends on the Isle of Harris, DI Shona Fallon was stepping out of a neglected terraced house in mid-Ulster. Ignoring the expletive laden barbs aimed at her back, she reached her car and glanced at her DS. 'You drive. I need to make a call.'

As they pulled away, ignoring the taunts from a group of boys, she dialled Alex Lillico.

'Alex, it's Shona. I've just left Iain Lynch's last known address. There was a girl there with a couple of kids. She claims he's left the country.'

'Oh, aye. Where to?'

'The poor darlin' couldn't remember. If it had been the old days, I would have shoved her against a wall and pushed my fist under her ribcage until her memory recovered, but hey ho. There are other ways to get that information.'

'Still, if he's on the run, it sounds like Lynch is our guy.'

'Aye. I'll go bang on the doors of some known associates and update you in due course.'

'Cool. And the trawler?'

'Is away on a two-week mackerel fishing trip in the North Atlantic. However, I did get a radio link to the skipper.'

'I bet he was as cooperative as Lynch's girlfriend.'

'Actually, we had a nice wee chat about the incident, and he explained how they'd had a system-wide electrical fault. Apparently, he decided to anchor in a sheltered bay while they identified the dodgy part and did a complete restart of the boat's system.'

'He'd got his story worked out in advance.'

'He had. So, I wished him the top of the mornin' and let him think I'd bought the whole tale.'

'But you haven't?'

'I can tell a liar, even if he's a thousand miles away. Tell me, did your researcher happen to find a log of where the *Argonaut* came from before her nighttime layover in Wigtownshire?'

'Let me check.' Lillico tabbed to his emails and called up the last dozen from Eliza. 'Yes. We've got her transponder movements for one month before and one month after. We're still trying to identify any moment when they might have rendezvoused with another vessel.'

'If you get any hits, ping those to me, there's a good fella.'

Around the time Fallon was updating Lillico, Lorna was glaring at Katie across her kitchen table while they flexed their fingers. Then, steadying their elbows on the table they clasped hands.

'Don't start 'til I'm ready,' Lorna snapped.

'You're a criminal, girl,' Katie retorted. 'You've had all the second chances you're gonna get.'

'Oh, listen to her,' mocked Lorna. 'The bully in her silly harlequins.'

'I'm so gonna whip your arse,' said Katie. 'Oh, wait a second. That's nipping me.' She broke their grip and swiftly took off the rings that adorning her right hand. Pushing them aside, she pulled her game-face back on and stared coldly at Lorna. 'Ready or not, here I come.'

Lorna felt the full force of Katie's hand press against hers and just managed to keep her arm upright. Most important of all, she kept fear from her face while she watched Katie's bicep bulge. 'That the best you got?' she sneered.

'Okay, so that's what you did in prison! You finally found time to work out.'

Lorna pressed her face across the table at Katie. 'And then some.' She pushed hard into the wrestle and for a second, Katie lost some ground.

'Not … lost to you … since I was nine years old,' hissed Katie. 'Not … gonna … happen now.' Then, with a heave, she found some extra force and slapped Lorna's arm flat against the table.

'Okay, okay,' Lorna laughed. 'But I almost had you.'

'Never,' sniffed Katie. 'Not for a second.'

'Now you've asserted dominance in your traditional manner, are you gonna keep your promise and help me finish the upstairs bedroom?'

'I thought your new pals did all that,' said Katie, flexing her hand to encourage the blood flow.

'They made a great start, but there's still lots to do.'

'In fact, I'm not sure why I'm here. Now you've got a gaggle of magical besties at your beck and call, do you still need your oldest friend?'

Lorna stood and embraced her. 'Until the day when I beat you in an arm wrestle, you remain indispensable.'

Katie laughed and pushed her away. 'Any nice men in this new squad?'

'Nice?' Lorna queried.

'You know. Fit, braw, tidy. Basically, would you do it with any of them?'

Lorna blushed. 'You're looking at the oldest virgin in Morayshire.'

'No way! And you're not even minging.'

'Ach, you …'

'There is someone,' called Katie, triumphantly. 'I can tell by your blushes. One of those laddies has caught your eye.'

Lorna spiked her hands on her hips and shrugged theatrically.

'Is he married? I'll bet he's married. All the nice ones are at our age.'

'He's not married,' said Lorna.

'And what's his superpower?' She sprang closer to elbow Lorna in the ribs. 'Are you gonna tell me. I'll bet he's got a really …'

'I heard the doorbell,' said Lorna. 'Did you hear the doorbell? I'm sure I heard the doorbell.'

'Send them away. I still want to hear about his superpower,' cried Katie.

'I need to answer the door!'

She freed herself from Katie's clutches, and laughing, she stepped from the kitchen and down a short corridor. She opened the front door to a large, balding man in his early forties. Briefly, the unsmiling man held up his ID. 'Steven Blaine, Aberdeenshire Probation Service. Are you Lorna Cheyne?'

'I am.'

'This is a routine spot check on convicted offenders, as regulated by Scotland's Community Justice Act of 2016. May I come in please?'

Lorna glanced at her watch. 'At 8 pm in the evening?'

'Nine in the morning to nine in the evening. Those are the hours, Miss Cheyne.'

'But I have a friend here.'

The man lifted a hand to scratch his right ear. 'Did you read the material the probation service gave you before your release?'

'I did.'

'So, you'll understand the consequences of refusing a regulated visit?'

Lorna released an embarrassed smile. 'I just thought it would be a woman.' She felt movement beside her. It was Katie.

'Look, this sounds important. I'll just go.'

'You leavin' me to paint on my own?'

'Oops,' smiled Katie. 'Rain check. See you tomorrow, yeah?'

'Yep. Rematch please.' She waved Katie off and turned to the scowling Steven Blaine. 'Would you like a cup of tea?'

'Milk, and two sugars, please.'

She beckoned to him. 'Come in.'

Shifting his girth sideways to make it through the narrow hall, he followed her into the kitchen.

'Have a seat,' said Lorna. 'I'll pop the kettle on.'

'I'll stand if that's okay,' said Blaine. 'Been sitting in the car all day.'

She turned her back on him and leaned over the sink to fill the kettle. 'You must cover a large district?'

'Aberdeen to Nairn on a bad day. At least it's pretty countryside.'

'And do you always have to work this late?'

Blaine didn't answer. Instead, a hand came from behind her, pulling a strong-smelling cloth sharply against her nose and mouth. Immediately, Lorna felt her consciousness flicker. The logic in her brain knew she was in danger, but whatever Blaine was using, it had crashed that part of her awareness that would allow her to jump to safety. Moments later, she felt her knees buckle and Blaine guided her to the floor.

'Hey, stop that,' shouted a voice behind her.

The man immediately released the rag and stood to face the challenger. Without support, Lorna slumped to the floor. 'Oh, hi, Katie,' she mumbled through a chemically induced fog.

He locked eyes with Katie and for three long seconds, nobody moved. Then he lunged at her, just as Katie's hands shot up in self-defence. She deflected him a few times but with minimal room for manoeuvre, the man drove her back between the fridge and work surface. They locked fingers and even in this dream state, Lorna knew her friend would give a good account of herself. And indeed, Blaine grunted with effort while he pulled Katie into a position where he could do her some harm. Katie shook him off for a moment and jumped for the door. But he reached her before she could escape, throwing his arms around her shoulders to throw her to the floor. Katie's left elbow shot backwards, catching him full in the face and sending blood flying from his nose. He was angry now and turned to grab at Katie just as she pulled free from him. Bellowing, he propelled the tiny kitchen table across the floor with his thigh, cornering her next to the oven. And with hands outstretched, he charged at her. Katie seemed trapped, but in a deftly timed jolt, her right foot flew up, catching the man full in the crotch. As he pitched forward in pain, Katie's left knee came up like a piston, hitting him in the throat and jaw. Clutching his windpipe, he tumbled sideways against the table and staggered from there to the floor.

Katie stood, shaking, until she decided the threat had passed, then released a ragged breath. Lorna watched her friend gather something off the table then come round and slump, panting, on the kitchen floor beside her. With a little effort, they were able to get Lorna's head resting in Katie's lap.

'Forgot my rings,' said Katie, matter of factly, before jabbing a foot at the gasping figure. 'Who's the fat guy?'

'I dunno,' Lorna slurred. 'I think he works for someone who wants me dead.'

'Why?'

'Stole something from him. Long time ago.'

'The same guy who tried to kill us at the Bullers of Buchan?'

'Pr-wobbably.'

'What are we gonna do with him?'

'Did you kill him?'

'Not yet,' said Katie. 'But if he stands up again, I just might.'

'I'll give you a number. You can call my friend.'

'One of your magical besties?'

'Uh huh.'

'The special one?'

Lorna buried her face against Katie's thigh. 'Just call him, okay?'

Chapter 27

*Wigtown,
26th June 1746*

Dearest Mother,

Alas, our friends in Wigtownshire were no match for their lavish words. My visits to eight of their grand houses, made rich with cattle and trade, saw not a single door opened to me. Amidst rumours they might hand me to government bounty hunters, I decided to press deeper into this green wilderness until the time is right to return to thee.

Pray for me. I am fallen in with a group of lawless men. Despicable, landless creatures who know nothing of our Holy Mother but who stand apart as the only folk willing to share the road with me. They are fugitives from a different kind of war, cleared from the land to make way for the cattle that further enrich those same wealthy landowners. Despite their filth, my fellow travellers share their food with me, and I share with them what little I have been able to buy, or shamefully to steal. At night, I amuse these brigands with my dreadful playing on Richard's bagpipes. Indeed, just the other evening, a lass gave me a single kiss and a piece of stale bread in exchange for a promise I would not play another note that evening.

Do not be ashamed of me, Mother. To fight on in our most worthy cause, in whose name we have already given so much, I must survive.

*Thy wretched son,
Francis Towneley.*

Chapter 28

Alex Lillico sat in interview room seven alongside a member of the Aberdeenshire detective team. Opposite sat Billy Whyte and his solicitor.

'How's the nose, Billy?' said Lillico. 'Looks painful.'

'Piss off,' spat Billy.

'This makes our second wee chat in a fortnight,' said Lillico, smiling. 'One week you're bird watching in Wigtownshire and the next, you're trying to kidnap or kill a young woman in Morayshire. You do get around.'

Whyte's solicitor looked up from his notes. 'If there was a question there, DI Lillico, I didn't hear it.'

Lillico ignored him. 'Do you pay Stevie Blaine a fee?' he asked, directing his question at Whyte. 'You know, for using his name.'

Whyte sneered and looked away.

'Thing is, Billy. You've got all the imagination of a wasp. You use the same false name in every dubious endeavour and all the while you're leaving a tasty trail of nuts back to the man who I think is ultimately pulling your strings.'

Again, the solicitor squirmed. 'If this is an interview, Detective, I believe the principle is that you ask my client questions, rather than just sit there and insult him.'

'Okay,' said Lillico. 'Billy. Did you use a vaporised anaesthetic to disable Lorna Cheyne with the intention of abducting or killing her?'

'No comment.'

'Did you impersonate a probation officer, acting on behalf of Aberdeenshire council?'

'No comment.'

'And did you act on behalf of another person who intended you to cause harm to Miss Cheyne?'

'No comment.'

'And there you go,' said Lillico, addressing the solicitor. 'We could carry on in this vein, but really, life is too short.' He turned to Whyte. 'If you have nothing further to add, Mr Whyte, I'm now charging you for the attempted murder of Lorna Cheyne. Police Scotland will petition the court to refuse bail given the violent conduct in this case. You will be remanded in custody until we can arrange a court appearance. Do you understand?'

Billy Whyte nodded to confirm that he did, and for a second, Lillico observed relief on the man's face.

The following morning, Shona Fallon emerged from her flat on Balmoral Avenue in one of Belfast's leafier districts. As usual, she tossed her laptop bag in her car before preparing to make her preflight inspections. She wasn't looking forward to her working day. A stop off in Lisburn to pick up a junior member of her team, then another round of rapping on doors in one of the toughest areas of Loyalist Portadown. She'd be shouted at, have doors slammed in her face, and probably be spat at. And that's just when the good people of Edgarstown heard her name. She remembered hunting for suspects in that challenging district when she'd been a junior RUC officer, and these days, it wasn't much better in the PSNI. She completed her check of the wheel arches and was about to grab the extendable mirror from her boot when her mobile rang.

'DI Fallon,' she said briskly.

'Shona,' the voice, breathing into the phone. 'Hear you've been looking for me.'

'Who's speaking, please?'

'Yesterday you were on my patch banging on doors. Takin' a chance there, lassie.'

Fallon paused her checks and leant on the car roof. 'Lemme guess. Iain Lynch?'

'Maybe. Maybe not. For now, why don't you just call me, The Quartermaster.'

'Oh, spare me the theatrics, Iain. This is the 2020s, not the 1980s.'

'Oh, is it love? Is that why you sleep with a gun under your pillow and check beneath your car every morning?'

Fallon glanced back at her house. Did Lynch really know she slept with a gun at night or was that just a lucky guess?

'They never did find the guy,' Lynch said, conversationally.

'What guy?'

'The one that finished your daddy at Holycross.'

'You listen to me, you pathetic little turd …'

'Thing is, I know the fella. He's an old man now, but he used to brag about doin' your old da.'

Fallon was improvising now, grappling with her laptop bag, pulling out the device and frantically emailing a colleague, to demand an immediate trace for the number calling her work phone.

'He used to make a joke about it. "Mind that wee Catholic girl," he'd say. "She's aye as fear't and useless as a fart in the wind."' Lynch stopped to laugh. 'And that's true, isn't it Shona? Didn't do a very good job looking after you old da?'

'Oh, you think you're such a big man, Lynch. But you're old school. Anyone who ever knew your name forgot it a long time ago.' She knew she sounded breathless, but DS Martin had acknowledged her message and confirmed the call trace was running. All she had to do was keep Lynch talking.

'Let's chat about Scotland,' she barked. 'Are there not enough beaches in Ireland that you have to go taking your shite to Wigtownshire?'

'Well, that was unfortunate, the way that cliff opened like that. It's all these storms we're having. I blame global warming.'

The location data for Lynch's call pinged in and to her surprise and delight, it was less than a mile away. Armed response was enroute and she confirmed she'd meet them there. Jumping into the car, she started the engine.

'Of course, Iain, you'll know by now, we have your guns.'

Lynch laughed. 'Plenty more where those come frae.' He paused. 'I can hear an engine. Are you driving?'

Fallon had found a gap in the traffic and reversed from her drive onto Balmoral Avenue. 'I'm on my way to work, moron.'

Lynch tutted. 'I do hope you took your usual precautions.'

Swinging into the northbound carriageway, Fallon started to accelerate. 'I'm always careful.'

'Always,' he said, playfully. 'You always check under your car. I like that about you. You're very consistent.' He left a pause. 'We'll likely not speak again. Say hi to your daddy for me.'

Abruptly, the line went dead, and Fallon took three seconds to ponder exactly what he'd implied. Then in a burst of panic, she leaned so hard on the brakes, smoke streamed from her tyres. A woman pushing a child's buggy stopped and stared. A man wearing joggers and sitting in a self-propelled wheelchair started to turn towards her. Behind her, a car blew its horn.

'Get away!' she yelled at the pedestrians. 'Suspected explosive device. Tell the traffic to move back!'

The people just stared at her and the driver behind her got out of his car.

'Go!' she screamed. 'Get away from this car.'

Stumbling to remember her training; stay in the car or flee? Use her phone or not? Frozen, she sat staring at her legs and wondering if she was about to be parted from them. In the distance, she could hear sirens and in the terror of the moment, she swung open her door and was violently sick.

Seventy-five minutes later an unfamiliar number dialled Lillico's number.

'DI Lillico.'

'Alex, it's Shona Fallon.

'You okay?' he asked after hearing her shivering introduction.

'I found Lynch. Or rather, he found me,' she explained. 'He, or someone in his circle, placed a dummy explosive device under my car this morning.'

'You sure? How can you be certain it was him?'

'They were watching me. The sneaky wee bastard distracted me from my normal routines. I was halfway to being dead before I realised what was happening.'

There was a brief silence on the other end of the line. 'I'm so sorry, Shona.'

'He phoned me and was bugging me about the case. I think he's warning me off.'

'But you're not hurt?'

'No. When I realised what was happening, I stopped in the middle of the street. Sat there for an hour ready to crap myself while the bomb squad did their thing.'

'And the device?'

'Was a plastic lunchbox with a big magnet inside. Point he was making, they can reach me, whoever "they" are.'

'Look, Shona, if you feel your life is in danger, no one will blame you if you take a rain check on this case.'

'You kidding? That road leads to anarchy, my friend. The only thing this morning changes for me is doubling my determination to make that little shit pay for what he's done.'

'Clearly, he's not working alone.'

'Indeed. And I'm going to find them.'

Six hours later, Fallon was back from Edgarstown. The door to door hadn't been as fruitless as expected and now she'd come by some new intel on Lynch. Snatching her phone, she decided to update Alex Lillico. 'Just seen your arrest report on Billy Whyte. Is this attempted abduction related in any way to our Wigtownshire case?'

'Not as far as I can see and the man himself isn't talking. Though …'

'Though what, Alex?'

'I got the weirdest sense that Whyte is happier tucked up in our detention centre than out on the street. He hasn't said so, but I think the man fears for his life.'

'If he's mixed up with hardline Loyalists, then you might be right.'

'Any word on Lynch?' asked Lillico.

'I've discovered the wee weasel spent most of last month in Boston. Looks like he's running his network from there.'

'I thought he was in Belfast this morning?'

'Nah. Some clever jiggery-pokery with the phones. He's miles away.'

'No chance of pulling him back?'

'We might have been handed a lucky break as he flew to Amsterdam three days ago.'

'Any idea where he is now?'

'Looks like he switched passports as his trail stops there. He'll likely have a Republic of Ireland documentation and could be darting around the EU with minimal checks.'

'Meaning there's no way of finding him?'

Fallon snorted. 'With my resources? No chance. That fella is invisible until he pops his head up from whatever hole he's hiding in.'

'There must be people helping him?'

'There are and we've got some names,' Fallon confirmed. 'They've not been on the radar for a while, but I know where to look for them.'

'Okay. Be careful.'

'Might take me a week or more to find the wee minger, but I'll be in touch as soon as I track him down.'

Chapter 29

'I hate caves,' Gill heard Fiona say.

'You afraid of the dark?' asked Joey.

'It's the thought of all that rock above my head. That at any moment ...' she let her fingers splay out in front of her. 'The whole lot could come tumbling down.'

'It's a stable environment,' said Joey. 'We wouldn't be here if it wasn't safe.'

'Oh yeah? Remind me how was it found again?'

Donnie stepped in to answer. 'A rockfall caused by coastal erosion exposing the cave entrance.'

Joey scowled in Gill's direction. 'And there's all these wee shakes we're getting along the Great Glen Fault.'

'Super,' said Fiona, not sounding like she meant it. 'Shall we crack on, guys? Before I have second thoughts about this.'

Gill was standing ten steps away finishing a call. Fiona beckoned him over and he joined Murray, Donnie and Joey to study a laminated map of the caverns, constructed from Murray's radar scans. 'The green bits are locations we know for certain,' she began. '*Delta* cavern, plus the linked chambers of *Echo* through to *Lima* caverns. Then the red bits are unexplored terrain, mainly at the back of the ossuary where you think there's another cave system.'

'We had a quick look back there,' said Murray. 'There's an active watercourse so it probably floods from time to time. No sign the inhabitants ever colonised further back than the ossuary.'

'Great. Let's focus on the central chambers.' Fiona glanced around the faces. 'You guys aren't trained archaeologists, so let's summarise again what we're after. Joey, you have the walls. What are you looking for?'

'I've to record all etchings and any cave decoration we find, photographing and recording the exact position of each piece.'

Fiona nodded. 'Donnie. You have sediments. What's the brief?'

Donnie tapped the map. 'I've got to go to each of the coordinates you've listed and take core samples of all the mud, shit and stuff on the floor. Pop it all in those plastic test tubes you gave me.'

'Aye. And some of them will be bland because stuff gets mixed up. But some of these sediments will be gold dust because their layers will represent a timeline of the cave's occupation. What they ate. What they burned for heat and light. It's essential you do those carefully.'

Donnie shrugged. 'I'm on it.'

'Gill. You're on artefacts. Photograph, record and box them for recovery.'

'Aye. And Mhairi will take anything we find for analysis.'

'Where is she taking those?' asked Fiona.

'She's hired a van and will be acting as our courier,' said Gill. 'Tomorrow afternoon I'll go with her to take the first batch up to Glasgow Uni. After that, she'll shuttle back and forward as many times as we need her.'

Fiona nodded. 'Because the site is rapidly eroding, Historic Scotland has advised us to remove items rather than preserve *in situ*.' She pointed at Murray. 'As our most experienced cave expert, you're going to study the cavern's development. Records things like erosion by human feet, indicating high trafficked areas, or tool marks suggesting where the caves expanded. It might seem mundane, but some guy sitting at a computer many years from now might be able to build a realistic model of how this place evolved.'

'Got it,' said Murray.

'I'll keep the register – what we find and where. So, I'll be the one bossing you about and telling you where you're needed next. Oh, and I've bagged the ossuary,' sighed Fiona. 'Because I love saving the best bits for myself.'

'You're welcome to it,' muttered Murray.

'And for clarity, outwith the ossuary, remind me where the human remains are located?'

Murray leaned over the map. 'There's a man of normal human dimensions, here, in this uppermost gallery. He's accompanied by a diminutive adult female.'

'Then there are two tiny females, here and here,' said Donnie. 'They're all alone, God bless 'em.'

'Okay,' said Fiona. 'The Fiscal has given permission for us to recover these bodies to Lossuary. Let's do that today. Face masks and gloves when handling human remains, people, as we don't know what killed them.'

'And a big health & safety reminder,' said Murray. 'Despite the fact we've got a big new pump keeping our access channel clear in all points in the tide, we must only enter the caverns on a strict rota basis. There must always be one person on the outside, as per the schedule. Plus, one-hour check-ins with that day's holder of the rock radio.'

Fiona nodded and glanced around at the group. 'That's us all set. Everybody grab a box and let's get started.'

The following afternoon, Gill helped Mhairi load the van with a first set of clear plastic crates before the trip up to Glasgow University in the west side of the city. They were meeting Saul Neville, a PhD student who'd offered to analyse the items recovered during the cave dig. Grabbing a large plastic box each, they made their way through to a lab in an older part of the university.

'Goodness,' said Gill, casting his gaze around the room. 'This place hasn't changed a bit.'

'You've worked here?' asked Saul after they'd made their introductions.

'No, but I've had cause to visit on occasions. During my postgrad, and more recently when *Mys.Scot* excavated an old coaching inn discovered when the Byres Road site was being redeveloped.'

'Ah, the mummies,' said Saul. 'Discovered under what is now the ARC building. We still have one in the Hunterian Museum.'

Gill tipped a hand towards his colleague. 'Mhairi had just joined us at the time. She did the legwork that confirmed the medical hypothesis.'

Saul smiled at Mhairi and Gill could see straight away he was slightly in awe of her. 'Is Egyptology your specialism?' he asked.

'Persia was more my area,' Mhairi replied. 'Though these days I do ghosts, faked gold hoards and fairies. Yeah, I can turn my hand to pretty much anything.'

'And Mhairi is going to be your main contact on this dig,' Gill added. 'Simply because I'm often not available.'

'Too busy being trapped under sandstone blocks, or escaping burning farmhouses,' Mhairi offered by way of explanation.

Gill gave a pained smile. 'I'll try very hard not to die.'

'Well,' said Saul, giving himself a little shake. 'Shall we see what you've got for me?'

'We've emailed you the logbook,' said Mhairi, switching back into professional mode. 'So, all the numbered pieces will tally with the catalogue we sent you. There's quite a bit so Gill will talk you through the priority finds.'

'Box one,' said Gill, opening the first plastic crate. 'These are the bagpipes I mentioned to you, assuming that's what they are. We'd like you to confirm that assumption and gather any clues as to when and where they were made.'

'They certainly look like pipes,' said Saul. 'And I can see right away that they're at least eighteenth century.'

'How do you know that?' asked Mhairi.

Saul popped off the box lid and ran a gloved finger along one of the pieces of wood. 'The earliest bagpipes only had a single drone.'

'Drone?' asked Gill.

'It's the upwardly protruding piece of pipe that produces a constant harmonising note that the player then supplements using the chanter.' He smiled shyly at Mhairi. 'That's the wee pipe with the holes in.'

'A constant harmonising note,' Mhairi repeated. 'That's what we're calling it now?'

'You're not a fan?'

'I'm an accordion player,' said Mhairi solemnly. 'I've heard many a fine ballad ruined by some kid who thinks he can play the pipes.'

Saul blinked at her then pointed back into the box. 'Anyway, a second drone was added in the sixteenth century and the third and largest from the 1700s, like the example in Gill's crate.'

'Will you be able to tell what it's made from?' asked Mhairi.

'It'll almost certainly be elderberry. That species grows nice straight stems that can be easily hollowed out. But, yes, I'll check. Should be able to give you a date and possibly a location, assuming the wood analysis gives me robust data points.'

'Next up is box two,' said Gill. 'This contains the remaining garment fabric from our deceased piper.'

'Are those buttons?' asked Saul, pointing at a separate plastic bag held within the box.

'Aye. We've gathered a clutch of other buttons from around the cave, but these ones were part of the piper's garb. Have a quick look if you want.'

They watched as Saul extracted the bag and shook the buttons onto the palm of his hand. 'Nice,' he said. 'They look like pewter to me. Should be well preserved.'

'You sure? I studied them under a magnifying glass under good light. They looked quite corroded.'

Saul shook his head. 'No, Pewter is mainly tin, alloyed with other metals. These wee bumps you're seeing might be hiding an insignia or something. I'll clean them up and let you know.'

'Brilliant,' Gill moved across to the third box. This one was densely packed with cloth bags. 'We've got lots of odds and ends. We'd like your observations on what you see and what they might tell us about the cave inhabitants.'

'Sure. Can you give me a little more context?'

'I don't want to influence your analysis, but suffice to say, this group lived a foraging style existence. I'd be curious to know for example if they manufactured anything.'

'Great.' He passed them both a pair of gloves. 'In a moment, you can help me lay out the pipes for an initial assessment.'

Chapter 30

Midway through the following afternoon, Gill was prepping for an update with Tony when he had a message from Mhairi requesting a call.

'Gill. We just received the first batch of carbon dating from the lab samples.'

'Lossuary kept their promise on the quick turnaround. How did we get on?'

'They're pleased with the sample quality. While the ossuary was damp, it was free from soil bacteria. They took extracts of tooth enamel, and their estimates are plus or minus two years.'

'Excellent. And how long was the cavern colony active?'

'The earliest date detected so far was 1595 and the latest was 1749.'

Gill whistled. 'That's the best part of two hundred years. And now we need to figure out why they were there.'

'The lab already has one clue for us.'

'Okay. Hit me.'

'They had a skeletal specialist start laying out the ossuary remains, and they noted short leg and arm bones.'

'Dwarfism,' murmured Gill. 'We've seen that in the few bodies we collected.'

'Achondroplasia to give it its full name,' said Mhairi. 'Almost all the remains recovered are exhibiting the condition.'

'The founding fathers must have carried the faulty gene,' mused Gill.

'That's what I'd imagine. They'll have DNA analysis on the adults by early next week. That'll help us build a family tree.'

'Thanks, Mhairi. This is very helpful.'

'Another thing. I recall reading a mention of dwarfism in one of Rory Carmichael's blogs. Might be worth checking if he has an insight.'

'Yeah, thanks. I'll read as much of his material as I can tonight.'

'I'm going to pop in tomorrow around 2 pm to pick up the next batch of boxes,' said Mhairi. 'Will you still be on site?'

'Absolutely. See you then.'

During their afternoon phone call, Gill could hear tension in Cassy's voice. 'Tony's gagging for an update. You okay if I pull him in?'

Gill agreed and waited for Tony to join the call before updating them on the progress of the dig. 'In terms of artefacts, the caves are quite rich. There are household items consistent with seventeenth and eighteenth centuries, but all of it very worn.'

'As in corroded?' checked Tony.

'No. I've noted that their most treasured items were already spoilt by wear and tear. Basically, what I'm interpreting is this community's extreme poverty.'

'What about human remains?' asked Cassy.

'We've got four complete skeletons, three of which are remains of people less than one hundred and twenty centimetres. The ossuary contained dozens of parcels of bones and fragments, and the Falkirk lab is working on them now.'

'Why so few in the main habitation?' asked Tony.

'Our theory is the colony suffered a rapid population crash, and until the last gasp, there were always enough fit individuals around to deal with the bodies.'

'Meaning they were sharing a cave with their dead kin,' said Cassy. 'That's sick.'

'Not in their immediate living space, but yes, the smell of decomposition must have been noticeable. Historically, there were many human cultures where that was common practice.'

Tony cleared his throat. 'The big question, Gill, is how you're going to run this story?'

Gill had thought about this, so he leapt straight in. 'We'll simply use the facts to illustrate an underground community of diminutive adults.'

Cassy wasn't happy. 'If we tout a headline that hints at the discovery of a fairy kingdom, we're gonna get laughed at.'

'So, we avoid using words like fairy, or Fae, or anything that implies we're wandering in a fantasy novel.'

'But isn't that what excited you, Gill? You all but said you'd discovered dead fairies.'

Gill fell back on the defensive. 'I don't think I used exactly those words. We might imply a Fae interpretation, rather than shout it out loud. Now we're getting some tangible results from the cave I'm going to have a second meeting with my local expert down here. Tease out his interpretation.'

'The chap in the Robin Hood bunnet?' Cassy mumbled. 'Sounds like a head case.'

'Eccentric,' said Gill. 'But guarded. My sense is he has more to say.'

'Okay,' Tony concluded. 'Look, I've got to go on another call. I trust you to find the headline amidst all this. But be on notice, the pair of you, that I want to comment on the lead article before it goes to press. I don't want to be in a position where I'm defending something outrageous that I haven't even seen.'

Gill acknowledged Tony's command and waited until his boss dropped out of the call before releasing a pent-up breath.

'He's nervous,' said Cassy. 'To be honest, we all are.'
'About what?'
'We started this dig as an investigation of rare Scottish cave art,' Cassy sighed. 'Then you started muttering about the Fae, and from there we skipped to personifying an impoverished dwarf community as fairies. I'm really worried it could horribly backfire.'

'I won't be mocking them, Cass. I want to know who they were and why they lived where they did. Was it out of choice or were they hounded to the margins? Those people had a story, and I'd like to celebrate it.'

'You know what I mean, Gill.'

'Who were the Fae, Cass? That's the question I'm starting to ask myself. I mean, if you try to block out contemporary interpretations in movies and books, really, who were they?'

'Well,' Cassy said. 'If you answer that question and can do it in a way that doesn't get us all cancelled, then you might actually have a story.'

Gill dropped the heat out of his voice. 'For what it's worth, Cass, I agree with you. And I'm giving you my solemn promise, I won't link these bodies with Fae mythology unless I have solid corroboration.'

'Glad to hear it,' said Cassy. 'And while you're feeling so magnanimous, here's a second reminder you're needed in Dundee next week to prep that cemetery work you were so excited about?'

Gill swore under his breath, mindful he'd been neglecting a long-planned dig. 'Yeah. Might need to push that back a little.'

'Gill, we busted a gut with Dundee Council to grant access to this dig. And it's a quarter mile from your front door. As I recall, you were really keen.'

'And I'll get to it, Cass. I just need to get Wigtownshire over the line.'

'I don't know if they'll offer you any flexibility. It's going to be a construction site, remember?'

'I know the site manager. I'll give him a shout and figure out if we have any wiggle room. It's just …'

'Just what, Gill?'

'It's an old graveyard. It'll be hard going and aside from crumbling tombs, I doubt it will give us any more than a four-page spread.'

'Gill, this is local. It means it's our reputation on the line. If you're thinking of bailing on it, you need to do it soon. Give them time to find somebody else.'

'No, I'll do it. I'm struggling to muster any enthusiasm, that's all.'

'Okay, well, I'm going to hold you to that.'

'What about you, Cass. Fancy being involved?'

'Will there be human remains?'

Gill blinked twice. 'It's a graveyard. Pretty sure we'll come across a few old bones.'

'Then I'll run the show from here. Though Zack said he's keen to help.'

'How do you feel about your son volunteering?'

'If it keeps him out of trouble at the end of the school holidays, I'm all for it.'

'That would be great. Lovely to work with your wee fella.'

'My "wee fella" is almost sixteen. He's as tall as you.'

'Well, sign him up. I'll need all the help I can get.'

Early the following afternoon, Gill was taking a break from the dig and resting on the beach outside *Alpha* cavern while he sucked on a water bottle and enjoyed the sun on his face. Seeing Mhairi strolling down the track towards the site, he decided to meet her halfway and when he got closer, he could see she was smiling.

'This really is a lovely spot,' she said scanning the shingle beach that backed the deeper part of the bay.

'Aye, but with all the cave work, I'm beginning to tire of it.'

'Well, I finally got a couple of hours to research Clanyard Bay,' she announced, 'and I think I can rejuvenate your affection for this remote nook.'

'Excellent. What do you have for me?'

'I've a story angle on the bagpipes you found. It's an old wives' tale about a thriving rural community at this end of the Wigtownshire peninsula. Does that ring any bells?'

Gill considered her question. 'Most of the villages around here are tiny, but if you look closely, there's a ruined castle adjacent to Clanyard farm. It's possible it supported a substantial settlement at one time.'

'Anyway, the story goes that this village was bothered by evil fairies that lived in a cave at Clanyard Bay. That's here, right?'

'Spot on.'

'The story goes that one day a lone piper returned from a battle. He was begging for food and lodging and was almost turned away, but then the local laird realised his daughter was missing. Fearing her abduction by the evil fairies, he promised the soldier a reward if he entered the cave to look for her. Reasoning that dealing with the Fae couldn't be worse than enduring a battlefield, the soldier agreed. He entered a sea cave, watched by the town's elders, however, neither he nor the Laird's daughter were ever seen again.'

'Bloody hell,' said Gill. 'And he definitely carried bagpipes?'

'The legend says that if you stand on the cliffs on a stormy night, you can hear him playing in the cave system far below.'

'That's wild,' said Gill. 'Listen, we found the pipes beside the bones of the only full-sized adult so I'd like you to get a rush on this guy's DNA. See if we can figure out where he came from.'

'Sure. I can do that.'

'And if we get a date, have a think about what war he was fleeing from. Aside from Scottish battles, the location of these caves means he might have survived a conflict in Ireland or England.'

'Good plan. But whoever our mysterious piper was, he kept his side of the laird's bargain.'

'How so?'

Mhairi leaned in so close to whisper in Gill's ear that her breath tickled. 'After the piper entered the cave, the legend ends by saying the evil fairies were never heard from again.'

Chapter 31

Before he left the caves on Thursday afternoon, Gill alerted Fiona that he'd start the next day in Wigtown. With the work progressing ahead of schedule, she seemed relaxed about his temporary absence, so on Friday morning, he phoned Carmichael and requested to meet. On this particular day, the expert wasn't manning his fairy trail, but he did tell Gill where to find him.

Parking up on the lower reaches of Wigtown, Gill joined a dusty track and walked for a mile, following signs for the harbour. This he discovered was an unusual place, effectively a stone dry dock just big enough to accommodate a single merchant ship from the days of sail. With its sheer walls, cargo could have loaded on and off with ease before the ship rejoined the River Bladnoch at high tide, free to sail the short distance back to open sea.

With no sign of Carmichael, Gill texted him, then followed his directions to a large bird hide, two hundred metres closer to the river mouth. Here he found his quarry, sitting with binoculars and scanning a nearby reedbed.

'Do you hear that?' asked Carmichael, as Gill sat down.

Gill listened, and in his mind's eye, he was transported back to a family holiday in France, somewhere deep in

Provence. As the sun had gone down, the cicadas had serenaded his family, chirping all night in the heat.

'Insects?' he asked, noting that the temperature here was twenty degrees cooler than it would be in Provence just now.

'Grasshopper warblers,' Carmichael beamed. 'They're quite rare. This reedbed is one of the best places to see them in the country.

'Cool. May I see?'

He accepted binoculars and followed Carmichael's directions until he spotted a small, olive-coloured bird, clutching a reed stem. He studied it for a few moments before passing the glasses back to their owner. 'Beautiful.'

'I agree. There's excellent birding around here, although these warblers are my personal favourites.'

Gill slid a few feet along the bench away from Rory and turned to face him. 'Last night, I buried myself in your older blogs.'

'Oh, aye.' Carmichael lifted his glasses back to his eyes. 'The ones that hastened the end of my ecclesiastical career?'

'Well, I think I've finally understood why you're so cagey about the Fae.'

'I told you,' said Carmichael, evenly. 'I do believe in fairies, just not the Hollywood version.'

'In one article you claim they're human, but not ordinary humans. Instead, you suggest they are the dregs of society, so far removed from mainstream lifestyles that they became characterised as monsters.'

'Not monsters, Gill. I prefer words like imps, elves, pixies and goblins.' He held up a hand. 'They weren't bad people; just the insignificant wretches that didn't look like the honest, hardworking folk of mainstream society. People, and especially, young people, driven to live so far from civilization they became cave and forest dwellers.'

'But we've always had poor people, Rory. And no one else characterises the poor as Fae.'

Carmichael sniffed. 'I think today we abhor our poor in different ways.'

'I'm not sure what you mean.'

'Well think about it. Today we have rough sleepers. They're not exactly held in high esteem.'

'I know some charity folk who work quite hard for the homeless.'

'And I'm sure they're very generous,' said Carmichael. 'Until the moment comes when they've a homeless person trying to kip in their garden.'

'I guess.'

'And before us, the Victorians had workhouses. Before that, our biggest cities had slums.' He laid down his binoculars and scanned the reeds for movement. 'But here's the crucial question, Gill, and I want you to think about this. If we go way back in time, what did we do with our rural poor?'

'I'm not sure I grasp your question.'

'Think of it this way,' said Carmichael, putting away his glasses. 'These days we plonk our rural poor in distant housing schemes with inadequate transport links and wonder why many struggle to find work. But in olden times, ask yourself, what did agricultural communities do with their sick and disabled?'

'I imagine most families struggled on as best they could?'

'Did they, Gill? Imagine yourself as a father of a dirt-poor family from three hundred years ago. Now imagine rapid agricultural change gets your family thrown off their land to make way for industrialised cattle rearing. And when they're clinging to life by their fingernails, now add a child born with abnormalities or a congenital disorder.'

Gill considered this. 'Like dwarfism?'

Carmichael nodded. 'Now you're catching my drift.'

Gill shook his head. 'Personally, I couldn't have behaved like that.'

'You can't conceive of it today, because your belly is full, and for all I know you've a house full of healthy children. But if you'd already suffered years of tumult and near starvation, Gill? Can you not comprehend why some families might abandon their children?'

Gill chewed his lip but said nothing.

Carmichael responded by glancing at his watch. 'Almost lunchtime. What would you say to a quick pint in the Bladnoch Inn?'

'I can only have one as I'm back in the cave this afternoon,' Gill grunted. 'But as a consultancy fee, I can buy you some lunch.'

'Now you've read my theory,' said Carmichael. 'And you haven't dismissed it out of hand. Seems to me that my ideas aren't preposterous to you.'

'I've been digging at Clanyard since we last spoke,' said Gill as they settled down with their pints. 'And I've made a few disturbing discoveries.'

'Oh, aye?'

'Last night, I read your blog asserting the *wee folk* weren't the baby stealers our forbears made them out to be.'

Carmichael sipped his drink but said nothing.

'If I understand your hypothesis, you're saying that seventeenth-century families, burdened by children with life-shortening genetic conditions, sometimes dumped their unwanted offspring in caves. The most fortunate rejects encountered cavern-dwelling societies like Clanyard, and were raised by them?'

Carmichael sighed and nodded. 'If families were desperate enough, Gill. And I mean, literally having to decide if their children lived or starved, is it unreasonable?'

'Then to add insult to injury, when these orphan communities begged, foraged and stole to survive, you say they became persecuted by the society that had discarded them.'

'They'd been expected to die. No one anticipated they'd have the strength of character to overcome their predicament. To bind together as a nascent community, then become thorns in the side of the families who'd rejected them.'

'But do you have evidence?' asked Gill.

'I was about to ask you the same thing,' Carmichael shot back.

'Bones in a cave won't be enough to endorse your theory. Do you have anything else?'

Carmichael peered down into his beer, the colour of burnt amber. 'We have the legends, of course. But I have more than that. I was a minister on the Wigtownshire peninsula. Did I tell you that?'

'Yes, though you didn't say where.'

'I covered a cluster of parishes, from *The Rhins* to Stranraer. A dozen wee churches in various states of social and physical disrepair.' His eyes flashed to the ceiling. 'Most of them are shut now, but a good few years ago, I gathered up the parish records to be digitised. It was a tedious job. Fetching old books from cupboards and lofts. Thumbing through them so we could identify any missing volumes and have a last search for …'

Gill peered at the man, as his voice trailed off. 'What did you find?'

Carmichael shifted uncomfortably. 'I was tasked with photographing the records and sending the images up to head office.' He paused. 'But then I got reading some of the records. People's lives; their births, deaths and marriages. For a few weeks, I lost myself in it. Following families through the roll call of their lives. And during this exercise, I spotted something.' Carmichael stopped to remember. 'On the register, there's a space to record the cause of death.' He glanced at Gill. 'You can imagine what killed folk back in the seventeenth and eighteenth centuries. Consumption. Tuberculosis. Smallpox. Farm accidents. But there was a shorthand in a few cases. "BC" for breast cancer. "SF" for scarlet fever. And that's when I saw the letters, "GF."'

'Meaning what?' asked Gill.

'Over the space of a decade, one Parish, near Portpatrick I think, used the notation, "GF" for the deaths of seven infants less than five years old.'

'What did that designation mean?' asked Gill, sensing Carmichael's discomfort.

'I managed to chase down an old man whose grandfather had been a parish clerk in the mid-nineteenth century. He talked about the *Guid Folk* taking one of his kin. When I quizzed him what he meant, the conversation abruptly came to an end. But I've researched the phrase, and its implications are quite disturbing.'

Gill waited patiently for Carmichael to build up to his big finale.

'It implies that the children recorded as "GF" were left outdoors to the mercy of the Fae.'

Carmichael paused to study Gill's reaction.

Gill laid down his glass. 'Damnit.'

'What?' barked Carmichael.

'That might tally with what I've discovered.'

'You've found the remains of some of these unfortunates?'

'Rory, this must be a secret for now. Until my research is clearer.'

Carmichael gave a single defiant nod. 'Your comments are safe with me.'

'If what you're saying is true, then it does indeed appear that a proportion of those infants survived into their adult years.'

'And they lived underground? Just like the old tales?'

'We're running a bunch of tests, but in the Clanyard community at least, it's starting to look that way.'

'Dear, God,' murmured Carmichael. 'I've nursed my theory, but the very thought of this being true leaves me sick to my stomach.'

'I don't want it to be true either,' said Gill. 'To think of those poor children abandoned; forced to scratch for a living if they survived at all. Then personified as evil Fae, despised and rejected and chased to the margins to die.'

'Aye,' spat Carmichael, standing up to order another beer. 'That's how shame-filled people manage their guilt. They demonise the people they've pushed away.'

Driving back to the dig site, Gill called Cassy. 'I know you're about to dash into the publisher's meeting, but I have some news.'

'Sure, but you're gonna need to be quick.'

'Firstly, Mhairi has uncovered a local legend mentioning a vagrant soldier. He might be the deceased piper in our cave.'

'Okay,' said Cassy. 'But a myth is just a myth. We'd need a little more on this guy if you're using his existence to endorse your fairy hypothesis.'

'Absolutely. We're trying to obtain his DNA and clothing samples that might help understand where he came from.'

'And the second thing?' asked Cassy, impatiently.

'Many years ago, Rory Carmichael collected parish registers for digitisation. He mentioned notation against a cluster of infant deaths. He claims this is evidence of families disposing of sick children by handing them over to the Fae, or *Guid Folk* in the local vernacular.'

'Grief, Gill. You do stumble across the cheeriest of tales.'

'Aye, well. That's a claim we can confirm or deny by doing our own check on parish records. When she's not dashing up and down to Glasgow with Fiona's boxes, that'll be Mhairi's main job for next week.'

'For your sake, let's hope they're written on cuneiform tablets.' Gill could hear the background rumble of voices and pictured her at the conference room door. 'Are you staying down there this weekend or heading home?' she asked.

'Home. We all need a break from the cave.'

'Glad to hear it. Have a good one. Gotta dash.'

Chapter 32

'Look at that bloody thing,' said DI Fallon to no one in particular. It was Sunday evening on the eleventh of July and she and her team were sitting in the Belfast control centre watching video feed from three drones. 'It's like the tower of feckin' Babel.'

'A monument to misunderstanding,' said DC Keenan, the only other Catholic member on Fallon's team.

The object of their wrath was the Edgarstown Bonfire; a stack of wooden pallets, towering one hundred metres high on a footprint the size of a family home. Constructed with engineering precision, it was being readied for celebrations at sunset. Tomorrow was "The Twelfth" when the annual celebration of Loyalist culture reached its zenith.

'I think what you're experiencing is a moment of cultural alienation,' said DS Martin. 'And maybe a little bit of jealousy.' He shook his head. 'Us Proddies just build better bonfires than you shamrock huggers.'

Keenan wasn't finished. 'Think of the carbon footprint then. All that timber, gone in an instant, and for what?'

'An act of remembrance,' said Martin, evenly. 'The protestant community in this wee province still celebrates historical landmarks the rest of the British Isles has long forgotten.'

'By hoisting a big burning, middle finger, at the rest of us,' murmured Fallon, her eyes flitting between the images. 'A place where Loyalist hard men go to see and be seen.'

The team watched in silence for ten minutes. On their screens, they were watching a big crowd gathering and little coloured boxes darted around the images while the facial recognition software collected pattern data and filed it for immediate processing.

'Got a hit,' called Keenan, suddenly. 'Approaching target site from Craigwell Avenue.'

'And two more,' said Martin. 'Stepping out of the terrace on Corcain Road.'

'Well, would you look at that,' mused Fallon. 'It's the man himself, back from his holidays.'

Martin spun in his chair. 'What do you want to do, boss?'

'Ignore the others. All eyes on Lynch. Have the snatch team stand by.'

DI Fallon chose to stand, leaning against the wall of the interrogation room. It was Monday morning and her bag man, DS Martin, was sticking to the regs. Seated opposite him were Iain Lynch and his solicitor. It was the start of their third hour-long session watching Lynch stare at his hands.

'Bet you wish you'd stayed in Boston,' said Fallon, in a conversational tone. 'Because now you're stuck in here and not outside enjoying the Twelfth of July with all those bands, and big drums, and hoards of eejits dressed like Victorian sailors. Oh, and you missed last night's bonfire. I'm sooo sorry about that.'

'Piss off,' Lynch hissed.

'Yeah, we watched the fire via the drones while you were being brought in.' She shook her head. 'All that hard work, gone in a matter of minutes.'

Lynch said nothing.

'Mind you, it's what people like you do.'

'Do what?'

'Burn things to the ground. Kind of an Ulster tradition.'

'My client has an exemplary record. We deplore your insinuation.'

Fallon waved a hand in front of her face. 'We both know your client had his slate wiped clean after the Good Friday Agreement. But don't pretend for a second that we've forgotten what he did; what he was part of. And yet, here he is again, ready to bring the guns and ammunition to kick the war in Ireland into a whole new phase.'

Lynch sneered and looked away. 'You know nothing.'

The solicitor looked at his watch. 'Keep insulting him if you must, but I think our time here is almost up.'

Fallon pushed off from the wall and lazily sat down. 'You're wrong about that. Terrorist offences on the British mainland, you see. You can bank on me to detain Mr Lynch for a while yet. And when I'm done, Police Scotland have booked him for most of August.'

Lynch sat back and folded his arms. 'Keep me as long as you want, but you're getting nothing.'

Fallon let her face fill with theatrical shock. 'You honestly think you're gonna walk away from this? For starters, we have your voice recording of the Balmoral Avenue incident. Threatening the life of a police officer; that'll get you years, my friend. And that's before we get to guns in Wigtownshire.'

'No comment.'

'What's puzzling me is why you warned me off the case?' Lynch didn't respond, so she ploughed on. 'The Scots have better evidence on you than your worst nightmare.'

'I'll expect that to be fully disclosed,' snapped the solicitor.

Fallon shrugged. 'You'll need to ask them about that. Meanwhile, if we find anything in your Portstewart beach house, we'll obviously let you know.'

Lynch diverted his gaze from her.

She peered at her adversary and smiled. 'I'm likin' your body language, Iain. You look good and stressed. You didn't think we'd find out about Portstewart? Think you'd just present yourself as a simple *Porty-down* fella? No, we're gonna take your beach house back to the bare walls if we must, and I think you know what we're going to find.'

She waited to see if he would bite. 'Still not for talking? No problem. We'll drop you back in the clink. And when we're done in Portstewart, we're off to Lurgan to do the same at your mum's. And I'll tell you what, for nothing. This case is massive, Iain, and if you think we're ever gonna stop, then you should have legged it up that stack of pallets and jumped while you had the chance.'

Fallon stopped when her phone buzzed with a message. She read it and showed it to DS Martin. When they were both on their feet, she turned and wiggled her phone at Lynch. 'Do you see what I see?'

Lynch squinted at her screen. 'What's that?'

'Screenshot from a colleague of mine in Scotland from a moment in time two months ago. There aren't any landmarks so let me explain by saying this image represents two boats in the mid-Atlantic somewhere. The blue dot is your pal Chris Kearny aboard the *Argonaut*. The red dot is another trawler that has steamed all the way up from Africa.'

Lynch swallowed but said nothing.

Fallon tapped her screen. 'We're closing in on you, Iain. If you want to get on the right side of this, you need to start talking.'

His face glistened with a thin sheen of sweat. His mouth moved a few times before he finally spoke. 'No comment.'

'Suit yourself. Keep silent for another twenty-four hours and your life is gonna be like that bonfire. A heap of smoking ashes.'

'Alex,' said Fallon when he picked up the call. 'Perfect timing with your screenshot.'

'Thought that might be useful. What happens now?'

'We're holding Lynch in Belfast while we build a case against him. Key to that will be the *Argonaut* which is due back in Kilkeel in four days.' She glanced at DS Martin beside her. 'To help with that little chat can you give us any more context on that mid-ocean meet-up?'

'My researcher in Bathgate had a breakthrough when she traced the movement of the *Argonaut* in the weeks before her Wigtownshire layover. A week before anchoring at Clanyard Bay, the *Argonaut* experienced an earlier bout of electrical problems and sat motionless in international waters. Surprise, surprise, her transponder disappeared for four hours.'

'Where was that exactly?' asked Fallon.

'East of the Azores,' said Lillico. 'Pelagic tuna fishery, apparently.'

'And what's that other dot, steaming towards her?'

'That's the *Tallie Diamond*. Another purse seiner, operating out of … gimme your best guess, please, Shona?'

'South Africa,' breathed Fallon.

'And it's transponder also disappeared,' added Lillico. 'More electrical trouble. Must be like the Bermuda Triangle in there.'

'But they had enough time to make a ship-to-ship transfer?'

'They did,' Lillico confirmed. 'Let me know how you get on in Kilkeel.'

Chapter 33

Gill was midway through his drive down from Dundee to Clanyard on Monday morning when Mhairi's text came in, saying, 'Call me when you get this.'

'DNA results are back on the cavern skeletons,' she began.

'How many in the end?' asked Gill.

'The lab estimates north of seventy individuals who lived and died in the cave over a span of one hundred and sixty years.' Over the next couple of minutes, Mhairi relayed everything the bones had revealed about the lives and deaths of the cave inhabitants.

Gill listened soberly, then asked, 'Do the results confirm chronic achondroplasia throughout the community?'

'They do.'

'There must have been considerable inbreeding.'

'Maybe, but not among the colonists.'

'What do you mean?'

'They're still constructing a family tree and while they've identified some individuals as siblings of others in the colony, only two are directly descended from earlier residents.'

Gill flinched. 'That confirms they were getting new recruits by another route.'

'You thinking of the old tales about the little people stealing babies?' said Mhairi

Gill rubbed his chin. 'That theory doesn't stand up to logic because under that scenario the bulk of the population would have been able-bodied. Guess again.'

'But ... if they were mainly dwarfs ...'

'In the period we're talking about, isolated parts of Scotland suffered inbreeding. I've read anecdotally that the gene causing achondroplasia was endemic in parts of Wigtownshire. Meaning lots of impoverished families had to contend with the disease.'

'Oh, that's dreadful,' said Mhairi, suddenly catching Gill's hint. 'You're saying these people were abandoned in the cave?'

'I'm leaning that way. Three hundred years ago, dwarfism was endemic in this area. I believe that when the condition presented in growing children, some were abandoned in Clanyard Bay.'

After Mhairi hung up, the revelations from the DNA data lay heavily on Gill. Local myths had alluded to it and now he'd physical evidence proving the Clanyard community had been built from discarded children. While he continued driving south that morning, he realised this discovery created a very unsettling possibility. These tragic past crimes now called out to him over the centuries and drew his attention to the plight of young Annie Wallace who'd fallen down a hole in the ground and almost lost her life in the very same cave. Gill reminded himself, he was an archaeologist, and hadn't come to Wigtownshire to report on her disappearance. And a year ago, he might have kept this unsavoury idea from germinating in his mind. But he was a father now, the guardian of his own precious child, and mindful of every child's welfare. If someone had done wrong by Annie, he needed to act.

He'd not been trying to overhear conversations where he'd heard mentions of Annie's address, but he'd still got a rough idea where she lived, and it wasn't wasted on him that he would pass her village on his way back Clanyard Bay. Making a small detour, he arrived in the small community of Sandcrest and found it awash with nature's rich gifts. In a sheltered position at the apex of Luce Bay, it was blessed with a long sandy beach and, if the trees were anything to go by, a mild temperate climate very unlike the rest of Scotland. But where he might have expected to see hotels and guest houses, dotted with restaurants and interesting shops, the village was bleak and lifeless. Turning into Luce Bay Drive, he passed a row of glum houses until he came to a long, low cottage with its curtains drawn. It had once been pebble-dashed, but now the render had crumbled in places exposing the underlying brickwork. The garden was a mixture of compressed hardcore and brambles, and the rotting remains of an old Ford Focus rested on its rims, with rubbish piled high against the inside windows.

He slowed his car to a standstill and asked himself why he was here. According to Lillico, Annie had said nothing about her time in the cave although the theory about the dogs' home and the child slipping into a new sinkhole seemed plausible. Nor was there any suggestion that anyone might have meant her harm. And yet, for the lass to have walked so far from home, and tumble into a newly opened gap in the ground seemed more than unfortunate.

The sound of someone rapping on his passenger window dragged him from his musings. Turning to find two women, the nearest was a vacant-faced woman of about forty. The other he realised was Joannie, the wild white-haired lady he'd seen three weeks ago in Portpatrick's Crown Hotel. And by her expression, she wasn't about to be friendly. To such an extent that Gill considered just driving on. But he was facing the wrong way down a dead-end street, so if they chose, the women could confront him when he turned around and made for the exit. Choosing acquiescence over confrontation, he wound down his window.

'Hey, archie-thingey,' barked Joannie. 'Wha' you lookin' at?'

Hearing her anger, the other woman backed away.

'I was just passing,' said Gill, half truthfully.

'And ye stopped ta tak a wee gawp?'

Gill winced. 'I've thought a lot about Annie these past few days. I suppose part of me wonders how she's doing?'

'Well enough, considerin'. But she's no wanting tae talk tae the like o' yous.'

'I didn't want to interview her. I was just ...'

'Interview? You said you dug stuff up. Now you're sayin' you're wan o' they journos?'

'I am a journalist, yes. But not on this kind of story.'

Joannie thrust an accusing finger through the open window. 'That wee lassie has had more than enough tae contend with in her short life. She don't need the likes of yous makin' it any harder.'

'I'm sorry,' said Gill. 'I didn't mean to offend you by stopping by. I'll go now.'

'Aye, do that. An' if I see ya agin, I'll hex you.'

Gill raised an eyebrow at this and for a moment, his crystal armour flickered around his body. She seemed to see this and took an astonished step backwards. Gill held her ragged gaze for long enough to demonstrate he wasn't afraid of her, or her curses. But she quickly found her feet and unleashed another barrage of abuse. So, he rolled up the window and ignored her taunts while he carefully made a three-point turn. As soon as he was clear of the village, he dialled Alex Lillico.

'What's up, Gill?'

'Hey, Alex. I'm probably sticking my nose in where it's not wanted, but I'm wondering if Annie Wallace has any significant health issues that precede her time in the cave?'

'Seriously, Gill? You know I couldn't tell you about that.'

'I hear you. But if she does, then there's an alarming discovery in the Clanyard cave that you need to be aware of.'

As soon as Lillico finished his call with Gill, he contacted the ward where Annie was still recuperating. Fortunately, he was able to catch Annie's consultant just as she arrived on her shift.

'Keira Maitland,' said the woman, briskly.

'Thanks for taking my call. It's DI Lillico here. I need to ask you a question about Annie if I may?'

'Go ahead, Detective. But I warn you, she still not speaking about her experience.'

'Okay. We'll come back to that in a moment. For now, I recall you mentioned Annie has a serious congenital disorder. Could you tell me how that condition would present?'

'She suffers from Batten disease. It's a very challenging condition that can develop in children as young as five or as old as ten. The children physically regress. They suffer vision loss, seizures, and delayed developmental milestones. As the disease progresses, they can suffer behavioural and learning problems, and eventually loss of language and motor skills.'

'And where is Annie on that spectrum?'

'The poor wee thing was diagnosed six months ago. She had a seizure at school which led to a battery of tests. Early signs are the disease is advancing quickly.'

'I see.'

'What's your concern?'

Lillico sighed. 'I've received credible insight that someone known to her may have placed Annie into that cave. That in effect, she was being left to die.'

'That's a terrible suggestion, DI Lillico.'

'It is. And if it's true, Annie needs to tell us, otherwise we risk another attempt on her life.'

'Well, I'm sorry, but if you lot go bursting into her room with your suits and badges, you will traumatise the girl.'

'I agree, so can I ask you, is there anyone she trusts? Anyone who could gently nudge at this line of enquiry?'

Maitland thought for a second. 'She's grown quite fond of one of our physios. I heard them both laughing together yesterday afternoon.'

'Anything would help,' said Lillico. 'And be aware, if Annie was endangered by a family member, then she may have experienced threats or incentives to buy her silence.'

'I hear you. I'll make enquiries and let you know how we get on.'

Chapter 34

Emerging from the cave that afternoon for a breath of fresh air, Gill felt himself washed by sunlight and relief. They were almost finished with the dig and Fiona was steering them towards a final list of tasks. He'd repressed his claustrophobia to make himself useful to her, but increasingly, found himself slipping out for a long, welcome look at the sky. While he was there, he checked his messages. One from Mhairi held a tantalising reference to the Piper of Clanyard Bay.

'What you got for me, Mhairi?' he asked as his call picked up.

'Good news/bad news. Unfortunately, carbon dates on the Piper's bones are inconclusive. Best guess, his remains date from sometime in the eighteenth century.'

'And the good news?'

'Firstly, we got a reasonable crack at his DNA. It's not showing a distinct regional bias, but it is clean enough to make a familial connection.'

'We'd need find them first,' mused Gill.

'And I might be able to help with that. Do you remember the piper's buttons? Saul has done a good job cleaning them up. Hang on, I'll send you an image.'

Gill glanced at his phone and saw only two bars of reception. 'I doubt I'll receive it here but email me anyway and I'll look at it later. Meantime, can you describe what you're seeing?'

'We think the buttons have a family crest. Imagine a metal helmet from the Middle Ages in a side profile. Got that?'

'Sure.'

'Now imagine three pentangle star shapes layered beneath the helmet.'

'Sorry, Mhairi, did you say pentagrams?'

'No. Think of the star on Captain America's shield.'

'Got you. Have you had a chance to see if it correlates with anything, past or present?'

'Not yet. I might outsource that task if it's okay. There are a zillion family crests in Europe and a lot of them look quite similar.'

'Sure. Go for it. Anything else?'

'Saul confirms the bagpipes are real and the elderberry pipes carbon date to between 1710 and 1730.'

'Excellent. I sense we're getting closer to our man. Let me know if you get a hit on that family crest.'

During the drive from Sandcrest up to Stranraer, DI Lillico and PC Hart endured a torrent of abuse from Annie Wallace's great-aunt Joan. It was an irony then that once they seated her in interview room three, she suddenly fell silent, refusing even to confirm her name and address, despite her legal representative cajoling her to cooperate.

'You were telling us on the way over that we're interfering with the old ways, Joan. What old ways were you referring to?'

Joan Wallace scowled and said nothing.

'Did you lower Annie into the cave, Joan?' said Hart. 'Were you planning to leave her there to die?'

Again, no answer.

'I have a witness in Portpatrick who reports you said Annie should have remained in that cave to meet her fate. Do you remember saying that?'

'Damn journos are always makin' up lies,' she muttered.

'Sergeant Dewar says a dog walker reported a light above the caves the night after Annie disappeared. Was that you, Joan? Did you go back to feed Annie? Had you changed your mind and decided to rescue your niece?'

This time, Joan shook her head and studiously looked away.

Lillico lowered his voice. 'Are you aware Annie is terrified of you?'

Joan turned and glowered at him.

'That even now, she's petrified that you might come to her hospital bed and steal her away.'

'She is no,' spat Joan. 'She's ma wee bairn.'

'Well, as things stand, you'll never see her again. And unless you give us solid evidence that you acted alone, there's a risk the child protection service will remove Annie from her family.'

'That's no fair on Bram and Karen! And no' very fair on the bairn.'

'Nevertheless, Annie has confided to a member of the medical team that you removed her from her home on the morning of the fourth of June. Then you travelled by bus to Drummore on a promise you'd go and visit the dogs' home. But instead, you walked across the peninsula and tricked Annie into letting you lower her into the cave.'

'Didnae tak any bus.'

Lillico pulled up an image on his laptop and spun it around so Joan could see. 'To corroborate Annie's story, we spoke to the bus company. They supplied clear CCTV footage of you both, boarding at Sandcrest and getting off, one mile before Drummore.'

Joan opened her mouth to protest, then shut it again.

'You don't have to say anything, because I've got enough evidence to charge you. But it's still in your power to decide if Annie remains with her parents or is taken into care.'

'The *Guid Folk* were ready for her,' she said, firmly. 'As a sign, they'd opened up yon hole tae tak ma wee bairn to their hearts.'

'You're admitting you lowered her into the cave?' pressed Lillico, relieved at last to be making a breakthrough.

Joan cast a sideways glance at her solicitor. 'Ah dinnae see what business it is o' yours.'

'But why?' demanded PC Hart, deviating from the script Lillico had proposed.

'The docktors cud dae nae mare for her. Ah ken the *Guid Folk* wid either heal her or lay the lass tae rest.'

'You honestly believe that?'

Joan nodded decisively. 'Ah do.'

'And who are these *Guid Folk*?' asked Lillico.

Joan shook her head. 'If ya dinnae ken, am nae goin' tae tell ya.'

'Fairies?' he pushed.

Joan shook her body in irritation. 'That's wan word for them.'

Lillico nodded to buy himself time. Joan Wallace was eccentric, but that didn't make her insane, so he found himself wondering what a judge or jury would make of her ramblings. 'There's no such thing as fairies, Joan. Or at least, not the type who care for sick children. Maybe in some perverted way there was an intended kindness in what you did. Knowing that Annie will likely endure diminishing quality of life and early death, maybe you were trying to spare her that?'

'Her folks, ken. They dinnae want tae watch their lassie die.'

'So, instead of letting the medical profession do their best by Annie, did you set out to kill her?'

'That's no wha happened,' she shouted.

'Really?' said Lillico. 'Well, I'm confident I can prove it.'

'Go yoursel',' she mumbled.

'And the last part of the puzzle is this,' said Lillico. 'We know from various witness statements that Bram and Karen were anxious about Annie. With a child carrying a dangerous illness, neither of them let her wander unsupervised. You boarded the bus with Annie just after nine in the morning, and nobody raised the alarm until the early evening. And to my mind, that means either Bram, or Karen, or both colluded with you.'

'Annie needs her folk, Mr Lillico. Don't you be sendin' both o' them tae jeyoll.'

Lillico shrugged. 'One of them facilitated Annie's attempted murder. If I don't know which parent, then I'll recommend to the Fiscal that he protects her from both.'

Joan's solicitor leaned over to her client. 'You don't need to answer that question.'

Joan nodded, then seemed to brush the advice away. 'It were Karen.'

PC Hart shifted uncomfortably in her seat. 'Why, Joan? What mother would give up on her child like that?'

Joan nodded, long and slow while she navigated her response. 'Because, lass, Karen's lost ay hope,' she said eventually. 'We talked it o'er and decided like adults, we cannae allow this family tae suffer mare pain.'

Chapter 35

On his last break of the day, Gill emerged from the dig and noticed a missed call from Mhairi.

'That crest, Gill,' she said when he returned her call. 'I've tied it to a family called Towneley in Burnley.'

Gill ran a hand across his forehead. 'But that's in Lancashire.'

'Correct.'

'Sorry, but what would a Lancastrian be doing two hundred miles away in a Wigtownshire cave? And why did he spend his last breath snuggled up with a set of bagpipes?'

'No idea,' said Mhairi. 'Just passing on what we know. I guess the jacket could have been stolen, like everything else in that cave.'

'Yeah, maybe. Have you researched the Towneleys?'

'Just a little. They were a big force in Lancashire until they fell on hard times in the early to mid-eighteenth century. Their manor house still exists, called Towneley Hall. It's a wedding venue these days and has a small museum.'

Gill's mental juices started to flow. 'When you say, "fell on hard times," can you be more precise?'

'Had all their lands confiscated. Punishment for some political dispute. That's all I know.' Mhairi paused. 'What's got you thinking?'

'Those dates would fit with the second Jacobite rebellion. Maybe our man was with an English regiment. Perhaps in some skirmish around Culloden, or in the chaos afterwards, he lost his jacket. For example, our piper could have taken it from his body and fled south.'

'Plausible. Do you want me to sniff around? See if there's anyone at Towneley Hall who could put their hands on the family records?'

'Please. Burnley is only a couple of hours south of here. If you can get me an appointment, I could call in person.'

'Okay, I might just catch someone before home-time. I'll text you either way to let you know.'

'How are we getting on?' asked Murray, while they were tidying up that afternoon.

'Definite picture emerging,' Gill replied. 'We're hypothesising the population down here established and then supplemented by abandoned children.'

Murray shook his head. 'That's terrible, man. What on earth did they eat?'

'Most seaweed growing around the UK is edible after a little cooking. And based on the middens, we're seeing fishbones, shellfish, seabirds and small mammals. Occasionally something larger, like sheep or deer, snatched from the fields.'

'And they went undetected for how long?'

'You're presuming the people on the surface weren't aware of them, while the legends suggest they were. Maybe the colony was a dirty local secret no one talked about.'

'But they've been dead for ages, yeah?'

Gill nodded. 'The oldest bones we have date from the late eighteenth century. There was some kind of cataclysm. Maybe an infectious disease or a collapse in the food supply. We saw the effects of that the day we first came in here. Precious goods being hoarded by the collapsing population who concentrated in the best bunks higher in the main gallery.'

'And your mysterious piper?'

'He gets a special mention in the local folklore. We might never know whether he decided to come down here and couldn't get out, or if he simply decided to stay.'

'Maybe they kept him prisoner?'

Gill shook his head. 'Doubt it. With food as tight as it must have been, keeping a prisoner would have been unaffordable.'

'Incredible though, to think there was a secret society down here for what, two hundred years?'

'Tolerated and ignored rather than secret. The rejects of society, discarded to live out of sight.'

'Awful,' said Murray. 'So, what happens next?'

'My magazine has done all it can afford to do, and so far, there's no interest from the various institutions who'd normally get excited by this kind of thing. Everyone is so short of cash. So, we'll give it a couple of weeks and then seal the cave. We'll let the sea pool flood again and stick a big metal door over the front.'

'What?' spluttered Joey. 'Is the Fiscal not coming to investigate the bones?'

'He's accepted Lillico's report of the situation, and we'll send the pathology data on all the bones we recovered.'

'Doesn't feel right,' said Joey, turning to walk away. 'We should find out who's to blame and make their descendants pay for it.'

Murray watched him go. 'Sorry, Gill. Joey's idealistic streak lies close to the surface.'

'No problem,' said Gill. 'I share his anger. Listen, I need to shoot off for twenty-four hours to pursue a lead on our mysterious piper. You okay working with Fiona?'

'Aye, we're solid. Will I see you tomorrow before we wrap up?'

'Definitely.'

'You driving?' asked Lillico the following morning as Gill picked up.

'Aye. On my way to Burnley to investigate something I found in the caves. What's happening with you?'

'Just wanted to thank you for your tip-off on Annie. The broad thrust of your theory was correct.'

'Not a tip as such,' Gill responded. 'More of an insight. Are you able to tell me what happened?'

Gill listened to a short silence while Lillico deliberated how much he could tell. 'The older lady you mentioned to me, Mrs Joan Wallace, she was the prime mover in it all.'

'I can imagine.'

'And unfortunately, she's implicated Annie's mother as an accomplice.'

'Oh, Alex. That's dreadful. What would drive them to something like this?'

'The family has been in a tailspin for years. Both of Annie's parents worked on the ferries out of Stranraer, but when that closed in 2011, they were made redundant. Karen became a care worker for a time but had to give it up when she fell pregnant with Annie. Bram has only had casual work in the years since his job ended and is now on long-term sickness benefit.'

'And then came Annie's illness,' Gill observed.

'The kid endured a battery of tests. Every time they got their hopes up about a line of treatment, Annie took another turn for the worse.'

'And this Auntie Joan?'

'Lives in part of the Wallace's house. Sees herself as the matriarch of the clan, and really Gill, that's all I can say for now.'

Chapter 36

After a brief stopover in Dumfries to collect a wedding outfit, it took Gill two hours driving south on the M6 to reach a fine old building nestled in one hundred acres of trees and ornamental gardens. Towneley Hall was on the outskirts of Burnley and an hour to the north of Greater Manchester. It had been the Towneleys' family home for centuries until its present-day reincarnation as a classy wedding venue. Mhairi's bid to get Gill a short-notice visit had paid off, but this interview was coming at a price. Slamming his car door, he caught sight of his reflection in the paintwork. He hadn't worn a kilt since his own wedding day and while that had been a natural moment, this felt strange, like he was debasing himself in search of a story.

'I'd be happy to honour your request,' Mrs Littleton had explained during their call the previous evening. 'But perhaps in return, you could help us with some promotional work?'

'Sure,' Gill had replied. 'What do you need?'

'Even south of the border, you've a degree of name recognition, Mr McArdle. A short photoshoot with a minor celebrity like yourself would bring the hotel valued publicity.'

So, Gill had swallowed what little pride this "minor celebrity" could normally muster and agreed to her proposal. And now he was here, the sooner he got it over with, the sooner he could discern if his dash to find a dress-hire shop in Dumfries was worth the expense. Introducing himself to Freda Littleton a few minutes later, he encountered a well-mannered lady, with a head full of permed white hair and a string of pearls, hung in a double loop around her neck. Quite a striking woman, she'd a twinkle in her eye and Gill imagined she was quite delighted with the deal they'd struck.

'Are you part of the family?' asked Gill.

'In a distant sense. My mother was a granddaughter of the last Towneley and remembered coming to family events in this building when she was a young thing. These days the new owners like to have me around so I can name-drop with their clients, even though I'm just on the staff.'

'I see.'

'And are you married, Mr McArdle?'

'I am.'

'Pity. I was hoping I could boast about our venue. See if I could lure you back.'

'Sorry. Today, I'm just here for the history.'

She led them into a large, oak-panelled room. 'This is our guest lounge. You'll see there are alcoves with some of the family's more special treasures on display.' She gesticulated around the walls. 'And these suits of armour are all genuine, but let me tell you, they're a beast to keep clean.'

'They're stunning, though it's your archive that most interests me.'

'And I'll take you there presently.' She paused. 'I wonder first if we could address the question of our reciprocal arrangement?'

Gill pointed at his Highland dress. 'I'm ready when you are.'

'Great. I'll fetch Bobby.'

Bobby, it turned out was the venue's marketing assistant, and though he was equipped with only a modest camera, he quite fancied himself as a David Bailey. Starting first in the lounge, he had Gill pose in front of the tiny museum's exhibits, before propping him, with whisky in hand, staring into a log fire, lit especially for the occasion. The next few shots were routine; mainly Freda showing him around the facilities and greeting the "bride and groom." These he discovered were not actually a married couple but were members of the catering staff who'd been paid twenty quid each to dress up and look happy. Suddenly bursting with creative zest, Bobby's camera chased them from ballroom to bedroom, and back to a rather grand bar at the heart of the hotel and eventually, out into the ornamental gardens where the couple poured Gill a generous glass of fake champagne.

Reunited with his whisky, Gill was marched to the centre of the lawn, where in a final humiliation, Bobby posed him leaning against a moss-covered, concrete unicorn. Gill struck a string of mocking, funny and serious poses with the statue, that ended with him offering the whisky to its snout. When Bobby announced that was the end of the "shoot," Gill finally took a sniff of the glass and knocked it back in one. He was all out of fun, realising he'd sold himself for a dram of Macallan and hasty rummage in Freda's paperwork.

With that ordeal behind him, Freda led him into a study and granted free range over the family's archives. She brought him a coffee press a few minutes later and promised to be back in ninety minutes to whisk him off to lunch.

The archive he discovered to his pleasant surprise was a wall of fireproof filing cabinets supported by a competently organised database. Using the login credentials provided, he was able to open a record of the Towneley family tree.

Tabbing to the appropriate era, Gill started to jot down the male names in the first half of the eighteenth century. Many of course had died in childhood. Three had gone to the colonies while a merry few had made it through to ripe old age. In all this, three names stood out. John Towneley who died in London on the second of March 1746 and his youngest son, Richard, whose recorded date of death was the sixteenth of April 1746. The place of his death was given only as "Scotland," but Gill gave himself a mental high five. That date was the Battle of Culloden.

The third name was Francis, the eldest son of John. Glancing at his record, it didn't list the date of his demise, recording only a question mark. Certain he was on the trail of something, Gill picked out the file references for the three men and started to dig in the paper records for more information.

'Excellent archive,' Gill commented later that afternoon while he contemplated another bite of the very fine roast beef sandwich. 'Everything is beautifully preserved, and the digital record makes it easy to navigate.'

'We spent quite a bit of money getting it organised after the house was sold,' said Freda. 'Myself and others in my generation had bundles in lofts, and shoeboxes bulging with bits and pieces. Goodness knows how much we managed to lose over the years, but it was a blessing the new owners saw value in collecting the remaining records.'

'I suppose, a place like this,' said Gill, waving a hand around the old dining room, 'the history is part of its value. You do well to look after it.'

'I'm glad you think so. And have you found what you're looking for?'

'I'm making progress.' He laid down his sandwich and peered at her. 'But although I've found the names of the people I'm looking for, I'm missing most of their details.'

'Details, Mr McArdle?'

'Some of your ancestors have files full of information. Medical records. Minutes of meetings. Legal proceedings. Accounts for properties bought and sold. And enough handwritten correspondence to keep me deciphering their spidery script until my dying day.'

'But not the people you're looking for?'

'Unfortunately, no.' Over the next few minutes, Gill concentrated on John Towneley and his two sons, none of whom had anything recorded other than dates of birth and death, and not even that for Francis.

'I see,' she said, laying down her cutlery. 'And you suspect this Richard Towneley died at Culloden?'

'I do. I've asked my researcher in Dundee to get into the government archives to try and determine what regiment he was with, but although the British records are good, they're not always comprehensive.'

Freda took a deep breath and released it. 'I'm afraid she's wasting her time.'

'How do you mean?'

'My ancestors didn't fight with the government. They were Jacobites.'

Gill suppressed his surprise.

'And those documents you are looking for were probably seized by the government during the period when my family was being punished for supporting the rebellion,' Freda continued.

'What form did that take?'

'Confiscation of land, in the main. We were left with a large house but no means to support it, so our demise was slow and painful over the next two centuries. And the elder John Towneley had a third son, another John. He was exiled to the colonies, though he returned in later life.'

Gill nodded. He'd known of course that a quarter of the fighting men on the government's side at Culloden were Scottish. He'd not been aware of English soldiers fighting for the rebellion. 'I'm sorry,' he said. 'Conflict extends so much further than the battlefields.'

She looked away and her expression didn't tell him if she agreed with him or not.

'Listen. I've come down here during an archaeological dig because I've found a body.'

She looked up sharply. 'At Culloden?'

'No. Somewhere in Wigtownshire. Based on my research today, I think it might be Francis.'

'Do you have any proof?'

Gill reached inside his waistcoat pocket and fished out the image Mhairi had sent him of the buttons. Under good light, the helmet in profile underscored by three stars was clearly visible.

'On the way in, I noticed this crest is carved into the stonework above the front door,' said Gill. 'And in other places around this building.'

'Yes,' she said, slightly absentmindedly as she tapped his phone screen. 'I suppose it might suggest a tentative link. What are you planning to do with this information?'

Gill tried to give her what he thought was his most winning smile. 'I've no political or religious bone to pick. I'm a historian and I just want to report the facts. And at a human level, if we have found Francis, I'd love to know what brought him to spend the last years of his life, living in a cave in Wigtownshire.'

Freda shuddered. 'It sounds awful. The poor man must have feared for his life.'

'We'll probably never know,' said Gill. 'But I'm wondering if there might be any clues buried in your archive.'

Freda picked up her napkin and dabbed her face. 'There are other documents. They're in the cabinets, but not listed in the digital catalogue.'

'What kind of documents?'

'Letters, mainly. Some of it is quite political. Some of it …' she paused to gather her thoughts. 'Suffice to say, given how harshly people from past generations seem judged these days by contemporary ethics, my family might not be treated kindly if these letters were ever published.'

'Are you worried about being trolled?'

'It's not as if the family divested a fleet of slave ships to buy into an animal testing firm.' Her eyes darted to his. 'The events are too long ago to damage a family that's already been ruined. I suppose I'm more concerned how you might portray my ancestors on a human level.'

Gill nodded. 'If I give you my solemn assurance not to pass judgment on them, may I see those letters?'

Freda lingered over her decision. 'For the sake of Francis, you may.'

Gill spent the rest of the afternoon working in the Towneley archive and it was early evening before he saw Freda again.

'How are you doing?' she asked.

'Getting there,' said Gill, looking at her over the top of the glasses he increasingly had to wear on days like this. 'It's tricky. The family used the same Christian names over and over again, and a good many of the letters aren't dated.'

'What about postmarks?'

'For the most part, they don't exist. The postal system during the period I'm targeting was still run on a "receiver pays" model. Anyone sending a letter would pass it to the person holding the local mail contract who in turn would put it on a mail coach. In due course, if the address was legible, it would be delivered, and the receiver would decide if they wanted it or not. The sorting office was crude by today's standards, and dates didn't appear until later.'

'How will you know if you have a letter from the Francis Towneley you are looking for?'

'I've used what clues I can to put the correspondence in date order. Where I don't have dates, I'm estimating the age of the paper or the handwriting style.' Gill nodded at one pile. 'And I'm setting aside any letter sent by someone called Francis that is either undated or dated within the mid-eighteenth century.'

Freda hefted her eyebrows. 'That's quite a pile.'

He grunted. 'Next step is to read them. See if we can find something from our man.'

She nodded curtly. 'I'm off duty shortly. I'll come and give you a hand.'

Somewhere in the house, a grand clock mechanically greeted the midnight hour. Accepting a letter from Freda, Gill added it to the sequence in front of him. Of the five letters they'd found, Freda had found two and although she was dry-eyed, he'd noticed how the distant family tragedy had softened her posture.

'All that suffering,' she said, sadly. 'What was it for?'

'Duty, faith and property,' said Gill. 'And a hierarchy of needs.'

She drew her forefinger across her eyelids and suddenly looked very tired. 'Explain that.'

'Depends where you were on the social ladder,' Gill said. 'For the tenant farmers in the Scottish Highlands, duty meant if your laird said come and fight, you either obeyed him or risked starvation. For a government soldier, your pay packet depended on doing what was asked of you.'

'You think the common man didn't care about politics or religion?'

'I suspect, as a farmer or a soldier, you had more pressing matters. But many advocated a personal faith because that's what led Protestantism to overthrow Catholicism in the first place.'

'And the lords and lairds?'

'In England as in Scotland, they acted out of a combination of personal preference for one form of religion or the other, while keeping a wary eye on any government that could kick them off their land if they backed the wrong horse.'

'Witness the Towneleys,' Freda acknowledged.

'Indeed.'

'Shall we summarise where we've got to, and then I'm going to bed?'

Gill picked up the first letter with gloved hands. 'John, Richard and Francis report they've joined the Manchester Regiment and that the Jacobites have taken Carlisle without a shot being fired. The Manchesters comprised English recruits to the Catholic cause during the Bonnie Prince's foray into England.'

'But then the prince retreats as he hasn't enough men to capture London and risks being outflanked by a government army marching north,' added Freda.

'The next letter says the Towneleys survived the government attack on Carlisle where most of the Manchester Regiment was killed. However, John is captured and sent to London for trial. Francis reports that he and his brother are escaping north with a group of Irish mercenaries to prepare for the next battle.'

'John is executed in March 1746, and the next significant date is Culloden.'

'The fourth letter is from Francis alone,' Gill continued. 'He reports that his brother died on the battlefield and that he is fulfilling his sibling's last wish, by taking the young man's bagpipes while he waits for the Jacobites to regroup.'

'Which of course, they don't,' Freda recalled.

'Some months have passed between this letter and the last. Francis is on the road and can trust no one. He hopes to be home by Christmas.'

'And finally?'

Gill turned to the last letter. 'He says he has posted this letter in Wigtownshire. He reports the roads are still not safe and that he is hiding out with a group of men and women more desperate and wretched than himself.'

'And that's the last we hear from him?'

Gill took a deep breath and looked at the pile of undated correspondence. 'Unless we've overlooked one.'

Freda nodded. 'You're welcome to try again in the morning. In the meantime, the hotel is almost empty mid-week. Let me fetch you a key to one of the rooms.'

Chapter 37

Portpatrick,
May 1747

Dearest Mother,

Didst thou think I was dead? Perhaps after my last letter, thou didst hope I was. Truly I had fallen to the lowest of the low, and since then, I am tumbled further.

I live now in a sea cave, far from civilization. But I do not live alone for I found a community of discarded souls who live short, brutal lives, nourished only by the love they render to each other. They steal, beg, and barter, and somehow, day by day, they survive. They are a most sorry lot, diminutive as if their bodies are arrested in perpetual childhood. Cursed and expelled from good society, I have become their mascot of sorts. Whenever we need interaction with the outside world, I am the one who goes, walking in rags to the town of Portpatrick to exchange barrows of wreck we find upon the seashore. The men of that town turn their backs on me. Children gape until their mothers usher them inside. I come, make my trade, and leave again to keep company with the little people who have become my family.

Our cause, which once worked powerfully within me, drawing me to the battlefield, to save our faith and restore the lands stolen from us by a Pope-hating king, no longer burns. I am wearied by the deaths I witnessed, and the pain inflicted on my fellow man, and for what? So that a French prince can walk down an avenue founded on the broken bodies of the poor and reign upon a bloodied throne? I went to war to win back our estate and the good standing of our family name, but now I struggle to reason the Towneleys' grievance as a true injustice. Now, when I see real suffering all around, I understand why we were despised. Common girls in the marketplace turned their backs on thee because we had munificent wealth, while they had barely enough to live. I think perhaps we saw injustice in our circumstances where in fact, there was none. And all around us, poverty and disease were nourished by our utter selfishness.

Art thou ashamed of me? I shall not write again unless I hear from thee. If thou choosest, leave a letter for me in the care of the Crowne Hotel in Portpatrick. Do not worry about the fee—I have paid for thy letter after a day spent begging, and if thou never writest, then that is a shilling in another man's hungry pocket. And please pray for me, for these days I am wracked by a cough that makes my lungs bleed.

Until I hear from thee,
Francis Towneley.

Chapter 38

'There you have it,' said Freda the following morning, as they stood by Gill's car. 'His last letter. So very sad.'

'Did his mother ever reply?' asked Gill as he passed back Towneley's letter.

She shook her head. 'There's no mention that she ever did, and we've no record he ever wrote again.'

'She must have felt ashamed of him.'

Freda's gaze left his face and out over the gardens. 'Maybe. Personally, I feel proud of him.'

'Interesting. Tell me why?'

'Francis left Burnley as a young man prepared to use violence to restore society to an earlier and outmoded religious age. The subtext of his letters suggests the family were more concerned about recovering their land than restoring a Catholic monarchy. Once he'd experienced the death and destruction of war and found himself in the company of people he'd formerly despised, he renounced violence and came to regard the cave dwellers as his family.'

'It was tough in there,' said Gill. 'We found evidence suggesting malnutrition and disease. They'd very few home comforts.'

Freda sighed. 'How did he die?'

'His remains are still being examined. Best guess would be consumption or tuberculosis.'

'I see. And what will happen to his body after all this analysis?'

'I daresay he could be returned to you. The Procurator might request a DNA sample from his nearest living kin, as a formality.'

'My family line traces back to the younger John, so yes, please send me a kit.'

Gill gave her a businesslike nod. 'This has been very helpful. Thank you.'

'And I want to give you this,' said Freda, passing him a small plastic wallet.

'What is it?'

'The memory card from Bobby's camera,' Freda sighed. 'You came all the way down here to do my family a great service and I, mistakenly, turned our encounter into a transaction. Please, take it, and my apologies for subjecting you to such vulgar treatment.'

Gill winked at her and refused the card. 'It's okay. Minor celebrities like me need as much publicity as they can get.'

She briefly hid her face in embarrassment, then reached out and touched his arm. 'Are you returning to the caves?'

'Yes. And I need to dash because our dig finishes later today.'

'Bear with me,' she said before darting off into the ornamental gardens where Gill had posed with the wedding party. She returned a few minutes later bearing a single white rosebud.

'This is an *Alba Maxima*; believed to be the original Yorkshire white rose. Francis mentioned in his first letter he was wearing one from the garden when he left Towneley

Hall.' She pointed at the manicured landscaping. 'The plants have changed a lot over the years, but we're very particular about our roses. There's a strong possibility this flower is directly descended from the one where Francis plucked his own.'

'It's beautiful,' said Gill.

'Would you lay it in the cave for me. Close to where he died.' Her head drooped. 'It's my way of saying sorry.'

'I will.'

Formally, they shook hands, then Gill turned around and drove back towards the northbound motorway.

Midway through his drive back to the dig, Gill had a call from Mhairi.

'Hey, Gill. That's me finished at Clanyard. Unless you need me to hang around, I'll leave now and drop the last boxes with Saul in Glasgow before he goes home for the day.'

'That's perfect. I'm sure he'll be delighted to see you.' He listened to Mhairi giggle with delight then pressed her on a request. 'Quick question. Have you had a chance to dig into the parish records I mentioned?'

'Massive task, Gill. It could take weeks to scroll through the digitised archives.'

'No worries. We can outsource that work.'

'However, I did take the specific examples Carmichael gave you and I can confirm his assertion that "GF" is noted against a cluster of infant deaths.'

Gill left a pause. 'Which means these kids weren't just secretly left to die. Their communities were aware and therefore, complicit.'

'Yeah, sorry.' Mhairi paused. 'It's quite sad.'

'It is, but thanks for checking. And Mhairi, thank you for all your help on this project.'

'Ach, I was due a little on-site work. When you listen to Cassy moaning about it, it makes me wonder what all the fuss was all about.'

'Sorry we didn't get you any cuneiform tablets to translate.'

'No problem. There was mystery enough in that cave.' She fell silent a moment. 'Which reminds me, have you had a chance to open the detailed email from Lossuary?'

'Not yet. I've been in meetings.'

'Well, whoever he was, it turns out he was a bit of a killer.'

'What do you mean?'

'If you recall, the carbon dating suggested the Clanyard community ended suddenly between 1745 and 1785.'

'Aye, and I know that Towneley fought at Culloden, so that narrows the window even further.'

'The DNA results confirm tuberculosis was widespread in the community. And based on his bones, the infection was most advanced in our mystery piper.'

Gill felt stung on Francis Towneley's behalf. 'How can they know that?'

'The tuberculosis mycobacterium leaves identifiable genetic markers that persist in the sufferer's skeletal remains,' Mhairi continued. 'And there are physical signs too, like bone lesions.'

'You think Towneley brought tuberculosis into the community?'

'It's possible. If he was a soldier during the final Jacobite rebellion, he would have mixed with men from all over Scotland and Ireland, whereas the community he entered was utterly isolated from the world.'

'Thanks, Mhairi. That's a useful insight. Could you do me a favour and get a DNA kit mailed to Freda Littleton. She gave her verbal consent this morning and it would be final confirmation of a familial connection between our piper and the Towneleys of Burnley.'

'Sure. I'll get that sent.'

'Great. All being well, I'll see you in the office tomorrow for the Publisher's Meeting.'

After Mhairi signed off, Gill felt tired and heavy. He was travelling along the busy A75 from Dumfries towards the port town of Cairnryan and took the opportunity to slide into one of the many laybys. Then he got out and leaned against his car. A terrible realisation was dawning on him. Francis Towneley mentioned in his last letter to his mother that he wasn't well. Mhairi's data confirmed his likely death from tuberculosis, and now there was evidence suggesting he'd communicated the infection to the rest of the Clanyard population. Towneley had travelled the length of the country moving from one tragedy to another, implicitly experiencing rejection from his own birth family. Finally, he'd found a community that had taken this weary soldier to its heart. Then one by one, the disease he carried had killed them all.

It was 4 pm before Gill drove into their makeshift car park at Clanyard. The piles of gear lying around confirmed the dig was finishing on schedule.

'Oh, there he is,' said Fiona, cresting the hilltop as Gill was locking his car.

'Hey, beautiful. Did I miss much?'

Fiona tossed an armful of tools into the open doors of her van. 'Once we got past the dragon's eggs and journeyed on a diamond the size of a minivan into the centre of the Earth, it was all quite tame.'

'That boring, huh?'

'Nothing new if that's what you're asking. A few wee odds and ends. When we ran out of artefacts to collect, we switched our effort to collecting soil samples.' She nodded at the rose in his hands. 'That for me?'

'Actually, for the Piper of Clanyard Bay.'

'Oh, aye?'

'Long story. Basically, I met his distant niece.' He held up the flower. 'She asked me to lay this where he died.'

'Great. If you're quick, you might still catch Murray in the caves. He was muttering about taking down the lighting rigs as soon as we're done.'

Gill jerked his head in the direction of the beach. 'Good tip. I'll go right away.'

'Gill,' called Fiona, when he made to move off. 'What about your hard hat and safety suit?'

'I'm only going in and out.'

'Oh, come on, man. We have this gear for a reason.'

Frustrated, Gill couldn't help but glance at his watch. He'd hoped to be back in Dundee tonight and it was already later than he hoped. 'Yeah, I know you're right.'

'Look, I'll help you suit up, but after that, if you'll excuse me, I promised to meet an old Uni friend tonight in Kirkcudbright, so I need to hit the road.'

'No problem. Thanks for all you've done and take care on the drive back north.'

Chapter 39

'Hey Gill,' said Murray. He was standing in the centre of the cavern, coiling wire cables.

'Hey Murray. Bumped into Fiona on the way in. She seems pleased with the dig.'

'Definitely. We put our backs into it.' Murray paused to throw Gill a roguish smile. 'Where did you disappear to these last two days?'

'Down in Burnley. Following a lead on our deceased piper.'

'He was English?'

Briefly, Gill gave Murray a potted history of his visit to Towneley Hall with its efficient archive and luxurious menu.

'While you were gallivanting, Fiona and the guys did a great job. So, unless you've anything new for us, it's time to wrap this up.'

'She was telling me …' Gill stopped, distracted by a small skittering noise from somewhere behind him. 'What was that?'

Murray started laughing 'You're twitchy all of a sudden. You know that's perfectly normal at the end of a cavern expedition?'

'What?'

'The lighting rig has pumped so much heat in here the last few days, we're starting to see the cave dry out.'

'Okay.'

Murray nodded at the white flower clutched in Gill's left hand. 'What's with that?'

Gill held up Freda's white rose. 'Do I have time for one small act of remembrance?'

'Do you need long?'

'Just a few minutes.'

Murray clapped him on the shoulder. 'I'll finish here. Then you can help me carry the last of the gear to the van.'

He turned back to dismantling the last lighting rig, leaving Gill to clamber up to the ledge where Francis Towneley, the Piper of Clanyard Bay, had breathed his last. Kneeling at the mouth of Towneley's chamber, he reached in and carefully placed the rose where the body had lain.

In this dark corner, the tragedy of what happened here fell heavily upon Gill. 'At the end, when you were dying, I wonder if you realised what you'd done?' Gill whispered, thinking of how awful it must have been for Francis. The position of his remains showed that the piper and his partner were among the last to die, with the bones of the others already packing the ossuary. And Gill felt anger. Anger at the soldier's mother who saw violence as a legitimate way to recover the family's riches. Anger at the generals like the Bonnie Prince who expended the lives of men, rich and poor, to bid for a bloodied throne. Anger at the laird who, who rather than help a troubled soldier, only offered to do so once the man had conducted an act of human pest control. Proud men and women, stepping on the bodies of the poor so their already privileged lives could become even richer.

'Gill,' yelled Murry's voice. 'Are you almost done?'

'Coming,' he shouted back.

As Gill reversed out of the hollow, the rock beneath him shivered. He froze for a second, wondering if he was giddy, or if in fact, he'd felt anything at all. But then a distant boom echoed inside *Delta* cavern, the sound rumbling through the rocks, like the sound of a hundred-tonne metal door swinging gently closed. From somewhere below him, he heard Murray's urgent voice.

'Gill! Where are you?'

'Up here. The piper's grotto. What was that noise?'

'Nothing good. Come on. We're leaving.'

Another boom. Further away this time but somehow expending more energy. This one was enough to dislodge loose fragments of rock which slithered down the sloping stone shelves and onto the floor. Something crashed into the remaining lighting rig, knocking it sideways, and Gill saw Murray's torch beam make a frantic dash towards the exit.

'Shit,' the man hissed in the dark.

'What's up?' asked Gill when he reached the floor.

'Those big boulders linking this room with *Charlie* cavern have closed together.'

Gill felt a lurch in his stomach. 'Why would they do that?'

'Earthquake, Gill. Just a tiny tremor but enough to bugger up our exit. Get over here and help me look for another way out.'

Gill picked his way over the stones to where Murray's torch was darting here and there around an obelisk of weathered stone that had toppled out of the upright and squeezed the gap between *Delta* cavern and the rest of the system. Standing beneath it, Gill felt a sudden sense of dread.

'I can hear the sea,' Murray muttered. 'Just need to get a fix on it.'

'Murray?'

'We'll turn our torches off in a second. See if we can detect any daylight.'

Gill's senses flared. 'Murray!'

'Ah, man. Donnie will be worried about us. As soon as we figure out what to do, I need to call him on the rock radio.'

'Murray. That big slab above your head. I don't think anything's supporting it.'

'What?'

Unable to bear it any longer, Gill sprang forward; grabbing Murray by his jacket hood and dragging him three steps backwards until they both stumbled and fell. Gill immediately rolled away from him and crouched at the centre of *Delta* cavern, sweeping his torch beam above their heads. But Murray was angry now and leapt at Gill, with a fist raised.

'What's with you, damn sassenach?'

'I … I…' gasped Gill, just as the obelisk lost its battle with gravity and crashed down on where they'd just been standing. A slew of rubble followed it, causing Murray to yell in pain.

'Donnie to *Delta* cavern. What is your situation, over?'

'Good work. You've got a connection,' whispered Murray through gritted teeth.

'Donnie. It's Gill. We hear you.'

'What's happening? I've been trying for an hour. Over.'

'There was a rock fall. The radio took a bump. Taken us this long to get the electrode to connect to the receiver.'

'I heard a couple of bangs. Are you guys alright?'

'I am. But Murray got hit by falling debris and I think his left ankle's fractured.'

'Shit. Can you get him out?'

'That's a negative for now. The whole seaward side of *Delta* has collapsed.'

'What about above or behind you?' Anything at all? Take a second, Gill, and look for light.'

Gill switched off his torch and looked. 'Nothing.'

'Right. Save your batteries. I'm going for help. I will call you in exactly one hour. Do your best to keep my boss comfortable and hydrated.'

'I will,' said Gill. '*Delta* cavern out.'

One hour later, Gill switched on the radio and waited for Donnie's call back. It took another fifteen minutes before the radio crackled to life. 'Gill, Murray? Donnie here. You guys online?'

Gill passed the mic to Murray. 'We're here, Don.'

They heard a gasp of relief from Donnie.

'Aye, the thermal network in these new suits adds extra weight,' Murray continued. 'But I'll never complain about that again.'

'How's your leg?'

'Twisted and bruised, but not bleeding. I'm chewing through the few painkillers we had in our first aid kits. Sooner you get us out the better.'

'Okay.' Donnie paused. 'Can you put me on to Gill? I need to discuss that with him.'

'Sure. Here you go.'

Gill took the radio. 'Hey, Donnie.'

'Listen, Gill. We have a problem.'

Gill felt a shiver go down his spine as he stood up and took a few steps away from Murray. 'What's happening?'

'That tremor was a Scotland-wide event. Thankfully, it wasn't big, and it centred on the Great Glen. Information is sketchy but it sounds like it's affecting road, rail and power, from Argyll right up to Inverness.'

'Casualties?'

'No idea, Gill, but emergency services are focused on the glen. When I finally got through to an operator, I won't say she didn't exactly give a shit, but I did establish that two guys stuck in a collapsed sea cave wasn't going to be high on her list of priorities.'

Gill pressed his left hand against his forehead until it started to hurt. 'You got any suggestions?'

'You've got air and water, right?'

Gill nodded, even though Donnie couldn't see him. 'There's freshwater pooling close to where I'm standing. And we've still got that cool draught, so there's air coming from somewhere.'

'You've enough calories in your emergency kit to keep you ticking over for up to a week.' Gill heard Donnie swallow. 'It's your batteries that will be the problem. I reckon you'll have six hours at most on your main torch. Another four or five on your head torch if you don't run down the suit battery by running your onboard heating.'

Gill groaned. 'So, we'll need to switch our torches off immediately if we're going to find water.'

'Yep. That's about it.'

'I'm going to ask you an honest question. Do you think it's likely we'll be rescued?'

Donnie didn't answer straight away. 'Depends how bad things are up north, but if heavy equipment and specialist rescue teams are required, you might have quite a wait.'

'Meanwhile, without food and light, our energy levels are going to drop quickly.'

'Sorry, Gill, but roughly speaking, your energy will drop by half every day.'

Gill's mind struggled to compute how much danger they were in. 'Okay. I'll brief Murray. Can you call us again in an hour?'

Gill and Murray sat side by side in complete darkness. It was 8 pm and the only sound they could hear was the drip, drip, drip of water and the occasional clatter of small stones dropping out of the rockfall. Even the sound of the sea crashing against the rocks seemed far away.

'Thank you,' said Murray after a while. 'For dragging me out of there.'

'You're welcome.'

Gill listened to the sound of Murray scratching the stubble on his face. 'How did you know?'

'Know what?'

'That the roof was about to cave in?'

Gill sighed. The only bright side to this predicament was that there seemed to be a Creator who wasn't quite done with him. 'Had an instinct,' he said.

'Well, grand job, pal.'

'The air we're feeling on our faces. It must be coming from somewhere, right?'

'Aye, a gap, or a hundred wee gaps. Who knows.'

'You guys used ground-penetrating radar on the second day. You showed me the resulting map.'

Murray snorted. 'That wasn't a map. We were simply looking for three-dimensional spaces linked to *Delta* cavern, and we got two hundred metres away from the sea before we decided we'd everything we needed.'

'Reminds me of the rumours about these caves stretching from coast to coast across the peninsula.'

Murray's laugh cut short with a huff of pain. 'I know what you're thinking. You're under the misimpression you can follow the air through a series of linked chambers until you come out the other side.'

'Well, I …'

'And because you're an archaeologist, maybe you'll come to a gallery with its high roof supported by carved lions, and the floor will be strewn with heaps of treasure?'

Gill rubbed his nose. 'I'm just saying that looking for an exit might be better than sitting here getting weaker and weaker.'

Murray grunted while he rearranged his seating position. 'Take an expert's advice, Gill. You'll die scared and alone if you try a stunt like that.'

'Maybe, but it's worth a punt.'

'Two and a half kilometres, shore to shore. And that's if you found a tunnel running in a straight line. But it won't be a straight line. It will be small cavities about the size of a twisted phonebox, linked by crawl spaces too small for a domestic cat. No way you'd make it through.'

'Maybe. Why shouldn't I take a look?'

'Oh, yeah. And who's going to stay and look after the casualty?'

'You can keep the radio. I wouldn't be able to carry it anyway.'

Murray shifted his position again and immediately sucked his teeth in pain. 'I'm pulling rank, Gill. No way I'm letting you do that.'

Gill took a second to ensure his voice sounded even. 'I've got a wife and son out there, Murray. I need to get back to them. And if I can't drag your sorry arse out the front door of this place, then I need to find the tradesman's entrance.'

'Just don't, Gill.'

But Gill was already standing up. 'The moment I hit a blocked door I'll turn around.'

'Gill.' Murray's headlamp flicked on.

'Yes?'

'At some point you'll need your phone, which means it must survive what's ahead of you. There's a waterproof case in your left breast pocket. Find it and place your phone inside, then open your survival suit and use the Velcro straps to clamp your phone against your inner left thigh.'

Gill fished for the tool in question. 'Got it.'

'And when you're scoping out the caverns, use your voice. The longer the echo, the bigger the space. And here. Take my big hand torch.'

'You'll need it.'

'I'm not going anywhere. While you, my foolish friend, are stepping into hell.'

Gill released an anxious laugh. 'Tell Donnie I'll be in touch by mobile once I make it to fresh air.'

'Sure.'

'Anything you want topside while I'm out?'

'Roast beef sandwiches,' Murray shot back. 'From that nice hotel in Burnley.'

'With or without mustard?'

'Just be safe, Gill.'

Chapter 40

Gill stood at the back of the cave near the ossuary and held his breath. The wall alcoves in the chamber now lay empty, but Gill wasn't here to look for bones. It was around this spot he'd most intensely felt a draught in his face. Not from the ossuary itself, but from a crevasse just off to his left. Joey had explored this area and while a rough passage continued for thirty metres, there was no sign of habitation. On that basis, the route had not attracted further investigation. Knowing that the named caverns had all been carefully explored, this virgin territory was now Gill's best chance to discover an exit. Taking a deep breath, he squeezed into the narrow crevasse.

It took him twenty minutes to reach the most distant point explored by Joey. Stepping into uncharted territory, he discovered there was a three-metre drop to reach the floor of what he christened *Victor* cavern. Descending slowly, he placed his feet carefully, knowing that breaking a leg down here would be the end of him. Glancing his torch beam off the walls he found there was a continuous smooth roof, hinting at regular periods of water erosion. The floor however was strewn with rubble that rose and fell between where he stood and the limits of his beam. Wondering how far this natural tunnel went, he remembered Murray's advice to use his voice.

'Aura. Are you here?' he called out into the darkness. And sure enough, his voice echoed back at him over several seconds. This was a big chamber; dark and deep. He was off to a good start.

Splashing through knee-high standing water, he called out again. 'Aura, I could really use your help.'

Again, his voice rumbled away, then back to him. But for now, it went unanswered, so he climbed one of the rubble mounds and squatting below the ceiling, used his torch to peer down the length of the chamber. In the event, he couldn't see much but had a growing sense that this channel extended some distance. It ran almost due east, which passed as a superhighway in this situation. He was about to set off when he instinctively paused again.

'Aura. Do I go straight ahead?'

No answer came and with the time pressure on his resources, he was keen to keep moving. But again, something in his psyche forced him to wait.

'Anything, Aura. A laugh, or a light. Even a big scary angel on a motorbike would be great just now.'

And again, nothing.

His urge to move forward was almost overwhelming, so why then did he stay still? He looked around, hunting for clues, but there was nothing, except rocks and the sound of running water. The only other possible exit was a dark space hinting at another cavity two metres above this level. It was little more than a diagonal crack from which a small stream discharged its water into the main channel.

'Aura. Please tell me you're not asking me to climb up there?'

He turned his back on the crawl space, but his attention kept falling back to it. 'Tell me there's a better way?'

The compulsion to explore the space became too strong to ignore. Reluctantly, Gill climbed down from his perch and stood surveying how he might reach up to the cavity.

'This is madness,' he called out. 'Two and a half kilometres, that way,' he yelled, pointing in the direction of the main watercourse. 'Tell me why I should go up here?'

'*Up here – up here – up here.*' The echoes of his voice died away and left a heavy silence. He sighed and started to climb.

'Just taking a look,' he muttered, grasping for a handhold and thrusting his right boot into a cavity. Pushing himself up, he made uncertain progress as he edged closer to the ledge above his head. He was almost there when his left boot sprang free from his toe hold. Gill emitted a tiny gasp of terror, as his left arm suddenly had to bear his weight. Immediately he felt a streak of pain as a tendon tore in his wrist. Fighting to maintain his balance while his body lurched, Murray's torch spooled out of his pocket and crashed, irredeemably, onto the hard surface below. Gill groaned and fought to take the pressure off his damaged wrist. It would be impossible to hold this position for very long, so he dug in again with his left foot and pushed hard until the fingertips on his right hand reached the ledge. He had to use both hands to pull himself up and now both arms throbbed with pain. He reached for the packet of painkillers in his first aid kit before remembering he'd donated them to Murray.

Making do with just rubbing his wrists, he peered back over the ledge. The drop back onto the floor of *Victor* cavern looked even worse from up here. With his damaged arm, he wasn't sure he could retrace his steps and do it safely, so for now, he needed to press on.

The small watercourse had eroded an adequate crawl space and for the first few minutes, he was able to limp along on all fours. But then it narrowed, and he had to drop onto his belly, dragging himself forward, jiggling his knees and elbows to achieve forward progress. The cavity tightened still further and with his chest pressed flat against the rock, the water flowing towards him soon penetrated his suit. Running cold against his chest, around his midriff and a few minutes later, starting to chill his feet. He groaned, forcing himself to hum a *Black Scabbard* guitar riff while he battled his brain not to panic. But he'd found himself in too many tight places over the years and knew this hole was worse than anything he'd ever imagined. The way forward was getting ever tighter, and his mind fretted about another earth tremor, waiting to crush him in the dark. He stopped humming, needing to force air out of his lungs so he could compress his chest and drag himself through the next section. With scuffing and pushing, wriggling and tugging he managed to achieve this, but the walls were so tight now, and his body tired and sore. If he couldn't go forward, he doubted he had the strength to go back. An image of Salina and Josh, playing on their living room floor flashed through his mind, and faced with the realistic possibility he would never see them again, he began to sob.

Pushing his palms against the rock in front of him, he tried to retreat. But his suit rucked beneath him, blocking movement. And though he pushed with all his remaining might, his arms shaking with exhaustion, his body didn't move. And he knew with a chest-crushing certainty, he was stuck.

'Please, Aura,' he whispered. 'I was sure you were telling me to come this way … Please … Where are you?'

Chapter 41

Entering the industrial campus around Kilkeel harbour, Fallon remembered visiting this place with her father, back in the days when dozens of wooden-hulled trawlers had packed the berths. Constructed in the mid-twentieth century, in liveries of black, blue, red and green, these little ships had endured ugly modifications when fishing technologies changed over the years. Most of those old boats were gone now, replaced with large ocean-going ships and a fleet of small, purpose-built dredgers. The harbour itself was a ribbon of deep moorings, reinforced with steel piling, along a stretch of the River Whitewater where it entered the Irish Sea.

Arriving early on this Friday morning, she met DS Martin on the harbourside and entered the long, low shed of the fish market via a back door. Despite the early hour, four large boats were busy unloading, the most distant of which was the *Argonaut*. Nodding at Martin, they strode through the fish market, bustling with buyers, their cold hands stuffed in pockets, and raucous with auctioneers bawling out their commodities over the noise of gas-powered forklifts.

'Chris Kearney?' asked Fallon, approaching a man unloading the most distant boat.

'Skipper's still on board,' said the lad, gesticulating with a gloved hand towards the wheelhouse towering above the holds.

She nodded her thanks and tiptoed along the gangplank and onto the boat.

Climbing two flights of metal stairs, she swung open the door of the wheelhouse without knocking. 'Kearney?' she barked at an older man, while she brandished her warrant card. Kearney clamped a cigarette between his lips while he supervised another lad of about seventeen, operating the gantry as they swung fish boxes onto the quayside.

'Who's asking,' he said without turning to look at her.

'DI Shona Fallon. We spoke over the radio three weeks ago. I've come to ask you a few follow-up questions about your unscheduled layover in Clanyard Bay in early May.'

'Oh aye? I think I told you everything when we last spoke.'

'Really? I've had time to do a little more digging since then. Are you sure you don't want to add to your statement?'

Kearney flicked his chin at his young assistant. 'Give us a second, Ronan. Oh, and phone Uncle Jake and ask him to give me a call at his earliest convenience. Need to chat to him about the crew rota.'

The boy nodded, and with a dark look at the two police officers, removed himself from the room. Kearney waited until the door had closed behind him before he spoke again. 'Much as I try to think, I doubt there's more I can tell you, officers. We were having electrical problems on the seventh of May. We anchored in a sheltered spot that I now know was Clanyard Bay. Had a complete shutdown while our sparky replaced a couple of fried circuits and got us up and running again.'

'Happen a lot?' asked DS Martin. 'These shutdowns?'

Kearney's small blue eyes studied the sergeant. 'Not a lot. A few times over the years.'

'Any before the Clanyard incident?'

Kearney's eyes darted to the ceiling. 'Once, I recall.'

'Whereabouts were you?'

'At sea.'

'Exactly where at sea?'

Kearney looked away and out the window where the two lads were standing on the quayside. One of them was scrolling on his phone while the other was more old-school and was actually making a phone call. 'Somewhere off Spain, I believe. I'd need to check my records.'

'Yes, please, Mr Kearny. Latitude and longitude by degrees, minutes and seconds.'

Kearny sighed in frustration. 'And if I don't want to give you that information?'

'Then I'll arrest you and we'll trot off to the local station. Meanwhile, I'll impound the *Argonaut* to allow a thorough search.'

'We're going back to sea tomorrow.'

'Not if I arrest you, you're not.'

Kearny jettisoned his cigarette and moved over to a keyboard and screen. After a few minutes of irritable tapping, he paused to study the screen and jotted down the coordinates Fallon was looking for. Fallon responded by comparing them to another set she had in an email on her phone.

'Well, well. Quite a little party out there. Did you and the South African guys chat rugby while your electricians were sorting out your various electrical problems?'

'I think,' said Kearny slowly, 'that if we're going to talk anymore, I'd like a solicitor present.'

'Good idea,' Fallon shot back. 'There'll be consequences for switching off your AIS transponder. And of course, there's your proximity to Clanyard Bay last month. There's enough guilt by association to justify us taking a forensics team through your vessel.'

Kearney rubbed his forehead. 'Told you, we're going to sea.'

'Should have thought about that before becoming a weapons courier.' Fallon walked a circuit of the wheelhouse with its starship-styled banks of switches and instrumentation. Then she stopped and glared at Kearny. 'Did you know Iain Lynch is back from Boston? He's currently in a Belfast Police Station, helping us with our enquiries.'

She watched as the redness in Kearney's cheeks dimmed a little.

'Okay. We're done here,' said Kearny. 'All you're gonna get from me is "no comment" until hell freezes over.'

Fallon nodded sympathetically. 'Probably for the best.' Walking towards the door, she ran her hand down a sleek array of screens displaying navigational data. 'What does it cost to leave a boat like this tied up for a day? Or a week? Or a month?'

But Kearny was done talking and Fallon turned to address DS Martin. 'I'll call for a couple of uniforms to secure this place until forensics have done their thing.'

'What about a warrant, boss?'

'I'm gonna skip over to Kilkeel nick to get that done. You keep an eye on the party here, and I'll be back with the paperwork in an hour.'

'And the suspect?'

Fallon glared at Kearney. 'Finish offloading your catch. I'll be back shortly to check if you've changed your mind.'

She studied his face for a few moments waiting for any indication he'd answer her questions, but the man's cold blue eyes were unyielding. Leaving the wheelhouse behind, she descended the stairs and stepped back out into the fish market before marching back through the long rows of ice-topped fish boxes towards her car. It took a few seconds to locate her vehicle as the yard had filled with traders attending the rolling auction on the harbourside. She eventually found it sandwiched between two long white vans. Reaching for her keys, she was caught completely off guard when someone yanked a cloth hood over her head. At the exact same moment, strong arms gripped her from behind.

'Don't,' said a deep Ulster voice behind her as she struggled vainly. 'We just want to talk.'

'Get the hell away from me.'

'Listen, Shona. If we meant you harm, you'd be dead already. Now, are you gonna be a good girl or do I need to shake you up a bit?'

'Who are you?'

The man laughed. 'Let's just say, I'm taking you to have a chat with Uncle Jake.'

Fallon kicked herself when she remembered Kearney's command to his lieutenant. And like a helpless bird in a net, she surrendered to the inevitable.

'That's more like it,' he grunted. She heard one of the van doors open and seconds later, she was bodily lifted inside. With her vision still completely masked, she was pushed into a sitting position. Then her captors sat solidly to her left and her right so that her hips and elbows were pinned between them.

'Phone?' someone demanded.

'Right jacket pocket,' she replied, meekly. 'The password is 17, 02, 78.'

Forcefully, hands reached for the device. After a minute's silence, it was thrust back into her pocket, and she assumed it had been powered down.

'All yours, boss,' said the guy on her left.

'How's about you, DI Fallon?' said an educated voice.

'Pure dead brilliant,' spat Fallon through the cloth bag. 'Which is more than you're going to be when I'm done with you.'

'I need to speak to you about a situation,' said the voice, ignoring her hollow threats.

'Abducting a police officer,' spat Fallon with more courage than she felt. 'Let's talk about that for starters.'

'Let's not,' said the voice. 'We'll make much faster progress if we stick to the issues at hand.'

She considered this for a second. 'Okay. Try me.'

'Iain Lynch. You have him in custody in Belfast.'

'Yes.'

'And you assume he's running guns for Loyalist paramilitaries?'

'I do.'

'That's the first misconception I need to correct. Lynch doesn't work for us. To be clear, he did, back in the day, but the man is a liability, and we ceased using his services a long time ago.'

'How very noble of you.'

'I'm not trying to be noble, Shona. I'm fighting to protect a way of life.'

'If Lynch doesn't work for your lot, then who?'

'He's a freelance smuggler. Done some modest stuff over the years, mainly in the Balkans and Africa. This is the first time we've seen him operating on home soil.'

'Why should I believe you?'

'I've no care whether you believe me or not,' the voice said calmly. 'But we'll see what happens to Mr Lynch once he leaves custody. Whether you release him, or he ends up on remand, he's about to discover he's just made a very bad life choice.'

'You're going to kill him?'

'I couldn't possibly comment,' said the voice evenly. 'What I really need to talk to you about is the crew of the *Argonaut*.'

'What about them?'

'They aren't in on Lynch's little games. Their skipper is being compelled.'

'Kearney is a gun runner. That's on the record and he needs to face justice.'

The man laughed again. 'You talk about justice. Listen, one of Lynch's goons sent Kearney's little kiddie home from nursery with a bullet in her lunchbox. He wants our poor fisherman to think his family are in danger.' He sighed. 'You don't threaten kiddies, Shona. That's another reason we'll be taking him out of play.'

'Thanks for the heads up. Now I know you've got a kill notice out on Lynch, I can protect him.'

The voice laughed. 'After that wee stunt on Balmoral Avenue? I'd have thought you'd be glad to know the man wasn't far from his last sunrise.'

'I don't like him, but I need Lynch as part of an ongoing investigation.'

'Do you mean, persuading him to reveal the ultimate client for his guns?'

'Yes.'

'I'll tell you what, darlin'. If I give you the identity of the client, will you leave the *Argonaut* out of this?'

Fallon wanted, desperately, to agree. 'I can't give you that assurance.'

'Okay. Then we don't have a deal. And that, my friend, means you're steering into trouble.'

'Give me a name,' Fallon pleaded. 'If you do that, I'll call off the forensics search and let the *Argonaut* go to sea tomorrow. Maybe, by the time they come back, the game will have moved on.'

The voice was silent while he considered her offer. 'I'm surprised, and a little disappointed,' he said at last.

'By what?'

'A boatload of guns shows up in Scotland and you cops just follow the same old logic and assume the clients are Loyalist headcases, back to their old tricks.'

'If the shoe fits …'

'It's three decades since the last war in Ireland,' he said sadly. 'Do you really think we'll fight the next one with bombs and bullets? The world has moved on, DI Fallon. In the event of any move to a united Ireland, I've tools to deploy that will take the Irish state back to the stone age, with never a shot fired. People like you would be well-minded remembering that.'

Fallon swallowed but said nothing.

'All clear, boss,' said a voice to her far left, and instantly, she was propelled to her feet by the men sitting on either side of her. The van door opened, and she was bodily lifted back out onto the tarmac.

Behind her, the educated voice whispered in her ear. 'Two last things. Firstly, when you hear the van doors close, do not move, and do not remove the hood for one full minute. Your failure to comply will result in … life-changing injuries.'

Fallon nodded.

The voice leaned in so close she could feel his breath tickling her ear. 'In a second, I'm going to tell you who ordered those guns. And after today, if our paths cross again, DI Fallon, I'll expect you to remember you're now in my debt.'

DS Martin stood uncomfortably, waiting for the forensics team to arrive. Kearney hadn't relaxed since Fallon left to sort the paperwork, and now the trapped skipper paced the wheelhouse throwing barbed glances at his guard. If Martin had been a betting man, he'd have wagered a confrontation wasn't far away. Unbuttoning his jacket and spreading the two sides apart to reveal the butt of his revolver, snug in its holster, he reminded Kearney that only one of them was armed.

He almost jumped out of his skin when DI Fallon stepped halfway through the wheelhouse door and tugged his sleeve. 'Let's go.'

Martin gave his head a little shake. 'What about forensics?'

'I've scrubbed that. We've got other fish to fry.' She turned to Kearny. 'Did you like that? I'm on a trawler and I'm really stressed, but I still managed to make a joke about fish.'

Kearny didn't respond, not even when Fallon nodded in his direction. 'Be good. You know we'll be watching.' She paused. 'And for what it's worth, tell your kiddie I'm sorry about what happened to her.'

DS Martin followed her out of the vessel and trotted to catch up as she strode back towards her car. 'What's happening, boss?'

'I just had intelligence to alert me to a credible threat to Iain Lynch's life, so you're going to Belfast to make sure no one blows his brains out.'

'And what about you?'

'Another piece of intelligence. I haven't validated it yet, so I'm off to Scotland to turn over some damp stones.'

Chapter 42

Trapped in the rock and too tired for emotion, Gill's sobs passed quickly, and in his exhausted state he drifted off to sleep. Dreams came, and in them he saw another archaeologist, many centuries from now, discovering his plastic-coated remains entombed in the rock. Ironically, because dreams are often ironic, he knew the future scientist had researched the records and found an old myth about a magazine editor who'd gone hunting for fairies and lost himself in the Clanyard caves. In the last scene in this perfectly choreographed dream, Gill took the perspective of someone standing by a glass case containing his own blackened bones. It was disappointing, he thought, to have gone to so much trouble, yet ending up in the back room of a regional museum, with water, dripping, dripping, dripping from the ceiling.

Gill awoke, startled, in the confined space, feeling real water falling on his face. Forgetting where he was, he tried to sit up and banged his head on the rock. Recoiling into a foetal crouch, he fumbled for his torch. Spilling light into this tiny space reminded him of his hopeless situation. As panic threatened to engulf him again, he tried distracting himself by wondering how history would actually remember him. But he quickly realised, he didn't care. The only opinions that were dear to him were those in the here and now. His friends and colleagues, his wife and son. Anger growled in his throat, and he resolved not to die in this place as some inconsequential footnote to history. He was an *armour-bearer* and there had to be more to his living and dying that this. What had Solomon said? Choose to wear the armour every day? At the start of this dangerous new day, Gill resolved to do just that; mentally dressing himself and speaking out the promises *The Book* declared over his life. And as his conviction grew, he felt the breastplate manifesting across his chest, around his sides and over his back, the rocks around him splintering as the armour demanded space to expand. His feet too became invigorated, gripped by the crystal armour and rejuvenated to push him forward in the confined space. As his face brushed painfully against a rock, the helmet manifested, crushing the obstacle. With fresh energy and renewed determination to make it home, Gill started to push forward again. An iron man, sheathed in supernatural metal.

After twenty minutes of sustained effort, he squeezed upwards through another five metres of impossible rock and found the cavity beginning to widen. Finally, somewhere ahead of him, hope shone in the darkness.

Up ahead, a long way distant, a pinprick of light punctured the black cavern. Or at least, he thought it was light. Perhaps through the remains of his dream, he was imagining it. His torchlight perhaps, being refracted back into his eyes in one last cruel twist of physics. But it was something to shoot for and it meant pressing forward, which he did now, pushing with his toes, dragging with his fingertips. Experiencing anger boiling in one side of his brain while panic clawed at the other, he channelled both into a last all-or-nothing explosion of energy that would either set him free or entomb him forever beneath forty metres of solid rock.

The channel was faintly uphill, and as it suddenly widened Gill glimpsed the flat surface of a pool. This was the source of the water that had gradually been filling his suit. But the armour had faded again, and his protective clothing was cut to ribbons by the journey. No matter – the light still shone. He was just surveying the pool when his hand torch flickered a few times, then went out. He shouldered his arms free of the rock tube's cold embrace and used this new flexibility to shake the torch, tap it, open it up and try jiggling the batteries. But it was no good. It was dead.

He had one last source of light, though how long it would last was uncertain. Switching his head torch back on, he was at least able to illuminate his immediate vicinity. The water in the pool seemed clear but of almost infinite depth. Already soaked to the skin, Gill pushed aside any misgivings because it wasn't as if he had any choice other than to launch out into the water. Fortunately, his ragged suit still had neutral buoyancy, so he was able to gently kick and splash himself into forward motion. And this he did, for several minutes. When he arrived at the far side, he was dismayed to find the opposing wall was not only smooth but that it was perceptibly concave so that now it arched above him. It was as if he'd swum up the spout of a gigantic teapot and slithered into the tepid remains of the tea. Now he was on the other side with nothing to grip.

'You have got to be kidding me,' he yelled into the darkness.

Like a trapped bug, he wearily began to swim around the edge of the bowl. First one direction, then the other until he was almost back at his entry point. But finally, he found a ledge of sorts he could crawl onto, and another beyond that. He heaved himself up until he was clear of the water and looked about him. The distant light was still visible. Closer now, but barely a pinhole twinkling in the dark. Dragging himself back onto his feet, he used his emergency knife to cut away the remains of his suit. Then, using the fading beam from his head torch, Gill wearily picked his way towards his goal.

When he was almost upon it, the light disappeared.

'I was beginning to worry about you,' said a familiar voice.

Suddenly overcome by excruciating tiredness, Gill almost dropped to his knees. 'Could've used your help two hours ago, and a hundred times since.'

'I brought the light,' said Raphael. 'The proof that if you just kept going …'

'Talking of light,' said Gill, cutting across him.

'Sorry. I forget humans can't see in the dark. My apologies.' There was a click, and Raphael promptly illuminated the area around them using a torch that looked remarkably like the one Gill had abandoned in the pool.

Gill stretched his arms towards Raphael and stumbled into an untidy embrace. Resting his head just below the angel's chin Gill stood like that for several long minutes. 'That was the shittiest moment of my whole damn life,' he mumbled.

'Nonsense,' said Raphael, clumsily stroking the back of Gill's head. 'It's good practise for you.'

'Please tell me you're joking,' Gill groaned.

Raphael gripped Gill's shoulders and pushed him away. 'Your courage. Your tenacity. Your ability to follow the smallest clues. The odds of the Armour Group surviving to see another Christmas are improving all the time.'

'Surviving?'

'You're a worthy *Sword-Bearer*, Gill McArdle.'

Gill dragged his right hand across his face to wipe off the residue he'd accumulated during his escape. 'Too many questions, Raphael, and not enough time. There's an injured man back there and I need to alert his team.'

'Good. I'll walk with you.'

'How long have I been in here?'

'Twelve hours. It's a lovely day outside, though it's to rain later. Now, which way are we walking?'

Gill's shoulders sagged. 'I kinda hoped you would help with that bit.'

'Use your senses, Gill.'

Gill nodded, and weary to his bones, he closed his eyes. Letting his senses heighten, he realised he could smell seawater. And far, far away, he could hear the cry of gulls.

Gill tried to pinpoint the sound of the birds. 'It's this way.'

Raphael nodded and they started walking. 'You took an age coming up that tube.'

Gill pressed his cold hands under his armpits. 'No offence, but you seem off your game today.'

'We are busy,' said the angel. 'Very, very busy. And as we're close to the end now, I will take my leave and attend to others who need my assurance.'

'The earth tremors,' remembered Gill.

'Exactly,' Raphael confirmed. 'People are scared.'

'Tell me about it,' moaned Gill. 'But thank you for the light. And the man hug ...' But somewhere mid-sentence he blinked, and Raphael was gone. In his place was the faint glimmer of daylight. Gill realised the sea cave must have run parallel to the shore. Given its twists and turns; he may not be more than a few hundred metres north of his original position. Would he emerge into a rockpool, to be dashed with towering waves? Or would he step onto a ledge twenty metres above the water alongside nesting gulls? Honestly, he wasn't that bothered. Compared to what he'd just been through, he'd handle it.

In the event, Gill emerged just a few metres above the waterline. 'I can see you,' shouted Donnie breathlessly. 'I have a fix on your position.'

Thanks to Murray's tip, Gill's phone had survived the soakings and beatings that now ravaged his body. He called Donnie first, alerting him to his likely position. Donnie had been on the high cliff path, working with Joey to find another route into the collapsed cave.

'Excellent,' said Gill. 'Don't suppose you could borrow a boat?'

'Sure. We have an emergency rib we can inflate. Hold tight. Be with you in twenty minutes.'

Gill hung up and found himself a comfortable place to sit until help arrived. Checking he still had battery and reception, he leaned back against the rock and dialled Salina.

One hour after calling Donnie, and finally free of his wet clothes, Gill sat draped in towels while he sipped tea from a flask and basked in the late afternoon sunshine. In the distance, he could see Donnie and Joey securing their tiny rib close to the ledge that had been Gill's escape route. After a flurry of activity, they were on their way to rescue Murray McGovern. Gill's responsibility was to act as their safety guy. Beside him was the rock radio he'd use to receive their hourly calls until all three were out of the cavern.

Under intense questioning, Gill had recounted his journey from *Delta* cavern and through the watercourses until he'd emerged from another sea cave two hundred metres up the shore. He'd spoken in grave tones about the perils the men would face, and how tight the passages would be. And while Joey wasn't exactly dismissive, he explained that it wasn't something they hadn't already done "like, a thousand times before."

Seeing Gill's stung expression, Donnie had conceded that finding the route on his own and without experience had been little short of miraculous. Their journey in and out would take twelve hours. It would be physically taxing but wouldn't hold particular terror as Gill had already demonstrated the route was feasible. Assessing the obstacles, they'd prepared the gear they would need to haul their boss through the confined spaces and out to safety. They were just about to set off when Donnie turned and asked. 'When you decided to leave the main east-west watercourse and clamber up to that narrow gap, what made you do that?'

'Tap on the shoulder from my guardian angel,' Gill had fired back.

'You're the first person to find that route,' Donnie remarked while he fired up the engine. 'That means you get to name it.'

Gill had thought for a second. 'The eye of the needle,' he'd announced. With a nod of acknowledgment, the men left, giving Gill twelve hours to wait and recuperate.

His phone rang, shaking him out of his reverie. It was Salina.

'Sorry I missed your call,' she said. 'You doing okay?'

'Got delayed exiting the cave. Had to manage a workaround.'

'But you're alright?'

'Brief chat with Raphael at the midway point, but yes, I'm sitting on a beach in brilliant sunshine. How are you?'

'We're okay. Did you hear about the Great Glen?'

'Just the mention of the tremors. And of course, we felt it underground. What's happening?'

'There are a few old buildings down. Especially in West Coast towns. The government has shut the A9 to reserve it for emergency vehicles. Dundee seems fine though the power went off a couple of times and the internet is up and down.'

'Josh alright?'

'Oblivious to danger. Just like his father.'

Gill laughed, knowing he wasn't immune to terror. 'Listen, we're delayed here today. I'm gonna stay off the roads and crash at my B&B tonight. All being well, I'll be with you both by lunchtime tomorrow.'

Chapter 43

Lillico rushed to collect Fallon off the 2 pm ferry in Cairnryan on that Friday afternoon. Traffic coming off the ferry was light as the Scottish Government had banned all non-essential travel. A slew of emergency vehicles emerged from the ship and joined the long road winding north. While Lillico waited for the sole foot passenger, he spotted Fallon, dashing through security. They jumped in his car and drove under blue lights the short distance to Stranraer. Waiting for them were the three local Wigtownshire officers, plus Chief Superintendent Macfarlane, attending the meeting via a video link.

While the senior officer shuffled notes and settled in his chair, Fallon jerked a thumb over her shoulder towards the cells. 'What happened to our armed officers?'

PC Hart looked at PC Laferty and sullenly folded her arms.

The Chief Super evidently overheard Fallon. 'You might not have noticed while you were back in Ireland, DI Fallon, but we've had a few local difficulties over here.'

'The earth tremors,' observed Fallon.

'So, I've redeployed those officers. And the question that really needs answering is why the hell DI Lillico hasn't arranged for the weapons' transfer to Edinburgh?'

'Keeping them handy for further forensics,' said Lillico.

'My arse,' bellowed Macfarlane. 'I'm overruling you, Detective. I've dispatched a team. They should be with you in an hour. Give them full cooperation while they remove the weapons to a safe store.'

'I understand, sir.'

'I hope you do, because it's my experience you're not a team player, Detective. Fix that attitude if you don't want to find yourself at the wrong end of a disciplinary notice.'

'Sir, I just feel …'

But Macfarlane wasn't finished. 'And DI Fallon. As you're on hand, please update us on the gun cache investigation.'

Briefly, Fallon recounted her team's arrest of Iain Lynch and the compelling evidence that the *Argonaut* had transported the guns.

'And this fellow, Lynch. He's the smoking gun that links the weapons cache to Loyalist terrorists?'

'That's the way it looks on paper, sir.'

'Very well. In which case, I think Police Scotland has done all it can on this enquiry. I'm going to pass it over to the PSNI and let you Ulster lads and lassies take it from here.'

'I'm sure we'll be delighted,' Fallon said evenly.

Macfarlane nodded once and broke the connection without another word.

Fallon turned to Lillico. 'He doesn't like me, which is fine, but he REALLY dislikes you.'

Lillico shrugged. 'A couple of years back, he and I crossed swords on a matter of ethics.'

'Which leads me to my next question.' Fallon jerked her head towards the cell where the weapons lay unguarded. 'You planning to let his people take them?'

Lillico found himself trapped in a moment of indecision. 'DCI Wiley is the one who's been cagey about sending them to Edinburgh. But Macfarlane has issued a direct order and I've no solid basis to disobey.'

Fallon shook her head. 'Actually, I think DCI Wiley might be right.'

'You're the person who's been twitchy about keeping the guns in Stranraer,' observed DS Dewar.

'We've had this all wrong from the start,' said Fallon. 'Lynch's historic links to Loyalist terrorists, the location of the gun stash and the identity of the final customer. We … sorry … I, looked for the easy answer and like the stupid eejit that I am, I took their bait.'

'All the evidence points to Ulster-based terrorists,' said Dewar. 'You said so yourself.'

Fallon shook her head. 'Before I left Kilkeel this morning, I was briefly detained by an active terrorist cell. Their reason for apprehending me was to deplore Lynch's gun-running endeavours and to give me a solid lead on the actual customer, here in Scotland.'

'You know who's ordered the guns?' asked Dewar.

'Not the end client, but certainly the name of his quartermaster.'

Dewar reddened with frustration. 'Damnit, DI Fallon. Who?'

'The man who ordered and paid for them was Billy Whyte,' said Fallon, matter of factly.

'Whyte is an Ulster Loyalist?' barked Dewar.

'That's the way it's meant to look,' said Fallon. 'But those guns were destined for a Scottish terror group, and they still might end up there if we don't secure them.'

'Whyte is in custody in Aberdeen on other charges,' said Lillico. 'Even if he was receiving the guns, he's out of the game.'

Fallon shook her head. 'Which means nothing because there'll be other players. People who Whyte could call on in the event the guns were captured.'

The room was silent for a few moments until Fallon pointed at Lillico. 'You're the only one who doesn't seem surprised by this.'

'I'm thinking, that's all.' Lillico fiddled with his phone. 'DCI Wiley has alluded to strange goings on in Edinburgh. You okay if I run this past him?'

'Can you trust your boss?'

'He's been reluctant to see the weapons transferred to the central belt. He's concerned they'll fall into the wrong hands.'

Fallon nodded. 'I'm starting to agree with him. Let's see what he has to say about Macfarlane's orders.'

Lillico nodded and made the call.

'What?' barked Wiley a few seconds later.

'I'm with DI Fallon. She's back from Ireland with credible evidence the guns weren't going to Ireland. That in fact, they were for Scottish terrorists.'

Wiley chewed on this for a few moments. 'Ah, that's not good news.'

'Thing is, boss. Chief Super Macfarlane pulled your armed response team. He's sending his own guys to take the cache.'

To Lillico's surprise, Wiley cackled happily. 'There were rumours, and now you've forced his hand, Alex. He's out in the open. Well done, lad.'

'Rumours, boss?'

'A senior officer, tapping colleagues on the shoulder. Sounding them out on aggressive support for independence.'

'What are you implying, George?'

'No time to explain. We'll get our heads together on Fallon's evidence at our first opportunity, but right now, you have one priority. Under no circumstances are you to let Macfarlane's men take those guns.'

'They're coming here, George. Macfarlane thinks they'll be with us in an hour.'

'Then improvise, Alex. Throw them in the sea if you have to.'

'Okay. I'll secure the weapons, but then you and I really need to talk.'

Lillico hung up and relayed the conversation to Fallon and the others.

Fallon dropped her hands to her sides. 'A senior officer, collaborating with terrorists?'

Lillico glanced at Fallon. 'He obviously suspects DSI Macfarlane.'

'This feckin' country is starting to feel more and more like home. And worst of all, we don't know who we can trust,'

'At the moment, no, we don't.'

'Meaning the guns might yet fall into the hands of terrorist forces.'

Lillico folded his arms. 'We can't let that happen. Not until we know for sure.'

'We can't protect them here,' snapped Fallon. 'Macfarlane's team are armed and potentially hostile.'

'Agreed,' said Lillico. 'Anyone got any ideas?'

PCs Hart and Lafferty shook their heads, but DS Dewar was running his fingers through his stubble while he formed a thought. 'Years ago, before I was a copper, I used to work in the now defunct *British Linen Bank*. But when it closed, it lay empty for a few years before it became a hotel.' He nodded while he remembered. 'They called it, *The Old Bank Hotel*, which makes sense I suppose.'

'God, give me strength,' whispered Fallon.

'Thing is, it still has its vault. The thing is massive. It was too heavy to shift without demolishing the building.'

'And you're thinking we could stash the guns there?' asked Lillico.

Dewar shrugged. 'I know the owner. Assuming I get hold of him, I'm sure he'd loan me the keys.'

Fallon made a show of looking at her watch. 'Whatever we're going to do, we need to do it quickly.'

Chapter 44

When Donnie and Joey reappeared with Murray, the dusky July sun had surrendered to a weather-front driving mist in from the sea. Dressed in dry clothes and wrapped in a blanket, Gill fended off the evening chill while the small rib motored up to the shore.

'How're you doing?' he asked Murray, catching a rope from the boat and pulling it onto the sand.

'Pretty sore, but I'll live.' He paused to give Gill a grateful nod. 'Thanks to you.'

'You're the real hero, boss,' said Joey. 'Keepin' it together in there. You're a proper pro.'

'We've put a splint on his ankle,' explained Donnie. 'He can walk if someone helps him keep his weight off it.'

'We'll have to do the hospital run ourselves,' observed Gill. 'I spoke to a dispatcher and the ambulance service is on standby for Highland call-outs.'

'Aye, and we've encountered something else.' Donnie nodded at his brother. 'Show him.'

Joey beckoned Gill forward and pointed at two long grey cases on the deck. 'We found guns in that cave of yours.'

Gill looked up at Joey's face. 'What cave?'

'The last one before you come out into the daylight.'

'But I was through there. I didn't see any guns.'

'You were exhausted, pal. Probably stepped right over them.'

'They're just like the last lot,' said Murray. 'We need to get them to the police.'

'Leave them, Murray,' urged Gill. 'I can call DI Lillico, and he'll collect them.'

'With all that's going on, it could be days before the cops come down here and there's no way I'm leaving a crate of M16s lying on a beach,' barked Donnie. 'We need to put them with the others.' He glanced at Gill. 'Stranraer police station, right?'

'Aye, but let me take care of that. It might save a few awkward questions at the other end.'

Donnie and Joey looked at each other for a few seconds before Donnie nodded. 'Makes sense.' They stood aside and watched as Gill made the call.

'Alex, sorry for phoning so late, but we've found another small arms cache.' Gill was silent for a few seconds while he listened to Lillico's response. 'Maybe you could send a vehicle?'

Gill stared at Donnie while he processed Lillico's response. 'No? Can I bring them to you? For obvious reasons, we don't want to leave them lying around.'

Gill screwed up his face. 'You're where?'

He shrugged. 'Okay, well whatever the big secret is, I need to drop the guns with you tonight while the boys take Murray to hospital.'

Gill worked for a moment to shorten a very long story. 'Yeah, he took a knock during the tremors. He was trapped for almost thirty hours, and we've just evacuated him.'

'Okay. We're moving now. I should be with you in an hour.'

'That you off to Stranraer?' asked Donnie, after Gill hung up.

'No. A secure unit in a different town. Apparently, it's got a big safe.'

'Oh, aye. Whereabouts?'

'It's a secret, apparently. I've to drive east in the A75 and he'll tell me when I'm closer.'

'Right,' said Donnie, after the merest pause. 'Gill. Can you help Murray up the hill to our truck? Joey and I will lug the gun cases, then we can all go our separate ways.'

The three men helped Murray to his feet and positioned him so that he could lean against Gill. That way, with the help of an improvised crutch, he could keep the weight off his damaged leg. Immediately it was slow going, with Murray leaning hard on Gill's right arm while he dragged himself through each painful step. For their part, Donnie and Joey each snatched a gun case and moved with comparative ease up towards the cars. As Gill watched them stride ahead, he noticed something in their posture he didn't expect to see. Instead of two men, wearied to their bones by a difficult cave rescue, they were marching with new-found energy. Ignoring Murray's grunts and gasps, he asked Aura to show him what needed to be seen, and in that moment, she reminded him of the first occasion he'd set foot in the cave.

'I hadn't realised you were aware,' Gill said in a conversational tone.

'Of what?' gasped Murray, as they staggered up the gradient towards the cars.

'The gun cache. DI Lillico was very confidential about it. But you guys seem to know the make and everything.'

'Ach, one of the forensics girls was a bit of a chatterbox. Told us all about it when her boss's back was turned.'

Gill had only met the forensics people briefly, and they'd worn face masks and paper suits, but he was pretty certain they'd both been men.

'Oh, aye. Was that Abigail or Ruth you were talking to?'

'Had their faces covered,' groaned Murray.

'Abigail was Asian and Ruth was black.'

Murray sounded exasperated. 'Why does it matter?'

'I'm curious. It's what makes me a good journalist.'

'Okay. The Asian kid, so it must have been Abigail.'

'Another thing that's bothering me,' said Gill, easing Murray to sit down on a boulder so they could both rest. 'Why would there be a second cache of guns in such an inaccessible cave? I mean, now you've seen it for yourself, I'm sure you'd agree that would be incredibly impractical.'

'Maybe they tried there first then found a better spot down in Clanyard Bay.'

Gill shook his head. 'They'd have done their research. No one would smuggle guns ashore without having a clear plan.'

'Honestly, Gill. Let's just leave it for the authorities.'

Gill opened his mouth to respond but the roar of a large engine and big tyres rucking in gravel interrupted him. He leapt up to see the source of the noise. 'Murray, why have the lads driven away in your truck?'

He heard a grunt behind him, but before Gill could turn around, Murray's good leg swung hard against Gill's calves and sent him crashing onto his back. The world went black for a second and when Gill's senses returned, Murray was rummaging through his pockets. Finding Gill's phone, the man hurled it away into the long grasses. Then Murray fished out his own phone and called a number he had on speed dial.

'Boss?' came Donnie's voice over the phone's speaker. In the background was the sound of a big diesel engine being pushed to its limits. 'What's up?'

'McArdle's on to us,' said Murray. 'I've bought you a couple of hours, but you need to get this done.'

'I hear you.'

Murray grunted in pain and took a second to take pressure off his left leg. 'Any word on where the cops moved the guns?'

'Macfarlane's mole came good. She's distracting her colleague while the remaining three officers shift the gear to *The Old Bank Hotel* in Wigtown.'

'Excellent. It's down to you guys now.'

Donnie left a pause. 'What about you?'

Murray glanced back at Gill. 'I can look after myself.' Then he hung up, and after a few seconds consideration, he flung his own phone far away into the undergrowth.

Still sprawled on the ground with his head and shoulders aching, Gill struggled onto his side to gape at the man. 'I busted my arse to get you rescued.'

Murray looked tired and sore. 'This cause is bigger than my life or yours.'

'No way I'm letting you take the guns.'

Murray shook his head. 'You're too late.'

Gill rolled over and started to clamber to his feet, but Murray's right hand flew out and clasped Gill's ankle, jerking him to the ground. Gill struck back at him and Murray yelped in pain. Kicking wildly, Gill fought to free his leg, but Murray's vice-like grip started to haul Gill towards him. Panicking about what Murray would do to him once his body was in range of his opponent's fists, Gill quickly ran out of options. In that instant, the crystal armour suddenly manifested, covering Gill's feet and ankles. For a few short seconds, both men fell into shocked immobility.

'Got a message for you,' gasped Gill.

'Oh, yeah?' jeered Murray, starting to pull Gill towards him again. 'What's that?'

With one powerful blow, Gill's armoured boot crashed against Murray's face, sending him sprawling backwards. Gill struggled onto his feet, terrified he might have killed the man and hobbled over to confirm his opponent was bloodied but breathing. He'd deal with Murray later. First, he needed to reach Lillico.

Leaving Murray, Gill scrambled up the track and arrived at his car, his shoulders sagging when he saw that all four tyres had been slashed. With no phone and no vehicle, how would he warn Lillico of the imminent threat? There was a farmhouse nearby and he could reach if he ran for ten minutes, but it was a risk to assume he'd raise the occupants at this late hour. He took the half-dozen steps back to the cliff top while he pleaded with Aura for help. Would she alert Solomon to reach out to Lillico? Or perhaps Ailsa or Adina would receive a sudden awareness of danger? As he stared down at Murray, the man began to stir, and far below him in the grass, a mobile phone screen suddenly illuminated. Keeping his eyes on the device, Gill hobbled towards the light. It was his own, the screen cracked, but with a message from Salina asking if he'd reached his B&B. He'd respond to her in just a moment. First, there was somebody else he needed to call.

Chapter 45

Lillico and his small team were stretched to breaking point. As soon as PCs Hart and Lafferty finished loading the van in Stranraer, they were summoned away on another emergency, leaving Lillico, Dewar and Fallon to drive to Wigtown and transfer the weapons inside *The Old Bank Hotel*. With Fallon insisting that only she was equipped to guard the van, it took Lillico and Dewar twenty-five trips between the van and the vault to shift the weapons, and another nine to carry the ammunition.

'I'm fit for a heart attack,' moaned Dewar while he leaned against the door of the vault, sweat pouring from his face.

'All the same, this was a good idea,' said Lillico, nodding at the vault. 'Can we lock it?'

Dewar nodded and held up an ancient metal key as long as his hand. 'I'll check it now.'

'Great. If you get a second, can you clean down a rifle each for you and me?'

Dewar nodded wearily. 'What happens next?'

Lillico patted his jacket, feeling for his phone. 'I'm off out to my car. And if I can get hold of him, I'm going to push my boss for clarity.'

'That's the van all locked up,' said Fallon, striding into the vault and passing keys to Dewar.

'Great. Make yourself at home. I'll be back in a second.'

Urging his tired body to more action, Lillico jogged through the old bank and out to his car. Dropping heavily onto the driver's seat, he reached across to the glove compartment and pulled out his phone. Settling in for as long as it would take, he caught Wiley on the fourth attempt.

'Did you move the guns?' barked Wiley, dispensing with any formalities.

'Moved to a secure location, just down the road in a place called …'

'Don't tell me,' Wiley cut in. 'I'd like plausible deniability on this.'

'I've come back to my car to find fifteen missed calls from the Chief Super, George. So, I'm glad for your sake you're keeping out of it because it feels like I'm making a career-ending move here.'

'Relax, Alex. I'm going to take responsibility for this. In the meantime, all you need to know is you're doing the right thing.'

'Am I? Disobeying a direct order from the most senior officer in our chain of command?'

'The key thing for you to understand is that those guns can't reach Edinburgh.'

'George, what is going on?'

'You've been busy on a case, I get that, but do you ever listen to the news?'

'Honestly, boss? I'm just not getting that kind of downtime.'

'These latest rumbles have created lots of anxiety on both sides of the Great Glen. Allegations being bandied around accusing the Holyrood government of knowing more about the earthquake risk in the region than it's letting on.

Consequently, Scotland's First Minister lost a vote of confidence this afternoon and has resigned. It's hard to tell what's going to happen next, but if the forecasts are right, Rodderick Canmore, MSP, will be our First Minister by this time tomorrow.'

'That's politics, boss. It doesn't affect us.'

'Thing is, it does, Alex. There's a lot of weird shit going on and I find myself looking around Police Scotland and wondering who the hell I can trust.'

'And is that a feeling in your water, sir, or do you have some solid evidence?'

Wiley released a ragged breath. 'There's confusion, Alex. Especially about your Wigtownshire gun cache. One senior officer gives an order then someone more senior countermands it. I'm hearing rumours of shouting matches in the oak-panelled offices of this organisation.'

'Is this all because of pressure on resources created by the tremors?'

'That's where it started, but now it's way more than that.' He paused. 'This is more than your regular day-to-day bureaucracy or incompetence. But let's leave that for a second. Have you identified the route the smugglers used?'

'The rifles were bought on the black market by a former quartermaster for Ulster Loyalists. He took delivery in the mid-Atlantic by switching the weapons from a South African trawler to one owned by a Loyalist sympathiser. They delivered the cache to Wigtownshire, with the main buyer keeping an eye on the cargo.'

'You didn't see the handover to the Scottish client?'

'No, but we observed an operative in the area, associated with Roddy Canmore. So, it appears the handover was only hours or days away.'

'Canmore?' Wiley sounded startled. 'Can you prove that connection?'

'Not conclusively, and Billy Whyte refused to cooperate the first time I interviewed him. But a few days later, the eejit managed to get caught during the attempted abduction of Lorna Cheyne. Remember her?'

'The amazing disappearing woman? I thought she was locked away at His Majesty's pleasure?'

'Released four weeks ago.'

'And does she have a role in this gun thing?'

'None. During her safe-cracking days, Canmore was one of her victims. Maybe he's just trying to settle old scores.'

'Don't go writing that in a report,' Wiley grumbled. 'Not unless you have incontrovertible proof.'

'Suffice to say, Billy Whyte is in custody and he's going nowhere. I've enough evidence to secure his conviction for the Cheyne attack and Billy must be fretting that one of these days, Canmore might start seeing him as a loose end.'

Wiley shook his head. 'If Canmore is driving this, he's taking some big risks.'

'Can I ask, boss, is Canmore the big case you're working on?'

Wiley chewed on that question for a second. 'Not directly, but now you have me wondering. In the meantime, the only thing I need from you, Detective, is to keep those guns away from Edinburgh. Don't let another police unit take them from you without my approval.'

'Okay.'

'That's all I want to say for now.' Wiley muttered. 'Keep a lid on things there. I'll be in touch as soon as there's news.'

The call rang off and Lillico swore lightly under his breath. They'd be sitting on their hands in Wigtown until Wiley got this figured out. He reached for his door handle but froze when he felt a puff of air against his left cheek. Whipping his head around, he found Lorna, sitting motionless in his passenger seat.

'Hi, Alex,' she said, with a shy little wave.

He blinked twice at her. 'Is this a social call or …'

Lorna swallowed. 'Gill phoned. He says he's stuck at the caves and urgently needs you to know that militants are about to attack *The Old Bank*.'

'Attacked? By whom?'

'The cave team, Murray and his lads. They want to recover the guns for Canmore's people. They'll be in Wigtown in a few minutes.'

'What? Murray?'

'Yes. Gill said they attacked him, but to tell you he's okay.'

'And you decided to bring this news in person?'

Lorna flicked her shoulders. 'Your number's been engaged for the last half hour.'

He studied her expression and found an urgent honesty in her eyes. 'Thank you for coming. That was very kind.'

'It's this new armour,' she murmured. 'I feel compelled to do the right thing.'

'Okay. It helps that I know what Murray's crew look like.' He released a juddering breath and checked all his mirrors. 'Right, I need to tell the officers inside we've got trouble … wait, Lorna. Lie down.'

'What?'

'Murray's truck is coming from behind us. Drop lower so they don't see us.'

They both bent sideways, their faces pressed together in the confined space. Lillico took Lorna's free hand in his and they held each other's gaze while the big truck and its trailer lumbered slowly passed. When the immediate threat had receded, Lorma pulled his hand against her face.

'I like you, Alex.'

Lillico's eyes flashed to hers. 'I like you too.'

'But there's someone else. I can see the hesitation in your eyes.'

'There is,' he said, wrong-footed by this sudden intimacy. 'Though I'm not sure she feels the same about me.'

She smiled sadly and gently kissed his forehead. 'You should tell me about her. I'm sure she's nice.'

'We'll talk, Lorna. Right now, I've got to dash.'

'I understand. Take care, Alex.' And with that, Lorna jumped away.

Chapter 46

Lillico heard an urgent rapping sound against the driver's window. 'You lost a contact lens or something,' shouted Shona Fallon from outside the car. 'I thought you were calling Edinburgh?'

Lillico unwound himself from the empty space where Lorna had been and ran down the window. 'I did.'

'What did they say?'

Lillico shook his head and focused on the immediate threat. 'Murray McGovern's boys are coming for the guns. My boss says we've to stop them.'

Fallon shook her head. 'Who's coming?'

'Murray and his team; they were the sentries all along. As soon as guns were discovered, a senior officer inserted Murray as our cave specialist to look for a chance to recover the weapons. They know the guns are here and they passed this spot thirty seconds ago.'

'Right Lillico. Inside please. We need to make a plan.'

Lillico scrambled out of his car and followed Fallon into the building. She slammed the door behind them, locking it before turning right and marching down a long corridor into a faded room with high ceilings. The vault was accessed via a door in the rear wall where DS Dewar was testing an ancient steel key in an antique lock.

'When does our armed response unit get here?' Fallon demanded.

Lillico shook his head. 'DCI Wiley says DSI Macfarlane despatched a crew to Stranraer, but they'll probably be diverted here. But honestly, Shona, I can't say with any confidence which side they'll be on.'

'But Wiley's sending a crew, right?'

Lillico shook his head. 'There isn't enough time.'

Fallon's eyes blinked a couple of times before she pushed off her leaning post. 'Meaning we're facing overwhelming odds?'

Lillico swallowed. 'That about sums it up.'

Fallon nodded urgently at Dewar. 'Okay, then. We need to lock this and bail.'

Lillico wasn't quite sure he'd heard her right. 'You've been playing hardball since you got here, Shona. And now, when the people you came to catch turn their guns on you, suddenly it's time to run away?'

'At the end of the day, this is a job, DI Lillico. I signed up to fight crime, not die in the process.' She nodded anxiously at the bank safe, piled high with weaponry. 'We lock that room and throw away the key. That's all we can do.'

'Might be a problem with that,' muttered Dewar.

'What?'

'When I asked my pal if we could borrow his vault, I neglected to check if the damn thing still works.'

'Meaning,' gasped Fallon, 'we've shifted the guns over here for nothing?'

'As I recall,' wheezed Dewar as he twisted the old key with all his strength, 'it was Lillico and I who did the heavy lifting.'

'Either way, we leave now, while there's still time.'

Lillico strode into the safe and flipped open one of the boxes. 'You go if you want to. Personally, I'm guarding the guns.'

Fallon was still staring, caught between panic and terror, watching Lillico grapple with a rifle. 'It needs cleaned you idiot,' she barked. 'Go find me some old rags and I'll do it.'

'And I'll check for something I can spray to get this thing loosened up,' said Dewar.

Lillico dashed off and returned three minutes later with a fistful of cloth napkins. Fallon had already disassembled the weapon, and he watched her frantically wiping down the components. 'We don't have the manpower; we don't have the training …'

'Can't find anything,' Dewar reported.

'Shit,' whispered Fallon, dropping the reassembled rifle back on the stack and glancing into the down the long corridor that ran the length of the old building.

Lillico picked up the M16 that Fallon had just cleaned and slid a magazine into the breech. Then he held it aloft for DS Dewar, who after a moment's pause marched forward and took it. 'You know how to use this?'

Dewar shuddered. 'If it comes down to it, I think I'll remember pretty quick.'

'Okay. Take a position over the rear of the house and I'll watch the front.' He waited for Dewar to acknowledge the order and scuttle off. Then he turned to Fallon. 'What's it going to be, Shona? Are you going to run, fight, or hide?'

With a look of horror on her face, Fallon sank quietly to her knees. 'I can't do this, Alex. I'm sorry, but if you knew … I can't.'

At the same moment as Lorna was briefing Lillico outside *The Old Bank Hotel*, Joey drove slowly down Wigtown High Street while Donnie cast his eyes around the unfamiliar town.

'Pull over,' said Donnie. 'I want to study the street plan for a second.'

Joey pulled up beside the town's Mercat cross. 'Looks nice,' he said, glancing around the town centre's wide expanse where two rows of grey granite houses faced each other across a carefully tended green space. 'We should come back here sometime.'

'Head in the game, bro. Keep an eye out for cops.'

'Still, I could see myself living somewhere like this.'

'We're not house-hunting you moron.' He nodded at the road. 'Get moving again. Drive straight ahead then this road becomes Bank Street, then it's the last building on the right.'

'Edge of town,' murmured Joey, moving off again. 'Perfect.'

They drove carefully down the length of the High Street and passed a town hall that wouldn't have looked out of place in a mid-sized communist city, before joining a narrower street. This one was also lined with stone houses, albeit of a humbler design. Joey glanced right as they passed a formidable grey house that had once been a hotel. There was a car outside he'd maybe seen one of the officers drive, but really, he wasn't sure.

'Pull into the church car park. We'll cross the road and approach the property from the rear.'

'I hear you,' said Joey, before moving the vehicle discreetly down the street and parking up.

'Who're you texting?' asked Joey as Donnie's thumbs flew over his phone screen.

'Reinforcements,' he muttered. 'Just in case.'

Sliding the truck into a gravelled space in front of the church, they unhooked their trailer before Donnie pushed it as far out of sight as he could. Quickly, he and his brother pulled on dark jackets, balaclavas and thin gloves. Joey opened the gun case, taking a rifle for himself and another for his brother.

'These definitely the ones you cleaned?' asked Donnie.

'They wouldn't satisfy our old Lieutenant, but they'll get the job done.'

Donnie nodded and they both started filling their pockets with ammunition.

'Will that be enough?' asked Joey, reaching for a fifth magazine.

'Keep to the plan, bro. We get in there and gather the cops in one room. I'll keep them covered while you bring the truck round front. Then we use our hostages to load the trailer.' He tapped his forehead in Joey's direction. 'Got it?'

His brother signalled he understood and together, they moved off.

The persistent mizzle coming in off the sea added a sullen darkness to the unseasonably cold July evening. The long grass was wet, and Donnie began to wonder if they shouldn't just have banged on the front door. And that wasn't the only thing that was bothering him.

'For an improvised police station, it's bloody dark,' he hissed.

'Maybe they've left the guns and gone home,' Joey whispered.

'We can hope. Switching to night vision,' he said, pulling the light-enhancing goggles down over his eyes.

'Movement,' said Joey. 'First floor. The window on the left side is open.'

Donnie considered his actions. 'Okay. I see him. I'll flush him out and if necessary, you take the shot.'

After his brother clapped his back and moved to crouch beside a tree, Donnie broke cover and strode across the debris of an abandoned garden. Immediately, the figure at the window snapped to attention.

'Armed police. Drop your weapon,' shouted a voice from the house.

Donnie paused and slowly raised his hands. Stepping into a patch of ground thinly illuminated by some distant street lighting, he called up to the house. 'What's the problem, officer?'

'Drop the rifle,' shouted the male voice. 'Do it now.'

Donnie stopped walking and slowly raised his hands until a single shot from Joey found its mark and the figure behind the glass spun away.

With no other resistance being offered, Donnie charged forward. He'd spotted a weather-beaten wooden door and without hesitating he shouldered it. Moments later, Joey was beside him in the stripped remains of what must once have been the hotel kitchen. They paused to listen, but the only sound was the painful cries of the injured officer, somewhere in the house.

'Sorry,' said Joey, pointing at the keening sound above their heads. 'I just winged him.'

'Go shut him up,' Donnie instructed. 'And I'll find the safe.'

Chapter 47

In the moments before Donnie and Joey began their attack, DI Fallon was crouching in a corner avoiding Lillico's glare. 'I can't, Alex. I just can't.'

Instead of a blunt riposte, his hand fell gently upon her shoulder. 'It's okay, Shona. I get it. But if you're not in the fight, you need to hide.'

Fallon remembered the last time she'd hidden during a firefight, and now, they were coming for her again.

'My father …' she began, trailing off before the words she wanted came out.

'What about him?' asked Lillico, moving to one side to peek around the door frame.

'My father …' *and as the stress of the last few days exploded into panic, DI Shona Fallon found herself back into a moment three decades before. She was a probationary constable in Belfast, while her father was a Detective Sergeant. She still lived at home and when their shifts overlapped, they'd travel to work together, with her father coaching her in a strict safety discipline. 'Check your weapon. Check your car. Check your street for unfamiliar vehicles. Check for anything out of the ordinary.' And they'd done it every day, religiously. Until the day they were ambushed driving down the Crumlin Road in Ardoyne. In a terraced street intersected by multiple narrow lanes, a big white van had abruptly reversed out in front of them, causing her father to swerve and crash into the gates of Holy Cross Church. Behind them, another car swung around to block their exit, and gunmen appeared.*

'Three shooters,' yelled her father. 'M16s. Lie low, Shona.'

Under the crackle of gunfire, she'd stumbled from the car, crawling on hands and knees to take shelter behind a low wall. Beside her, using his car as a flimsy shield, her father returned fire. Using his Glock, he squeezed off single rounds and ducked for cover, dodging bursts springing from his attacker's semi-automatic weapons. And when there was a lull, he'd jump up and fire three, until the moment came when he emitted a single low grunt and stopped shooting.

Curled into a foetal position, she realised no one was shooting anymore, and in the distance, she could hear sirens. She was desperate to check on her father but didn't want to give away her location. That was until she heard footsteps crunching across the broken glass and pausing at the tumbled gates. The footsteps started again and seconds later she felt a gun barrel press against her temple.

'I got your daddy's gun,' said a masked figure. 'Now he doesn't need it anymore, shall we find out if he had any ammo left?'

Shona opened her eyes and turned to face the masked figure. She could see his eyes through the slit in his mask. Certain eyes. Hateful eyes. And she watched his right arm stiffen as he took the shot. The click of the gun revealed it to be empty, and the man sighed, before grabbing her jacket collar and yanking her into a kneeling posture.

'Don't know what saints you pray to, girl, but they're looking out for you today,' he whispered, with the stale smell of cheese and onion crisps on his breath. 'And I've got a message for you and all other good Catholic boys and girls who should be fighting for a united Ireland. Stay out of the RUC or be prepared to pay the price.'

Then he shook himself free of her and after a shout of warning from one of his accomplices, dashed to his vehicle.

'Are you listening to me?' Lillico's voice was urgent now. Crashing out of her remembered trauma, she discovered he was shaking her. 'Shona, I think you're going into shock.'

She peered up at him through wet eyes. 'My father …'

She didn't get to finish her sentence before a gunshot was followed by a scream of pain from a distant room and the tinkle of broken glass.

Lillico stooped and dragged her to her feet. 'Sounds like they got Archie. I need to help him so it's time for you to hide,' he shouted, before releasing her and turning again to peer down the corridor. He yanked another rifle off the stack and scrabbled on the left side for the safety catch.

Fallon watched him fumbling with the unfamiliar weapon and realised he was on the cusp of a fatal mistake. 'Wait, Lillico. You look like a kid trying to point a bazooka. If you're safer around revolvers, take mine.'

'No way I'm giving you a rifle in your condition.'

'I've been here before,' whispered Fallon. 'This time, I know what to do.'

'Are you sure?' he hissed, urgently.

'My head's in the game,' she said. 'Go help DS Dewar and I'll guard the guns.'

Lillico regarded the Glock she'd extracted from her holster and took it from her in exchange for the M16. In response to his worried look, she took a competent grasp on the weapon and started to strip it down.

'Be a good fella,' she said, with uncertain humour. 'Hold those bastards off while I get this feckin' thing cleaned down.'

Lillico nodded once then checked the corridor before darting off to assist the injured DS Dewar. All alone in the once grand room, she took a second to review the surroundings and chose the best defensive position. With that decision made, her hands flew around the weapon, stripping, cleaning, assembling; finding comfort in a tactile discipline that might just save her life.

'Love you, Dad,' she whispered, before taking a firm grip on the gun.

Once the shooting started, Donnie realised they'd need to move quickly. His time in the armed forces had been brief and he'd never fought for real. But he had played a tonne of video games and knew how to clear a building. It was simple - as you stepped towards a doorway, you started firing – releasing a spray of bullets before the guy on the other side even saw you coming. He knew he was making a racket, but on the other hand, God help anyone who came knocking to complain about the noise. He watched as the door frame of the next room shattered into splinters, knowing instinctively anyone on the other side would be dead or injured. Then he changed the magazine before moving forward again, repeating the process in the hotel's foyer, a storeroom and the reception area. By now, he was dominating a wide corridor that ran the length of the building, and which emptied into a large room that had presumably been the defunct bank's retail floor. Always moving forward, sending bursts of bullets into each approaching doorway, he knew that's where the vault would be. And finally, he entered the once grand room. An ornate tiled floor was complemented by high doorways and intricately carved coving around the ceiling. And in the far corner stood the safe. He grinned when he saw the door was wide open.

Behind him, he heard Joey shout in a distant part of the building, followed by a single shot. And he was beginning to wonder if the cop who'd challenged them was the only one in the building. He tiptoed over to the vault's doorway and sucked his breath. With just him and his brother, it would take dozens of trips to move the guns. They'd have to abandon the ammo as they had neither the time nor the space to shift it. Eyes fixed on the prize, Donnie stepped into the safe and laid a hand on the first stack of rifle boxes.

'Armed police,' said a shaky voice behind him. 'Stay exactly as you are, or I will open fire.'

Instinctively, Donnie's right hand flashed back from the stack to his rifle butt, and the copper behind him didn't shoot.

'I know what you're thinking,' said the woman's voice. 'If I turn fast enough, can I get a shot in before she does? And honestly, you need to make your own decision on that. But here's another thought for you. Those guns are as dirty as hell. That's why the thing is hot in your hands, and you can smell it too, like a car tyre burning on a Loyalist bonfire. So, you gotta ask yourself; even if you can take the shot, will that old gun still fire? Your choice, my friend, but if I were you, I'd toss it to one side, then kneel with your hands behind your head.'

Lillico's confrontation with Joey was short and bloody. Tracking the man's noisy footsteps through the upper storey, he'd discovered the shooter poised over the fallen figure of DS Dewar and preparing to take a kill shot. Technically, Lillico didn't need to shout a warning because he'd heard Dewar do that at the start of the conflict. Nor did he have time to moralise, or anguish over how this decision might impact him in the years to come. It was either Dewar, or

Joey, and the accuracy of Lillico's shot would underline the clarity of his thinking.

'Drop it,' said Lillico, knowing full well he couldn't shoot this man in cold blood.

Joey froze, glancing slowly to his right to assess the new threat. As he spun around, both men fired simultaneously. Lillico felt the kick of a bullet as his crystal helmet flashed around his head just as Joey staggered backwards and slumped to the floor. Lillico swallowed anxiously, trying to force saliva into his parched throat, then sprang to Dewar's side. The man was alive, but the shoulder-shattering injury meant he needed immediate medical attention. With one eye on the door, Lillico called his control centre and reported the injured officer. Assuring Dewar that help was on its way, Lillico made one last check on Joey before turning again for the gun safe. Frequent and sustained bursts of automatic gunfire made it sound like Fallon was fighting an army, and Lillico's skin ran cold when a minute later, the firing stopped.

Picking his way silently through the shattered building, he finally came to the safe. Donnie lay sprawled backwards over the guns, surveyed by Fallon, her face and clothes splattered with blood while she stared at the man she'd killed. Gently, Lillico put a hand on her shoulder. She flinched, then relaxed again when she saw his face.

'What I was trying to say when we were so rudely interrupted,' she began. 'Is that my father died serving a cause he believed in. I guess, when it's your time, I can think of worse ways to go.'

Gently, Lillico pulled her back, then closed the safe. 'We need to help DS Dewar. And when we've got him to safety, we need to figure out what to do with these guns.'

Chapter 48

Angus Macfarlane pushed back from his desk and walked over to the window. News was coming in thick and fast, and he needed to make a decision before the finger of suspicion moved irrevocably to him. The armed response team under his command had reached Stranraer and informed him the weapons cache had moved. A local PC Lafferty was less than helpful while he spun some yarn about their local sergeant helping the Northern Irish detective to move the rifles to a secret location. Then PC Hart, Macfarlane's local eyes and ears, had surreptitiously passed them a note, revealing where the guns had gone. From there, news came in sporadically from Murray's crew, arriving at Wigtown and approaching the derelict hotel. For a time, it looked like they'd be successful, and Macfarlane had redirected his armed response unit to assist in Wigtown. Over the next half hour, bulletins flashed across his screen as caller after caller reported a gun battle in *The Old Bank Hotel.* And when he heard nothing more from the scene on his private line, he had to assume Murray's crew had failed. By then his team was approaching the town, moving fast under blue lights. The quandary for Macfarlane was that his unit might come into conflict with another police team of unknown strength already dug in to defend the guns. And now his screen alerted him that yet another firearms unit under the command of a different DSI, was now enroute from Dumfries. Admitting defeat, he issued an order for his crew to return to base and prepared himself to make an uncomfortable phone call.

'DSI Macfarlane for Roddy Canmore,' he said, flatly, while he waited nervously for the receptionist to put him through.

'Angus,' said Canmore. 'Two seconds and I'll call you back.'

Macfarlane hung up and waited until an unfamiliar mobile number illuminated his screen. 'At this late moment in the evening, I can only assume you're calling about my missing parcel?' said Canmore's voice.

Macfarlane cleared his throat and prepared to play Canmore's little game. 'You can, sir. We made efforts to retrieve it, but it appears to have been lost in the system somewhere.'

Canmore's voice was calm and level. 'That is disappointing. It was my impression you had this under control.'

'There's a Detective Inspector Lillico seconded to the Southern Division. I'm afraid he's been less than cooperative.'

'I'm aware of him, Angus,' Canmore murmured. 'Though I can't be involved in police matters so I will leave any disciplinary matters to your discretion.'

'Leave him to me, sir. In the meantime, we must treat your parcel as lost.'

'Guessed as much. I did contact the supplier in Ireland to arrange an alternative delivery, but it appears he's gone out of business.'

'I'm sorry to hear that.'

'No matter. I'll investigate sourcing replacement product, straight from wholesaler.'

'And you'll employ a different courier?'

'Absolutely. I'm arranging that as we speak.'

'I hope, sir, this debacle won't count against me.'

'Not at all, Angus. I think on reflection the error was mine. I should have invited your logistical expertise a little earlier in the process. The machinations at Holyrood will keep me busy for the next few days. Let's get our heads together next week and we can make a rigorous plan for a future delivery.' Canmore paused. 'I'm concerned that in all the excitement, my very best operative may face criminal charges. Will there be any way you can help with that?'

Macfarlane cleared his throat. 'I think, sir, it would be best if you maintained your distance from Billy Whyte. The Fiscal in Aberdeen is very confident he can secure a conviction.'

'No, no. Whyte is utterly expendable. Murray McGovern is the man I'm concerned about.'

Macfarlane thought about this for a moment. 'His lads confirmed McGovern didn't attend the Wigtown raid due to an injury he suffered in the cave. That means the Fiscal mightn't have enough evidence to construct a charge.'

'Excellent. And Whyte? Where do you think he'll serve his time?'

'Barlinnie, sir.'

'Pity. It's a dangerous jail, Barlinnie,' said Canmore, thoughtfully. 'I believe that's where you sent the Drumchapel boys.'

'Indeed, sir.'

'Very good, Angus. I'll leave you to carry on.'

Macfarlane listened as the call dropped, and surmised it had gone as well as he'd hoped. But DI Lillico would know that his DSI had moved against him and that made him a threat. One way or another, he needed to take Lillico out of play.

Chapter 49

Murray was shocked awake when Gill tossed water in his face.

'Sorry,' said Gill. 'Needed to check you're still alive.'

Murray rubbed his bruised jaw. 'What the hell did you hit me with?'

Gill looked over the man's head and out to the ink-black sea. 'I've some martial arts training.'

Murray grunted. 'Doubted you had that in you.'

'How's your leg?'

'Sore as hell. If I don't get to hospital soon, I'm going to be in trouble.'

'Should've thought about that before you had your boys slash my tyres.'

Murray slumped back on the ground and let out a juddering sigh. 'Greater good and all that.'

'Greater good? You'd pursue Scottish independence with guns rather than the ballot box?'

Murry grunted painfully. 'Worked for most of the rest of the British colonies. It's time we got ourselves a backbone.'

'Does this have anything to do with Roddy Canmore?'

'When there isn't a good man to get the job done, you need a strong man to do a good job.'

'Even if it stokes violence?'

'Gotta buy ourselves out of this mess, McArdle. Once we're running our own affairs, we can sort this country out.'

'Honestly, is that what he said to you? Not that it matters. After this little stunt, you're going to prison for a long time.'

Murray laughed. 'You really think that?' He pointed at his damaged leg. 'By the time this has fully healed, I'll be a free man again, living in an independent country.'

'I don't get it,' protested Gill. 'Why the guns? It's not as if Canmore can shoot his way to independence. That doesn't work with the British government – look at Ireland.'

Murray started to snigger, before gasping as another wave of pain shot up his leg. 'Roddy is a little more strategic than our friends over the water.'

'Yeah, well. It won't be much of a show without his weapons.'

Murray dragged up his left arm and peered at his watch. 'My boys will have them away by now.'

Gill reached into his pocket and pulled out his phone and jiggled it in front of Murray. 'Don't think so. I managed to call for reinforcements.'

For the first time, Gill saw a glimmer of concern pass Murray's face. 'Any chance you could go to the farmhouse? See if you could get me some painkillers?'

Gill shook his head. 'I promised DI Lillico I'd keep an eye on you. So, we wait until he gets here.'

'How would I get away?' Murray sounded desperate now. 'Come on, man. Show a little compassion.'

Gill looked right back at him. 'Give me something to use against Canmore and you can have all the compassion I have to offer.'

Murray looked away and shuddered.

'Yeah,' said Gill. 'Thought so. But the offer's open until the blue flashing lights turn up.' He stopped to read a news page he'd opened on his phone. 'But I think we're still way down their list of priorities.'

Murray looked like he was about to complain some more, but Gill held up a hand when his phone started to ring. Seeing the caller, he took a few steps away from his wounded foe. 'Alex, glad to hear your voce. How are things?'

Gill listened soberly while Lillico reported on the confrontation with Murray's crew, and the injury to DS Dewar, who was now on his way to the local A&E. Once Lillico brought Gill up to speed, he asked if there was anything he could do to help.

'My most pressing problem is the guns,' said Lillico. 'Right now, there's a Dumfries-based unit guarding our perimeter but I'm very reluctant to hand them the weapons cache.'

'You can't move them?'

'We don't have a big enough vehicle, and honestly, within Police Scotland right now, I don't know who's on our side.'

Gill kicked at the turf while he grasped an idea that would address Lillico's logistical problem. 'Do you have the authority to move the stash?'

'Wiley does,' said Lillico nervously. 'Until Macfarlane or one of Canmore's other lackeys countermands him.'

'Could we transfer the guns to a civilian vehicle?'

Lillico paused. 'What are you proposing, Gill?'

'Okay. She won't like it, but I think I know who can help.'

'This is completely out of order,' muttered Fiona as she and Gill hoisted another pair of rifle boxes between them. It was early Saturday morning, and the July sun had already been battling through last night's clouds for hours.

Gill nodded a cheerful 'Hello' to a pair of startled birdwatchers who stepped out of his way as they dragged their umpteenth load from the back of Fiona's van. 'Needs must,' he grunted.

'First, you've made me a defacto gun runner in whatever the hell you and Lillico were doing in Wigtown, and now you're making me pollute this gorgeous coastline.'

'Humanity has dumped a lot of metal in the sea, Fiona. In this case, when you think about the alternatives, I think we're justified.'

They dropped the boxes on the quayside of Wigtown's pocket harbour and one by one, launched the weapons into the deeply silted basin of the River Bladnoch.

'And your terrorist friends might just come back and get them,' Fiona complained, wiping her hands on her trousers.

Gill shook his head. 'No amount of grease will prevent the damage sand and sea water will inflict on a precision instrument like an M16. You might as well be dipping them in acid.'

'Gonna be so pissed off if we get arrested.'

'We're operating under DI Lillico's instructions,' said Gill as they wandered back to the van where Murray sweated uncomfortably on top of a pile of rifle boxes.

'For pity's sake, get me some help,' he moaned.

'Just tidying up your mess, pal,' said Gill. 'After that, your comfort and safety will be our highest priority.'

'Another twenty runs at least,' said Fiona, looking at the pile. 'Do you think it's okay to leave him unguarded?'

'We're a mile from anywhere down a single-track road.' Gill stopped to stare at Murray. 'Honestly? Just let him try.'

Gill slammed the rear doors to the ambulance and moments later, its blue lights illuminated as it pulled away. Inside, Murray McGovern was finally receiving first aid under the watchful eyes of DI Lillico. During his back-and-forwards to the van, Gill felt sorry for his wounded foe. The deaths of his men had hit him hard. That he'd also had to witness the disposal of the gun cache underscored the futility of their deaths.

'Where to?' asked Fiona, drawing weary arms to her hips.

'Could you drop me at Clanyard Bay?' asked Gill. 'Salina was able to organise someone to fix my car.'

'No one coming to arrest us?'

Gill gave her a weary smile. 'Not yet.'

'Good,' she said, curtly. 'And after I've served as your personal chauffeur, I'm definitely going home.'

'Thanks, Fi. Me too.'

'The day of the earth tremor,' said Fiona a few minutes later. 'Did you manage to deliver that white rose?'

'Just before it all kicked off,' said Gill, remembering his ordeal in the caves.

'And you said it was for the piper?'

'Do you remember the pewter buttons we discovered beside the piper's bones?'

'Aye.'

'They led us to identify the piper as a Jacobite soldier called Francis Towneley.'

'No way!'

'Have to wait for the final DNA comparison with one of his living relatives, but based on the family's archive, we're sure it's him.' He nodded across at Fiona, still sweaty after

their exertion, and her hands tightly gripping her wheel.
'Wanna hear about him?'

'Sounds better than anything else you've had me do today.'

Over the next hour, Gill described Towneley's call to war, his participation in the last battle on British soil, and his chaotic flight to safety. They spoke about the colony, the piper and the wicked laird, and when he'd said his piece, Fiona fell silent to focus on the road.

As Fiona's van rumbled back to Clanyard, Gill pondered the power of the old lairds and the meagre compassion they held for their subjects. Whether it was the Bonnie Prince sending loyal highlanders to die in bloody rebellions, or the governing class in Edinburgh crushing any threat to their wealth, the result was the same. As Wigtown and all its troubles fell away behind them, Gill knew with deeper certainty that a new laird was laying claim to Scotland. This was another man with no compassion for the little people that stood between him and power. And if he was able to corrupt the tools of government, Canmore's bid to control Scotland might be successful. If he subverted law and order, and the Armour Group couldn't stop him, Gill suddenly realised the merit of ripping part of Scotland away from this self-appointed laird. And this he realised was the potential power of *The Torn Isle*.

Chapter 50

After thanking Fiona and waving her off, Gill stood on the cliff top and stared out over Clanyard Bay. His tyres had been replaced and even though he was ready for the road, something held him back. Gazing down at the cave entrance, now blocked for another aeon by the latest rockfall, he wondered how history would judge this moment, or whether it would remember anything at all. He was pondering this when his phone rang and unusually, it was Solomon.

'What's happening, Solie? We having voice calls now? You couldn't you think of a suitable cryptic text?'

'I've been on edge for the last twenty-four hours,' snapped Solomon. 'I knew it would be you, and this is the first time I've felt peaceful about dialling your number.'

'I was finishing a cave excavation when we experienced the earth tremors. A rockfall blocked our exit and I had to crawl through tiny channels to find my way out,' said Gill. 'That was fun. Oh, and then three men I was working with turned out to be Nationalist terrorists.'

'Just another day at the office,' said Solomon.

'I hope there won't be another like it anytime soon.'

'As exciting as that all sounds, that wasn't what was bothering me.'

Gill shook his head in silent disbelief. 'Okay. Go on.'

'Messages have been pinging in all day from the various chapters of *The Vigil*. Every group has fixated on a single image that no one can interpret.'

'They're all seeing the same thing?'

'Yes, Gill. Orkney, Stornoway, Kirkintilloch and Portree. I've asked Aura but she won't reveal what it means.'

'Tell me. Let me see if I can help.'

'Different groups, Gill. And they all saw you holding a single white rose, dipped in blood.'

Gill sighed. 'It means, I'm ready.'

'Ready for what?'

'To declare *The Torn Isle*, if that's what's necessary.'

Solomon paused. 'I see. What's your reasoning for this change of heart?'

'I've spent two days this week getting to know a man from the eighteenth century who chose armed rebellion as his means for achieving his life goals. He was on his deathbed before he discovered he'd been manipulated by powerful men more selfish than him. And bringing that story up to date, I believe we now have high heidyins in Edinburgh inciting a bloody rebellion of their own. And the prime mover in all that doesn't care who dies under his chariot wheels.'

'And you're planning to resist his rebellion, Gill?'

'I might just start one of my own.'

'By declaring *The Torn Isle*?'

'If that's what it takes to frustrate him.'

'Explain the white rose?'

'It's a family emblem of sorts. It represents the men of a Catholic family called Towneley, who went to war to win back their lands and prestige.'

'That's all very well, but what does it mean, Gill?'

Gill sighed. 'The rose is a reference to all the people of pure motives who are being manipulated.'

'And the blood?'

'The price to be paid by anyone caught up in this rebellion.'

'And you think this is happening?'

'Lillico and I have evidence that it is.'

Solomon left a long pause. 'If we have Aura's approval I'll back you, Gill.'

'Thank you, Solie. Let's see what the next few days bring.'

Solomon was quiet again and for a moment, Gill wondered if she'd hung up. 'Following this revelation, you must talk to Adina.'

'What about?'

'I've always believed, when the purpose of the Armour Group became clear, she would be the first to see it.'

'I remember you saying that.'

'It's my instinct she has news for you.'

Gill sighed. Adina had alluded to as much herself. 'I'll speak to her, Solie. I'll do it right now.'

After closing his call with Solomon, Gill took a few seconds to centre himself before tapping Adina's number. He had no inkling what her news would be, but suddenly his chest felt tight.

'Gill,' said Adina, brightly.

'Sorry for phoning so early on a Saturday.'

'No problem. Where are you?'

'In Wigtownshire. I'm about to drive home.'

'Wigtown,' began Adina. 'There were two men killed and one arrested. Do you know anything about that?'

'More than I can tell you right now,' said Gill, glancing down at the cave.

Adina seemed to contemplate this. 'Okay.'

'And the reason for my call is that I think it's time you told me the information you've been holding back.'

Adina cleared her throat. 'What if I told you that Roddy Canmore plans to disrupt Scotland's democracy?'

'I'd find that very plausible.'

'Because of what happened in Wigtownshire?'

'While I was down here, I got caught up at the margins of a case Alex was working on. He has evidence that a senior officer tried to obstruct his efforts to secure a weapons cache.'

'I see.'

'But the part I don't know is what he would've done with these guns if we hadn't kept them from him.'

He heard Adina swallow. 'I might be able to help with that.'

'Go on.'

'Aura wouldn't let me say. Until today.'

'Adina?'

'Two years ago, Lorna obtained a USB stick packed with private documents from Roddy Canmore's safe. She passed them to me, and I decrypted them. They're working documents that explore how Canmore might agitate his way to an independent Scotland.'

'Rather than seek another independence referendum?'

'You don't understand. He's planning to disrupt the rule of law. Those men in Wigtown? I suspect they're the tip of the iceberg. And the weapons? Who knows how many more his faction has stashed.'

Gill shuddered. 'You're telling me, Canmore is planning a coup?'

'I doubt he'll ever call it that, but it's a good enough word.'

'In twenty-first century, United Kingdom?'

'Look around you, Gill. I'm not a native of the UK but "united" isn't the word I'd ever use to describe this country.'

'But the use of force, Adina? He'll never get away with it.'

'Doesn't mean he isn't about to try. What little I've heard about Wigtown fits the strategy he's proposed. You mentioned a weapons cache. It sounds like this was some kind of logistical preparation that went wrong.'

Gill drew his free hand to his brow. 'If this was Canmore's preparations, do you know when he'll trigger his plans?'

'He's waiting for the right moment. Either a change of government in Westminster or some crisis bestowing him with a chance to make a dash for power.'

'Adina, why is Aura only revealing this now?' asked Gill.

'I wasn't to tell you. That was her instruction, until she gave me permission to speak.'

'And the rest of the Armour Group?'

'It's time to tell them all.'

Gill agreed. 'I'll speak to Lillico, Ailsa and Solomon.'

'Okay, and I'll catch Lorna and Charlie. Then I'll show you Canmore's files when we're all together.'

'Thank you.' He paused to find the right words. 'I met Raphael this week.'

'I take it you weren't sitting in the sun with a glass of lemonade?'

'I was … enduring a moment of crisis. But the point is this, and Adina, this is really important. Raphael said the Armour Group's survival in the coming conflict can't be taken for granted.'

Adina's pause was painful. 'Oh, dear God.'

'So, we need some kind of backup plan.'

'Oh, Gill, what are you proposing?'

'He might be reluctant to admit it, but your husband will still have a way of reaching MI5. You need to tell him about Canmore's files in case we're suddenly taken out of the game.'

'I'm not sure having British domestic intelligence tramping all over this is going to help, Gill.'

'I hear your concerns, and I'll leave it with you. I'm just saying, as a piece of contingency planning, we shouldn't rule it out.'

Adina released a ragged sigh. 'I'll consider that. In the meantime, take care, Gill.'

Chapter 51

Gill and Salina lay sprawled in each other's arms. In the three hours since he'd finally arrived home, Gill had showered and changed before immersing himself in his family. He and Sal had fed Josh, but rather than lay their son in his bed, they both held a strong desire for the three of them to be together. So, they laid their sleeping child on cushions beside them and talked quietly into the evening.

'All your blethering about fairies,' said Salina with a mischievous smile. 'Did you ever work out if they were good or evil?'

Gill sighed. 'The only thing I know for certain is they were small. The rest depends on your point of view.'

Salina tilted her head. 'Explain, please?'

'Some people called them, the *Guid Folk*, and I guess that makes sense if you were superstitious about these little people. If you wanted to be in their favour, you'd speak nicely about them. And if you'd abandoned a child to their care, you'd want to justify to yourself you'd done the right thing.'

'While others saw them as evil?'

'They were diminutive and destitute. I've no doubt their strange lifestyles unnerved the people who'd rather not have had them in the local neighbourhood. No doubt they stole stuff when they were desperate and because they'd no voice in the community, all manner of bad luck could be blamed on them.'

'That sounds sad.'

'It's our humanity, Sal. Collectively we make a lot of decisions that disadvantage sections of society, and rather than fix the problem, we demonise the people we've most harmed.'

'Can we at least agree that your days as a cave explorer are over?' she asked with a straight face.

'Those twelve hours underground were the worst moments of my life. I lay there unable to go backwards and struggling to move forwards. Honestly, Sal, for a time, I almost lost it.'

'And yet, you didn't.'

'I put on the armour, at the last minute when I was utterly at my wits' end.'

'These latest tremors,' said Salina, squeezing his hand. 'Should we be worried?'

'There's lots of disruption, but at least nobody died,' said Gill. 'And it only measured 3.4 on the Richter scale. That's still tiny.'

'Aye, but it was a tremor that size that crashed the silt columns in Loch Ness.'

'That was a one-time thing. It can't happen again.'

'But we're seeing a pattern, Gill. And I don't know about you, but I think governments north and south of the border are being very quiet on the subject.'

'I agree. And it's cost us one First Minister already, so I'm curious to see how Canmore addresses the subject.' He paused to stroke some hair from her eyes. 'Which reminds me. I need to meet with the Armour Group tomorrow. Something urgent has come up.'

'Sure. When will you be back?'

'I'd like you to come with me.'

'What's the meeting about?'

Gill measured his response. 'Adina has important information for us.'

'Tell me more about it, then I'll decide.'

'I'll tell you everything I know in a second. Let me put our wee man in his bed.'

Gill gathered their sleeping son and leaned him across to Salina so she could kiss the top of his head. Then he stepped out of the room and climbed the stairs to the first floor. He laid Josh in his cot and moved to the window to close the curtains. The evening sun was sinking over the Tay and the water between the bridges shimmered with a golden glow. Gripping the fabric, he discovered he was shaking and for a few moments, he wasn't sure what to do. Adina's information seemed to propel them towards a confrontation. And yet, if Aura hadn't restrained this news about Canmore's plans, how would they have sustained themselves these last two years, knowing this crisis was coming at them?

And he realised. In a moment of absolute certainty, this was the reason the Armour Group existed. This was the emergency they had anticipated, and danger was all around. Canmore would make his dash for glory, and like the Bonnie Prince three centuries earlier, the politician didn't mind if he walked through blood to reach his throne.

He felt someone brush the base of his back; their touch rising up his right side and across his shoulders before travelling down his left arm until the only sensation was at his fingertips. Aura manifested, in a shimmer of translucent light. She didn't laugh. Nor did she smile. Instead, she tilted her head and looked straight into his eyes. She uttered no words, but her expression asked, 'Are you ready, Gill?'

He swallowed, and the sensation of her presence disappeared.

Was he ready? Did he know her? Had he fully grasped the extent of his mission? Was his knowledge of *The Book* and the Nazarene going to make him worthy of the task? And as his little boy breathed peacefully in his cot beside him, he considered again what this could cost him.

He was still contemplating this when his phone rang. He glanced down in irritation and saw the caller was from an unknown number. In this emotionally heightened state, nothing in him wanted to take the call. But a crushing weight against his chest told him it was significant. This was the moment when it all began.

He lifted his phone and cleared his throat. 'Gill McArdle,' he said, tentatively.

Nobody spoke and for a few moments, Gill could only hear the caller's ragged breathing and the sound of urgent voices shouting in the background.

'Hello, caller. Who's there?' he asked.

He heard more erratic breathing. 'Gill. It's Rani.'

'Rani? Sorry, I didn't recognise the number.'

'It's Graham's phone. Listen. We have a problem.'

'What's up?'

Rani snatched a few deep breaths before speaking. 'Bru freaked out during the earth tremors. He ran off and didn't come back until today. He wasn't injured, just a few scuffs and scratches. But Gill, he was soaking wet, and this evening he's going into shock.'

'What? Are you sure?'

'Graham is with him now, but the way Bru is deteriorating, it's only safe for us to stay with him a few more minutes.'

'What's happening, Rani? Tell me exactly what you can see.'

'Do I need to bloody spell it out?' she shouted. 'Look, I've got a husband and child to protect, and I don't …'

In the background, Gill heard a powerful crash. 'Rani ….'

'Gill,' Rani yelled. 'Please. Just come.'

There came the crack of splintering timbers, then a child's desperate screaming. He heard Rani gasp, just as the call cut off.

Chapter 52

Editor's comment, Mysterious Scotland, Issue 61
I've discovered, I'm a 'little' person.

What do I mean by that? Well, I'm not a leader of anything other than this ultimately inconsequential magazine. I'm not vested in industry or politics, nor do I own a country estate, and the origins of my family name are humble indeed. My influence is informal, in the views I hold, and in my freedom to explain myself upon these pages.

When I reflect on this, I realise I know other 'little' people. For example, the young men and women I meet through my literacy charity. They struggle to make their way in life as technological change devours the careers they thought they'd have, while new jobs demand skills they've yet to accrue.

And I suspect most of us are 'little' people.

We live our lives as best we can, providing for ourselves and our families. If we've any energy left, we expend it on a cause that's close to our heart like sport, or faith, or care for the environment.

There are always 'little' people, I hear you say, so where am I going with this? Let me explain.

During the disruption caused by the rumbles along the Great Glen Fault last month, I found myself far to the south of the action. Instead of being in the quake zone, I was in Wigtownshire, on the trail of fairies. Fairies! Suspend your incredulity for a second while I explain how I got there. To do this properly, I'm going back to the 16th of April 1746 and *the battle of Culloden. It's a famous date but many folks with a tenuous grasp of history assume Culloden was a battle between plucky Sottish highlanders and an invading English army. Mys.Scot readers are better read than that and know the battle pitted a diverse group of rebels against the united parliament of Great Britain. As the two armies faced off, there were Scottish regiments on the government side, and a lessor known fact was that some English fighters sided with the Jacobites. One such man was Francis Towneley from Burnley in Lancashire. Towneley's family was Catholic and wanted to see a Catholic monarch restored to Britain. With this goal, coupled with a desire to recover lands confiscated during his family's support for an earlier Jacobite rebellion, Francis and his kin followed the Bonnie Prince and went to war.*

As one of the few survivors of the Manchester regiment that rallied to Bonnie Prince Charlie, the unfortunate Francis soon left his father and brother dead on the battlefield. Following the Prince's order to disperse, he went on the run. His exact movements are unknown, but we do have snippets of correspondence in letters to his mother over the following year. His last letter home was in May 1747, and after this, Francis was never heard from again.

Hold that thought for a second while I turn to the fairies. In the pages that follow, I report on Mys.Scot's excavation in a Wigtownshire sea cave. And not just any cave because this one is immersed in Fae mythology. Amongst the remains of seventy people who were diminutive in the extreme, we found evidence of a long-established community. Okay, so they were small, but did that really make them fairies? Read our article by Mys.Scot contributor, Rory Carmichael before making up your mind. Rory argues that much of this folklore stems from an abhorrent historical practice of abandoning human children burdened with congenital disorders.

To grasp this, you need to remember that the eighteenth century was a time of rapid agricultural change that saw many families driven to starvation. Forced off the land and into destitution, perhaps we can comprehend the reasons why families might expel their weakest members. These poor abandoned children, these 'little' people, living in forests and caves, forced to beg, borrow and steal to survive. They were expected to die, and I'm sure many did, but the survivors in Wigtownshire, many of whom suffered from dwarfism, formed their own community. To the rest of human society, they were like us, but not us. Alien and feared, all manner of bad luck was blamed on them. We found evidence of this in our cave, and we also found some pewter buttons. With the help of DNA analysis and hard work by our diligent researchers, we've discovered those buttons belonged to the same Francis Towneley who fought at Culloden.

Back to Towneley. His reputation says he carried bagpipes, the remains of which we also found in the cave. And he appears in a local legend called the 'Fairy Piper of Clanyard Bay.' This describes how a destitute soldier, searching for food and board, was recruited by a Wigtownshire laird to enter the cave and pacify a hoard of evil fairies. But instead of killing them, our piper found himself identifying with these discarded children. As a refugee and the ultimate rough sleeper, perhaps Francis recognised himself in their rejected lives. Perhaps he came to see more value in their efforts to fashion an equitable underground society than serving the whims of the Bonnie Prince. We'll never know what the man was thinking, though I can imagine his reasoning. He left Burnley, using violence to recover his family's wealth and oblige his fellow Britons to subscribe to a strict form of religious practice. But in the end, he chose to die in a destitute community where the only membership code was an uncritical acceptance of each other.

Before you accuse me of scorning the Jacobite cause, let me acknowledge the huge and eternal harm done to the Highlanders and their culture in the wake of Culloden. The Bonnie Prince used violence in the bid for his throne and didn't mind tramping through blood to get there. Meanwhile, the British generals who opposed him enacted a cultural scorched-earth policy to sustain their grip on power. And I imagine it was ever thus in Scotland and across the world. Princes and generals pick fights and make wars, while the 'little' people end up crushed beneath their chariot wheels. Would it be brazen of me to suggest that in twenty-first century Scotland, we'll do well if we remember that, so history never repeats itself?

So join me, on a fairy trail through this month's issue. I can't promise you tiny houses, glittery wands, or gossamer wings, but I can introduce you to one community that sparked our most pervasive myth. And if you are fortunate enough to call this land your home, I will introduce you to Mysterious Scotland's 'little' people. Perhaps through the eyes of a different place or a different time, I might even introduce you to yourself.

The End

If you have enjoyed 'The Crystal Armour,' I would be so grateful if you could leave a review on the site where you bought the book. And please stay in touch via Facebook or The Reader's Syndicate while *Mysterious Scotland* reaches its gripping climax in book 9.

Tormod Cockburn

The final adventure is …

The Torn Isle

Will Gill McArdle tear up Scotland in his desire to save it?

While the Highlands north of the Great Glen are recovering from recent earth tremors, much of Scotland senses there's worse to come. Returning from a futile trip to Lewis, Gill busies himself in an archaeological dig close to his home. It's routine work – recovering bones from an old graveyard that's listed for redevelopment. Routine, until something unusual is discovered, hinting at a far darker secret buried beneath the ancient tombs.

Meanwhile, the Armour Group is assembled and ready to face the coming storm. And although they've got remarkable power on their side, their enemy knows who they are, and is about to unleash a force of his own. When the crisis erupts, and Canmore springs his trap, he knows exactly where to find them. As Gill fights to rally his team, terrible news arrives from the isles. A live waterhorse walks upon Hebridean soil and its destination can only be, The Temple of the Isles.

Join the Reader's Syndicate at TormodCockburn.com
Or click on any of the thumbnails

Mysterious Scotland Reader's Syndicate

Join our Reader's Syndicate at TormodCockburn.com for new publication alerts and for free material. There are three character-based stories, plus a novella explaining the origins of the waterhorse bones Gill found on Harris. All are free and exclusively available to members of the Syndicate.

Mys.Scot

Acknowledgements

My thanks to my editorial team, James, Audrey, Julia, Kath and Woodeene, all authors, or authors in the making. During its development, this book often ran away with me, like a wild horse on a moor, and you guys helped steer it back on track.

Thanks to Rhea Wild for her equestrian expertise, and for bringing Bru so forcefully to life. Any missteps in the application of your advice are all mine.

I trawled through heaps of fairy myth until I found one tale that resonated with the story I had in mind. So, my thanks to everyone online who has documented the 'Ghost Piper of Clanyard Bay.'

Finally, as an inspiration and a memorial, I remember Francis Murphy. A family friend and a serving officer in the RUC, murdered on 21st February 1985.

MYSTERIOUS SCOTLAND

IN AUDIOBOOK FORMAT

AVAILABLE FROM AMAZON AUDIBLE AND ITUNES

Printed in Great Britain
by Amazon